ANNE LYLE

The PRINCE of LIES

NIGHT'S MASQUE VOL III

ANGRY
ROBOT

ANGRY ROBOT
A member of the Osprey Group

Lace Market House,
54-56 High Pavement,
Nottingham NG1 1HW
UK

www.angryrobotbooks.com
Last chances

An Angry Robot paperback original 2013
1

A catalogue record for this book is available
from the British Library.

ISBN 978 0 85766 280 4
Ebook ISBN 978 0 85766 282 8

Set in Meridien by EpubServices

Printed and bound by CPI Group (UK) Ltd, Croydon, CR0 4YY.

PART ONE

"Seems he a dove? his feathers are but borrowed,
For he's disposed as the hateful raven:
Is he a lamb? his skin is surely lent him,
For he's inclined as is the ravenous wolf.
Who cannot steal a shape that means deceit?"

William Shakespeare, Henry VI pt 2

CHAPTER I

Mal reined in his mount and rested his gloved hands on the saddlebow, letting the gelding snatch a mouthful of new spring grass from the roadside. From here he could see the whole of London laid out below him, from the crumbling splendour of the Tower in the east to the gilded turrets of Whitehall Palace in the west, with Southwark a grubby stain on the farther bank of the Thames.

"See? I told you we weren't lost. Stretch your legs if you like. I won't be a moment."

Sandy said nothing, only stared at the city as if he could close the distance by sheer force of will. Which admittedly he could, if he wanted to.

"And don't go disappearing on me," Mal added in a low voice. "I don't need you affrighting half of London by using your magics in broad daylight."

"I am not such a fool as that. Brother."

"Well. Good, then."

He dismounted and strolled over to the nearest bush. A hawthorn, vivid green leaves bursting from the bud, clusters of white flowers already open. In his mind's eye he saw the design inked into his left shoulder: a roundel of flowers and thorns, a reminder of the sacred grove back in Vinland where skraylings went to die and be reborn... No. Pissing on a hawthorn was sacrilegious whichever way you looked at it. He moved further into the thicket, where a great clump of holly

7

stood like a fortress within a curtain wall of gorse and brambles. Did everything on this godforsaken heath have thorns? He unbuttoned his breeches and sighed, breath frosting the air.

A voice from the road behind him. And not Sandy's. Mal hurriedly refastened his clothing and padded back to the road, drawing his rapier silently.

"Hold! Or..." The man with a pistol to Sandy's head looked from one to the other, taking in their identical dark wavy hair and neatly trimmed beards. "Or your brother's a dead man. He is your brother, right?"

"Twins, as you see," Mal said, letting the tip of his rapier droop towards the ground as if on the verge of surrendering it. The fellow looked desperate enough to kill: hollow of cheek and with scabby red skin showing through his ripped and filthy finery. Stolen from other victims, no doubt.

"So if I shoot him," the footpad said, "do you die as well?"

Mal shrugged. "I'm not eager to test that hypothesis."

"Oi, don't you try and maze me with no fancy Latin."

"Actually," said Sandy, "it's Greek. From–"

"Shut up!" The pistol began to shake. "Shut up, the pair of you. Hand over the chinks. Now. And that pretty pigsticker. Bet it's worth ten times what you've got in your purse."

"You've a fine eye," Mal said, throwing his rapier onto the ground about halfway between them. The curving lines of the hilt flashed as they caught the afternoon sunlight. That gave him an idea...

"And the knife," the footpad said. "Come on, I can see the hilt sticking out behind your back."

The dagger joined its mate on the grass.

"Get on with it!"

Mal hefted his purse for a moment then tossed to the footpad in a high arc. The fool went to catch it with his free hand – and looked straight up into the sun. Sandy stepped aside and Mal ducked forward, snatching up the rapier and lunging in a single fluid movement that ended with the point of his blade pressing into the tender flesh under the man's chin.

"Once you pull the trigger," Mal said, "it'll take at least two heartbeats for the powder to ignite and the gun to fire. How many do you think it'll take for me to open your veins?"

The footpad's throat worked as he weighed the relative consequences of speaking and staying silent. After a moment he lowered the pistol.

"Drop it on the ground," Mal told him. "Carefully."

He did so, never taking his eyes off Mal. Sandy stepped behind him and took the man's head in both hands. The footpad whimpered and squirmed in Sandy's grasp, and his eyes rolled back in his skull.

"What are you doing?" Mal strode over and laid a hand on his brother's arm. "I told you–"

Sandy released the footpad, who fell to the ground in an untidy heap.

"–not to use magic openly."

"There is no one here to see us."

"There's him. Assuming you haven't killed him."

Mal sheathed his sword and crouched beside the man, taking hold of his jaw and turning his head from side to side. Drool trickled out between the slack lips, but the footpad appeared to still be breathing.

"You know I can't do that," Sandy replied.

"Do I? I'm not certain what you're capable of any more." Mal retrieved his fallen purse and straightened up.

"You're afraid, aren't you? Afraid of becoming like me."

Mal looked away, unable to meet his brother's eye. It was hard to keep secrets from someone when you shared a soul.

"You didn't need to do it. I had him disarmed and at swordspoint."

"He could have been an assassin."

"Him?" Mal shook his head over the sorry figure on the ground. "He's naught but a common thief. Plenty of them on the roads into London; the only wonder is we haven't been troubled by any before now."

"Still, I had to be sure."

"And was he?"

Sandy pulled a face. "No."

"Don't fret yourself. We were in London for weeks after we first got back from France; if someone was set on killing me, they'd have tried it before now." He stepped over the man, picked up his dagger and returned it to its sheath. "No, whoever sent that assassin after me on Raleigh's ship seems to have backed off. Probably doesn't want to upset the prince."

"The boy is barely four years old; I cannot think he leads our enemies yet."

"Not Henry; his father, Robert." Mal looked around for the horses. "It's a good hour's ride to Southwark. If we want to talk to the skraylings before Youssef's ship docks, we'd best hurry."

The suburb of Southwark had grown outwards in all directions except one. On its eastern edge the boundary was still the stream just past Morgan's Lane, crossed by a wooden bridge. The common land beyond lay as empty as ever, apart from a few grazing cattle and of course the skrayling encampment. Evidently no one was so desperate for land that they wanted to build within a stone's throw of the aliens.

"Remember," Mal said as they drew near the gates, "we offer help first, ask favours after."

He dismounted and stepped onto the near end of the bridge across the moat surrounding the camp. He recalled his very first visit here, trailing after Ambassador Kiiren in the pouring rain, shirt sticking to the bloody welts on his back. The fact that he had been the first human to set foot inside the compound had been lost on him at the time. He wondered if others had been admitted since then, though he knew of none for certain apart from himself and Sandy. The skraylings kept to themselves, even more so now they knew that traitors within their own people had infiltrated the English aristocracy in the past and might try to do so again.

"Sir Maliverny Catlyn and Alexander Catlyn, to see Outspeaker Adjaan," he said to the guard. The title still sounded foolish to his own ears, but there it was. The Queen had decided his actions in Venice had deserved a knighthood, and who was he to gainsay her?

The skrayling's tattooed face remained impassive, but he bowed politely and waved them through. Mal breathed a sigh of relief. He had not been sure they would be welcome here in the wake of Ambassador Kiiren's death, which was why he had not visited the skraylings upon his return to England. Only the necessity of protecting his family drove him to it now, and though the skraylings were a peaceable folk for the most part and he did not fear an attack, still he could not help but glance about him, hand on rapier hilt, as they entered the compound.

The camp was much as Mal remembered it: an area of about two acres filled with domed tents of a heavy canvas patterned in cream and black triangles, zigzags and interlocking squares. In the centre a great pavilion rose amongst the smaller tents, and trees grew here and there, hung with the blown-glass spheres the skraylings used for lamps. This early in the evening the trees were dark, but already a lamp-tender was passing among them with his ladder, emptying out the spent lightwater into a bucket that glowed faintly when he passed into the shadow of a tent.

"Do you know this new outspeaker?" Mal asked his brother as they dismounted.

"Adjaan?" Sandy shook his head. "The name is not familiar to me."

A movement in the crowd caught Mal's eye and he shifted his grip on the rapier hilt, but it was only a young skrayling in a clerk's brown tunic and trousers. The lad stumbled to a halt, his amber eyes wide at the sight of the visitors, then he seemed to remember himself and made a hesitant obeisance, hands raised palms outwards.

"Erishen-*tuur*?"

"*Hä*," Sandy replied, returning the obeisance.

Mal forced a smile. Erishen was the name of the skrayling soul that had reincarnated in the twins. He supposed he should find it reassuring that at least some of the skraylings still considered the Catlyn brothers near-kinsmen, but it made him uneasy nonetheless.

The clerk rattled something off in Vinlandic and beckoned to the two men.

"He says the outspeaker will see us now," Sandy told Mal. "She is in her office."

"She?" Mal caught his brother's arm, slowing him down so that they were out of earshot of the young clerk. "I thought female skraylings never ventured across the ocean?"

"Times change," Sandy replied. "Even for us."

Mal bit back a comment. If Sandy now thought of himself as more skrayling than human, was that not Mal's own fault as much as anyone's? He was the one who had handed his brother over to the creatures to be "cured" of his madness.

The clerk led them along a raised wooden causeway to a cabin on the far side of the compound. It resembled the skraylings' dome-shaped tents, except that it was roofed with a spiral of wooden tiles shaped like fish scales, and its walls were carved in simple lines to emphasise the grain of the timber. Folding doors on all sides let in the spring air and revealed its inhabitant kneeling at a low table heaped with books and papers. Turquoise-blue lamps hung from the ceiling, giving the cabin interior the appearance of an underwater cave. Sandy muttered something under his breath but Mal had no time to ask him what he meant, since Outspeaker Adjaan was already rising to greet them.

She was tall as skraylings went, though she still barely reached Mal's chin, and broader than most. Her face was an even bluish-grey, lacking the mottled pattern that male skraylings enhanced with tattooed lines, and she wore a robe of deep lapis blue over tunic and trousers of the same colour. Mal recalled Ambassador Kiiren's explanation of his own garb: that male outspeakers dressed as women to form a bridge between the two sexes, who normally lived apart. He wondered what had brought Adjaan here to live among her menfolk. Nothing good, he suspected.

"Gentlemen. Welcome to my humble *lirraan*." Adjaan bowed, a little awkwardly. Her English however was flawless, with even less of an accent than Kiiren's.

"*Senlirren-tuur*." Sandy returned the courtesy in the skrayling fashion, palms forward and head turned to one side to expose his throat.

Mal did likewise, and Adjaan replied in Vinlandic. He racked his brains, willing the words to mean something, but unlike his brother he had limited access to Erishen's powers and even less to his memories.

"Forgive me," Adjaan said in English. "It was impolite of me to use the language of my kinfolk, when we are the strangers here. Please, sit." She went over to the brazier in the rear doorway and picked up a wooden-handled jug that steamed in the cool evening air. "What brings you back to London so soon?"

"Soon?" Mal sat down cross-legged on the near side of the table. "We have been in Derbyshire all winter."

Adjaan cleared a space on the corner of the table and set down the jug. "How old are you?"

"We will be thirty years old in November," Mal said.

"Not these bodies. How long have you walked in the worlds? Five hundred years? Six?"

"About that," Sandy said. "I was born in the Ninth Cycle–"

"Then a few turns of the moon is but a moment, yes?"

She took out three cups of translucent porcelain and filled them. *Aniig*, Mal realised, the herbal brew favoured by the skraylings, though he had never drunk it hot before. At least not in this body, as Adjaan would no doubt be quick to point out.

"To answer your question, honoured one," Sandy said, taking a cup, "we are here with good news of our findings in the north."

"Or lack of findings," Mal put in.

"You found no *hrrith*?"

"None. If our brother Charles ever hunted the devourers, as he claimed, they are long gone."

"They were there once," Sandy added. "I saw his scars. But my brother is right, they are long gone."

"Well, that is good news." Adjaan cupped her *aniig* in her hands but did not drink. "I would not like to think of those creatures roaming any land, especially not the home of our good friends the English."

"We are still good friends?" Mal asked.

"Of course." She gestured to her cabin. "I would not have come all this way if we did not wish to continue in friendship with you."

She smiled, showing even white teeth, but something about her expression did not convince Mal.

"And is that all your news?" she went on. "It seems a long way to come, to say you have found nothing."

"Well, since we no longer have aught to do in the north," Mal said, "we thought we might be of help here."

"Indeed." Adjaan continued to smile, but her tone was icy.

Mal put down his cup. "The guisers are our enemies as well as yours, honoured one. And I have vowed to drive them from England."

"You? A *kiaqnehet*?"

The word meant broken soul, abomination. Mal ignored the insult. Their mission was more important than petty squabblings over skrayling dogma.

"My brother has been teaching me. How do you think we determined there were no devourers – no *hrrith* – in our lands?"

"Show me."

"Now?"

"Why not now? It will be quiet; even your enemies are unlikely to be around at this time of day."

She motioned to Sandy, who stood up and began closing the doors of the hut. Mal laid his hands in his lap and closed his eyes, forcing himself to breathe more slowly. No, not forcing. That would not work. He breathed again, focusing on the play of light and colour behind his eyelids, letting his imagination draw pictures. The colours rippled and flowed past him, so that he felt as if he were running down a narrow alley with high walls on either side... A moment later he stepped out onto the familiar open plain of the dreamlands, twilit and silent.

"A little clumsy," said a voice at his side, "but better than I expected."

He turned to see Adjaan, and Sandy beyond her. She was as tall as them both now, or perhaps they were as short as her; it was hard to judge size in this featureless place.

The dreamlands were not entirely empty, of course, not even at this hour. A scatter of golden lights on a nearby slope marked the city full of humans, and closer at hand the paler glow of skrayling dreamwalkers, some resting, some circling the compound.

"We patrol day and night," Adjaan said. "Not a soul enters or leaves this compound without me knowing."

"How far do they range?" Sandy asked.

"Not far. Our purpose is to guard our own people, not yours."

Mal crouched and ran a hand through the cold, colourless grass. The earth – if such you could call it – felt different here: more alive, or perhaps less substantial.

"So, you feel it." Adjaan nodded in approval.

"What is it?" he asked, straightening up.

"The price of staying in one place too long."

She snapped her fingers in his face. Mal blinked – and opened his eyes to the blue-green light of the skrayling lamps. Adjaan gave a hissing laugh.

"You will need better self-control than that, Catlyn-*tuur*, if you wish to fight our enemies."

Mal picked up the cup of *aniig* and sipped the cooling liquid. Adjaan reminded him of his fencing-master, never satisfied with his pupils' rate of improvement. *He only wishes you to reach your full potential.* Easy for father to say. He wasn't the one hobbling down the stairs like an old man, hamstrings protesting from an afternoon of naught but footwork.

"Catlyn-*tuur*?"

Mal blinked again, and realised Adjaan was addressing him.

"Sorry, honoured one. You are right, I need better control."

She smiled, more kindly. "Fortunately Erishen-*tuur* is remarkably adept for a *kiaqnehet*. And the renegades are fewer than we feared."

"You're sure?"

"We can never be sure, but yes. By my reckoning there are no more than a handful in and around the city."

Mal leaned forward. "Who are they?"

"Alas, that I cannot tell you. Jathekkil we know, of course, though he is as yet too weak to be a danger."

"Prince Henry." The Queen's four year-old grandson hosted the soul of their old enemy Jathekkil, formerly incarnated as the late Duke of Suffolk.

"Indeed. Doubtless he has an *amayi*, but if so they are being very discreet; at any rate we have not been able to confirm it."

Mal nodded. Skraylings did not marry but some took life-mates, *amayiä*, who watched over them during the vulnerable years before and after reincarnation. Erishen and Kiiren were just such a pair; he should not be surprised that Jathekkil had a companion too.

"There is one who spends a great deal of time at the palace and seldom leaves London," Adjaan went on. "It could be he. And there are one or two who come and go, or perhaps several."

"Then we have a good chance at success." Mal was unable to suppress a grin of triumph.

"You have a chance, yes."

"And the skraylings will help?"

"We will prevent any more of our people from joining their ranks, and our patrols here will discourage activity in your capital, but more than that I cannot promise. Our position here is fragile enough; if those in power knew what was truly occurring in their peaceful kingdom…"

"Of course, honoured one. Discretion is paramount." Ever since the trouble in Venice there had been more and more reports of witch-hunts, some as far afield as Germany and Scotland. He had no wish to bring such horrors to his own country. "Even so, the aid you describe will be invaluable."

They drank their *aniig* in silence for a few moments.

"And what will you do when the *senzadheneth*, the guisers, are gone?" Adjaan asked, just as the silence threatened to go on too long for courtesy.

"I had not looked that far ahead," Mal lied, putting down his cup. "But now that you mention it… We are ourselves renegades, in a sense. We would gladly surrender to the elders' justice, to be reborn among the skraylings if we can."

"You and your brother are *kiaqneheth*. Surely you understand that this is not possible?"

"Jathekkil thought it was," Sandy said. "By killing one of us–"

Adjaan made a dismissive gesture. "Even if it could be done, it would not avail you. The penalty for taking human form is destruction, you know that."

"And what of our *amayi*, Kiiren? Must he too be condemned for our sins?"

Her topaz eyes narrowed. "Outspeaker Kiiren is not lost?"

"No, honoured one," Mal said. "He has been reborn in human flesh, as we were–"

"*Kiiren senzadh.*"

The distaste in her voice made him wince, but he pressed on nonetheless.

"Yes, honoured one. We brought him back with us from Venice. That is, we took him as far as my estate in Provence, and my wife has charge of him now. But with all the trouble in France, she has decided to bring him here to England despite the dangers."

"Oh? And what business is he of mine, this human child of yours, this…" she looked from one twin to the other "…guiser?"

"It was not his wish to break our laws, honoured one," said Sandy, "any more than it was mine. He is young, scarcely more than a century in this world, and does not deserve exile. Please, let him go back to our homeland and rejoin our people."

"And why should I allow this? As a favour to you, who unleashed *hrrith* in the streets of Venice and dashed all our hopes of an alliance with that city?"

"No, of course not."

"Then you cannot be disappointed when I refuse."

Mal bowed his head in submission. There was no point arguing the matter, not now. Perhaps if the outspeaker were allowed time to consider…

"Come on, Sandy." He got to his feet. "We should be going. The *Hayreddin* will be arriving soon."

Sandy opened his mouth to protest, but Mal took hold of his brother's hand and used the skin-to-skin contact to send thoughts of reassurance and urge him to silence. Sandy's eyes widened at this unexpected display of power. After a moment Mal felt an answering wave of agreement tinged with pride. He smiled and bade the puzzled outspeaker farewell.

"Don't worry," Mal said in a low voice as they led their horses out of the compound. "I haven't given up yet."

"But Kiiren–" Sandy looked contrite. "I mean Kit… It's not safe for him here."

"You think he would be any safer on Sark? Or back in Vinland? The guisers here in England aren't our only enemies; they have Christ knows how many allies and would-be recruits among the skraylings. He'll be safer with us, at least for now. When he is older perhaps we can petition the skraylings again."

Sandy halted, twisting his mount's reins absentmindedly between his hands.

"You're right." He looked up and gave Mal a watery smile. "I'm glad Adjaan said no."

Mal patted his brother on the shoulder. "Come on, let's go and bring him home."

CHAPTER II

By the time they reached Botolph's Wharf, the *Hayreddin* was riding at anchor, her sails reefed against a stiff breeze blowing up the Thames. Hailing the captain, Mal jogged up the gangplank with more enthusiasm than he had ever boarded a vessel in his life.

"Catlyn!" Youssef embraced him, then stepped back to hold him at arm's length. "You look pale. These northern climes do not suit you, I think."

"You look as hale as ever, you old rogue," Mal replied. "Well, there might be one or two more grey hairs in your beard, but it's hard to be certain among so many."

Youssef gave him a friendly buffet on the arm.

"I could say the same of you, friend." He glanced at Sandy. "I suppose you gentlemen want to see your family?"

Not waiting for an answer, Youssef led them down to the tiny cabin where Mal and Ned had once stayed on the journey to Venice. The Moor inclined his head in silent invitation. Mal reached out a shaking hand and opened the door. Immediately his eyes lit upon the one face he had been seeking: his wife, Coby. Her expression brightened and she leapt to her feet, slipping into Mal's arms like a hand into a glove. He pressed his cheek against her headdress, wishing he could bury his face in her pale hair that always smelt of chamomile and woodsmoke, but it did not do for a married woman to go bareheaded, especially on a ship full of men.

19

Sandy pushed past them with scarcely a word of apology.

"Where is my *amayi*?"

Susanna, their Venetian nursemaid, curtsied and gestured to a sea chest that had been turned into a makeshift cot. Kit lay sprawled on a blanket, thumb in his mouth, dark lashes fluttering as he slept. Mal smiled down at him for a moment. Strange how like Sandy and himself the boy looked, despite not being of their blood. Kiiren had chosen well.

"We'll take a wherry over to Southwark," he said, "and stay at Ned's—"

"No." Coby twisted in his arms and looked towards Sandy, who had scooped up the sleeping child and was cradling him as tenderly as any mother. "We should go straight to Rushdale Hall. Tonight."

"What's the matter?" He cupped her chin in one hand and gazed into her sea-grey eyes, resisting the temptation to probe her thoughts. He was not his brother.

"I don't want anyone to see Kit. Not yet."

He drew her out into the passageway and closed the door behind them.

"Is there something wrong with the boy?" he asked in a low voice.

"No, nothing. But we don't want the guisers to guess he's—" she looked around, as if suspecting spies even here "—who he is, do we?"

"I suppose not."

"So it's best they believe he was born in Provence, after we were married, and not in Venice."

"I still don't understand. How would they know?"

She sighed. "If he was born in France, he would be scarcely a year and a half old now, not nearly two."

"So?"

"So a child of his age grows quickly. Someone might notice that he's very forward for his supposed age, and put two and two together."

"Oh."

"In a year or so, a few months here or there won't matter so much. But right now..." She shrugged.

"You think of everything, don't you?"

"Someone has to."

"And what about Susanna?"

"What do you mean?"

"Why do we have a Venetian nursemaid, if he was born in France?"

Coby stared up at him, crestfallen. "I didn't think of that."

"No matter, my love." He kissed her brow. "Where we are going, they scarce know a Frenchman from a Turk."

He ushered her back into the cabin.

"Sandy, wait here with the womenfolk. I'll be back before curfew with a coach and our luggage."

He snapped a bow to the ladies and made his way back to the quayside. Perhaps he could hire a coach at the livery stables where they had left their horses, though he would still have to go back to Southwark to get his and Sandy's belongings. He set off up the street, eyes flicking from one passerby to the next. Any of these people could be a guiser spy, but what could they report back? That he and his brother had met a ship out of Marseille? Perhaps with a few well-placed lies, their enemies could be fooled into thinking they were leaving for France…

"Evening," a voice growled from the shadows of a nearby alley. Its owner stepped out into the street: a nondescript man of middling years in the rough jerkin and hose of a labourer.

"Baines. What are you doing here?"

"Our esteemed employer sent me to deliver a message as soon as she heard you was back in London. I wondered what you was up to, visiting your heathen friends, so I followed."

"You were spying on me."

The intelligencer grinned unpleasantly. "Just doing my job."

"So, you're here now. What's the message?"

"You're to join her for supper on Thursday night. At the house in Seething Lane."

Mal cursed under his breath. It was a good week's travel to his estate in Derbyshire, which meant he would have to send Coby on ahead of him with only Sandy for protection. Still, with their main target still in London, perhaps the guisers would leave his family alone.

"Very well. Now, if you'll excuse me, I'll be about my own business. Alone."

Baines gave him a mocking bow and disappeared back into the shadows. Mal headed for the livery stable, his former good humour souring like milk in a dairymaid's bucket.

He returned to the *Hayreddin* an hour later with a hired coach and both horses. Night was falling, long shadows melting into the permanent gloom of the capital's alleys: the perfect time to smuggle his family ashore unnoticed. Wrapping his cloak closer against the evening chill, he boarded the French galiote and made his way down to the cabin. The prospect of breaking the bad news to his wife slowed his steps, but there was nothing else for it. He forced a smile and opened the cabin door.

Kit was awake and sitting on Sandy's lap, listening to his uncle tell him a story. Mal leant against the doorpost for a moment, wondering how many times this scene had played out across the centuries. Five hundred years, Sandy – or rather Erishen – had said, though not always with Kiiren. There must have been other *amayiä* before that, their names lost among the brothers' fractured memories.

"Come," Mal said, reluctantly interrupting the tale. "Curfew will be upon us soon, and I want you out of the city before the gates close."

He led his wife up onto the deck, followed by Sandy carrying Kit half-hidden under his cloak and Susanna trailing in their wake. Youssef barked instructions to his men in a mixture of French and Arabic, and four of them disappeared into the ship, re-emerging a few moments later with the women's baggage.

"Did you bring enough?" Mal said, looking back at them.

"Most of it is Kit's," Coby said with a sigh. "You would not believe how tiresome it is to travel with a small child. Susanna is a saint for bearing with all the work."

"Better than her old life in Venice, surely?"

"Of course," Coby said. "How could she not prefer honest employment to a life of wickedness?"

Mal suppressed a grin. Tempting as it was to point out his wife's hypocrisy, he did not want to spoil their last few moments together. Though perhaps it was time to break the ill news? No, he would wait until they were in the coach. Best not to draw attention to themselves.

Kit stirred briefly as they got into the coach, blinked up at his uncle and settled down again with a beatific smile on his chubby features. Susanna sat stiff as a poker on the bench beside them, not taking her eyes off Kit.

They travelled in companionable silence for a while, Coby resting her head on Mal's shoulder as they bounced along the cobbled streets. It was slow going up the hill to Bishopsgate, the horses straining at the traces and the coachman cursing like a Billingsgate fishwife.

"There's something I have to tell you," Mal said at last, swallowing his dread. "I'm not coming to Rushdale with you."

Coby's head jerked up. "What?"

Mal held up his hands to forestall her protests. "I am sorry, my love. Business keeps me here in the capital–"

"What business?"

"You know what business. The same as always."

"But – I've not seen you in months. Can it not be delayed?"

He told her about Lady Frances's invitation. Coby's expression became grave.

"She hardly ever visits her father's house, not since he died," Mal went on. "If she wants to meet me there instead of at Whitehall Palace, there must be something badly amiss."

The coach slowed to a halt. Mal stuck his head out of the window and discovered they had reached the city gates.

"I'll come north as soon as I can," he said, and leant over to kiss her farewell.

For a moment he thought she would deny him, then she melted into his arms and kissed him with such fervour that he was sorely tempted to go north after all. When the coach started moving again, he gently disentangled himself from his wife's embrace, nodded farewell to his brother and leapt down into the street.

The coachman's lad handed him Hector's reins and he sprang into the saddle with a muttered curse. He would have to ride hard to get across London Bridge before the Great Stone Gate closed, and right now he could hardly see a damned thing. Wiping his eyes with the back of his sleeve, he kicked the gelding into a trot.

On Thursday evening Mal made his way to Seething Lane, near the Tower of London. The house near the end of the street belonged to his employer, the daughter of the late spymaster Sir Francis Walsingham, and was still used by Mal and his confederates for clandestine meetings. He wondered again what was so important that Lady Frances would return to her old home.

At his knock the door was opened by a servant in smart new livery, rather than one of the usual intelligencers. This did not bode well at all. He let the man take his cloak and usher him into the candlelit chamber.

"Sir Maliverny." Lady Frances stepped forward to greet him. "How good to see you again."

"My lady." Mal bowed deeply. "You look well."

It was no empty flattery; though past the first bloom of youth she was still handsome, and her flushed cheeks and the sparkle in her brown eyes appeared to owe more to health than fashionable cosmetics.

"And you also." She stepped to one side. "I believe you know my lord the Duke of Suffolk?"

Mal froze as Blaise Grey unfolded his lanky frame from the high-backed chair where he had been sitting concealed from view. The duke got to his feet with the aid of a silver-topped cane and gave Mal a curt bow. His curly dark-blond hair was as untouched by grey as when they had been undergraduates together, but the chronic pain of an old sword wound had scored lines into his handsome features.

I suppose I should feel guilty about that, but I count it fair recompense for the torment he and his father inflicted on me.

"My lord."

"Catlyn. It has been too long." The duke held out his free hand towards Lady Frances, who smiled and laid her own upon it as if posing for a portrait. "It seems we are to be business partners after all."

Mal glanced from one to the other. "The Queen approved your marriage."

"Of course," Grey said. "I was never one of her favourites, even at the height of my powers. I think she only procrastinated so that my dear Frances could stay with Princess Juliana a little longer."

"Then you have my congratulations," Mal said, forcing a smile.

"And you mine. A knighthood, an estate, a wife and a son, all within the space of a couple of years? How swiftly you have risen, since you came to me begging for work."

Mal was saved from having to frame a polite response by the arrival of another of the liveried servants.

"Supper is served, my lord."

They crossed the entrance hall to the dining room, which had also been woken from its long slumber and made fit for its new master. Silver plate and Venetian glass, laid out along the long polished table in quantities enough to furnish twice their company, reflected back the light of an extravagant number of candles. The servant lifted the lids from an array of dishes, filling the air with the savoury scent of meats, herbs and spices.

Lady Frances made small talk until the servant had withdrawn, whilst the two gentlemen glowered at one another over their plates of beef olives. Mal sipped his wine – predictably excellent – and wondered how he was going to walk away from this situation still breathing. Damn Grey! Of all the women at court to choose from, why did he have to pick Walsingham's daughter? She was as old as him, with only one surviving daughter from her previous marriage, so she was hardly a good prospect for breeding an heir. On the other hand, scurrilous gossip at court implied that Grey's injuries had made him impotent, so perhaps he had already resigned himself to the end of his line. And with Walsingham's daughter came control of her late father's spy network – an invaluable asset for an ambitious man like Grey.

"You may of course continue to use this house for meetings." Grey said, setting down his knife. "I am anxious for business to continue as usual. Under my supervision, of course."

Mal glanced at Lady Frances, but she had eyes only for her husband. Can she really be in love with him, and perhaps he with her? It was a comforting explanation for the turn of events, but not one he dared trust in.

"Of course, my lord," he said. "I will send regular reports. Are you familiar with our customary ciphers?"

Grey hesitated just long enough for Mal to guess that the answer was no.

"Lady Frances has provided me with the necessary keys," Grey said. "Compared to my work on the alleged skrayling texts you and your brother translated for me, Walsingham's ciphers are child's play."

Mal ignored the insult. Unless Grey had been feigning all along, his ignorance of the book's contents was proof he was merely human; the text had been written in a double cipher that only guisers could read. A cruel irony that his old enemy should be one of the few men he could truly trust.

"I hope you found the translation satisfactory, my lord."

"Satisfactory? I dare say a tale of the Norsemen's voyages would be of interest to an explorer or antiquarian, but it is of no use to me. Why my father thought it so important, I cannot fathom."

"Your father was trying to root out an anti-skrayling conspiracy, my lord." A lie, but one that came close enough to the truth to still make sense to Grey. Mal was not about to put his head in the noose by trying once more to convince Blaise of his father's true nature. "To own any documents of potential use in that fight and be unable to read them… it would tax the patience of any man."

"I don't know why he didn't ask his skrayling friends to translate them."

"Perhaps he feared traitors amongst the skraylings themselves."

Grey frowned and took a sip of wine. "Why would they side with humans against their own kind?"

"Who knows? They are still largely a mystery to me." That at least was not a lie.

"No matter. If my father's notebooks cannot avail me, I am certain I will find what I need in Sir Francis's records. I swore to Prince Robert I would uncover my father's lieutenants within the Huntsmen, and I shall."

So that's what all this is about: a crusade founded on misplaced filial loyalty and desperate self-preservation. Mal feigned an air of sympathy.

"Alas, my lord, if only it were that straightforward. The Huntsmen are troublemakers, to be sure, but they are mere footsoldiers, and their aim is simple: to rid England of the skraylings. The men I seek – that your father sought – have a much greater prize in mind."

Grey's eyes narrowed. "What do you mean?"

"Breaking our alliance with the skraylings is only a means to an end. The end of the Tudor line."

"Most abominable treason! Do you have proof of this?"

"Not yet, my lord. But ever since I returned to England last summer, I have been doing everything in my power to infiltrate their ranks, starting with my late brother Charles's associates in Derbyshire. It took a great deal of tact and guile, considering I am now famed for helping strengthen England's alliance with the skraylings, but I have persuaded a few key men that it is all part of a longer term plan to destroy them. I'm afraid they really are very gullible at times."

"Why have you reported none of this to me?" Lady Frances asked.

"Forgive me, my lady. I was not certain of my success until very recently, nor even of which men were truly traitors and which only idle malcontents. I would not black the reputation of any man without at least some evidence."

"I want a list," Grey said. "The names of everyone you have spoken to, with details of any gatherings or other potentially seditious activities they were involved in."

"Of course, my lord." An edited list, naturally. He was hardly going to reveal his most useful intelligence, at least not just yet. "Although their activities of late have been limited to boasting about their glorious past and drinking inordinate quantities of bad sack. With the skraylings mewed up in their camp two hundred miles away, they have little else to do nowadays."

When they had finished supper, Grey suggested they retire to the parlour. Lady Frances excused herself, saying she was expected back at Richmond Palace early the next day, and bade both of them good night. In the entrance hall Mal tried to make his own farewells, but Grey forestalled him and steered him into the parlour, closing the door behind them.

"Let's not beat about the bush, Catlyn," the duke said. "I don't like you, you don't like me, but we have little choice but to cooperate in this matter."

"I would be happy to withdraw from your service, my lord, if you would prefer. You can of course count on my complete discretion."

Grey eased himself into the fireside chair. "Can I indeed? But who says I want to be rid of you?"

"My lord?"

"I need—" Grey made the word sound like it choked him to say it "—a man with your experience of Walsingham's men. My wife... that is, my wife-to-be, has done a remarkable job of it for a woman, but it is not proper that she continue to consort with such ruffians."

"That is why she asked me to act as her lieutenant," Mal said.

"Indeed. And no doubt you know far more about them than she: not just their skills, but their weaknesses that our enemies could use to their advantage. Every man has his price, Catlyn."

"I will provide you with a full report, my lord. Every particular known to me."

"Good." Grey rocked his cane back and forth thoughtfully. "Including your friends?"

"My lord?"

"I am well aware of your... companions. I saw them at my father's house, and met one of them subsequently. A lad of about sixteen, and two more a little older. I believe one of them is an actor?"

"Aye, my lord. Gabriel Parrish, formerly with your father's company of players. Though he is as much a playwright as an actor these days."

"No matter. You will provide full and accurate details of these three, as well as the other men in Lady Frances's service." This time it was not a question.

"If it please my lord. Although the youngest one, Jacob Hendricks, has gone back to his family in the Low Countries, I believe. I have not seen him this past year or more."

Grey leaned forward. "If he knows your business, he is a weak spot in our defences. All the more so since we have no control over him. In fact, I think you should recall him to your service."

Mal was tempted to say that "Jacob" was dead, but his wife might need the disguise again some day.

"Aye, my lord."

"You anticipate some difficulty?"

"No, my lord, but it may take some time."

"Give it your highest priority, after making your reports on the others."

"Aye, my lord."

Grey waved a hand irritably in his direction.

"Enough for one night. I have much still to do."

Mal bowed and withdrew, his thoughts already racing ahead of him to Southwark. Grey was not the only man with much to do tonight.

The Sign of the Parley stood in one of the many new streets that had spread southwards from Bankside as the suburb's population soared. A timber-framed gatehouse with workshops either side fronted onto the street, with behind it a small courtyard, and the owners' house beyond that. The sign that gave the establishment its name – a mailed fist clutching a roll of paper – hung over the gateway; a jest of Ned's, but one that always gave Mal a pang of guilt. If he had not taken him to Venice, Ned would never have lost his right hand to the devourers. The brass-and-steel replacement designed by Coby was poor compensation for a man who had formerly earned his living as a scrivener, hence Mal's sponsorship of Ned to become a master of the Worshipful Company of Stationers and his purchase of this house-cum-workshop in which his friend could practice his new trade.

The print shop had closed up for the day, so Mal let himself in by the wicket gate. As he crossed the yard a blonde head poked out of the upstairs window. Mal broke into a smile – the very man he sought. If anyone could dream up a few fictional weaknesses to present to Grey, it was a playwright.

"Catlyn!" Parrish called down. "How went your enterprise?"

"Middling well. But I need to talk to you."

"Sorry, I have business with the Prince's Men tonight. Is tomorrow soon enough?"

"Tomorrow will do. Where's Ned?"

"In the shop, I think. He's been working late on a rush job."

Mal saluted him and went through the back door of the shop. Immediately his nose was met by the sharp bitter smell of ink and the vanilla must of paper. He picked his way around the stacks of pamphlets and boxes of type and eventually found Ned at his desk in the office. The younger man looked up from his ledgers and broke into a grin.

"Good news, I hope?"

"When is there ever good news in our line of work?" Mal replied. "I see you've been busy."

"Burbage got wind of a half-arsed copy of *Romeo and Juliet* doing the rounds, so he wants us to have an official version to sell in its place. I've been manning the press on our other jobs so we can get it typeset in time."

He yawned and flexed his ink-stained left hand. The right rested motionless on the ledger, the edges of its intricate brass joints shining like molten gold in the lamplight.

"You deserve a beer," Mal said. "And I need one."

"All right. I'm about done here anyway."

Mal followed Ned across the yard to the kitchen. The fire had been banked for the night, but Mal lit a spill from the embers and touched it to a candle stub whilst Ned moved about the darkened room with the ease of familiarity.

"So," Ned said, bringing two leather jacks of beer to the kitchen table, "what's afoot?"

Mal told him about Grey, everything except the instruction to report on the other agents. Ned interrupted from time to time, often with questions that Mal had no answer to, and cursed Grey at regular intervals. At last the tale was done and they sat in silence, drinking their beer.

"You reckon there's any way we can get out of it?" Ned got to his feet and went to refill their tankards.

"Working for Grey? No, I doubt it. Besides, this could be the very chance we've been looking for."

Ned looked up from the beer tap. "How so?"

"Right now we only know one guiser's identity for certain. Prince Henry, the Duke of Suffolk as was."

"Blaise's father."

Mal nodded. "Coby said that Grey had a substantial collection of his father's paperwork, not just that book Sandy stole. And now we have an ally within his very household."

"It's a good start. But wasn't the book useless?"

"Aye, but there could be other evidence: letters from their fellow conspirators, perhaps even a diary. But getting our hands on that will take time. In the meantime, I need you to redouble your efforts."

"I'm doing my best, Mal–"

"I know, but if Grey gets his hands on Walsingham's papers, that could be the last we see of them. I can stall him for a while, tell him I need them in order to compile the reports he wants, but after that…"

"All right. One of my journeymen has a nephew looking for an apprenticeship, so I dare say I could take a bit more time away from the presses."

"Thank you." Mal drained his tankard. "I'll do what I can to help, but I don't have your eye for handwriting, you know that. And if I don't get up to Derbyshire before the summer's out, my wife will have my guts for lute-strings."

CHAPTER III

Someone was knocking on his bedchamber door. Or perhaps the palace was falling down. Mal rather hoped it was the latter, so that it wouldn't be his problem.

"Go away," he groaned, and buried his face in the bolster.

The knocking came again. More like hammering, to tell the truth. Only one person could knock like that. And if he'd bothered coming all the way to Whitehall, it must be important. Mal cursed under his breath. This was all he needed.

"Come in!"

He struggled upright, tangling his legs in the sheets. It had been a warm night for May and he was wearing naught but what he had been born in. A little self-consciously he pulled the sheet up around his waist.

"I don't know why you're bothering," Ned said, closing the door behind him. "It's nothing I haven't seen before."

Mal made the sign of the fig at him.

"Pass me that decanter," he said, waving at the dresser on the other side of the room.

"Aye, milord. Whatever you say, milord." Despite his tone Ned obeyed, tucking the sheaf of papers he was carrying under his right arm so that he could lift the flagon with his good hand. "You look as crapulous as a cardinal. Late night, was it?"

Mal rubbed a hand over his face. "Could say that. Southampton dragged us all to the new theatre in Blackfriars, and then back here for a late supper. A very late supper."

"You love every moment of it," Ned replied. "Swanning around with the flower of the court. *Sir* Maliverny Catlyn, intimate of the Prince of Wales."

"Robert wasn't there. He said he had more important things to do. And no, I don't love it. I'm too old for this game." He took a gulp of the wine. It had gone a little sour overnight; perhaps he should send for sugar? Perhaps not. The sourness suited his humour. "Why are you here, anyway?"

"I have a letter for you. From your wife."

Mal took it, pressed his lips to the creased paper and tucked it under the bolster. Was it only two weeks since he had left them? It felt more like a year.

"Aren't you going to read it?"

"Later." He would savour her words in private, without Ned breathing down his neck. "You didn't come all this way so early in the morning just to bring me that letter, did you?"

"Early? It's almost noon."

"You haven't answered my question."

Ned sat down on the end of the bed with a sigh. "I have the information you wanted. But you're not going to like it."

"Oh?"

"I went through all the papers you sent me, looking for mentions of the late duke and his intimates."

"And?"

"One name seemed out of place. Sir William Selby."

"Selby, Selby…" Mal scratched his brow. "Sounds familiar, but I can't think where from."

"He's a Member of Parliament for Northumberland, owns a small estate down in Kent. In and out of London all the time."

"That fits the pattern. Still, small fry by the sounds of it. So what's the bad news?"

"Ten, fifteen years ago, he was a captain in the Berwick garrison, where he passed on letters from Scottish spies to our late master, Sir Francis Walsingham."

"An intelligencer? He's not still active, though, is he?" Mal said.

"Perhaps not. I had to dig deep into Walsingham's old records to make the connection." Ned shook his head. "Christ's balls, Mal! What if he's not out of the game? He was doing this long before we were; he could be in league with someone like Baines and we'd never know."

Mal slapped Ned on the shoulder. "Don't look downcast! We can use this to our advantage."

"How?"

"Leave that to me. But thank you. For the first time since we returned to England, we have a glimpse of the enemy."

The manor of Ightham Mote lay some thirty miles southwest of London, near the town of Sevenoaks. Mal's intelligencers' reports had led him to expect a fortified manorhouse with thick stone walls falling sheer to a moat, and in that he was not disappointed. The outward-facing windows were small, and the only entrance lay across a narrow wooden bridge. Mal's conviction that here was a guiser stronghold deepened. There was still a risk that he was wrong, of course, and that all his careful planning of the past few weeks would come to naught, but he had delayed long enough. He had to start somewhere, and Walsingham had taught him that to break a conspiracy apart, you always targeted the weakest link.

He reined Hector to a halt at the bridge's near end and dismounted. The planks of the bridge sounded hollowly under his booted feet; a sign of age, or was it deliberate, to make it harder to approach the house unnoticed? He wished there had been a way to find out more about the house before coming here, but too much attention would only have aroused Selby's suspicions. Strangers were conspicuous in a quiet village like Ightham.

The low entrance door opened at his approach and a middle-aged man in russet livery greeted him.

"The master will see you in the great hall," the porter added with a sniff, looking him up and down. Mal supposed he must look dusty and rumpled from his ride. "I'll send a boy to tend to your horse."

Mal stepped into the gatehouse and made a show of dusting himself down whilst surreptitiously glancing around. A hook near the doorway held a large iron key; stronghold or no, it appeared they did not lock the door during daylight hours. Careless of Selby, but it would save a good deal of trouble later.

The porter showed him across the courtyard and into a spacious chamber with a wide stone fireplace and half-panelled walls. A liver-and-white spotted hound lazed before the fire, but at Mal's entrance it raised its head and growled.

"Quiet, lad," a voice said from the opposite doorway.

Mal turned to see a well-dressed man of about forty with receding hair and doleful blue eyes. "Sir William?"

"Aye. And you must be Sir Maliverny Catlyn."

A moment's awkward pause, then Selby gestured to one of the heavily carved chairs by the fire. Mal edged around the hound and sat down.

"Let's get to the point, shall we, Catlyn? You said you had a business proposition for me, one you needed to discuss in private."

"Aye." *Carefully does it now. There's still a chance that Selby is no more than he appears: an ex-soldier come into a handsome inheritance. How oddly alike we are.* "I believe we have some acquaintances in common. The late Sir Francis Walsingham, for one."

Selby smiled and leaned back in his chair. "Alas, poor Sir Francis. I don't think I saw him after he fell sick in the winter of ninety-four, and I ceased working for him some years before that."

"Did you know that Lord Grey has taken over his intelligence network, since his betrothal to Walsingham's daughter?"

"No, I did not."

There was no hint of duplicity in Selby's expression. If anything he sounded worried.

"Then we have common cause," Mal said. "Grey has sworn to Robert that he will hunt down his father's former associates."

"And what business is that of mine?"

"You are named in a good many of Walsingham's papers, in conjunction with the duke."

A curious expression crossed Selby's features, amusement warring with sudden dread. "I dare say there's been some mistake."

"No mistake, Selby. And if I can find you out, so can he."

"Why are you telling me all this? Do you expect a reward? Some favour in return? I have little influence except my vote in parliament."

"I told you, we have common cause." Mal stretched out his damp boots towards the fire. The hound twitched an eyebrow but otherwise ignored him. "How's Prince Henry these days?"

"What? How should I know? I am no hanger-on at court." Selby looked ruffled now. "Are you accusing me of something, Catlyn?"

"Not at all. I just thought we might share an interest in the prince's welfare. The line of succession is so important, is it not?"

Selby sprang to his feet. "If you have come here to recruit me into some treasonous scheme, sir, you can leave now."

Mal held up his hands placatingly. "You misunderstand me, Sir William. I know you have a special fondness for our young prince, that is all. As you did for the late Duke of Suffolk."

Selby hesitated, and his look of outrage softened into a smile. Mal breathed a quiet sigh of relief. They had been on the right trail, then. Selby sat down again.

"Go on."

"Let there be no more deceit or coyness between us, Sir William," Mal said. "I know what you are, and I think you know more about me than you are letting on."

"I know you to be a friend of the skraylings. Is that true?"

"A necessary deception," Mal said. "My brother and I needed to earn their trust so that we could discover their plans. It took time, but now we have achieved that, we can make our next move."

"Which is?"

"Ah, now, that would be telling. How do I know we can trust you?"

"I might ask you the same question."

Damn it, we could dance around one another half the night. "Tonight. We will dreamwalk together, then there will be no secrets between us."

He waited for Selby to claim he knew nothing of dreamwalking, afraid he had mistaken this country knight after all. Selby reached over and rang a bell by the fireplace.

"Bring us wine," he told the servant who appeared a few moments later. "And make up a bed for Sir Maliverny. He'll be staying the night."

Mal inclined his head in thanks, hiding a smile of relief. *Christ's blood, but this plan had better work, otherwise we're all as fucked as a tupenny whore.*

As soon as he retired to bed, Mal lit a candle and waved it back and forth thrice at his bedchamber window, praying his allies would take the hint and come soon. He took off his doublet, shoes and stockings, repeated the signal and then sat down on the bed to wait for the household to settle down for the night. There were not a great many of them, as far as he could tell, but most were men between twenty and forty. Nothing unusual in that, but it meant they were likely to put up a fight. Most likely none of them were guisers, though, apart from their master. At least so Mal hoped. Otherwise… well, they would deal with that problem if it came to it. Slaughtering the entire household was not part of the plan.

As soon as all was quiet, he crept barefoot down the stairs and let himself out into the courtyard. The hound lay with its nose poking out of the kennel, snoring and twitching in its sleep. Mal tiptoed across the cold, damp cobbles, praying silently. He was going to have to do this skin-to-skin, or Selby would notice immediately. The fellow was probably already waiting in the dreamlands; much more delay and he would become suspicious.

The hound wuffled to itself but did not stir. Mal crouched and laid a hand on the beast's head, reaching out to touch its dreaming mind with his own. A barrage of scents overwhelmed him, he was running on all fours through long wet grass… Holding onto his sense of self he led the hound further into deep, dreamless sleep, the way Sandy had showed him. It wouldn't last more than a few minutes, but that should be enough. He crossed the yard and slipped into the short wide passageway that led to the front door.

"Can I help you, sir?"

Candlelight flooded the passage, and Mal froze. A girl of about eighteen, dressed in a servant's cap and apron, stood in a side doorway.

Mal yawned prodigiously. "I'm afraid I couldn't find a pisspot in my chamber."

"I'm very sorry, sir. I'll fetch one for you, shall I?"

"I don't want to be any trouble. I'll just go outside and do it in the moat–"

"Oh, it's no trouble, sir. Just you wait there."

"If you're going to the kitchens, a flagon of small ale wouldn't go amiss," Mal called after her.

When he was sure she had gone, he eased back the bolts on the front door, taking care not to make a sound. Finally he took down the door key from its hook, turned it in the lock and quickly replaced it.

Hearing footsteps approach, he stepped back towards the courtyard. The maidservant emerged from the side door, dangling an empty pisspot from one hand and carrying a pewter tankard in the other.

"Most excellent wench!" Mal drawled, blocking her path back inside. He held out his left hand, and she dutifully gave him the tankard. "Perhaps you would come up to my chamber and stow yon crock safely?"

She clutched the pisspot to her chest. "If you insist, my lord."

"I am no lord, merely a knight of the realm." He took a swig of the ale. "The Prince of Wales himself dubbed me, you know."

The girl smiled politely.

"Come, give me the pisspot," Mal said, "and I'll retire alone. There's no pleasure in a reluctant woman."

She held out the pot, her arm trembling, and Mal took it from her gently.

"Now, get you gone," he said with a jerk of his head towards the door, "and we'll tell your master no more of this little adventure, eh?"

"No, sir. Thank you, sir."

Mal swept a bow, flourishing the pisspot, and made his way back up to his room. Poor child, he'd given her quite a fright, but at least it had kept her eyes away from the door. Now there was nothing more to do but wait.

He used the pisspot, slid it under his bed and lay down. This next part would be cold and uncomfortable, but they had to make it look convincing, at least until Selby was under control.

He closed his eyes, knowing he could not put this off much longer. Taking a deep breath he put all thoughts of his waiting allies aside and focused on the skraylings. The guisers must have some idea of what was happening in the camp, so it was hardly a betrayal. He recalled his first visit there, with Kiiren – no, he mustn't think of Kiiren either. Adjaan, that was safer. He conjured up a vision of the female outspeaker, kneeling at her desk.

"This is your plan?" Selby said, materialising silently at his side. "To bring skrayling women to England?"

"We need more recruits, don't we, if we are to take over? A period of stability will allow that. And once the womenfolk see what humans are really like, surely they will easily be convinced that we are in the right?"

Selby smiled at him. "Your enthusiasm is gratifying, Catlyn, but–"

Mal jerked awake, certain he had heard a shot. The hound in the courtyard yelped, and the gun spoke again. Damn those idiots, they'll wake half the neighbourhood! He snatched up his dagger and ran across the landing to Selby's bedchamber, flattening himself against the wall just as the door opened.

Selby poked his head out.

"What's going on down there?"

Mal put the blade to Selby's throat, pressing just hard enough to break the skin. There, let him magic his way out with cold steel tainting his blood.

"You duplicitous whoreson," Selby hissed. "Jathekkil should have ripped your crippled soul from your body when he had the chance."

Shouting and sounds of fighting came from below. William Frogmore and his Huntsmen, subduing the servants with brutal efficiency. This was the part of his plan he had not told Grey about;

the duke would hardly approve of employing the very villains he had promised the Prince of Wales he would hunt down.

Moments later three men in nondescript dark clothing, their lower faces covered by kerchiefs, pounded up the stairs. Mal nodded to their leader, but continued to hold Selby at knifepoint until one of the Huntsmen had him gagged and in iron manacles. Mal stood patiently whilst the "robbers" tied his own hands behind his back and gagged him, then Frogmore led both captives downstairs to the courtyard, where the servants were being held at gunpoint. Selby struggled and jerked his head towards Mal. Frogmore cuffed him hard, making him stumble. Mal feigned concern, but his need for acting was short-lived. Amid the jeering laughter of the Huntsmen, he was seized and thrown over a horse's back like a sack of meal.

One of the men swung himself into the saddle behind Mal and the raiding party set off into the Kentish countryside. They passed out of sight of the manorhouse and cut across a field of half-rotted wheat stubble. What was Frogmore playing at? Surely this was far enough from the manorhouse that they could dispense with the ruse and let him ride in comfort.

About half an hour later they halted under a twisted oak. The ground before them fell steeply for a dozen feet then levelled out to a broad, grassy riverbank, the waters beyond silver-limned by the rising moon. Mal was hauled off his horse and he sank to his knees, head reeling from hanging upside-down for so long. He watched Selby stumble down the slope towards a waiting boat, flanked by Frogmore's men. When they were out of earshot, someone untied Mal's bonds and he pulled the gag down, licking his dry lips.

"Damn it, Frogmore," he muttered, "you didn't have to carry me all the way."

Frogmore held out a hand and hauled him to his feet.

"Had to make it look good. Speaking of which…"

Mal saw the punch coming, too late, and tried to dodge. His foot slipped on a mossy tree root and he couldn't avoid Frogmore's fist slamming into his nose. He heard rather than felt the snap of cartilage.

"Christ's balls!" He dabbed at the blood running down into his moustache. The young cur was enjoying this far too much.

Frogmore shrugged. "You wanted your escape to look convincing. Sir."

"Get to the boat," Mal told him. "I don't suppose you could leave me a horse for the journey back to Ightham?"

The servants believed him, of course. They could hardly not, when he turned up rain-soaked and bloody-nosed some hours after the attack. He quickly changed into a borrowed shirt and his own clothes before leading the hue-and-cry back to the river bank. Of course the Huntsmen had long gone by then, but they had left evidence of their work. Mal swore under his breath. Someone had been creative with his instructions. A little too creative.

A little way along the ridge from where he had "escaped", blackened timbers jutted from the earth: an X-shaped framework to which a man's body was chained, upside-down. A fire had been set beneath it and the victim's clothes and hair had already burned away, falling in sooty pieces into the ashes. For a moment Mal wondered if the bastards had done something similar to Erishen's previous body, after… He pushed the thought aside. This was no innocent victim burned alive, only a hanged corpse of Selby's height and build, dressed in his clothes to leave evidence: buttons, belt buckles, perhaps even rings. The Huntsmen were thorough, but not totally immune to temptation.

Selby's steward halted, his expression needing no words. Somewhere behind them, one of the younger men was violently sick.

"Who would do such a thing?" the steward said at last.

"Witchhunters?" This was the last thing Mal wanted, but it seemed the only way to deflect suspicion from his allies. "Perhaps the madness has crossed the Narrow Sea."

"But why our master?" another man demanded. "Who would think him a witch?"

"How should I know?" Mal took in the assembled servants with a look. "Has he been behaving strangely of late? Any peculiar instructions or absences?"

There were some shaken heads and mumbles of denial, but also one or two shared looks of enlightenment. If Selby had done anything in the least out of the ordinary – and as a guiser plotting to control the kingdom, he was certain to have done something odd at some point – gossip would soon turn it into symptoms of possession or devil-worship. That was how these things worked, after all.

"Put out the fire and retrieve the body," Mal said. "He should be given a Christian burial, whatever his murderers believed. Now, if you will excuse me, I have to get back to London and inform the Privy Council. If we have lawless bands of witchhunters roaming the country, someone needs to put a stop to it."

CHAPTER IV

Even with a change of horses it took Mal until well past noon to reach London. He prayed Selby was safely mewed up in the Tower by now, but he could not afford the luxury of a visit just yet. News of Selby's apparent death would reach the other guisers soon enough, and if Mal's story was to hold water he needed to act as if it were true. Which meant reporting the incident to the Privy Council in Whitehall Palace. The County Coroner for Kent would deal with the murder itself, but the nature of the attack was a more serious business. Damn the Huntsmen to the innermost circle of Hell! He had been a fool to think he could use them and not pay a heavy price. As soon as he was sure he had the last scrap of useful information out of them, Grey would get his list and could round them up at his leisure.

The city sweltered and stank in the August heat, its open sewers too dry to wash the filth away. Mal pressed a clove-scented handkerchief to his mouth until he reached the cleaner air of Westminster, guiding his mount with his knees and leaving the reins loose so the poor beast could shake away the flies that filled the air like smoke. If plague did not follow on the heels of this latest poor harvest, it would be a miracle. Suddenly he was very glad his family were far from the capital, where they would at least be spared such horrors.

It appeared that Prince Robert felt likewise. The courtyards of the palace of Whitehall lay empty, only a few bored guardsmen at each gate to keep the hungry, frightened populace at bay. Mal gave his name and business, and was told that the Privy Council had dispersed for the summer; only Lord Grey had remained behind to deal with affairs of state. At least that made matters simpler. The formalities could be adhered to without drawing undue attention, and by the time the council reconvened, Selby would have been taken care of. Permanently.

Mal was show into a dining parlour that formed part of the councillors' suite of chambers in the palace. The same room in which he had been questioned by Walsingham after his escape from Grey's own father. He wondered if the duke knew that and was using it to throw him off balance, or whether it was mere coincidence. Probably the latter: Grey might have a talent for interrogation, but he lacked his predecessor's subtlety.

The room was empty, however. No spymaster seated at the long oak dining table, no Baines standing by the door to prevent his departure. Mal made a discreet sweep of the room, looking for places where a hidden observer might lurk. No hollows behind the panels, nor concealed doors. The windows either side of the fireplace looked out onto a narrow courtyard, but the brick wall opposite was blank and the surrounding buildings' windows too far away for a good view into the dining parlour.

Halting footsteps sounded in the corridor, giving Mal time to turn to face the door.

"Catlyn." Grey paused in the doorway and looked around the room. "You came alone."

Since there were no servants about, Mal went to the head of the table and pulled out the chair for the duke. Grey limped over and sat down, slow as an old man. Probably putting half of it on, just to make a point. He left Grey to settle himself and closed the door, resisting the urge to look out into the corridor for spies. If anyone were observing, it would only draw attention, and by the looks of the rest of the palace there was no one around in any case.

"You expected me to bring our… acquaintance here, my lord?"

"Those were my instructions," Grey said. He undid the top two buttons on his doublet. "God's teeth but it's close today!"

"Shall I send for chilled wine?"

"Later. Let's get this business over with. About Selby…"

Mal ran his tongue round a mouth suddenly dry at the mention of wine.

"Forgive me, my lord. I thought you said to take him into safe custody, not bring him into the midst of our enemies."

"The palace is empty, as you must have seen. Where better to conceal him?"

"With respect, my lord, the Tower is a far more secure location."

"And are you certain that neither the Lieutenant of the Tower nor any of his men are members of this conspiracy?"

Mal stared at the reflection of the candlesticks in the table's polished surface. There were ways to uncover a guiser using the magics Sandy had taught him, but they required close contact and risked alerting the subject to one's suspicions. Only a handful of his intelligencers had been tested – and cleared – thus far.

"No, my lord."

Grey shook his head and tutted.

"But I do have men in the garrison," Mal added. "It was they who took the prisoner into custody, and they are under strict instructions not to let him speak except to his interrogators."

That much was true, if everything had gone to plan. The Huntsmen were no more keen to enter the Tower than Mal was to have them there, so he had arranged for Selby to be handed over to two of his most trusted agents on the outskirts of Tower Hamlets.

"Nonetheless, I do not appreciate independence in my subordinates," Grey said. "Next time you will follow your orders to the letter. Do you understand?"

"Yes, my lord."

"And I want the names of these men of yours at the Tower. I trust they were included in your reports?"

"Of course. If you have pen and paper to hand, I'll make a list for you."

Grey gestured towards a cupboard on the far side of the room. "And when you're done, I want a full written report of your doings in

Kent. No, make that two reports. An official one for the Privy Council, leaving out all this conspiracy nonsense, and the real one."

"What would you have the official report say, my lord?"

"Say whatever you like, as long as it puts them off the scent. For all we know, half of them could be in on the plot, eh?"

"Indeed, my lord."

Mal found paper, quills and ink and set about scratching down a list of names. At this rate Selby would be tortured and executed before he got another look at him. *Damn Grey and his reports! Should have run the bastard through good and proper instead of letting him live. Your honour will be the death of you, Mal Catlyn.*

Writing the reports for Grey took until nightfall, by which time Mal's right hand was stiff with cramp and his head pounding like a war drum. He had considered going back to Southwark and calling upon Parrish's talents once more, but the less his friends knew about the goings-on in Kent, the better. So he painstakingly composed each story in outline – with many crossings-out and amendments – then wrote them out in formal language before burning all his notes in the fireplace. Without their masters to run around after, the remaining servants would be even more likely to notice something amiss and use it to their advantage if they could.

He found a manservant to bring him supper, and retired to the chamber he had slept in during previous sojourns at court. With a pleasantly full belly at last, and a final cup of wine to hand, he stripped to his drawers and lay down on the bed. He fingered the smooth round beads at his throat, remembering the dead skraylings he had found in the watchtower on Corsica, and his thoughts strayed eastwards to another tower, older but much closer. For one drunken moment he considered removing his spirit-guard and dreamwalking in search of Selby, of probing his enemy's most secret thoughts as Sandy could do. With the palace empty, there might not be any other guisers in the whole of London, so now would be as good a time as–

No, dammit. The villain would be in irons, cut off from the dreamlands as effectively as any mortal man. That was a vital part of the plan.

No use for it; he would have to wait until the morrow. Yawning widely, he rolled over and surrendered to sleep.

The Tower of London was silent but for the croaking of ravens and screaming of kites as they squabbled over the meagre pickings on Traitor's Gate. There had been few prisoners here of late, and only one that Mal cared about.

He spared a glance for St Thomas's Tower, where the skrayling ambassador and his party had lodged several summers ago, then turned left into the inner ward and climbed the long slope to the green. An L-shaped timber-framed house was tucked into the corner of the south and west walls, facing the five hundred year-old bulk of the central keep. Mal went up to the front door and knocked. It felt like a lifetime since he had first come here, perplexed and unwilling, to discover he had been chosen as the ambassador's bodyguard. There was another Lieutenant of the Tower now; they were never allowed to stay in their post long, lest complacency made them corrupt. The Tower was reserved for the kingdom's most dangerous wrongdoers, many of whom were rich and powerful enough to bend even the most honest gaoler to their will.

His knock was answered at length by a servant, who ushered him through the antechamber with its portraits of former custodians (including, Mal noticed, a new one, of the previous incumbent, Sir James Leland), through the dining chamber that Leland had favoured as his office and up a narrow oak staircase to the first floor.

"Sir Maliverny Catlyn to see you, sir."

Mal bowed crisply, as befitted the situation, and straightened up.

"Sir Richard Berkeley?"

"The same." The new lieutenant was a short, spindly-calved man of three score years or more. What remained of his hair was as grey as his full, pointed beard and curled moustache. Disappointing. They needed a ruthless ally in this fight, and Mal doubted they would find one in Berkeley.

"Has Selby confessed yet?" Mal crossed to the window, wondering which tower's bowels contained the prisoner's cries. He had given strict orders that no one except his tormentors was to be able to hear the man scream.

"You young fellows nowadays don't beat about the bush, do you?" Berkeley replied. "Here, see for yourself."

He handed Mal a sheet of paper. A list of names. Lots of names.

"Damn it!" The paper crumpled in his hand, and it was all he could do not to throw it into the fire. "I thought I told you to get the truth out of him, not a list of every peer of the realm. This is useless."

"Topcliffe can be very... dedicated to his vocation," Berkeley said, turning pale. "I regret I have not the stomach to supervise his work."

"And Lord Grey? Has he been here since the prisoner arrived?"

"No, he has not. Should I have expected him?"

I would have. But perhaps Grey's appetite for causing pain died when he was forced to suffer it himself.

"I think I had better go and see for myself."

He shoved the wad of paper into his pocket, gave Berkeley the curtest of bows and strode out of the room without a backward glance.

Selby had been put in a small cell in the base of the Martin Tower; a filthy hole with naught but straw on the floor and a slop bucket in the corner. The prisoner was lying on a pile of straw like a discarded doll, evidently lacking the strength even to roll into a more comfortable position. If he could find one. England had only one torture implement in regular use – the rack – but Topcliffe had grown expert in its operation.

Mal's gaze fell upon Selby's arm, lying flung out towards the door as if in mute supplication. A heavy iron manacle with a few links trailing from its staple had been locked around his wrist, but it did not hide the cruel rope burns where Selby had been tied to the rack. A quick survey showed all four limbs in the same state. Mal looked again. The position of the burns suggested that the ropes could not have been tied in place whilst the shackles were around Selby's wrists and ankles. If it had been done one at a time, that would have been safe enough. If not…

"Gaoler!"

The prisoner did not stir. Mal went back to the door.

"Gaoler!"

A skinny Tower guard in ill-fitting livery shuffled into view. "My lord?"

"Where's Master Topcliffe?"

"Gone home, sir. Said he was done here."

"What about…" Mal reeled off the names of his agents, plus a couple of commonplace surnames for good measure.

"Off duty, sir. They was up all night with the prisoner."

He scratched a stubbly sideburn and flicked the results towards the prisoner.

"All?" Mal asked, trying to rein in his impatience. "Is no one here that saw the interrogation?"

"Yes, sir. Me, sir."

Mal looked him up and down. "You were called in to help subdue the prisoner?"

"No need for no subduing, sir. He came quiet as a lamb."

"Really."

"Aye, sir. He even thanked us as we took off his shackles."

"You took off his shackles. All of them?"

"Only for a moment, sir. Master Topcliffe said he couldn't do the racking proper like, not in shackles, but Sir Richard told him he had to. So we took 'em off and tied him up, then put 'em back on again."

Mal suppressed the urge to slam the stupid little man's head against the wall. It wasn't his fault after all. Thank God Berkeley had overruled Topcliffe. Still, it might have been enough.

"Leave us," he told the guard. "And close the door behind you. I may be in here some time."

"You're not going to torture him, are you, sir? Only Master Topcliffe gets paid by the hour, and he won't be too happy if someone else does his work for him."

Mal slammed the man against the cell wall.

"You can tell Master Topcliffe," he growled, leaning down so close he nearly gagged on the man's foul breath, "that if he had done his job properly, I wouldn't need to do it for him. Do you understand?"

The guard nodded. "Y-y-yes, my lord."

Mal let him go and he scuttled out of the cell before he could be reprimanded further. When the door had closed, Mal turned back to the prisoner, whose eyes were now open.

"I gather you heard all that?"

"Most of it," Selby rasped. "You were a fool to trust these feeble-minded creatures with such a task."

"A mistake I will not make again," Mal replied. He hunkered down, just out of Selby's reach. Even in his present enfeebled state, the man might still be desperate enough for a last attack.

"Shall I tell you what I told my friends about you?" Selby said with a sly smile.

"Everything you've said here is a lie. I have no wish to hear more such." Mal drew his dagger.

"I told them… Aaah!" Selby gasped as the dagger blade slid between his ribs. His smile faded to a look of hatred, then of panic as he realised Mal had not withdrawn the dagger.

"I'll just leave it there for a while, shall I?" Mal said, getting to his feet. He retrieved the unused slop-bucket, turned it upside down and sat on it. "This time I want to make sure you are absolutely, certainly dead. For all time."

It was but a short walk from the Tower to Saint Katherine's Stairs, and from there an equally short journey by wherry to the skrayling camp on the opposite bank. The camp was busier than Mal had seen it for a long time: several small boats were moored on the riverward side of the stockade, and the gates were wide open, albeit still guarded.

"*Kuru-an rrish.*" He made obeisance in the skrayling fashion, holding his hands palm forwards at his sides and turning his head to present his bare throat.

"*Kaal-an rrish, Catlyn-tuur.*"

"Adjaan-tuur is here?"

One of the guards inclined his head and waved Mal through the gate. Mal thanked him and made his way through the camp, ignoring the inquisitive and sometimes admiring looks he got from some of the inhabitants. Since meeting Adjaan he had come to understand why human males looked feminine to skrayling eyes, but it was still disconcerting.

The outspeaker herself was not in her cabin today. Eventually Mal found her seated under a beech tree at the other end of the camp, watching a group of skrayling men play a fast-moving ball game that looked like a cross between tennis and football. Adjaan hardly seemed to notice his arrival; her eyes were fixed on the players, a look of fierce concentration on her face. Mal sat down quietly next to her and waited.

After a few more tense passes, one side erupted in cheers, which Mal supposed meant they had won the game. The losers abased themselves and walked away, whilst the winners approached Adjaan. She scanned them all for several moments, and at last pointed to one of them and snapped her fingers.

The young skrayling flushed beneath his tattoos and bared his fangs in a grin. His team mates dispersed, their shoulders drooping in disappointment. Adjaan beckoned her chosen one forward and said something to him in low tones. He nodded and left, with a cocky swagger to his gait that Mal had never seen before in a skrayling. At last Adjaan turned to him.

"*Kaal-an rrish*, Catlyn-*tuur.*"

"*Kaal-an rrish*, Adjaan-*tuur.*"

"Did you enjoy the game?" She craned her neck, her eyes following the young skrayling as he disappeared between the tents.

"I... Yes, I suppose so. Though I cannot remember the rules."

Adjaan made a face. "Do not tell my kinfolk, but neither can I. Still, one cannot argue with tradition, eh? Not when the outcome is so pleasing."

Mal recalled something that Kiiren had once told him, about the skraylings using games and competitions to choose mates. Was that what had just happened here?

"You are well?" Adjaan asked, breaking into his train of thought. "And Erishen and Kiiren-*tuur* also?"

"Ah, yes, thank you, honoured one," he said, struggling to bring his thoughts back to the matter in hand. "Or at least, so I believe. I have not heard from Sandy – I mean Erishen – for a few weeks, but my wife sent his greetings in her last letter. And Kit too." He smiled to himself, remembering the inky scratch vaguely resembling a *K* at the bottom of the letter, guided by an adult's hand.

Adjaan nodded. "You are here on dreamwalker business."

So much for the pleasantries. "Am I so easy to read?"

"Yes."

There was no polite answer to that. Mal had to remind himself that this was not his old friend, but a stranger who had taken over his role within the clan.

"Very well, then," he said. "Let us get down to business."

He told Adjaan about Selby: his capture and interrogation, and the unfortunate removal of his irons for a brief but unknown period.

"Careless," Adjaan said. "You should have brought him to us for questioning."

"That would have been... difficult. The Huntsmen would never have willingly handed him over to you."

Adjaan muttered something under her breath. Mal wasn't sure the skraylings understood the concept of swearing, but the outspeaker's words had not sounded polite.

"And now you expect my people to... how do you say it? 'Clean up after you'?"

"Of course not, honoured one. But I thought your dreamwalkers might have observed something."

"When did this occur?"

"Yesterday, a little after sunset."

Adjaan took a deep breath and closed her eyes. Mal waited. And waited. He was tempted to remove his own spirit-guard and try to follow her into the dreamlands, but suspected that would not be considered polite.

Eventually Adjaan's eyes snapped open again.

"There was something, just the other side of the river."

Mal's heart sank. "What kind of 'something'?"

"Njaaren could not be certain. Our patrols pay little attention to what goes on in the city itself, unless it appears to be a direct threat to us."

"Please, honoured one; any information could be valuable."

"Yesterday Njaaren saw a white light flare and dance amongst the souls within the Tower, and when it was gone, so were some of the others."

"What others?"

"The off-duty guardsmen. They had woken."

"That could just have been devourers," Mal said with a shudder. He had once been chased across the dreamscape by the creatures, and seen them crash into the other dreaming minds around him, leaving nightmares in their wake.

"True. If this guiser was being hurt, as you say, the *hrrith* would have been drawn to him, and may have disturbed the sleep of the others. Or..." The skrayling gestured helplessly.

"Or it could have been Selby himself," Mal said.

"Yes. It would depend upon his skill, of course. You are sure the *senzadheneth* here are young and inexperienced?"

"For the most part, yes. Jathekkil..." Mal forced out the name of his enemy. "Jathekkil turned to dream-magic only as a last resort, after he had failed to learn what he wanted from me through more... mundane means. I have no reason to believe that any of the others are markedly more skilful than he."

"Then it seems unlikely he could have impressed a strong enough compulsion on any of the guardsmen."

"A compulsion to do what?"

Adjaan shrugged again. "To do whatever he needed."

"Like, tell the other guisers?"

"Yes. A simple image of the truth might suffice. If it was strong enough to make the man speak of it to those who might want to know."

Mal swore under his breath, earning an icy look from the outspeaker.

"Thank you for your help, Adjaan-*tuur*," he said, getting to his feet. "I will leave you to your meditations."

He left the camp deep in thought. If only he had been able to call on the skraylings to fence Selby in, none of this would have happened. But he doubted they would have agreed to it, and in any case it would surely have attracted the attention of the others. No, the plan had been a good one, given the tools at hand. He would simply have to rethink his next move.

CHAPTER V

Ned perused the printed sheet, chewing at his moustache. Out of the corner of his eye he watched the apprentice, Jack, who had brought him the piece. The lad looked fit to wet himself with fear.

"Well," he said at last. "It's better than your last attempt."

"Yes, sir. T-t-thank you, sir."

"But see here." Ned laid the sheet down on the table. "The spacing on the first word is all wrong. You want a number three 'A' on a word like that, then the 'W' will fit all snug against it. You have to take extra care with the capitals, or it looks a right old mess."

"Yes, sir, I'll try, sir."

Ned handed him the sheet. "Do it again. And start with an empty frame this time. You're going to have to reset nearly every line anyway, once you've got that first one right."

Jack scurried away, the offending sheet clutched in his hand. Ned sighed. He had no idea what the other apprentices had been telling the boy – some gruesome but all-too-believable story about how their master had come to lose his hand, perhaps – but he appeared terrified of Ned. Perhaps Jack's father beat him too often, or without reason. That sort of thing could make a boy fearful, if it did not make him a bully in his turn.

The doorbell jingled, and he looked around. A man in a sergeant's steel gorget and kettle helm stood in the doorway.

"Good morning, officer," Ned said, as calmly as he could manage. "What can I do for you?"

"Edmund Faulkner?"

"Yes."

The sergeant stepped further into the shop, making way for half a dozen of his men. So many. What did they think he had done?

"You four." The sergeant gestured to his men. "Take the back room. Round up everyone you can find. Journeymen, apprentices, the lot. Bradley, Moxon, start gathering up the evidence."

"Evidence?" Ned stepped between the soldiers and the door to the workshop. "Evidence of what?"

The sergeant glared at him. "Sedition. Treason. The usual stuff."

"But…"

"Out of my way, little man." The soldier pushed him aside.

Ned swung his right arm wildly, catching the man on the jawline with his brass-and-steel fist. The soldier swayed back a little then recovered his balance.

"You little–"

He aimed a punch for Ned's temple, but Ned was gone, ducking away and heading for the door. Something hit him from behind, and the next thing he knew, he was lying face down on the floor with one of the soldiers on top of him.

"I'm flattered, mate," he groaned, "but perhaps another time?"

The soldier grabbed him by the hair and slammed his face against the splintery planks. Ned hissed in pain, forcing himself to lie still.

"Right, get him up," the sergeant barked. "I want this place cleared and locked up within the hour."

Rough hands hauled Ned to his feet. The rest of the printers were gathered by the display shelves. One of the guardsmen had a split lip and another a swollen eye; gifts no doubt from Peter, the bull-like journeyman who wound the presses and had biceps as thick as Ned's thighs. Peter himself stood quiet and sullen, and Ned noticed that one of the soldiers had a hand on young Jack's shoulder.

"Is this all of them?" the sergeant asked Ned.

"I…" He scanned the pale faces. "No. John Harris isn't here."

"Where does he dwell?"

Ned gave him directions.

"We'll worry about him later." The sergeant favoured Ned with an unpleasant smile. "You might want to take a purse with you, unless you fancy braving the Common Side."

"You're taking us to the Marshalsea?"

Several of the printers swore, and one cried out, "We ain't done nothing!"

The sergeant ignored them. Ned went into the back office with a sinking heart, unlocked the strongbox and took out a bag of coins. The weight of metal felt good in his hand, like a weapon, but it would be a temporary defence at best. Even a short stay in the Marshalsea Prison could ruin a man, and a longer one was guaranteed to kill him.

Gabriel pushed his way through the crowd of players milling around the tiring house. As the principal actor in this new production he had his own dressing table at the back of the room, where the wooden-barred windows gave the best light for applying makeup. His costume hung on pegs nearby, covered in linen sheets to protect it from dust and grease. Gabriel lifted the plain fabric to reveal the magnificence beneath: a doublet and hose in cloth-of-gold, embroidered all over with fake pearls, and a scarlet cloak lined with white fur. They must have cost almost as much as the theatre itself, but a London audience expected a king to look like a king, especially when the players' patron was himself a prince.

"About time, Parrish!" A hand clapped Gabriel on the shoulder, and he turned to see Will Shakespeare grinning at him. "You know, I'm happy to take the role if you don't think you're up to it. I do have every line by heart, you know."

"I would hope so, since you wrote it," Gabriel replied. He looked around the tiring house in irritation. "Where's that wretched boy got to? I'll never be ready at this rate."

"Here, Master Parrish." Noll, Gabriel's former apprentice, scurried over. He'd had to give up acting when his voice broke, but Gabriel had found him work as a tireman with the Prince's Men.

Gabriel started unbuttoning his doublet.

"No," he told the boy, "don't uncover them yet. Wait until the last minute. In fact, leave the cloak until I'm about to go on stage."

He shrugged out of the doublet and handed it to Noll, then kicked off his shoes and unfastened his breeches. He was about to drop them when he heard raised voices out in the auditorium. He paused, a sudden chill running over his skin despite the muggy warmth of the tiring house. The other actors crowded back towards him as a group of armed men appeared at the stage door. Shakespeare stepped forward.

"Is something wrong, officers? I was assured that this play had been cleared by the Office of the Revels."

The leading guardsman glared at him. "Who are you?"

"William Shakespeare, poet and actor, at your service." He swept a bow.

"I don't know nothing about no Shakespeare," the guardsman said. "I'm here for a fellow by the name of Gabriel Parrish."

Gabriel froze. There was no way out except into the auditorium and through the main gates; unlike the Mirror, this older theatre had no back entrance.

"Come back at three," Shakespeare said. "The play will be over and you can do what you will with him."

"My orders was to take him now–"

"He's not going anywhere," Shakespeare said in his most reasonable tones. "Gentlemen, there will soon be more than a thousand people out there on those benches and in the yard, all watching my good friend Master Parrish like hawks."

"How do we know he won't try and give us the slip?"

"You can post your men at the doors, if you like, but I assure you, he won't be leaving. Will you, Parrish?"

Gabriel shook his head, not trusting his voice not to crack. How could he go through with the performance, knowing he would be arrested at the end of it?

"Even better than that," Shakespeare said, draping an arm around the sergeant's shoulders, "I'll have a stool set up for you on the edge of the stage, just like the noble lords have. The king is in nearly every scene, and you'll be within arm's reach of him at all times. You cannot say fairer than that, eh?"

The sergeant squinted at the playwright. "What's the play?"

"The History of King Richard the Second," Shakespeare said. "Newly written and never before performed in a public theatre."

"Are there battles, and bloody murder?"

"Oh yes," Shakespeare said. "Rebellion and regicide too."

He drew the sergeant aside, and winked at Gabriel as he turned away. Gabriel swallowed hard, and turned back to Noll.

"You heard Master Shakespeare. Come, transform me into a king."

A king who would be thrown into prison by the end of the play. Fate had a twisted sense of humour.

The Marshalsea Prison stood a little back from the street, its entrance dominated by a turreted lodge. Ned and his employees were marched through the main gate and into a bare side room opposite the porter's office. The door slammed shut behind them, and a key grated in the lock. Peter sank to the ground against the wall, and Jack huddled next to him.

"What now?" Ben, the other journeyman, asked.

Ned shrugged helplessly. His only previous experience of English prisons had been a short spell in the nearby Compter. Then there was that night in the Doge's cells in Venice... Ned shuddered and pushed the memory aside.

"They call this the Pound," said Nicholas, the oldest of Ned's three apprentices. He boosted himself up on the wall and grabbed the bars of the high narrow window, trying to see out. "They'll leave us here until they find a room for us."

"Better than this one?" Jack said, his expression hopeful.

Nicholas looked at their master and jumped down. "Aye, if we can pay for it."

"And if not?"

"If not they put us in the Common Side, where you'll count yourself lucky to have stale bread once a day, and the rats come in the night to eat your face."

He scrabbled in the air with fingers hooked like rats' claws and chittered àt Jack, who shrank back against Peter's side.

"Stop affrighting the boy," Ben said.

"It's naught but the truth."

"And how come you know so much about it?"

"My father died here," Nicholas said softly. "Fell into debt, couldn't pay back his creditors fast enough to get him out of here. He let the gaolers starve him to death rather than leave mother and me penniless."

No one had anything more to say after that, and they all sat in miserable silence, awaiting their fate. The church bells had tolled noon and were just starting to mark the quarter hour when the sound of the door being unlocked roused them all from their separate reveries.

A fat, ill-favoured man with a red nose and a scrubby, greying beard entered the Pound, flanked by two guards with cudgels. He flourished a scrap of paper ostentatiously.

"Edmund Faulkner, proprietor of the Sign of the Parley?"

"I am he," Ned replied, stepping forward.

"And these are your hirelings? Benjamin Wyatt, Peter Brown, Nicholas Piper, John Harris, John Fellowes?"

"Harris isn't here. He didn't turn up for work this morning."

The gaoler raised a bushy eyebrow. "Five, then. Perhaps six. Let's call it ten shillings a week for the lot, since the boy won't take up much room."

"Ten shillings for what?"

"A room in the Master's Side. Food will be extra, of course."

"Ten shillings? That's more than I pay this lot a month."

"Ten now, or twelve in arrears."

Ned sighed and took out his purse. "Ten it is, then."

The gaoler pocketed the coins and they were led out of the Pound and across a narrow gloomy yard, cut in two by a high wall that almost reached the top of the upper storey.

"What's on the other side?" Ned couldn't resist asking.

"The Commons."

"And why's the wall so high? To stop them getting out?"

"Oh God bless you, no, sir. That's so the folks on the Master's Side don't have to see 'em. Not a pretty sight, believe you me. But you keep paying, sir, and you won't have to find out, will you?"

The room was on the upper floor, just off a dark stairwell. No more than a dozen feet across in either direction, it held two beds and a battered worm-eaten chest with rusty hinges. There was no fireplace, and its single unglazed window looked out over the courtyard. Not much chance of escape, then. Once upon a time he might have chanced a climb up to the roof, but the loss of his hand had put paid to such adventures.

"Could be worse," Peter said, throwing himself down on one of the beds. "Could be six of us in here, not five."

"I don't know why you sound so cheerful," Nicholas replied. "If you hadn't noticed, we're in prison. Suspected of sedition. You know what that means."

He looked around the company, but no one answered.

"We'll all be questioned," he went on. "Probably tortured."

Jack turned pale.

"They can't do that," Peter said. "It's contrary to the statutes of the realm."

"Hark at the good doctor of law, there." Nicholas pulled a face. "What do you know, clotpole?"

"I may not be quick-tongued like some fellows," Peter replied, "but I can read as well as any of you. And I was a copyist at Lincoln's Inn Fields before I got apprenticed to Master Faulkner."

"Aye, we know, you were all set for a fine career before–"

"Enough." Ned glared at both apprentices. "Go on, Peter."

"Well," he said, "according to the law, they'll need written approval from the Privy Council, and that's only done in cases of suspected treason."

"That's all right, then," said Jack. "We haven't done nothing wrong, have we?"

Ned turned away and looked out of the window. Let them hold on to hope as long as they could. Sedition was close enough to treason to make no odds, and the permission of the council could easily be sought after the fact. He clenched his good hand around his metal fist. Sweet Jesu, let it not come to that.

"Where is Harris, anyway?" Nicholas said to no one in particular. "Strange he didn't come into work today. Suspicious, even."

"You think he betrayed us?" Ben asked.

"He'd never do a thing like that," said Jack. "He's my best friend."

They fell silent for a moment, and Ned imagined Peter looking crestfallen.

"I think," Nicholas said, "that he's a craven turncoat who cares more for his own good name than the wellbeing of his friends. He always thought he was better than us."

"That's not true," Ben said. "He's a good, conscientious worker, that's all. Master Faulkner was lucky to get him."

Ned smiled bitterly to himself. Anyone would think I wasn't here. God knows I wish it were so.

A stir of movement by the gatehouse caught his eye, and his heart leapt as a slight, fair-haired figure emerged into the yard, accompanying the fat gaoler. Gabriel. But was he a visitor, or had he been dragged into this mess? Ned watched the two men cross the yard, his stomach churning with fear. It felt like an eternity, but at last footsteps sounded on the stair outside, followed by the rattle of locks and bolts being unfastened. The door swung open and Gabriel stumbled over the threshold before it slammed shut behind him.

Ned crossed the cell and caught Gabriel, who clung to him for a moment like a drowning man to a timber. The actor smelt of sawdust and greasepaint and tobacco, and Ned swallowed past the tightness in his throat.

"They told me you've been accused of printing seditious ballads," Gabriel said, releasing him at last. He put his hands on Ned's shoulders and gazed into his eyes. "Tell me it isn't true."

"I swear, on my honour. For what that's worth."

"Then why–?"

Ned drew him aside. Jack had produced a set of knucklebones, and he and Nicholas were playing against one another in the space between the two beds, watched by their fellows.

"I was the one who kicked off that business in Kent. If Selby had connections among Walsingham's men, he could have found out. And we know he got a message out, before–"

Gabriel shook his head. "He couldn't have found out you were responsible. If he'd known before Mal arrived, things would not have gone half so smoothly. And there was no way he could have found out afterwards, surely?"

"Perhaps you're right. But what else could it be?"

"There haven't been any accusations of a, well, a more personal nature?"

Ned glanced at his employees. "You mean, you and me? No, not yet. Anyway, why arrest us for a different charge altogether, especially one so flimsy?"

They all turned as a key grated in the lock. The gaoler came in, bloodshot eyes sweeping over the prisoners. Two of his men stood in the doorway, arms folded.

"Well, now," the gaoler said softly, "which of you wants a go first? How about you in the corner, lad? Think we'll have you squealing soon as look at you."

Jack shrunk back against the wall, edging towards Peter. Ned stepped forward.

"Take me first."

"Oh, I don't think so. Grown man like you, we need to soften you up a bit first, let you see what happens to the men in your care if you break the law."

Ned stiffened, but did not step aside.

"In any case," the gaoler went on, "we're having to bring in something special for you." He laughed unpleasantly. "Bit tricky, racking a man with one arm, ain't it, lads?"

The two men behind him laughed in chorus with their leader.

"So, I'm afraid you'll have to wait your turn, Master Faulkner." He jerked his head towards Ben. "We'll start with him. He's your chief journeyman, isn't he? Bet he knows everything that goes on, better even than the master."

Ben paled, but stepped forward. Ned laid a hand on his arm as he walked past, thinking to say something reassuring, but words failed him. Ben pulled away, his face a mask of mistrust. *Dear God, let this not be happening.*

The door slammed behind them and the four men's footsteps retreated down the stairs. For several long moments the room was silent but for Jack's muffled sobbing as he curled up in the corner of the room, head buried in his arms.

"Cowards and filthy sodomites, the pair of you!" Nicholas pressed his back against the side of the door as if he could squeeze out through the narrow gap. "I hope they bugger you both with red hot irons until you plead for death."

Ned swallowed. The thought had crossed his own mind more than once; it was the kind of poetic justice that men like their captors would favour.

"I hope they take you next," Ned said to Nicholas in a low voice. "And be ready with plenty to tell them. They never believe a man's word against that of his master, not unless they torture him to be sure. Their threats to me were just words, meant to unman me; you'll they'll take apart without a second thought."

Nicholas turned as grey as the wall behind him. Ned went to stand by Gabriel, staring out at the yard.

"You don't really believe that, do you?" Gabriel murmured. "They'll come for us eventually, you know."

"I know. I just hope to God that Mal can get us a pardon before it's too late."

Grey was waiting for him in the library, as usual. Mal was sure the duke did it to put him on edge; a none-too-subtle reminder that it was from this place that Sandy had stolen a book of skrayling writings, and only Grey's restraint in not pressing charges stood between Mal's brother and the gallows. But then Grey had never been subtle. He might fancy himself the equal of Walsingham in guile, but though he bore a far finer coat of arms he relied too much on his status and influence. He was a siege engine, where he ought to be a dagger in the back. Still, sometimes a siege engine was exactly what you needed.

"I suppose you are here about Faulkner," Grey drawled, glancing over the papers on his desk.

Unsubtle. Not stupid. Always remember that. "It seems more than a little coincidental, don't you think, my lord? I make my move against the guisers, and a few days later one of my closest friends is arrested on false charges."

"False?"

"Of course. You don't think Ned is stupid enough to dabble in seditious writings, surely?"

Grey raised an eyebrow to indicate his opinion of Ned's wits. "You must have known the plotters might not be fooled by your felicitous 'escape' from the Huntsmen."

"What else was I to do? Once we suspected Selby of betraying our network, he had to be eliminated."

"There are other ways–"

"What other ways, my lord? Besides, I seem to recall you were happy to let me deal with it."

"Set a dog to catch foxes, that's what my father always said."

"Well, he should have known. After all, he was one of them." Mal knew it was the wrong thing to say, the moment the words left his mouth.

"Do you think it pleases me that two of my agents are now in prison under threat of torture?"

"No, my lord."

"The rack is a very effective device in loosening men's tongues. A little too effective. And your friends know a great deal that I would rather not have written down and passed on to our enemies. If Selby was a leak in our barrel, the interrogation of Faulkner and Parrish will be an axe to its side."

"I understand that, my lord."

"You do? Good. Then you know what must be done."

"My lord?"

Grey sighed. "Kill them, before they can talk."

Mal didn't trust himself to reply. To kill a stranger in cold blood was one thing, but two of his closest friends?

"It will be more difficult than with Marlowe, I appreciate that," the duke went on. "There are two to dispose of, and you will have to do it alone; the chief warder will be suspicious if you bring men along and ask to be left alone with the prisoners."

You don't say.

"And you will have to get out of the Marshalsea afterwards. Perhaps it would be better to let them arrest you on the scene. I can arrange a pardon for murder far more easily than for sedition."

Mal took a deep breath and forced himself to loosen his grip on the hilt of his rapier. If he tried to get out of this, Grey would just send someone else in his place. Someone like Baines, who would not balk at carrying out his orders to the letter.

"I will deal with it."

"Good." The duke stared at Mal for a moment. "You have my permission to leave, Catlyn."

"Thank you, my lord."

Mal gave him as curt a bow as he dared, turned on his heel and left the library. Servants scurried out of his path as he strode across the courtyard to the stables, and the groom was more than usually prompt in bringing Hector out. Mal paused for a moment, stroking the chestnut gelding's muzzle to calm himself. Damn Grey to the fiery pits of Hades! There had to be another way.

As he mounted and nudged Hector into a walk, the appalling truth struck him. If he could not find a way out of this, it was his duty to his friends as well as to Grey to give them a swift death. Better that than what awaited them: either a lingering death from the injuries inflicted by their torturer, or an even more hideous execution.

CHAPTER VI

Out in the Strand, Mal reined Hector to a halt for a moment before turning the gelding's head to the left. Whitehall might be empty, but he had ascertained that most of the court had gone no further than Richmond to escape the threat of plague.

"We're not beaten yet, lad," he murmured, patting Hector's neck.

The gelding jerked his head down as if in agreement, and set off towards Charing Cross.

Mal considered his options as he rode. Grey was not his only connection at court, nor even the most friendly to his cause; surely there was someone else he could prevail upon to secure a swift pardon for Ned and Gabriel? The Privy Council was sadly depleted of late, it was true. His own former patron, Sir Francis Walsingham, had not been replaced when he died, and three other members were so old and infirm they came seldom to court. That only left the current Secretary of State, Robert Cecil, who was an old rival of Sir Francis and thus unlikely to favour Mal's cause; the Lord High Admiral, whom he knew from his time as Ambassador Kiiren's bodyguard; the new Lord Chancellor, Sir Thomas Egerton; and the Prince of Wales himself.

The admiral he dismissed as too remote a connection and too little interested in the matter. The Prince of Wales might be persuaded to clemency, but it would likely be too slow a process; he was as cautious as his mother, and as proud as his late father. The Lord Chancellor was an unknown quantity; he was a former lawyer and had a reputation as a shrewd legislator, but whose side would he take in this case? There was only one way to find out.

By the time he neared Richmond, the sun was dipping below the palace's gilt-topped towers and setting the Thames ablaze. Mal followed the road round to the main entrance, where massive octagonal towers of pale stone flanked double doors of solid oak. Above them a gilded and painted bas-relief of the royal arms gleamed in the honey-thick light: golden lions and fleurs-de-lys on a quartered field of red and blue, supported by a larger lion and a unicorn, both with crowns around their necks. On one tower was the royal badge combining a portcullis and a Tudor rose; on the other, a red heart surmounted by a scroll bearing the single word *Loyal* – the late King Henry's personal emblem. These days the palace was the favourite residence of the Princess of Wales, but her husband visited often, mostly to avail himself of the hunting in the nearby park.

Leaving Hector with a palace groom, Mal crossed the main courtyard and slipped down a narrow passage between two buildings and through a plain arched door. A long corridor stretched left and right, but he carried straight on, eventually emerging behind the palace on the edge of its formal gardens. As he had hoped. A knot of men stood around the near end of the bowling alley, talking and laughing. All were richly dressed in the height of fashion: close-fitting silk doublets heavy with embroidery, a prince's ransom in lace at collar and cuffs, and curled hair arranged artfully over one shoulder. Mal assumed a carefree air and strolled over to greet them.

"My lords. Gentlemen."

The hangers-on parted to reveal Henry Wriothesley, Earl of Southampton and current darling of Robert's court.

"Catlyn, you old rogue! Where have you been these past few weeks?"

Though only a few years younger than Mal the earl looked scarcely more than a boy, with a thin sandy moustache and sparse beard. *No wonder close-trimmed whiskers are all the rage at court, if they seek to flatter this young coxcomb.*

"I might ask you the same, my lord. London is a dreary place without you."

"I don't know why you remain there. Christ's blood, if I had a pretty wife and a country estate to go home to, I'd leap at the chance."

Mal smiled politely. It was common knowledge that Southampton was so far in debt as to have been obliged to sell off some of his lands, as well as postpone his wedding to one of Princess Juliana's ladies-in-waiting.

"How would you like an estate in Ireland?" Southampton went on. "Essex and I have a mind to show that upstart Tyrone the edge of our blades. What say you join us?"

"I would be honoured, my lord, but alas I have business back in London."

"What business is more important than Her Majesty's?"

"You have me there, my lord." He could hardly tell the earl about his campaign against the guisers. Wriothesley's name had been on Selby's list, and though that meant nothing either way, one couldn't be too careful.

"Splendid! We'll show Raleigh a thing or two, eh?"

"Aye, my lord."

Southampton turned away, satisfied now that his will had prevailed. Mal cursed silently. The last thing he needed was to be caught in the middle of Essex and Raleigh's rivalry. Perhaps he could contrive a way out of it: a sudden illness, or an injury sustained in a duel. On the other hand, the invitation suggested an approach to his own problem.

"My lord, a question, if I may?"

Southampton waved a hand, which Mal took for encouragement, though the earl's attention remained on the game.

"A man of my station can hardly set out upon such a venture unaccompanied, but I am regrettably deprived of my two stoutest companions by an unfortunate turn of events."

"Oh?"

"The men who assisted me most ably on my mission to Venice have been arrested on charges of sedition. Wholly false charges, I would stake my reputation on it."

"I see," Southampton murmured. He clapped his hands as one of the players landed a ball just touching the jack. "Oh, well played, sir!"

"I understand," Mal went on, "that my lord Essex is well acquainted with the Lord Chancellor, and I wondered if he might be prevailed upon to intervene."

Southampton turned, and frowned at him. "Who are these men?"

"Ned Faulkner, a printer, and Gabriel Parrish, an actor and playwright."

The earl sniffed. "Hardly fit companions for a gentleman, Catlyn. Can you not bring someone else?"

Mal reined in his frustration.

"Assuredly, my lord. However it ill befits a gentleman to abandon those who have served him faithfully."

"Very well, I shall do what I can."

"You will? Thank you, my lord. I will be forever in your debt."

Southampton waved his hand dismissively. "I shall mention it to Essex next time I write to him."

Mal's heart sank. "He's not here?"

"He's in Southampton, reviewing our prospective fleet. But never fear; he'll be back before Christmas."

Mal made his obeisance and went to find lodgings for the night. Damn it! By the time Essex heard of the business and deigned to intervene, Ned and Gabriel could be dead. He was going to have to take matters into his own hands, and not in a way that Grey was likely to approve of.

It took Mal most of the next day to find his quarry, since discretion was vital to his plan, but by early evening he found himself outside a shabby lodging-house a few streets from Smithfield. The landlady let him in and directed him to the attic at the top of the house.

Mal took the stairs slowly, going over the plan for weaknesses. He was distracted, however, by the rhythmic creaking coming from the chamber ahead. Evidently the actor's evening of pleasure had begun early.

Mal grinned to himself and knocked on the door. When no answer came, he knocked again, louder.

"Shakespeare, are you in there?"

A sudden scuffle. He tried the door; it was unlocked. As he made to open it, however, he met resistance. He shoved hard and a man yelped and swore in pain. Mal shouldered his way into the actor's lodgings.

"God's light, man, what did you do that for?" Shakespeare was in his shirt and little else, hopping around on one foot. He glared at Mal, who shrugged an apology. "Who are you, anyway?"

"A friend of Gabriel Parrish."

Shakespeare's lodgings were as untidy as the man himself, dirty linens overflowing their basket and the remains of a meal on the floor by the bed, as if set out for the mice. The bed itself was a tangle of sheets and bolsters and… naked limbs? A young woman poked a tousled head out of the folds and gave him an appreciative look. Mal nodded back politely.

"Later, Nell." Shakespeare threw her a coin, and she snatched it from the air before climbing out of bed and retrieving her clothes. It was Mal's turn to be appreciative. Derbyshire was a long way away…

"You have news of Parrish?" Shakespeare said when his companion had left.

Mal went quietly over to the door and hauled it open, but there was no one there. He glimpsed Nell disappearing down the next turn of the stairs.

"I need your help," he said, shutting the door, "otherwise, one way or another, Parrish will die."

Shakespeare sat down on the bed and pulled on his hose.

"That would be a shame. He's a fine actor."

"And a rival playwright." Better test the waters now, before he took the man further into his confidence.

Shakespeare laughed. "Hardly. Oh, these new comedies bring in the crowds, but it's a passing fashion, you'll see. Blood and woe, that's what brings the penny stinkards in. Though come to think of it, why not combine the two?" He wandered over to his desk and snatched up a sheet of paper and a pen. "A wronged woman. Suicide. Deception. And all with a happy ending this time. Yes..."

"Shakespeare?"

"Hmm?"

"About Parrish. You'll help me, won't you?"

The actor put down his pen. "In what way?"

"I'm going to get Parrish, and Ned Faulkner and his men, out of the Marshalsea."

Shakespeare stared at him for a moment then burst out laughing.

"Do you take me for a fool? If you're caught you'll hang – or worse."

"I know," Mal replied softly.

"Then you have my answer. I know my liver is lily-white: I don't need an executioner to cut it out and show it to me."

"I understand." Mal chewed his lip as if in thought. *Gently does it.* "It is a great hazard, as you say, and only the finest actors in London could carry it off. Perhaps Parrish's old friends in the Admiral's Men would be willing to chance it..."

He turned back to the door and laid his hand upon the latch.

"Wait!"

Mal allowed himself a brief grin of triumph before schooling his features to hopeful innocence.

"You'll do it?"

"God help me, yes," Shakespeare said with a sigh. "We've lost too many fine talents already to these pinch-souled wardens of our morals. What do you want me to do?"

Shakespeare was as good as his word, though he did not come with them on the venture. He pointed out that as a regular actor in the city's foremost company, his face and voice were too well known for him to pass as a stranger. He did however introduce Mal to a number of players he claimed were reliable, along with a far less savoury fellow with a nice fist for paperwork, and lent him the key to the company's wardrobe.

"Just make sure you bring everything back straight away." Shakespeare said. "We've got a production of Henry the Sixth tomorrow afternoon, and we'll need those helmets."

"Don't worry. If we're not done by noon, we'll be in the Tower together and you'll have more to worry about than a few missing costumes."

"And that's meant to reassure me, is it?"

Mal patted him on the shoulder, took up his burdens and hurried out into the night. Good thing he'd brought Hector, or he might look a bit conspicuous hauling this lot around. Not to mention the likelihood of not getting back to Southwark before they closed the gates at either end of London Bridge.

The gelding looked at him askance as Mal threw the sack of costumes over his back. Mal patted his neck in reassurance and strapped a longer canvas-wrapped bundle alongside the sack. If only Coby still worked for a theatre company. As a tireman she had had far easier access to theatre costumes, and her other skills would have come in handy too. Still, he couldn't wish her to be in the middle of this lot. Better for her to be safe with Kit in Derbyshire. Assuming they were safe.

At the thought he paused, hands clenching on the rough sacking. If this were retaliation for the attack on Selby, Ned and Gabriel might not be the only targets. He fought the urge to throw the costumes in the gutter, leap onto Hector's back and ride for Derbyshire that very hour. No. He had entrusted his dear ones to Sandy all this time, and if anyone could deal with the guisers, it was his brother. Tomorrow would be soon enough to ride north, once his task here was done.

The following morning Mal met his accomplices in an alley behind a baker's and they all changed into their costumes. In scarlet jackets and steel breastplates, the four actors made as impressive a crew of Tower guardsmen as Mal could wish for. The halberds, on the other hand, would never pass muster. What had looked good enough by candlelight wouldn't fool a child in the unforgiving light of day.

"Leave them here," Mal said at last. "Better for the gaolers to wonder why we go unarmed, than to notice that we're carrying painted wood instead of real weapons."

He himself was not unarmed, though he had dulled his rapier hilt to make it less conspicuous. The last thing he wanted was for this to turn into a fight, but he felt naked without the weight of a sword at his side.

"Remember," he added, as the actors formed up in pairs. "Don't speak unless you're spoken to. I don't expect them to be suspicious of strange faces – the Tower militia is large enough that the gaolers are unlikely to see the same men every time – but I don't want them hearing anything out of place. Do you understand?"

"Yes, sir."

One of them put his hand up. "What if the gaolers do ask questions?"

Mal sighed. "You answer them as best you can, and as briefly. You're actors, aren't you? Surely you improvise your lines from time to time?"

The man nodded, and Mal turned smartly on his heel and marched out of the alley. With a scuffle of uneven footsteps and not a few muttered curses, the actors followed.

The porter seemed a little surprised by their arrival, but after a glance at Mal's forged papers he waved them through into the courtyard. The same procedure induced the duty gaoler on the Masters' Side to conduct them up to the room where Ned and his men were lodged.

As Mal stepped into the room, he caught Ned's eye and gave a quick shake of the head.

"Which of you men is Edmund Faulkner?"

The printers looked at him oddly, but the false guardsmen had crowded into the room behind Mal, blocking the gaoler's view.

"I am," Ned said.

"And Gabriel Parrish?"

"Here."

Mal gestured to his companions, who produced leg-irons and manacles and closed in on the two men.

"Where are you taking them?" one of the apprentices asked as the fettered prisoners were ushered out of the door.

"That's no concern of yours, cur." Mal aimed a backhanded blow at the youth's head, slowly enough to give him a chance to dodge.

"Get out of here, the lot of you. The Privy Council has no use for you small fry."

The printers stared at him for a moment, then two of the apprentices helped the older journeyman to his feet. Mal took care to keep his expression blank, though his heart went out to the man. He remembered all too well the pain such torments inflicted.

When the cell was empty Mal followed them down to the courtyard.

"Here, where are you taking those men?" One of the chief warders waddled across the yard towards them, beard bristling.

"Transfer to the Tower. Sir Richard Berkeley's orders."

"And you are…?"

"Captain John White." Mal puffed out his chest. "First week on the job, and I already drew the plum assignment."

"Have you a letter from Sir Richard, authorising the transfer?"

"Right here." Mal handed over the document. Thank the saints he had kept hold of Selby's confession with the lieutenant's counter-signature on the bottom; it had given the forger something to work from.

The gaoler squinted at the writing. "This isn't the usual clerk's hand."

Mal shrugged. "What's that to me?"

Over the gaoler's shoulder, he flashed a warning glance at Ned, who nodded back.

"In fact," the gaoler went on, "this doesn't look anything like–"

"Let me go, you bastards!" Ned yelled, pulling free of the actor-guards.

He flailed his manacled arms around, hitting the fat gaoler around the head with his metal hand. The man staggered a little.

"You men, get that prisoner under control!"

Mal put a hand under the gaoler's elbow, but withdrew it just as the man tried to put his weight on it. The gaoler fell to the cobbles with a strangled cry, the piece of paper crumpling in his fist, and Ned kicked him in the head with a yell of triumph.

"That's for Ben, you slack-gutted toad!"

"Enough! Seize him!" Mal snatched the forged warrant from the gaoler's hand and turned to the other warders. "See to your master, quick!"

Even as the prison warders began to move, Mal ushered his companions through the gates.

"Quick march! I want these villains in the Tower before they cause any more trouble."

They set off down St Olave's Street, taking care to avoid the riverbank just downstream of London Bridge where the real Tower guards moored their boats. A couple of hundred yards further on, Mal led them into a riverside alley as if heading for St Olave's Stairs, but turned aside at the last minute into a tiny courtyard, barely more than a space between three adjacent buildings whose overhanging upper stories blocked out the grimy sunlight.

"God's teeth, that was close," Mal said, taking off his helmet and wiping his brow. "Well done, Ned! And thank you too, lads, you did a splendid job."

He handed out payment to the actors, who bundled up their costumes in a couple of sacks and rolled up their shirt sleeves, instantly transforming themselves into a gang of labourers who could pass unnoticed in any riverside street. When they had gone, Mal unlocked his friends' shackles. Ned was grinning like an apprentice on holiday but Gabriel's face was pale in the gloom, his eyes almost expressionless, as if he dared not believe they had escaped. *A man after my own heart.*

"Well, gentlemen, time to get you out of here."

He led them back out into the alley and down to the river, where they caught a wherry downstream to the far eastern end of Southwark. Two horses were waiting for them at a livery stable in Bermondsey Street, along with saddlebags full of food and spare clothing. Mal pressed a purse into Ned's hand.

"That should be enough to see you safely to France," he said. "Here are your passports; at least the Privy Council never got around to revoking them."

"Where shall we go?" Ned asked. "Your estate in Provence?"

"No. That's the first place they'll look, if they do come for you. Go to Marseille, and pay Youssef to take you on from there."

"You think they'll come after us?"

"Probably not, but it's best not to assume. Get as far from England as you can, and if you write, do not tell me where you are. The less I know, the better."

"We cannot thank you enough for this," Ned said, embracing him.

"No thanks are needed; it was my actions that brought this disaster upon you in the first place."

"What about the print shop?"

"The soldiers took most of your stock, and I dare say the men won't want to work there after what happened. I'll sell off the equipment and set the money against that loan." He smiled at them both encouragingly. "Let the bastards think us defeated, at least for now."

"And you?" Parrish asked.

"I'm for the north. If the guisers are behind this attack on us, you and Ned might not be their only targets."

CHAPTER VII

Coby hitched up her skirt and climbed onto the stile, giving her an unparalleled view over Rushdale. The little river from which the valley got its name wound below her, skirting the outcroppings of pale grey limestone and falling in tiny cascades to pool amongst the thorn trees that edged the meadows. Swallows from the hall's outbuildings skimmed out over the grass, filling their bellies against the cold of winter. Thankfully the people of the estate had been able to do the same this year; though not bountiful, the harvest had not been as poor as they had feared.

"Up! Mamma, up!"

She turned and smiled down at her adopted son. At a little over two, Kit was walking well now and insisted on accompanying her on her daily hike up the hill, and she had shortened his smocks to prevent them getting too muddy. She bent down and picked him up, sitting him on the cross-rail of the stile and holding him tight around the waist. It was a long tumble down the slope on the other side.

"Mamma! Mamma! Baa-lambs!" He pointed at the sheep in the meadow below.

"Yes, my pet, baa-lambs. Though they're not babies any more. See, they're nearly as big as their mammas now."

She leant her cheek against his dark curls and closed her eyes, listening to the shrilling of the swallows and the bleating of the sheep. So quiet here, so unlike the clamour and stink of London. It reminded her of her childhood in the little town of Berchem, near Antwerp, though of course there were no hills there. She wondered if Mal ever came up here with his mother, when he was Kit's age. Perhaps not; managing twin boys must have been wearisome indeed.

"Daddy!"

Coby's eyes blinked open, and her heart skipped a beat. But she could see no one on the road.

"Are you sure, lambkin?"

He nodded vigorously, and now she could hear the sound of trotting hooves, faint but clear in the cold autumn air.

"It's probably just Father Whittam on his mule," she said, though Kit had grown out of the phase of referring to all men as "Daddy".

The rider reappeared from behind a row of trees: a tall dark-haired man on a chestnut horse, the plume on his low-crowned hat bobbing in time to the animal's gait. Coby bit back a squeal of delight.

"It is Daddy!"

Hardly daring to believe it, she scrambled down from the stile and lifted Kit onto her hip, then set off down the hill as fast as her feet would take her.

They reached the front courtyard of the manorhouse just as Mal was coming out of the stable. He broke into a run, and a moment later was hugging and kissing them both, and though he was covered in the dust of the road and stank of sweat and horse she didn't care.

"Praise God you're both safe," he said at last, holding them at arm's length. "I was so afraid–"

"What for?" She put Kit down. "You don't think–?""

He put a finger to his lips. "Let's not speak of it here. Where's Sandy?"

"Probably asleep. He spends every night keeping vigil over Kit."

"Very wise. Well, we won't disturb him now."

Susanna appeared at the front door of the house and immediately crouched and held out her arms. Kit ran to her, and they disappeared into the house together. Truly, Susanna looked far more like Kit's mother than Coby did, and she was genuinely attached to the boy. Perhaps it was not surprising, since the Italian girl had lost her own child just before they hired her.

"Come," Coby said, "why don't we walk in the garden and you can tell me all about it. Unless you'd rather rest a while?"

"No, I need to stretch my legs a little before I sit down. A walk would be perfect."

She put her arm in his and they strolled round the back of the house to the walled garden. Rows of apple and pear trees, pruned and trained so that they were no higher than Coby's chin, stood in ranks to catch the sun, a last few fruits glowing amongst their faded leaves. She glanced up at the house, but all the windows were closed against the damp air.

For long moments neither of them spoke, and Coby began to feel sure Mal had naught but bad news. The last she had heard, Ned and Gabriel had been arrested; were they now dead?

"I fear I may have done something a little rash," he said at last.

She listened in wonder as he told her of Grey's instructions, and his alternative solution.

"You broke them out of prison? My love, they'll arrest you the minute you set foot back in London."

"Then I won't go back."

"You have to. You said you would get rid of the guisers, no matter what it takes."

He slipped his arm around her waist. "You seem in a great hurry to be rid of me."

"I didn't mean right now," she sighed. "But one day."

"I know."

He bent his head and kissed her. At the touch of his lips, all thought of London friends and enemies fled, like autumn leaves blown before a gale. He was here, now, with her. That was all that mattered.

He took hold of her wrist and pulled her behind the yew hedge that bordered the herb beds. From the urgency with which he thrust his hips against hers, his intent was clear.

"What if the servants see us?" she whispered.

"Then they'll know their master is in love with his wife and overjoyed to be with her again."

He pulled up her skirts and thrust a hand beneath them. She gasped at the touch, and he drew back with a grin.

"What, still wearing drawers like a boy?"

"I feel naked without them."

"Naked. I like the sound of that word."

He pulled at the drawstring and let the loosened undergarment fall to the ground, then cupped a bare buttock in each hand.

"Aah, your hands are like ice!"

"Then let me warm them," he said, pulling her close and stifling any further complaint with another kiss.

She slipped a hand down between their bellies and began unbuttoning his breeches. Tempting as it was to take revenge by slipping her own cold fingers inside, she hadn't the heart for such cruelty. Instead she withdrew her hand as soon as the last button was undone, and let him press against her again.

"Oh sweet Mother of God, Mina, how I have missed thee!" he murmured, his breath hot in her ear.

And how I have longed to hear you call me by that name again.

He pushed her back against the damp orchard wall, lifted her up and thrust gently but determinedly inside her. *And they shall be one flesh.* She clung to him as he shuddered in his pleasure, both of them blind to everything but the need to drive away all memory of their separation. She whispered incoherent words of love and kissed his brow, and at last he released her, slumping against the wall with a mazed look on his face.

Coby glanced around to reassure herself they had not been seen, then retrieved her drawers and put them back on. By the time she was respectable again, Mal had fastened his own clothing and was standing by the wall with folded arms and a smug grin on his face.

"Now that was a warm welcome home," he said. "I should go away more often."

Coby plucked an apple from a nearby espalier and mimed aiming it at him. He pretended to duck and ran off laughing. She picked up her skirts and chased after him, finally catching up at the back door. He drew her in for another kiss, but she put a finger to his lips.

"Later. You need to go and see Sandy."

Mal frowned. "Why so grave? Is something wrong?"

"I don't know," she sighed. "I think... Well, you'll know when you see him."

He released her and strode into the house without another word. Coby stood on the back doorstep, hugging herself against his sudden, painful absence. *Why could I not have kept my mouth shut a little longer?* But he had to know, sooner or later.

Mal made his way up to the private apartments on the first floor. Sandy had taken the room they had shared as boys, at the end of the east wing. The larger chamber before it, which had once been Charles', looked now to have been converted to a nursery for Kit, though there was no sign of his son or the nursemaid. He crossed the room, stepping over a fallen toy horse on wheels, and knocked gently on the door.

"Sandy?"

No reply. He eased the door open. The room beyond was dark and the air over-warm and thick with the bitter, tobacco-like scent of *qoheetsakhan*, the skrayling dream-herb. Sandy lay on the bed, fully clothed, hands folded on his chest like a corpse. For a moment Mal thought his brother was dead and his wife had been unable to break the news, and an involuntary cry caught in his throat. Sandy's eyes snapped open.

"Sandy?" Mal all but ran over to the bed. "I'm here. Speak to me."

Sandy blinked up at him. "Brother. Back so soon?"

"What do you mean, soon? It's September."

Sandy sat up and rubbed his face. "September. Really?"

"Yes, really." Mal went over to the window and started opening the shutters. "What are you doing still in bed in the middle of the day, anyway?"

"Resting. I've been watching over Kit whilst he sleeps, since he's still too young to wear a spirit-guard–"

"Why?

"His soul needs to put down roots in the dreamlands, if it is ever to blossom. If we cut him off from it now, Kiiren will be lost to us. Perhaps forever."

"No, I meant why do you need to watch over him? There can't be that much danger, surely, not this far from London." He turned back to the room, blinking away the after-images of the sun's glare. "The guisers–"

He stared at his brother. If he had thought Sandy looked pale in the darkened room, it was nothing to what the cruel light of day revealed. Sandy's complexion was a sickly white, his skin sagging from features almost as gaunt as they had been back in Bedlam. His dark hair hung lank and tangled around his shoulders, and his beard hadn't been cut in weeks.

"Dear God, Sandy, have you not given one thought to yourself these past months?"

"I can't let them near him!" Sandy made to stand, but tottered and would have fallen if Mal had not dashed forward to catch him.

"You're no use to him like this. Come on, let's get some food inside you. I can look after Kit."

With Mal's help and encouragement Sandy's condition soon began to improve, and as the weeks passed they fell into a comfortable routine of alternating patrols in the dreamlands. As on their earlier explorations there was no sign of guiser activity, and the devourers kept to the shadows where they belonged. Mal began thinking of ways to persuade Sandy to ease off on the patrolling, so that he could go back to London without having to worry about a relapse. Perhaps Coby was right and they would arrest him the moment he set foot in the capital, but he couldn't hide here forever.

Christmas came, followed by the turn of the year and the traditional exchange of gifts. Mal gave his wife a bolt of blue-green Naples fustian for a new gown and Kit a hobby-horse with a real horsehair tail, both sent up secretly from London by Lady Frances. In return he received three new shirts with whitework collars and cuffs, and a bottle of neat's-foot oil with a child-sized thumbprint in the centre of its wax seal.

"Perhaps Daddy will show you how to look after your horsey's saddle and reins after dinner," Coby said as Mal kissed Kit's brow in thanks.

Kit said nothing, only waddled off with his skirts hitched up either side of the hobby horse.

"I have no gifts for either of you," Sandy said, clutching his own new shirt to his chest. "I had no money to buy anything, and I have been distracted–"

"No matter," Mal said. "You give us your time and love, every day. And night."

Sandy nodded his gratitude.

"In fact…" Mal took his brother by the elbow and let him out of earshot of Coby and Kit. "I need your help. Tonight."

"Oh?"

"I found something in the dreamlands, a few nights ago. At first I thought nothing of it, but it was there again last night when I patrolled. I think it could be the evidence we have been seeking all this time."

"Then Charles was telling the truth?"

"Yes. At least as he saw it."

"But why now, I wonder," Sandy said. He glanced over at Kit, who was galloping unsteadily around the room. "We searched very thoroughly when we first returned to England."

"That was what puzzled me. Surely the traces would have faded with time, not renewed themselves."

Sandy laughed. "It is no use applying your school-masters' logic to the dreamworld, brother. Dreams have no reason, or at least, their reasons are their own."

"Then I will let you interpret this mystery, since you are so much more knowledgeable than I."

Sandy looked up, his expression grave. "You have more knowledge than you know, if only you would dare open your heart to it."

"Last time I did that, people died. Or have you forgotten?"

"It was fear that made you hesitate," Sandy replied, reaching out to rest a hand on Mal's wrist. "And hesitation made you vulnerable. That is not what our fencing-master taught us."

"I know." It came out as barely more than a whisper. Mal cleared his throat. "Very well, I shall endeavour to be bold and grasp the nettle. Tonight."

••••

"This will be easier if we share a bed," Sandy said, leading the way through into his own chamber. "We don't need your wife coming in and waking you."

"If you insist," Mal replied.

It was strange being back in his own room with Sandy, undressing for bed and arguing over who got to use the tooth-stick first, as if the past fifteen years had never happened. The last time... the last time had been the night they were initiated into the Huntsmen. After that, Sandy had to be locked in a room by himself. Mal climbed into bed and stared up at the shadowy canopy, trying to empty his mind of the day's bustle and achieve the calmness that would allow him to step into the dreamlands without needing to fall asleep.

"Why don't I tell you a story," Sandy said, propping himself up on one elbow, "like Mother used to?"

"If you think it will help," Mal replied, trying to get comfortable. The mattress was lumpier than he remembered, and sagged in the wrong places.

Sandy began to tell his tale: something about an old man who lived alone in the woods, far from any clan or settlement, eating only berries and drinking water from the leaves of... Mal had a brief moment of clarity in which he realised his brother was not speaking English or any other Christian language, then all thought dissolved and darkness closed around him.

Mal kept his senses sharp as he walked at Sandy's side across the colourless ankle-deep grass. Hills rose around them, mimicking the landscape of the waking world. This early in the evening only a faint gleam here and there marked a sleeping child or an old man drowsing by his fire, which was why Mal had insisted on beginning so early. If there were guisers lurking after all, they would see them a mile off.

"Over that way," he said, pointing to a gap in the hills. Sandy broke into a run and leapt into the air, skimming effortlessly over the grass like thistledown on the wind. Mal cursed and tried to copy him, feeling his stomach lurch as his feet left the ground. Up he soared, so high he feared he would fall, but then Sandy was there holding his hand and they were flying side by side. Mal laughed. This was what he remembered from his childhood dreams, before the dark days when Sandy went away–

"Stay with me!" Sandy shouted in his ear. Mal blinked away a fog of silvery light. "You have to stay focused on the here-and-now, or you'll fall back into a dream or, worse still, wake up."

"Sorry."

They flew onward, over hills far taller than their counterparts in the waking world. The air should have been colder up here, but nothing in the dreamlands behaved quite as expected. The nacreous sky seemed a lot closer too, as if it were the ceiling of a gargantuan hall, not a crystalline sphere millions of miles across. Though if it were a ceiling, the painter had been drunk. Stars were meant to be twinkling pinpoints of light, not haphazard smears that swam in and out of focus when you tried to concentrate on them.

"Not so high!"

Mal turned his attention back to the land below them. There. A line of hills like a dog's back tooth. He soared around the tallest peak and into the valley beyond.

"Is this it?" Sandy gestured to a paler area of ground. "You were right. It is… most strange."

They touched down at the edge of the… whatever it was. At their feet the grass began to thin, revealing bare patches of what ought to have been earth but looked more like skin, riven by a thousand tiny creases that traced lines around the contours of the land. Some of the larger cracks emitted a faint golden light, as if dreaming minds lay just under the surface.

"It's like the thinness I saw at the skrayling camp," Mal said, "and yet different somehow."

"I've never seen anything like it before." Sandy knelt and touched a finger to one of the glowing cracks.

"Don't!" Mal shouted, but it was too late.

Sandy's arm was sucked into the crack, slamming his head against the ground. Mal slid his arms round his brother's chest and pulled. Sandy did not budge so much as a hair's breadth; Mal might as well have tried to lift a mountain.

"Wait! I can feel something. Hold on... now pull again!"

Mal heaved, bracing his feet either side of his brother's torso, and Sandy's arm slid from the crack with a sound like a cork being pulled from a bottle. They both tumbled backwards–

–and woke up in the curtained bed in their old room. Mal disentangled himself from Sandy and stumbled up from the bed in search of a candle. By the time he had it lit, Sandy was sitting up in bed, a puzzled look on his face, staring down at his cupped hands.

"What in God's name...? You brought something back with you?"

Sandy held out his hands. In the soft glow of the candlelight Mal could just make out a dark shape about the size of a hen's egg but flatter and more triangular, with a small circular depression near one end.

"Isn't that–?"

"The hagstone I found in the beck? Aye." Sandy grinned and held the stone up to the light. As Mal had guessed, the dent was a hole that went all the way through. "I thought it lost all these years."

"But what was it doing in the dreamlands? And how...?" Mal shrugged helplessly.

"I think... You remember I had to reach a long way down into the water to get it, right up to my chin? And you were holding onto me so I didn't fall in."

Mal nodded.

"I was thinking about that moment," Sandy went on. "When the crack pulled me in. And then I felt it."

"The stone."

"Yes. As soon as my fingers closed around it, the... whatever it was... let me go. As if it had done what it meant to do."

"Do what? Give you your old hagstone back?"

"No. Complete the memory."

"How do you know all this? You said you'd never seen anything like it before."

"I haven't. But it makes sense."

"A mad sort of dream sense, perhaps." Mal took the stone from Sandy's palm and peered through the hole.

"Hoping to see fairies?"

Mal laughed, but the words struck home. What if such stones were spyholes into the dreamlands?

"Give it here." Sandy held out his hand.

Mal passed the stone back, and his brother produced a length of string from somewhere and hung the stone up from the bed canopy.

"To keep away nightmares," he said softly.

"But what does it all mean?" Mal asked. "Have the dreamlands worn thin because the guisers were here so long?"

"I don't know. Something happened there, that's for certain. Something big and dangerous. Perhaps that's how the devourers got into the dale, back in Charles's day. The dreamworld wore thin and they broke through..."

"So why didn't we notice it before?"

"Perhaps it was there all along, half healed, only something made it worse again. Like when you scratch a scab off and make it bleed again."

"This thing," Mal said, thinking back to their journey across the dark plains. "This... wound. It must have some corresponding spot in the waking world, yes? Somewhere not too far from here."

Sandy's eyes widened. "Yes! Yes, that's it. If we can find out where the dreamers broke through from, it might tell us who they were and what they were really up to."

Mal stared at his reflection in the darkened window, recalling the times he had been pulled bodily into the dreamworld by Sandy. Was that how the damage had happened? Had their own passage left similar wounds, places where the veil of sleep was thin enough for nightmares to seep through? There was so much he still did not know about the strange magics he and his brother were heir to, and the more he learned, the less he wanted to know.

CHAPTER VIII

For the next three weeks they explored the surrounding Peaklands, heedless of the rain that continued to fall in grey sheets. Mal had thought their previous investigations thorough, but Sandy pressed on much further this time, pointing out that distances in the dreamlands could be deceptive. Soon they had exhausted every valley within a winter day's ride and were having to stay overnight in unfamiliar villages, but still they found nothing.

"We must have missed it," Mal said, one freezing cold day as they circled north towards Matlock. "Surely the devourers would never have strayed so far as Rushdale if they'd escaped around here."

Sandy sighed, his breath clouding the air. "You're probably right. Let's have dinner at the next inn and then head for home."

They followed an icy, rutted path down the hillside into a small village, no more than a huddle of cottages about a grey stone church. An ale-stake outside one of the houses drew Mal's eye, and he dismounted stiffly.

"A drink will warm us up, even if there's no food to be had," he said, leading his horse towards the church gate since there was no stable or even a hitching-post to be seen.

The alehouse was busy, there being little to do in the fields on these bitter winter days. The villagers fell silent as Mal entered, and exchanged glances and muttered curses as Sandy followed behind him. Mal ignored them; he was used to such receptions by now. Instead he bestowed his most charming smile upon the alewife, plied her with silver and soon took possession of two seats near the small fireplace, two jacks of very tolerable porter and a plate of bread and pickled onions.

"You're a long way from home, gentlemen," their hostess said, wiping her hands on her apron. "Up from Derby, are yer?"

"Yes," Mal said quickly, before Sandy could betray their purpose. "Looking for an old friend who used to live in these parts, name of Frogmore."

It was the first name that came to mind, but that didn't matter. It did the trick.

"No Frogmores round here, sir. Only gentlemen of your station hereabouts were the Shawes, but they've been gone these twenty year or more."

"Shawe?" Where had he heard that name before? "Oh, so they didn't sell their house to Frogmore after they left?"

The alewife gave a short laugh. "Not likely, sir. Shawe House is cursed. That's why they left. No one's lived there since."

"Cursed?"

"Haunted by vengeful spirits. Or demons. Old man Shawe was murdered in his bed; slashed to ribbons, they say."

"Could have been a wronged woman with a kitchen knife," Mal said, forcing a laugh.

No one else seemed to find his quip amusing. Mal turned his attention back to his dinner, and as soon as both their plates were empty they went back out into the cold.

"Demons, eh?" Mal said as they rode away from the tavern. "Where have we heard that before? Still, sounds like we're on the right track at last."

Mal stopped at the last house in the village and asked directions of a grubby-faced child of indeterminate sex, who ran indoors without a reply. A few moments later an old man came out.

"Shawe House, yer say? Well, ye're on the right road. Carry on about a mile and a half and yer'll come to a pair o' gates on yer left. Shawe House is at the end o' the lane – or what's left on it."

The directions were simple enough, and within half an hour they found themselves riding along an overgrown track between a double row of chestnut trees. After about a quarter of a mile the track opened out into what was probably once an entrance courtyard paved with brick, now turned to a copse of leafless sycamore undergrown with the frost-blackened remnants of last summer's nettles. Beyond stood the house itself: all sagging roof timbers, crumbling brick and empty windows.

They dismounted and tied their horses to one of the sturdier saplings. Mal drew his rapier; if Sandy was right, the devourers had come from here originally, and who knew but that more could have escaped through the reopened wound in the dreamlands? It should be safe enough in daylight, but the sun was sinking and they did not have much time. He waved Sandy behind him and approached the entrance to the manorhouse.

The front door had fallen in and its remnants rotted in the damp upland climate. Within, broken bricks and roof-tiles covered the floor in a thick layer, and a damp, mushroomy smell filled the air. Mal cast about him, all senses alert, but saw no sign of devourers.

They explored the rest of the manorhouse, but found only rot and destruction giving way to nature.

"Shawe," Mal muttered under his breath. "I know that name. John Shawe? Robert Shawe? Richard? William? Thomas?"

He ran through all the names he could think of, until–

"Matthew Shawe." That was it. Northumberland's protégé, friend of the astronomer Thomas Harriot. He beckoned Sandy over. "I know the son of the man who owned this house."

"You're sure?"

"He would have been but a child when the place was abandoned, but yes, I would wager good money on it. He is an alchemist; a pursuit he picked up from his father, perhaps?"

"Our people have knowledge far beyond that of Christian scholars. Though how alchemy relates to what happened in the dreamlands..." Sandy looked thoughtful. "There should be traces here."

"Can you not feel them?"

"I can try."

"Do it. I'll keep watch, just in case."

Sandy crouched in the rubble with his back against one of the crumbling walls and closed his eyes. Long minutes passed, and eventually Sandy's eyes began to move under their lids. He was dreaming. Mal waited impatiently, half an eye on the sun sinking behind the far wall. They had to leave soon, or–

A sharp intake of breath made him whirl, blade at the ready. Sandy was staring up at him.

"It's close. I felt…" He pointed towards the rear of the building. "There."

Mal held out a hand and hauled his brother to his feet, and they made their way quickly through the ruins. At the far end of a group of outbuildings stood one that had remained surprisingly intact.

"Of course," Mal said. "They would have kept it away from the main house. Too much risk of fire."

He heaved open the damp-swollen door. The dank air smelt faintly of charcoal and something else, bitter and metallic, but nothing could be seen within. Mal took out his flint and tinder, and improvised a torch from a piece of scrap timber that was drier than the rest. Holding his rapier in a middle guard to defend against an attack from any quarter, he advanced slowly over the threshold.

The building was a workshop of some kind, with thick walls and a hearth at the far end, and wooden shelving along each long wall. Most of the shelves had collapsed, leaving heaps of broken glass and earthenware at their feet, held together by a sticky mass that sprouted clumps of pale fungi. A table in the centre of the workshop had also collapsed in on itself. Mal crunched across the floor to the fireplace, and noted the oven-like structure to one side, its bronze door crusted with verdigris. Sandy stooped and picked something out of the rubble.

"Look at this." He held it out to Mal.

Torchlight glinted on a glass rod with vivid blue crystals fused to one end.

"Alchemy indeed," Mal said softly.

"But to what end?" Sandy replied. "Alchemy has many uses, but it cannot affect the dreamlands."

"Iron can. It cuts off our souls from that place, after all."

"You think they were searching for a way around that?"

"Perhaps," Mal said. "That could explain how the devourers got through. Though if the alchemist succeeded, why didn't Selby use his magic to escape, or at least call upon his friends for aid?"

"Maybe he did and they failed to get there in time. Or perhaps Shawe is still searching."

Mal wrapped the glass rod in his handkerchief and stowed it inside his doublet.

"Whatever happened, I need to get back to London and find out more."

Before Mal could make preparations to leave Rushdale, snow fell again, sealing them in for the best part of a month. The delay irked him, but he forced himself to at least appear cheerful, for his wife's sake as well as Kit's. The boy was growing fast, and revelled in the combined attention of his father and uncle. He clearly preferred the latter, but so far that was the only sign that the soul within him was Kiiren's. Mal had been worried that Kit might start babbling in Vinlandic or the ancient skrayling tongue before he learned English, and frighten the servants into thinking him a changeling, but Sandy assured him that it would be some years before Kiiren's memories started to assert themselves.

"It won't take as long as it did with me, thank goodness," Sandy said one afternoon, as they sat by the fire watching Kit and Susanna playing peekaboo over the back of a dining chair. "His soul is strong, and his death was less horrible than ours."

"It was horrible enough," Mal said, trying to banish the image of Kiiren screaming as the devourer tore out his guts.

"But we were there with him, at the end. That makes a big difference."

"If you say so."

It was hard to reconcile this merry child with the solemn ambassador he had known. There were times he almost forgot that Kit was not his own son, so natural did he seem with his adoptive mother. He wondered how deeply Coby would mourn – how they both would – when Kit grew up and left them, as he must do eventually. For all Grey's congratulations, they did not truly have a son and heir, not yet. Mal only hoped he had managed to get her with child this winter. She had not said anything so far, but perhaps she would not want to tell him until she was certain herself, and such things took time. Or so he had been led to believe. That was women's business, and he had only the haziest of ideas how things went once the man's part was done.

Thoughts of his wife sent him in search of her. With this break in the weather he had no more excuses to delay his journey south, and good reason to go. Food supplies were running low, and every ounce of flour and cheese and bacon had to be accounted for if they were not to starve before spring. The sooner he left, the sooner he would cease to be a burden on the household.

He found her in the kitchen, supervising the cooking of supper. Coby wiped her hands on her apron and left the cook to finish making the pastry.

"Can I help you, my lord?"

He smiled; ever the model of a dutiful wife in the servants' presence. If only they knew what mischief the two of them had wrought together in the past! He led her through the servants' hall and into the dining parlour, where they would not be overheard.

"I'm leaving tomorrow," he told her. "The road is as clear as it's likely to get this side of Easter, and it's bound to be fairer going once I get out of the Peaklands."

"Must you?" She slid her arms about his waist and laid her head upon his chest. "It feels like only a moment since you arrived."

"You know I have to," he replied, embracing her.

She looked up at him, her grey eyes bright with unshed tears. "Then we shall come with you. Kit's old enough now that no one is likely to question the exact month of his birth."

"I have to be sure it's safe first. Our enemies could still be waiting for me."

"But you'll write, won't you? I shan't sleep for worrying that you've been arrested, or worse."

"I promise," Mal said, and sealed the vow with a kiss. "And I'll send for you all as soon as I can. Better in Southwark under the eye of the skraylings, than a week's ride away."

The journey back to London took rather longer than a week, on roads thick with mud and slush and pocked with holes big enough to swallow horse and rider both. When Mal finally saw the smoke of the capital rising above the trees, relief threatened to overwhelm caution, and it took all his willpower not to urge Hector into a canter down the last stretch towards Bishopsgate.

Getting into the city was not the immediate problem, he reassured himself. Even if his description had been circulated after the Marshalsea incident, surely after six months the guards would have forgotten it? In any case, he was so bedaubed with mud that even his friends might not recognise him. No matter; there were plenty of bath-houses in Bankside where he might steam away the filth from his skin and the chill from his bones.

He guided Hector through traffic that rapidly thickened as it was funnelled into the suburb that lay outside the walls, past taverns and shops and the forbidding bulk of Bedlam. This close to the gate, he felt less certain of anonymity. He had travelled through here often when Sandy was locked up in the hospital, and long-serving guards might just remember his face, even if it took a while to attach a name to it. He pulled his cap down lower and slumped in his saddle, trying to look inconsequential but not furtive.

"You there!"

Mal's heart twisted against his ribs for a second, but he willed himself not to give any outward sign of alarm. A glance from under the brim of his hat revealed that the object of the gatekeepers' attention was a merchant whose wagon was scoring deep ruts in the mud.

"Got something extra in there, have you?" one of the men asked, lifting the canvas sheet lashed over a stack of barrels.

"Have you seen the shitty state of these cobbles?" the merchant replied, brandishing his hat. "It's a wonder I haven't lost a wheel. What do I pay my tolls for, if the parish doesn't maintain the road?"

"Then you won't mind paying double to help fund the next work crew, will you, sir?"

Mal left them to their arguing and slipped past, tossing a coin into the toll-collector's box. One line of defences breached; now there was just the rest of the city between himself and the relative safety of Southwark.

He half-expected the Sign of the Parley to be burnt down or damaged, but apart from the crude boarding-up of the shop windows on the ground floor, the building was much as he had left it. He let himself into the house. Dear God but it was a dreary place without his friends and family to brighten his homecoming! The kitchen stank of vinegar where the beer barrel had leaked and dripped its contents on the floor, and the upstairs rooms were hardly any better. He went into his bedchamber and pulled back the sheets on the bed, wrinkling his nose at the damp, mouldy linen. He would have to hire a maid to clean and air the place if his family were to live here.

He deposited his saddlebags and rapier on the chest at the foot of the bed, retrieved the package containing the alchemist's rod, then set off for the skrayling camp on foot. The bath-house would have to wait. After a week on the road with nothing to do but think over what he and Sandy had found, he was eager to move on with his investigations.

It began to rain as he walked along St Olave's Street, and by the time he reached Horseydown his hat and cloak were heavy with moisture. He was glad therefore to find Adjaan back in her cabin with the doors closed and a brazier warming the air. The outspeaker looked a little plumper than he remembered, with a distinct swell to her formerly flat bosom. Was this some masquerade to make herself look more human?

"Catlyn-*tuur*. Please, come in."

Mal kicked off his muddy boots and stepped over the threshold. As the outspeaker turned to let him pass, Mal could not help but stare at her bulging belly. Adjaan laughed and stroked the broad curve stretching her tunic.

"Have you never seen a woman with child before?"

"Forgive me, honoured one. I am still getting accustomed to seeing a woman here at all."

"As are my menfolk," she said with a sigh, and knelt by the brazier.

Mal hung up his hat and cloak and joined her.

"What brings you back to us?" she asked. "I heard from your theatre friends that you had fled the city."

"You know Shakespeare?"

"I like to acquaint myself with all your storytellers."

Mal drew forth the package of waxed cloth tied with string and laid it on the matting between them. Adjaan cocked her head on one side.

"A gift?"

"Not exactly. Please, open it, and tell me what you think."

Adjaan did so, revealing the crumpled handkerchief still wrapped around the glass rod. She peeled the fine linen away and held the rod up before her eyes. The deep blue crystals caught the light of the hanging lamps, seeming to glow from within like lightwater exposed to air. Adjaan sniffed delicately at the encrusted end.

"*Siiluhlankaar*. Interesting."

"What is it?"

"I do not know the English name. We call it 'sacred poison stone', because its making from ore gives off deadly fumes, but its colour makes it precious to us. Where did you find it?"

Mal told her about the alchemical workshop. She nodded thoughtfully.

"*Siiluhlankaar* has an interesting nature; it behaves a little like iron, even though it contains none."

"Like iron, but not iron? That explains a lot."

"It does?"

"My brother has an idea that the guisers may be trying to counteract the effect of iron on dreamwalking."

Adjaan's eyes widened, and she laid a hand on her belly in instinctive protection. "Do you think so?"

"I really don't know, honoured one. But I mean to find out."

"I will do whatever I can to help, of course, though alchemy is not my field of study."

"May I ask what is?"

"Language, of course. That is why I asked to come here to be my clan's outspeaker, against all our traditions. I wanted to learn your languages and discover if they are related to our own."

"And are they?"

"Alas, no. Not that I can discover. Everything about them is different."

She fell silent, stroking her belly. Mal wondered if the child within was a reincarnated skrayling, or waiting to be the vessel for one. Was that why she was really here? If one of the elders was too infirm to travel across the ocean, this might be his only alternative to extinction. And if more skrayling women came, might that not also be a solution to Sandy and Kit's problem one day? He dragged his thoughts back to the present. It would be many years before either of them was ready to reincarnate.

"Fascinating as such a subject is, honoured one, I am more interested in the *siiluhlankaar*." Mal held out his hand for the glass rod and Adjaan passed it back to him. "Do you know anyone who could tell me more about it?"

"There are few *tjirzadheneth* on this side of the great sea, and alchemy is only one craft of many. Still, I shall ask."

"Why would you need to seek among the reborn, honoured one?"

"Do you forget so much, Catlyn-*tuur*? Alchemy is the province of women, as with all crafts." She laughed softly. "I am sure Erishen has been a woman at least once in his many lifetimes."

Mal hid his embarrassment by carefully wrapping up the glass rod once more.

"Thank you, Adjaan-*tuur*," he said, getting to his feet and bowing.

Adjaan looked up at him, her amber eyes grave. "I am only sorry I could not do more."

"One more question, if I may, honoured one? Will any more skrayling women be coming over the ocean, to England or Sark?"

"Why do you ask?"

"I merely wondered if you were considering a permanent settlement. Since you are having a child here."

She shook her head. "These are your lands. We do not wish to take any of them from you."

"Not even a small island, freely given?"

"Lent to us only, I think. It is surely still your Queen's, to bestow where she wishes."

He had no answer to that, so he bowed and withdrew. Still, it had answered the question he had not asked. If Erishen and Kiiren wanted to become skraylings in their next lifetime, they would have to risk their lives on a voyage back to the New World.

CHAPTER IX

With Mal gone the house felt strangely empty, even though he had been but one man out of a household of more than a dozen. However, Coby was far too busy with spring chores to sit and mope. The arrival of March brought dry windy weather that was perfect for laundry, then there was the kitchen garden to prepare for the coming year: leeks and parsnips to harvested, beds to be cleared and re-sown with lettuce, spinach, onions, carrots and summer cabbage. Every night Coby fell into bed exhausted and with nothing but the prospect of longer, harder days ahead. Every morning she hoped for news from Mal, though she knew it would take at least two weeks for a letter to reach her.

To her relief Sandy came down to the hall for meals more often, but half the time he didn't respond to his own name and she could hardly call him "Erishen" in front of the servants. Once or twice she even caught him referring to his nephew as "Kiiren", and though she chided him, he appeared unrepentant. If they did not join Mal in London soon, she didn't know what she would do with him.

"I thought you might like to take Kit to see the new lambs," she said one day at dinner, some ten days after Mal's departure. "The path up towards Bleak Low should be dry enough by now."

Sandy's reply was interrupted by the sound of hoofbeats from the courtyard. Coby leapt up from her seat and ran to the front door, wiping her hands on her apron as she went.

Five horsemen, not one, drew to a halt in the centre of the courtyard. Nor was their leader her husband, though he was handsome enough, with dark wind-blown hair and grey eyes that sparkled with the exertion of his ride. He dismounted smoothly and bowed to Coby.

"Mistress Catlyn."

"Do I know you?"

"William Frogmore, at your service." He bowed again.

So, this was the Huntsman Mal had worked with in Kent.

"Ah, of course. Do come inside and refresh yourself," she said, forcing a smile. She glanced at Frogmore's companions and reluctantly added, "Your men, also."

In truth they were as hard-eyed a bunch of ruffians as she had seen in all her time in Southwark, with steel gorgets around their throats and pistols tucked into their belts. *Well, let them swagger; I am not afraid of them. I bet they've never even seen a devourer, let alone killed one.*

As they entered the hall, Susanna rose from her seat and Kit jumped down and hid behind her skirts, eyeing the new arrivals suspiciously.

"Catlyn?" Frogmore strode up to the dais.

Sandy nodded his acknowledgement, but made no further move. Frogmore glanced back at Coby, puzzled, then his features relaxed into a smile.

"Ah, you must be his brother, Alexander. Truly, the likeness is remarkable."

"So I am told."

Sandy's icy tones did not invite further pleasantries, and it was left to Coby to fill the silence.

"Do you not bring news of my husband, sir?"

"He is not here?"

She shook her head, not trusting herself to speak.

"That is a pity," Frogmore said. "I'd hoped to have words with him ere I return to my estate in Kent."

"He is gone to London. I'm surprised you did not see him on the road."

"Oh, I have been in Derbyshire some weeks, visiting old friends."

Sandy turned pale and looked as though he were about to say something impolitic.

"Why don't you take Kit up for his nap?" she said quickly. "Susanna has a good deal of sewing to do, don't you, my dear?"

The nursemaid nodded, her glance flicking over to the visitors. So, she didn't think much of them either.

Sandy beckoned to Kit, who dashed round the back of the chairs and flung his arms around his uncle's long legs.

"You will be down again for supper?" she murmured to Sandy as he bent to pick Kit up.

"If you insist."

"I do." She watched the three of them leave, then turned back to her guest. "You must forgive my brother-in-law. He takes his duty of guardianship very seriously."

"I understand. The enemy are devious, and even little children are not safe from their enchantments."

Somehow Coby managed to keep her expression blank.

"Indeed." The sooner these zealots were out of her house, the better she would like it. "Please, sit down. It's a long ride to Kent, and I would not see you leave on an empty belly."

"Perhaps we should stay a day or two," Frogmore said, stepping up onto the dais and taking Sandy's now-empty seat. "My men could go hunting in the morning, bring you some fresh meat for your table."

Frogmore's men took their places on the servants' table and began helping themselves to bread and beer. Coby resumed her own place at table, next to Frogmore.

"That's most generous," she said, "but I wouldn't want you to delay your homeward journey on our account. Do you not have a wife waiting for you?"

"Alas, my business affairs take up a great deal of my time. And God's work must come first, must it not?"

Coby could hardly disagree, but thankfully Frogmore soon turned the conversation to less contentious topics such as the prospect for the coming year's harvest. She offered her own inexpert opinions and withdrew to her own chamber as soon as it was courteous to do so. All this talk of country matters only made her homesick for London, and she was determined to leave soon, whether Mal sent for her or no. Either he was safe in London, in which case he would be glad to see them earlier than expected, or he was in trouble and the sooner she was there to help him, the better.

One thing was certain: she could not let Frogmore know of her plans. He would surely offer his services to escort them to London, and for all her bravado she would as soon take up with bandits as travel with the Huntsmen. Tempted as she was to send him on his way this very afternoon, however, it would be hard to do so without arousing his suspicions. No, she would let Frogmore and his men stay here tonight, then give them a good start in the morning before setting off herself. She smiled to herself. If Mal were in trouble, this was a job for intelligencer Jacob Hendricks, not Lady Jacomina Catlyn. And travelling in male guise would be safer in any case.

At the bottom of her clothes chest she found the old doublet and hose she had worn in her guise as Mal's valet. She shook them out and hung them up to air, then did the same for the shirt and hose to wear with them. The prospect of a chance to resume her old persona gave her a guilty thrill, and she glanced upwards apologetically. *Forgive me, Lord, for my sin of pride. But I was good at what I did.*

A trawl of the chests and cupboards produced more treasures: a worn leather belt and a knife in its sheath; leather shoes suitable for a man, also old but well-mended; her roll of skeleton keys; and a cherrywood box containing a pair of pistols that Mal had bought her for her eighteenth birthday. How long ago that seemed now, more like forty years than four. She put everything into an old satchel, ready to take down to the stables. After a moment's thought she added her jewellery box to the satchel and bundled up the gown made from her New Year's gift, along with a linen coif and other necessary items of feminine apparel. God willing, she would not need her disguise beyond the journey itself.

The rest of their preparations would have to wait until Frogmore had left; she could not risk him suspecting her purpose. With a last wistful glance at her old clothes, she shut the bedchamber door and locked it, then went back down to see to her guests.

••••

Despite his promise, Erishen did not go down to supper that night. Though the visitors might be too young to have participated in his own murder, he had no doubts they would turn on him and Kiiren the moment they suspected the truth. It had been madness to involve them in the fight against the guisers, but Mal would not be swayed.

"They might have more information about Shawe," he had said before leaving for London. "How can I let that chance slip through my fingers?"

"It seems to me that you are protecting them." Erishen replied. "I think they did something to you that night, when they daubed you in Tanijeel's blood. They made you one of their own."

"How can you say that? The memory still haunts me–"

"Then why do you not want revenge?"

"Trust me, we will have it. But it will have to be planned carefully. A single coordinated arrest, like the Templars of France long ago."

Erishen only hoped his brother had put the plan into motion by now. The thought of Frogmore and his friends riding south into a trap made him chuckle aloud, drawing Kiiren's attention.

"Come on, *amayi*, time for bed. You can sleep in my room tonight."

Susanna bade her charge good night and settled down to her mending. Erishen smiled to himself as he went through into the bedchamber. Ever since he had caught the nursemaid enjoying lustful dreams about his brother and diverted them to be about himself instead, she had been decidedly more compliant. The release from guilt had made her happier to serve his sister-in-law as well, so he considered it a job well done.

He shut the door behind him, and went to draw the bed-curtains against the chill evening air. Tomorrow the killers of his people would be gone and he and Kiiren could return to their familiar routine. Perhaps he would even take his *amayi* to see the young sheep. Childhood innocence was short for their kind, and all the more precious for it.

••••

Coby paced her bedchamber, unable to settle. Even with two locked doors between herself and her guests, the thought of stripping down to her shift made her stomach turn over. And what about Susanna? Had the girl the sense to lock her bedchamber door? She should go and check, but that would mean going through the guest chamber.

The clothes hanging up on the closet door caught her eye. What if she dressed as Jacob? Frogmore and his men might not even recognise her, and they would pay a male servant little attention. With pounding heart she undressed and slipped into the familiar garments. Her hair had grown long in the past couple of years, so she tied it with a ribbon at the nape of her neck and covered her head with a flat woollen cap. Finally she picked up the chamber pot, draped a linen towel over the top and went over to the door.

She pressed her ear to the wood, but could hear nothing. Slowly she turned the key and eased the door ajar. The next chamber was dark, but a light showed beneath the door opposite. Coby crept across the room and listened at the far door. A faint rustling, as of the pages of a book turning. Best to act like someone who had every right to be there. She seized the handle and opened the door.

Erishen woke with a start. He thought he had heard someone cry out, but the house was silent. Reaching out in the darkness he felt Kiiren sleeping at his side, sprawled carelessly on his back. Erishen eased out of bed and fumbled with flint and tinder, cursing the primitive humans for their ignorance of lightwater. A creak of floorboards from the outer room, and a muffled cry. Erishen stood between the door and the bed, unlit candlestick in hand.

The latch clicked up and the door swung open, letting in the warm, diffuse light of a lantern. Erishen could see only a dark shape behind it, but below the lantern a sword blade gleamed like molten gold.

"*Nehetsjelen!*" he hissed. "*Adringsjelen!*"

"Hold, demon! Depart that poor wretch's body or we will burn you from it!"

"I am not one of your demons," Erishen replied. "Though you may come to wish I were."

Behind him, Kiiren began to stir. The man with the lantern stepped into the room; as Erishen had suspected, it was Frogmore. One of his confederates filled the doorway behind him, also bearing a sword. Frogmore jerked his head to the side.

"Take the child; we will exorcise the demon from him after I have disposed of this one."

The second man edged round behind his leader, eyes darting nervously from Erishen to Kiiren and back.

"Touch him and I will destroy you," Erishen said softly.

The Huntsman lifted the cross hanging from his neck to his lips. "Our Father, who art in Heaven…"

Erishen reached out to Kiiren and felt the power of the dreamlands flood his limbs. A green glow filled the air behind him, mingling with the lamplight to give their attackers' faces a sickly yellow hue.

"I give you one last warning," Erishen told them.

The Huntsman charged the bed, sword hacking at Erishen, who ducked so that the blade whistled over his head and slammed into the bedpost. Erishen straightened and kicked him hard in the groin, so that he fell backwards, dropping his sword and groaning. That left only Frogmore. Erishen threw the candlestick at him, but his opponent was not so easily put off. Frogmore advanced on the bed, making short rapid feints with his blade. Erishen edged back until the bedframe pressed into his calves. If the steel touched him or his magic…

"Under the bed, *amayi*!" Erishen called over his shoulder. "Hide from the bad men!"

Frogmore took advantage of the distraction to lunge. Erishen dodged to one side and forward, embracing Frogmore like a long-lost friend. The Huntsman, taken aback by the move, hesitated just long enough for Erishen to raise a hand to the man's face and close the connection between them. As the sword fell from Frogmore's nerveless fingers, Erishen summoned his power and stepped into the dreamlands, taking Frogmore with him.

The young man's eyes widened in terror as he took in the nacreous sky and dark, desolate landscape. Erishen released him, and he began to back away.

"Where am I?"

"The home of your worst nightmares," Erishen said softly.

At those words, dark shapes began to stir in the shadows.

"Farewell."

Erishen stepped back into the waking world to see the remaining man down on elbows and knees, poking his sword blade under the bed.

"Come out, you little–!" His voice choked off as Erishen kicked him hard in the side.

Erishen steadied himself on the bedpost, his head swimming from the effort of transporting Frogmore against his will. The Huntsman rolled over and lashed out with both feet, knocking Erishen to the floor. He raised the sword in both hands – and the world filled with smoke and thunder.

A voice, half-familiar, though Erishen couldn't make out the words for the ringing in his ears. He sat up, looking round wildly for Kiiren.

"Are you hurt?"

A hand reached down out of the smoke, with a pale face behind it. Coby. She helped him to his feet.

"Where is Kiiren? Where is my *amayi*?"

Something slammed into his legs, almost knocking him over again.

"I'm here, Uncle Sandy."

Erishen picked the boy up and hugged him, eyes filling with tears. He wiped his face with his nightgown sleeve. The gunsmoke didn't seem to be clearing.

"Come on!" Coby tugged at his arm. "They've set fire to the house."

Coby left Sandy tearing sheets up and tying them into a makeshift rope, and ran back into the nursery. Susanna was stuffing Kit's clothes into a travel chest, her face set in hard lines.

"We have no time for that," Coby told her.

Susanna ignored her. Coby went to the farther door, opened it a crack and closed it again with a curse as smoke billowed into the room. No chance of getting out that way. She pulled Susanna away from the trunk and dragged her towards the door. Already the heat of the fire was palpable, ancient timbers and panels fuelling its fury.

In the bedchamber she found Sandy opening the window overlooking the courtyard.

"Wait!"

She pushed him to one side of the window, flattened herself against the opposite side and peered out. Figures moved in the courtyard below, but they were hard to make out in the darkness. Friend or foe?

"Let's try the other side," she said.

No movement there. She eased open the casement and scanned the outbuildings. *Please, Lord, let Frogmore not have brought a horde of confederates to surround the house and pick off anyone who tries to escape.* But there was no sign of Huntsmen, only the screaming of horses trapped in the stables. Coby knotted one end of their makeshift rope around the stone mullion that divided the bedchamber window into two arched sections.

"I will go first," Sandy said, "and you must throw Kiiren down to me."

"Very well."

He passed Kit to her and she stood back to let him scramble over the windowsill and down into the stable yard. Kit held out a hand, sobbing.

"Sssh, lambkin, you'll be with him again soon."

She leaned out of the window to see Sandy in the flowerbed below, arms raised. It wasn't easy to get Kit onto the windowsill, and letting go was even harder. For a long moment she stood there, holding him tight and blinking back the stinging tears.

"Come on!" Sandy shouted.

Taking a deep breath she lifted Kit free of the window and let go. He shrieked as he fell, but Sandy caught him and they tumbled to the ground in a joyful heap, laughing with relief.

"Now your turn," she said to Susanna.

The girl stared at her, wide-eyed. "No, I cannot. It is too far."

"No, it's not. Here, let me show you. And I will catch you at the bottom." She took Susanna by the shoulders. "Swear to me that you will follow."

"On my mother's soul," the girl whispered. "Please, mistress, hurry!"

Coby clambered over the narrow sill, thanking God for the protection of her breeches, and lowered herself down on the makeshift rope. The linen sheets scraped against her fingers, but the rough brick wall below the window offered plenty of footholds and she made the next couple of yards without difficulty. Her toes encountered a slight ledge, no more than two fingers' breadth deep, and she paused for a second. This was the stonework around the window below, which meant glass instead of bricks. No toeholds, and she was nearly out of sheet. With a muttered prayer she dropped down another yard, kicking forwards as she went. Glass cracked and leading buckled under the impact, but the window held, and a moment later she was standing on the sill below, heart pounding and gasping for breath. Letting go of the sheet she turned around and jumped the last couple of feet onto the gravel path, landing a little awkwardly and skinning the heel of one hand. She got to her feet and looked up.

"Susanna! Come down, it's quite easy!"

The girl's face appeared at the window, and for one horrible moment Coby thought she would refuse. Susanna began to cough as the fire spread into the bedchamber, and after a desperate glance back over her shoulder she scrambled over the windowsill. Coby stifled a laugh. Like the Venetian whore she had once been, Susanna was wearing knee-length drawers, and had tucked her nightgown into them to keep it out of the way. She clambered down the sheets as far as the ground-floor window, then Coby helped her the last few feet. Susanna crossed herself, muttering a prayer of thanks, and pulled her nightgown free to cover her legs once more.

Coby crouched and rummaged in her satchel for her powder-horn.

"Take Kit and hide in the garden," she told Sandy. "Susanna, go to the stables and let out the horses."

"Where are you going, mistress?"

"I'm going to find out if any of those bastards escaped my house."

"And if they did?" Sandy asked.

Coby looked up from loading her pistol. "Then they'll wish they hadn't."

She ran over to the corner of the house and flattened herself against the wall, clutching her pistol in one trembling hand. Shooting a man – even one threatening her son – had not been as easy as shooting a devourer, and she would rather not have to do it again. She edged closer to the corner and looked round. A low wailing came from the courtyard, and long shadows cast by the flames moved across the ground. Taking a deep breath she stepped out into the open.

The house was ablaze now, black smoke blotting out the sky and flames vying with the rising sun to light the surrounding gardens. Servants in varying states of undress and distress had gathered to watch the conflagration.

"Get away from the house," Coby shouted at them, weaving her way through the throng. She scanned the smoke-grimed faces. "Lynwood! Where is Lynwood?"

"Here, my lady," the steward wheezed, stepping forward. His silver-grey hair stuck up in a halo around his bald pate and he wore a long woollen gown dotted with singe-marks. He didn't seem to have noticed her own unorthodox garb. So much for a disguise. Then she realised that she had lost her cap on the climb down and her hair had come loose. She brushed it back distractedly.

"Have you seen our guests, Lynwood?"

"Three men rode away, my lady, not long ago. The other two I have not seen."

"One of them is dead, but William Frogmore himself..." She shrugged. "Perhaps he perished in the fire."

"I am sorry, my lady–"

"Don't be. He and his men started it." She looked around at the servants huddled over their scant piles of belongings. "Get everyone down to the lodge. There's nothing more we can do here."

At that moment several horses cantered around the side of the house and away down the drive. Susanna appeared close behind, smoke-stained but uninjured. Coby ran up and embraced her.

"The Huntsmen are gone. Come, let's find Kit."

Mal woke with a start and swept a hand across the empty side of the bed, wondering where his wife had got to. Probably fussing over Kit, even though that was Susanna's job. He smiled. She had taken to the boy better even than he'd hoped…

He blinked and looked around again. This was not Rushdale. The bed was too small, the windows and ceiling too low. He was in Southwark, in the house behind the Sign of the Parley.

He scrubbed a hand over his face, the remnants of the dream melting away even as he tried to recall them. A dream? More like a nightmare, a jumble of memories of the theatre fire from which he, Coby and Ambassador Kiiren had barely escaped with their lives. He could almost smell the smoke again, the stink of it on his clothes and in her hair… He shook his head. It was just the morning smell of the suburb, as the fires and furnaces were lit to power the tanneries, forges and other industries deemed too noxious to be allowed within the city itself.

There was nothing for it; he was awake now. With a groan of frustration he climbed out of bed, crossed to the washstand and splashed tepid water on his face. A trip to the barber's, perhaps, and then to court, to try and glean information about Shawe's whereabouts without arousing anyone's suspicions. At least the guisers hadn't tried to have him arrested yet. Perhaps he should write to Coby and let her know it was safe to come down to London. No, best to wait a little longer. They were safe enough where they were.

The household assembled in the park lodge a mile down the valley. A quick tally revealed only two servants missing, and there was still hope they might have fled into the hills and yet be found safe. However there was no food, and despite the chill of a March morning no one wanted to start a fire in the hearth.

"Send everyone home to their families," Coby told the steward. "I ought to take my son to London. His father should not hear the news from strangers."

"Of course, my lady."

"And set some of the men to round up the horses. The coach may be beyond saving, but we can still ride."

"Aye, my lady." He made his obeisance and shuffled away.

She was still wearing her boy's garb, of course, having lent her gown to Susanna. She had her jewellery box and some money, and they could clean themselves up at the first inn they came to. The important thing was to be on their way to London as soon as the horses could be found.

Whilst they waited, she took Sandy aside.

"What on Earth happened back there?" she whispered. "Did you see Frogmore?"

He grinned slyly. "I took him into the dreamlands and left him there."

"You what? Where is he now?"

"I don't know."

"You don't know?"

"I've never done it before. He might come out of his own accord, like a pea is expelled from the ripe pod. Or he might die there, or dissolve into nothing. In truth, I care not."

He smiled down at Kit. The boy had fallen asleep from sheer exhaustion despite his terrifying night, and now lay curled on a pile of sacking.

"Still, why Frogmore?" Coby said, trying not to think about what Sandy had just said. "I thought he was our friend."

"He was there at the capture of Selby, was he not?"

"Yes, but... You think Selby got into his mind, made him do this?"

"He must have done. Him, or one of the other renegades."

She shivered, thinking of how she had let the man into her home even though she had not entirely trusted him or his companions. "We have to warn Mal. If Frogmore could be turned traitor, more of the Huntsmen may do likewise."

"I agree. We should never have allied ourselves with them. Their hatred makes them weak."

Coby left him to watch over Kit. *If hatred makes the Huntsmen weak, then our love for one another makes us strong.* Strong enough to defeat them – and the guisers? She shook her head. Her feelings for Sandy bordered on fear, not love. Was he really any better than them, if he could send a man into oblivion without a second thought? She did not like to think ill of him, for Mal's sake, but she would be glad when Sandy was no longer her responsibility.

CHAPTER X

Mal stared at the sheet of paper on the desk before him, as if by sheer force of will he could make Selby's confession resolve itself to a list of the actual guisers instead of accusing half the court. Either the guilty were named alongside the innocent, or their names had been wilfully omitted, but there were so many on each side that neither approach looked fruitful. He slammed his fist down on the table, making the ink-bottle jump. Damn Selby! And damn Shawe, for being so elusive.

The alchemist had not been seen for many months, at least not by anyone within Mal's circle of acquaintance. Most likely he was hidden away at the home of his patron the Earl of Northumberland, but gaining entrance to Syon House would not be easy. Of Mal's acquaintances at court, Sir Walter Raleigh was wintering in Cornwall after being wounded in the Irish expedition last year, and whilst the Earl of Essex was related through marriage to Northumberland, the two men had little in do with one another. No, Mal's chief hope lay in Blaise Grey who, as a neighbour of Northumberland's, might reasonably be invited to dine with him at some point.

Unfortunately that plan rather required Mal to spend time with his new employer, something neither of them would take pleasure in. It could not be postponed any longer, however. He put Selby's confession aside, took down his cloak and hat and set off for the Strand at a brisk walk.

●●●●

At Suffolk House he was shown upstairs to a grand parlour with a gilded and painted ceiling. Lady Frances Grey and her mother-in-law, the Dowager Duchess of Suffolk, sat either side of the great marble hearth, a clutter of sewing baskets around their feet.

"Sir Maliverny! What a lovely surprise!"

Mal bowed as Lady Frances rose to greet him. "The pleasure is all mine, my lady."

"And how is that fine son of yours?"

"I left him in very good health, my lady."

"You must bring him to court soon," the dowager duchess said, "and your wife too. Blaise could do with a reminder of where his family duty lies."

"Of course, my lady," Mal replied with another bow.

Lady Frances cleared her throat. "If you came to see my husband, sir, I'm afraid he isn't here today. Affairs of state take up so much of his time."

Disappointment warred with relief in Mal's breast, and an idea came to him. Perhaps his journey needn't be wasted after all. He took Lady Frances by the elbow and guided her towards the window, out of earshot of the old duchess.

"In truth it is you I came to see, my lady," he said in a low voice.

"Oh?"

"I need to put a spy in the Earl of Northumberland's household, but it has to be someone completely unknown to our enemies. I therefore cannot assign any of my own men, lest Selby betrayed them, and my own presence in the vicinity of Syon House would be noted immediately."

Lady Frances's eyes sparkled with mischief.

"So you were hoping I might oblige, is that it?"

"I would not want you to put yourself in harm's way, my lady. But perhaps you have connections you can use?"

Lady Frances pursed her lips, and her dark brows drew together.

"There is someone. A gardener at Richmond Palace–"

"A gardener? How is he to help us? Syon House is on the other side of the river."

"And with it his lady-love, a maidservant in the Countess of Essex's service. Fear not, he is a quick-witted lad with a keen memory. I shall speak with him when I next visit the Princess of Wales."

"Thank you, my lady."

"And whilst you are here," she said more loudly, guiding him back towards the fireplace, "you must dine with us, so that you can tell us all about your family. I am so longing to meet Lady Catlyn; when will you bring her out of hiding, Sir Maliverny?"

"Very soon I assure you. But I need a household fit to receive her." He gave the duchess his most charming smile. "Perhaps you ladies would advise me?"

Dinner passed slowly, for the ladies were far more intent upon giving Mal instructions on the running of his household than on consuming the food on their plates. Mal tried to pay attention whilst discreetly wolfing his own meal; the Greys were wealthy enough to eat well even in times of famine, though in deference to the Lenten season there was more fish on the table than meat.

At last the meal ended and servants brought round fingerbowls and napkins. The dower duchess excused herself, saying she customarily read her Bible in private after meals, though Mal suspected a nap was a more likely habit. He felt drowsy himself, truth be told: his belly was fuller than it had been in months, and the house's tall glazed windows had distilled the spring sunshine into languid summer heat.

"What I wouldn't give," he said, as he escorted Lady Frances to the entrance hall, "for a cup of *caffè* right now. Just the thing for after dinner."

"*Caffè?*"

"An Eastern beverage I encountered in Venice. Most stimulating, though the bitter flavour takes a little getting used to." He ignored the pang of guilt at the memory of the equally stimulating company he had enjoyed it in. He had been a bachelor back then, entitled to his pleasures. "I wonder that the habit has not reached these shores yet."

"I dare say it shall, soon enough. Italian fashions are still very much the vogue at court."

The coolness of the marble-lined hall was clearing Mal's head a little, and he recalled his other pressing problem: the identity of Jathekkil's *amayi*. Surely some clue must lie within these walls, and it would be foolish to leave without at least trying to gain Lady Frances's aid in finding it. Not here, though; the hard stone magnified the slightest whisper. He inclined his head towards the parlour opposite.

"Might I have a word in private, my lady?"

Lady Frances said nothing, only gestured gracefully for him to lead the way. He ushered her inside and closed the door. It was risking gossip, even scandal, but he dare not risk the servants overhearing.

"My lady, has Lord Grey made any further progress in his own investigations?"

"I do not think so, not beyond what you have told him."

"Then he has not found anything useful in his father's papers?"

She shrugged helplessly.

"An unbiased eye might help," Mal went on. "Blaise loved his father, or at least respected him."

"As any man should."

"Of course. But loyalty can blind one to a loved one's flaws, can it not?" When she nodded thoughtfully, he pressed on. "Let me take a look at the late duke's papers, as many as we can find. Perhaps right away, before Lord Grey returns from court?"

Mal held his breath, praying that curiosity would get the better of her. He wanted to be there, to ensure that nothing incriminating was conveniently lost.

After a moment Lady Frances grinned like a naughty child. "Yes, why not? And I have an idea where to start."

She led him through room after room of the mansion's west wing until Mal was sure they would end up in the Thames. At last she opened a hidden door in the panelling and they went up a narrow flight of stairs to what must surely be the very top of the house. She halted at a low door and sorted through the keys on her chatelaine for a few moments. At last she found the one she was looking for, and the door creaked open into darkness.

"This is the family archive," Lady Frances said, coughing into her sleeve as a cloud of dust rose around them. "Every letter, household bill and account book since before the Black Death, according to the steward."

Mal stared in disbelief. Though low-ceilinged, the attic room was a good ten yards long and almost as wide, with one cobweb-festooned window at the gable end. And every square foot of floor was covered with stacks of mouldering paper, some of them as high as his waist.

"It could take a lifetime to sort through this lot, assuming the mice haven't eaten half of it already."

"You did say you wanted to see everything."

"I suppose I did, didn't I?" He picked up a handful of sheets from the nearest stack. Tailor's bills, unpaid by the look of them, and several decades old. "Are the late duke's personal letters here?"

"I'm not certain. They might still be in the library, if my husband has not finished with them."

"You've seen them?"

"Yes, in the desk. It has a great many pigeonholes and drawers."

"Locked drawers?"

"Some of them, yes." She looked abashed. "I could not find a key to fit them, and I could hardly ask Lord Grey."

"I think I can help you there. Please, show me."

A preliminary search of the desk revealed nothing more incriminating than a collection of letters written by Blaise to his father from school and university.

"How are you going to get into the drawers?" Lady Frances asked, unfolding one of the letters.

Mal extracted a number of skeleton keys from his boots, hat brim and dagger scabbard, placed there against the threat of arrest and imprisonment.

"Fear not, I've learnt a few tricks as part of my profession."

Taught to him by his wife, though he was hardly going to tell Lady Frances that. He began probing the first lock. Lady Frances put aside her husband's letters and came over to watch.

After a few tries the lock gave way, and its fellow yielded to the same skeleton key. The left hand drawer turned out to be empty, but the right hand one contained a small sheaf of letters in various hands, including several from Lord Burghley.

"Have you found anything?" Lady Frances asked.

Mal showed her the letters.

"Nothing strange about Burghley and my father-in-law exchanging letters," she said. "He was Lord Treasurer, after all, and had dealings with all the great lords of the realm."

"And too old, I think, to be a danger. He must be past his threescore years and ten by now."

"Nearer four score. And in poor health besides. Baron Buckhurst has had to take his place on the council."

Buckhurst. His name wasn't on Selby's list, nor was Burghley's. Was that significant? Come to think of it, none of the Privy Councillors were named. That boded ill. Mal began to feel more certain than ever that it was the omissions that mattered, not the names on the list.

On a hunch he pulled out both drawers, and let out a low whistle. The empty one was a hand's breadth shallower than the one he had found the letters in. A secret compartment! Remembering Baines's training, he took out his riding gloves and felt around cautiously. One could never rule out poisoned needles and other traps. There. The back panel tilted when you pushed on the top and sprang back into place when you let go.

"I'll need something to hold it open," he said, and drew his dagger.

A few moments later he was staring at a small bundle of letters tied with silk ribbon. Love letters? Hardly daring to trust his luck he pulled the ribbon loose and began reading.

Right honourable my good and dearest lord, my most humble and bountiful thanks for all your kind wishes for my health. The days wax long in your absence, and my heart is so afflicted that I curse the

sun for its mockery of my dark humour. I greatly fear that time will
soon be upon me when my soul shall be taken up to Heaven, but I
know that with your care I shall be delivered safe into a new life.

"This is it," he said, trying to keep his voice steady. "Clear evidence of Jathekkil's *amayi*."

"I know not that word, *amayi*. It is not Latin, though it sounds much like it."

"It is a skrayling word, my lady, meaning a trusted companion." When she looked puzzled, he recalled that she still believed the late duke had plotted against the skraylings, not that he was one of them. "Forgive me. I spend too much time with my brother. I forget that others do not understand our private speech."

He scanned to the end of the letter.

I pray most earnestly for your own good health and happiness.
Your very assured and loving kinsman, Wm Selby.
Sent this viijth day of June, 1575.

"No, this cannot be correct," he said aloud. "Selby was a young man when this letter was written. Why would he fear imminent death?"

He sorted through the other letters. This was the last, and some went back as far as the 1540s, written in a boyish hand.

"These are not from the man I arrested."

Lady Frances tapped a folded letter against her lips.

"Selby. Selby." Her dark brows drew together in concentration. "The late Sir William inherited Ightham from his uncle, also Sir William Selby."

Mal swore under his breath. "And did he die twenty-three years ago, as these letters suggest?"

Lady Frances shrugged. "Thereabouts, as I recall. I know not the precise date. Why?"

There was nothing for it but the truth, or some version of it that Lady Frances might believe.

"Our enemies believe in reincarnation, like the followers of Pythagoras. They choose their recruits from those they believe are their dead members reborn."

"Oh." Her eyes widened in shock. "Then they are heretics as well as traitors."

"Indeed, my lady. Now you understand why I must root them out." He shuffled the letters distractedly. "The person I seek is twenty years old or so. Most likely another courtier, and one more powerful than Selby, judging by their schemes so far."

"Oh dear Lord." Lady Frances turned pale and sat down.

"My lady?"

"The Earl of Rutland is courting my daughter Elizabeth. He is twenty-two years old, I believe."

Another guiser trying to get close to Grey's network? That was all they needed. "He is only one man. Who else can you think of?"

Lady Frances counted on her fingers. "There's Nottingham's eldest, Lord Howard of Effingham. He's only twenty-one, but he was elected to Parliament last year. Unfortunately his father's investiture as earl made him ineligible for the Commons, so he left for Ireland under the Earl of Essex."

"Hmm. A possible candidate, though it leaves the young prince vulnerable. Go on."

"Northumberland's brother Josceline is around two-and-twenty also."

"Christ's balls! How I would love that strutting codpiece to be discovered a traitor. I'd take great pleasure in gutting him myself."

Lady Frances ignored the outburst.

"And then there's Elizabeth de Vere, daughter of the Earl of Oxford," she went on. "She used to be lady-in-waiting to Princess Juliana, until she married Lord Derby."

"When was that?"

"Four years ago."

"The year after your father-in-law died, and less than a year after Prince Henry was born. Do you think perhaps someone wanted her away from court, and away from the prince?"

"If they did, they failed. She is more often at court than at her husband's home; indeed, it is quite the scandal. She is said to have had affairs with Sir Walter Raleigh and the Earl of Essex, though my sources have been unable to confirm it."

"The girl has spirit, then, and she's ambitious." *Reminds me of someone I once knew…* "Well, that's given me plenty of food for thought. Thank you, my lady."

Mal walked home, his mind awhirl. So, two generations of guisers in one family. Just like Sandy and Kit, and possibly the Shawes as well. After all, what better place to raise another guiser than within your own family? Damn it, he had been a fool not to think of it sooner. If he compared Selby's list against the names Lady Frances had suggested, it might reveal some pattern. Then there were the young candidates themselves. None were sufficiently well-placed to be influential at court, but perhaps not all guisers aimed for high office. A man of power was constrained by duty and could not always go where he pleased. Better to be a relative nobody, or a young wastrel like Jos Percy. Indeed the web of connections to Northumberland made the earl's brother a very plausible candidate.

As Mal neared the Sign of the Parley he noticed that the front gate was ajar. He paused in a doorway on the other side of the street. This was it. Should he run, or let them arrest him?

Long moments passed, with no sign of armed guards. At last the door opened and a fair-haired lad in travel-stained clothing stepped out into the street. Mal burst out laughing with relief, and ran across the road to greet his wife.

Coby hunched over the kitchen table, poking a spoon distractedly into her own pottage whilst watching Susanna feed Kit. It was a messy business, since Kit was old enough now to use a spoon himself, and provided harmless amusement for them all. Even Sandy managed a smile, though he was grey-faced from a sleepless week on the road.

As soon as they had finished supper Mal ushered her upstairs, insisting that the dishes could wait until morning. In truth she was only too glad to get out of the filthy clothes she had been wearing for the past few days, and her nakedness had the predictable effect on her husband.

"Not too sleepy yet?" he asked, getting into bed beside her.

She chuckled and ran her fingers through the dark wiry curls covering his chest. There were a few more silver ones than she remembered. "Perhaps not that sleepy..."

The night was mild and close, and sweat quickly pooled between their bodies as they moved together. She couldn't help but giggle as they parted with a loud squelch, like a boot being pulled out of mud.

"You find my lovemaking ridiculous, do you?" Mal pulled a face, barely visible in the late evening gloom.

For an answer she drew him closer and kissed him again.

"Oh, I have missed thee, good wife," he sighed when she let him go. "Though unless you have other garb in your saddlebags, methinks my wife had best disappear and we will put it about that her cousin Jacob is back in London."

"No, I have nothing else besides the gown I lent to Susanna," she said quietly, staring up at the shadowed canopy. "We were able to save very little from the fire."

He sat up in bed and ran his fingers through his hair.

"I cannot believe Frogmore betrayed us." His voice was steel-edged, as if a different man sat by her side than the one who had made gentle love to her. "Is there no one we can trust?"

"We have each other," she said. "And Sandy, and Kit."

"Aye."

She looked up at the bitter tone in his voice. "It wasn't your fault–"

"No? If I hadn't made such a bold move against Selby, the other guisers would never have taken their revenge on... on my loved ones." He slammed a hand against the bedpost, making Coby jump. "Damn it, you nearly died, and Kit and Sandy too. And Rushdale is..."

She reached out a hand to comfort him, but pulled it back. She knew he wouldn't thank her for fussing over him as if he were Kit with a scraped knee.

"The house can be rebuilt," she said softly. "We still have the land and all its income."

"I can't do it anymore." His voice was so low, she had to lean closer to make out his words.

"What do you mean?"

"I can't keep up this fight against the guisers. Not if…" He looked down at her. Coby swallowed. She had never seen him so wretched, not even after he had been tortured by the Venetians. "I can't lose you."

"We can't give up, not now–"

"Yes we can. We can go back to France, or even further. Venice wasn't so bad, was it?"

Coby shuddered at the memory of the devourers coursing through the narrow city streets, tearing people apart. London was dangerous enough, but no power on Earth would get her back to Venice. She reached out a hand and laid it on his.

"And what about all the other lives they will steal in our absence? If we stand by and let them do this blasphemous thing, how will we ever live with ourselves? What reason will we give, come Judgement Day, for abandoning our countrymen to their fates?"

"Perhaps you are right," he said after a moment. "But we cannot fight them alone. We need allies."

"Much good our alliances have done us so far."

"I was perhaps unwise to trust the Huntsmen," he said. "They are too easily swayed by their hatred of the skraylings, too easily manipulated into turning against anyone connected with them."

"Then who? Is there anyone we can trust? Anyone we can be sure is not a guiser, or one of their allies?"

"I don't know." He lay back down. "Let us sleep on it. Perhaps inspiration will strike when I am less weary."

Coby laid her head on his shoulder.

"Promise me one thing?"

"Hmm?"

"Promise you won't send me away again."

"I–"

"We have to stay together from now on," she said, levering herself up on one elbow and fixing him with her gaze. "If they come for us, I would rather die by your side than hundreds of miles away."

He hesitated, and she narrowed her eyes at him, preparing to argue further.

"Very well," he said at last. "I promise."

"Good. And I think Lady Catlyn will rise from the ashes after all. I can make more gowns easily enough, especially if I sell some of my jewellery."

"So anxious to be back in skirts?" he asked with a smile.

"No, but I will not give those villains the satisfaction of thinking they have us beaten. And in any case, you will need a pair of eyes – and ears – amongst the ladies of the court. This Lady Derby could just as easily be a guiser as any of the men."

"Very well. I'll ask Lady Frances, and perhaps she can exert her influence to get you a place in the Princess of Wales's household. But promise me you'll be careful."

She lay back down and snuggled close to him. "I'm always careful."

She refrained from adding, *It is you who needs to be careful, my love.*

CHAPTER XI

Soon after her arrival in London Coby went to Goody Watson's and bought the best second-hand clothing her budget would stretch to: a plain woollen bodice and skirts for Susanna, and a couple of silk gowns for herself. The latter were somewhat out of fashion and the embroidery needed mending but they were good enough for court, especially for the wife of a country knight. It would not do to dress above her station.

Thus transformed once more into Lady Catlyn, it was time to face her next challenge. Lady Frances Grey had agreed to consider recommending Coby to the Princess of Wales as a lady-in-waiting, but wanted to meet her first. On the following Thursday, therefore, Coby's mare was groomed and saddled, and she and Mal rode to Suffolk House to dine with the Greys.

The dinner itself passed in a blur of fine tableware and elaborate dishes flavoured with sugar and spices. Thankfully the duke did not share the current craze for the skraylings' hot pepper, but there were plenty of other delicacies on offer. Coby had been forced to learn to eat in a more ladylike fashion since giving up her boy's guise, but she still filled her plate with a gusto that raised a few eyebrows. She flushed and tried to eat as daintily as Lady Frances, cutting her food into tiny morsels that hardly needed any chewing.

At last the dishes were cleared away and the gentlemen retired to the library to discuss business.

"Won't you join me in taking a turn about the garden, Lady Catlyn?" Lady Frances said, getting to her feet. "It's such a fine afternoon."

"Is that wise, my dear, in your condition?" the dowager duchess asked. "We wouldn't want you to catch a chill."

"I'll send for a warm cloak," Lady Frances replied. "And Lady Catlyn will make sure I don't stay outside too long, won't you, my dear?"

"Assuredly, my lady." She glanced sidelong at Lady Frances, but if the duchess truly were with child, her condition had not advanced far enough to show.

The gardens of Suffolk House stretched down to the Thames. Coby had seen only glimpses of them, last time she was here with Sandy, and though they were barer at this time of year they had a stark elegance that fitted their mistress better. Low box hedges traced elaborate knot patterns around beds just starting to break into fresh leaf, with violets and daffodils adding a splash of colour to the gloom. At the corners of each bed, red-and-blue painted poles topped with the unicorn of Suffolk gleamed in the spring sunlight. A gilded pleasure-barge, almost as fine as the Queen's, rocked at its mooring place, ready to take the duke and duchess to their estate upriver or to one of the many royal palaces.

"So, your husband wishes you to spy for us at court," Lady Frances said.

"Um, yes, my lady. He is well aware of the great service you did your father in that respect."

"I would be happy to do so again, of course, but it appears that God has other plans for me." She stroked her stomacher and smiled in contentment. "I hope to provide my husband with an heir, as you have done for yours."

Coby had no answer to that.

"I must say," Lady Frances went on, "you look a great deal like that servant of Sir Maliverny's, the one he brought to my father's house before he went to Venice. What was his name...?"

"Jacob Hendricks, my lady. He's my cousin."

"Ah, well, that would explain it." The smile she gave Coby suggested she was not fooled. "A pity he had to leave your husband's service."

"Y-yes, my lady. He… he had news of my uncle and aunt, whom he feared had perished at sea, so of course Sir Maliverny had to let him go back to Antwerp to see them."

She wished it were the truth, but no news had ever come to her of her parents' fate, though she had made enquiries amongst the Dutch community in London for years afterwards.

"And yet I heard he was seen entering the Sign of the Parley not three weeks ago," Lady Frances said.

Coby froze, clutching her hands together and staring at the bright yellow trumpets of the daffodils that shook their heads in the breeze as if mocking her.

"My dear…" Lady Frances halted by a bower covered in climbing roses, their new leaves still dark crimson and folded against the frost. "If I am to recommend you to the Princess of Wales, I must have the truth from your own lips. Are you or are you not the same person I saw three years ago, in the service of Sir Maliverny Catlyn?"

Coby swallowed. If she lied now, would Lady Frances report her to the city authorities for lewd and unwomanly behaviour? But surely she would not cause a scandal over something that had happened so long ago? She licked lips suddenly gone dry as old leather.

"Yes, my lady."

"And are you a man or a woman?"

Coby felt a flush rise from her collar.

"A woman, my lady, upon mine honour."

"Well, that is something. I would not like to think that your husband was making fools of the entire court."

"No, my lady."

"And the child; he is yours?"

"No, my lady."

"You have taken your husband's bastard into your family?"

"Certainly not, my lady."

Lady Frances laughed. "Now that was the truth, if a little too near the knuckle, eh? Men are such wayward creatures…"

"Kit was born in wedlock," Coby said stiffly. "But... his parents were unable to look after him. Venice is a rich city but there are poor people to be found there too, as everywhere."

"So your son is an Italian pauper, whom you and your husband took in out of the kindness of your own heart."

"Yes, my lady." It was true, after a fashion. And perhaps other truths would bolster it. "My husband wanted an heir and I... I fear I may be barren."

"I am so sorry, my dear."

Coby nodded her thanks, a sudden overwhelming grief choking the words in her throat. Until she had said it aloud just now, she had not admitted the truth of it, not even to herself. But there it was. Three years of marriage, and no sign of a child. Perhaps it was a punishment from God after all, for her unnatural ambition in trying to live like a man.

She was vaguely aware of Lady Frances holding out an embroidered handkerchief, and realised that tears were spilling down her cheeks. She took it and blew her nose loudly.

"Well, you have proven yourself capable of great discretion already, and more than able to look after yourself. I shall write to Princess Juliana immediately, and recommend you to her."

Coby curtsied deeply. "Thank you, my lady."

"But I warn you, be on your guard. You may be well-versed in the ways of men's deceptions, but women are just as cunning and twice as ruthless. After all, we have so much more to lose, do we not?"

The Princess of Wales sat stiff-backed on a carved chair under a canopy bearing the arms of the Duchy of Lancaster – a legacy of her ancestors' heritage – quartered with the leopards and fleur-de-lys of the English royal coat of arms. Around her were seated her ladies-in-waiting in order of precedence: some on stools at the side of the low dais, others on cushions at her feet. Coby, as newest and least important of them, had a cushion off to one side and half-hidden behind a senior lady; a position that suited her very well, since it meant she could observe most of the royal party as well as those being presented to the princess.

Such observances were her only amusement in a life of stifling routine: dressing the princess when she rose, eating when she ate, amusing her when she grew bored, going to bed when she felt weary. How the other ladies endured it, Coby could not fathom. No wonder they were all obsessed with marriage. At least as head of a household they would have some control over their own lives, especially if their husband were often at court. Coby was a curiosity to them, a married woman who had nonetheless chosen service to the princess. Over the past few weeks she had had to use all her wits in fending off their endless questions and speculations, and she still was not sure she had convinced them she was not seeking an affair with a more powerful nobleman. This was particularly irksome as it put her at odds with Lady Derby, the one woman Coby had hoped to befriend. Lady Derby clearly considered her a rival, whilst simultaneously dismissing the possibility that any man could be interested in such a plain creature of common stock and no wealth. Coby was beginning to wish she had let "Lady Catlyn" die in the fire after all.

Her thoughts were diverted from such dark musings by a sudden blare of trumpets. She looked up, and was surprised to see Lady Frances Grey standing in the doorway, accompanied by a tall, skinny girl of about twelve or thirteen. They approached the princess and curtsied so deeply that Coby began to wonder how they would stand upright again.

"Your Highness, allow me to present my daughter, Elizabeth Sidney."

Coby tried not to stare. This child was the daughter being courted by the Earl of Rutland? She had heard that the aristocracy often married young, and here was proof of it. Come to think of it, Lady Frances was barely old enough to have a grown daughter.

"Come nearer, my dear. Let me get a good look at you."

The girl stepped carefully between the cushions, her face pale as milk against her dark hair.

"This is the child Rutland wants to marry?" Princess Juliana asked over the girl's head.

"Yes, Your Highness."

"Well, she'll need fattening up before she's fit for the marriage bed," the princess replied, frowning.

"I was hoping you might take her into your service," Lady Frances said.

"Another one?" The princess glanced at Coby, who flushed and looked down at her hands.

"As you know, Your Highness, I am with child and have not the strength to chase after a grown daughter. And her grandmother is not a well woman either."

"Very well. Send her to me next week." Juliana cocked her head on one side. "I don't suppose her courses have started yet?"

Elizabeth flushed scarlet.

"No, Your Highness," her mother replied.

"Hmm. Well, you can tell Rutland he can have her when they do, but no sooner."

Lady Frances and her daughter curtsied again and withdrew from the royal presence. Just before the duchess turned to leave, Coby swore she saw her wink in her direction. Was this some ploy of Lady Frances's, to bring Rutland within Coby's reach? If so it was a callous move, to use her own daughter as a pawn to draw out the guisers. Coby resolved to take the poor child under her wing and protect her as best she could from the harridans at court. The fact that Lady Frances was relying on her to do just that left a sour taste in her mouth, but what choice did she have?

The rest of the morning's business was of little interest to Coby: an artist who had been commissioned to paint new portraits of the princess's daughters; a delegation of scholars from the Cambridge college endowed by the princess, bearing a book of moral instruction dedicated to her, and a tailor with dolls dressed in the latest fashions from Spain and Italy. The latter were cooed over by the other ladies-in-waiting, their insistences that they could not do without such dresses for the coming year bringing a gleam of avarice to the man's eyes.

As the tailor departed, Princess Juliana's steward stepped forward.

"One final matter, Your Highness, and one that I think will give you great pleasure." He handed her a letter.

Princess Juliana cracked the seal and read.

"From my cousin Joaquim," she said, smiling. "And what is this? He sends a gift."

"What kind of gift, Your Highness?" Lady Derby asked. "Jewels, perhaps, or a popinjay from the Indies?"

"Better than that, Your Highness." The steward clapped his hands.

For a moment nothing happened. No sound of trumpets, no stamp of feet. Then the silence of the audience chamber was broken by a high, sweet voice, singing. Coby could not quite make out the words or the language; Portuguese, perhaps, like the princess? After a few moments the singer appeared in the doorway: a slender young man, dark of skin and hair and dressed in courtly finery.

"Bartolomeo Pellegrino, Your Highness. A castrato, all the way from Rome."

The ladies-in-waiting burst into excited whispers at this news. The Italians were famous, or perhaps infamous, for their eunuch singers, castrated before puberty to preserve their youthful voices. Enhanced by the power of an adult male's lungs, they were said to be the closest one could come on Earth to the voices of angels. Coby saw many of the ladies blush and heard them giggle about how handsome the young man was, and what a pity he was not a man entire.

The song died away, and Bartolomeo walked the length of the presence chamber to bow before the princess and her companions.

"I bring you greetings, Your Highness, from your noble cousin, and his heartfelt wishes for your health and happiness."

"Welcome to England, Signor Pellegrino. Please, come sit at my feet and tell me all the news of my uncle's court."

Coby quietly observed the young man during this exchange. It was true he was very handsome despite being unfashionably swarthy of complexion, with a wide brow, finely curled black hair and eyes of a striking jade green. His voice, as high as a woman's, had a soft Italian accent, though he spoke surprisingly good English. The other ladies hung on his every word, and laughed prettily at every slightest jest. Coby was content to watch and listen and note which of the ladies showed him the most favour. Lady Derby for one did not seem overly in awe of him, although she feigned interest well; mostly to please Princess Juliana, Coby suspected. Guiser or no, Lady Derby's ambitions stretched far higher than a court minstrel. Rumour had it that Prince Robert would be visiting soon, to hunt in the park. If so, Coby was ready to do whatever was necessary to keep him and Lady Derby under observation, and perhaps determine the lady's loyalties once and for all.

The days passed, but the Prince of Wales did not come to Richmond with his courtiers, nor did Mal visit on business of his own, and Coby began to regret this whole plan. She was making little headway with Lady Derby, who frequently disappeared on business of her own, often to Syon House according to the other ladies-in-waiting. Of course they all assumed she was visiting one of her lovers, or perhaps just gossiping with Essex's sister, but Coby became increasingly convinced that Lady Derby was in league with the alchemist, Matthew Shawe. Why else visit a house where neither Essex nor Raleigh had been seen in months?

She went to the window of her apartments, from which she could just see the corner of Syon House if she pressed her face against the glass. Cream stone battlements rose above the line of trees, like a child's wooden castle.

"Your son is very beautiful."

Coby looked around with a start. Bartolomeo stood in the doorway, his head cocked on one side. She followed his gaze to the bed, where Kit lay sprawled as carelessly as a puppy, one hand pressed to his plump cheek. Susanna, half-hidden by the long velvet curtains framing the other window, paused in her sewing. The arrival of a visitor was of no immediate concern to her, as long as Kit was not disturbed.

"Thank you," Coby said to the young man. When he did not immediately respond she added, "You speak very good English."

"I learnt it from songs. I like your English music: your William Byrd and John Dowland."

His voice was husky, like a boy's on the verge of breaking. Or like a girl pretending to be a boy. Coby wondered if that was what she had sounded like, when she was being Jacob. No wonder everyone had thought she was younger than she claimed to be.

Bartolomeo nodded towards Kit. "He looks like his father?"

"Yes," she said. "Yes, he does."

"A handsome man, then."

"You can tell me, when you see him for yourself."

"Oh?"

"He wrote to say he would visit soon."

"To see his son. And you."

"Yes."

She gestured to the stool at her side, where Susanna had been sitting until she complained that the light was not good enough. Bartolomeo sat down, folding his long elegant hands in his lap. This close, Coby see that his cheeks were as hairless as a girl's, and she couldn't help wondering if the rest of his body was the same. A warm flush crept up from her collar. She cleared her throat.

"How are you finding England?"

"Cold." Bartolomeo smiled, but Coby sensed a double meaning behind the word. Strange; the Princess had welcomed him, and the other ladies-in-waiting were already making wagers as to which of them he would fall in love with. Perhaps he was all too aware that he was no more than a pawn in their petty rivalries.

"We have had several bad winters in recent years," she said, "but it is certainly colder here than Italy."

"You have been to my country?"

"Only once. A journey to Venice, on the Queen's business."

"And how did you like it?"

"It was… different."

Bartolomeo laughed. "Now you know how I feel. Everything is different here, not just the weather: the churches, the manners, the food–"

"You do not like English food?"

"It is very…" He broke off, frowning, as if searching his memory for the right word. "Heavy," he said at last, patting his belly ruefully.

"Princess Juliana keeps a good table. The food here is richer than I have been used to, I must confess."

"You have not always been a lady?"

This time his dual meaning was surely unintended, yet it still gave Coby pause.

"No. My parents were not of gentle birth." Again, the Italian's questions pressed into areas she did not wish to become common currency around the court. "Tell me about your own travels. Have you been to Venice yourself?"

"Alas, no. I grew up in the countryside near Rome, and travelled to the Eternal City as a boy."

He fell silent, and Coby cursed herself for reminding him of his cruel treatment by the choirmasters.

"But more recently, you were in Portugal," she said.

"Yes, at the court of Prince Joaquim."

He proceeded to tell an amusing story about the prince's pet monkey, which liked to ride in a cart pulled by a little dog and which had been trained to laugh at all the prince's clever jests.

Kit stirred at their laughter, and Bartolomeo leapt to his feet.

"Please, forgive me, I did not mean to disturb your child–"

"There is nothing to forgive. He usually wakes from his nap around this time."

"Then I will leave him to your care. Good day, Signora Catalin."

He bowed and left before Coby could return the courtesy.

"Well, what do you make of that?" she said to no one in particular, staring at the closed door. "Surely he did not have to leave in such haste?"

She went over to the bed and held out her arms to Kit, but he scrambled down the far side and ran over to Susanna. The nursemaid put down her sewing and picked him up. Coby suppressed a pang of jealousy. After all, he was no more her son than he was Susanna's.

"You cannot trust that one, mistress," the girl said, setting Kit down on the window seat so he could look out into the garden.

"Oh? Why do you say that?"

"Because he lies. He says he has never been to Venice, and yet I would swear he is as Venetian as I am. I hear it in his voice."

"Venetian? But why would he lie about something like that?"

"Because he is here to spy on you, perhaps?"

Coby turned away. Why would the Venetians want to spy on her? It had been years since her little adventure in the republic, and anyway if they were interested in anyone, it would be Mal. He was the one who had wrecked all their plans for an alliance with the skraylings. But perhaps they meant to get to him through her and Kit, just as the guisers had done. She sighed. The last thing they needed was more enemies. She would write to her husband immediately and warn him. No, perhaps it was better not to. Bartolomeo could be using his closeness to the princess to read the correspondence passing through her couriers. Better to wait, and watch, and listen. Mal knew how to be circumspect on his own account, and soon he would be here and she could warn him in person. God willing, she would not have to wait too long.

CHAPTER XII

"I could murder some ale," Ned growled into his glass of mint tea.

Steam condensed on his face, mingling with the sweat that trickled down from his hairline. God's teeth but he hated this place! He had thought Marseille hot enough, but al-Jaza'ir could have been the borderlands of Hell. Was, for all he knew. Perhaps one day the parched ground would open up to reveal firepits full of damned souls, and he would be taken down to the fate that he knew awaited all his kind.

"Who needs ale?" Gabriel murmured, opening the little wooden box in front of him. Inside nestled several cherry-sized balls of *hashish*, a local sweetmeat made from date paste, hemp leaves and spices.

Ned reached out with his good hand and closed the lid.

"You've had enough of that already."

Gabriel squinted at him through gilt lashes. His high cheekbones were sun-scorched and flaking, and his fair hair bleached almost white, and yet he was as beautiful as ever, especially when he smiled. Nowadays though he only smiled after a morsel of *hashish*. The rest of the time he sank into melancholy, pining for his London friends – and the stage.

"All right." Ned took his hand away. "But only one more. Youssef will thrash us from here to the New World and back if we come aboard anything less than sober."

Gabriel paused with the sweetmeat halfway to his mouth.

"We're going to the New World?"

137

"No, just back to Marseille. God's teeth, Gabe, has that stuff stolen all your wits?"

The actor looked contrite and replaced the *hashish* in the box.

"You're right. I'm sorry, love."

"I'm sorry too. I wish I'd never dragged you into this mess." He looked around the tavern, if you could call it that in the absence of strong drink. "What's Youssef up to, anyway? I thought this was a quick in-and-out mission. Sell the goods, fill the hold and back to sea."

Gabriel shrugged. "You know our captain."

"Do we, though? He may be Mal's friend, but he says little enough to the rest of us."

"It's not easy when he speaks no English."

"True, but you speak a bit of French. Can't you worm your way into his confidence?"

"To what end? I don't want to spend the rest of my life scrubbing decks, Ned. We need to find proper work, something better suited to our talents." He leaned closer. "Mal must know people in Paris. What if you write to him...?"

"And how is he to reply? He made us promise not to tell him where we are."

Gabriel slumped back down in his seat, staring at the wooden box.

At that moment the curtain over the doorway lifted and Simon Danziger entered the tavern. Though only twenty years old, the Dutchman was already a seasoned member of the *Hayreddin*'s crew and its chief carpenter, having learned the craft from his father in Marseille. Danziger pulled off the scarf covering his straw-coloured hair and called for a pot of tea, and Ned beckoned him over to their table.

"What news?" Ned asked him as he pulled up a stool. "Do we sail soon?"

"Maybe," the carpenter replied, his English accented with a mixture of southern France and his native Holland. "Capitain Youssef is still haggling over that consignment of fine leather."

Gabriel pulled a face. Ned shot him a warning glance and poured Danziger a glass of tea.

"The better price he gets, the surer we are of another voyage, eh?"

"Maybe. Though perhaps I won't be sailing with Youssef much longer."

"Oh?" Gabriel leaned closer.

"I have a mind to start up here on my own account, if I can get the money together." He blew on his tea, and gave them a conspiratorial wink. "Build some proper ships, not these old-fashioned galleys the Moors seem so wedded to. I'm sick of puttering around the Mediterranean; with a full-rigged pinnace or two we could venture out into the Atlantic and take on the whole world."

"It'll take you years to accumulate that much money, surely, even if we were to spend all our time preying on the Spanish."

Danziger made a dismissive noise. "Youssef hasn't the balls for the kind of venture I'm planning."

"What sort of venture?" Ned asked.

"A little favour for the Pasha," Danziger replied in low tones. "Guaranteed to make us rich men. Are you in?"

"Yes," Gabriel said.

"No!" Ned added a heartbeat later.

"Yes or no, gentlemen?"

"Tell us what the favour is, then we'll decide."

"Very well. But not here. Too many ears twitching."

They finished their tea and followed Danziger out into the blinding sunlight. The street was nearly empty but for a one-armed beggar crouched in the shade between two buildings. The man seemed to be asleep, but when Ned tossed a coin at his feet the beggar's hand shot out and retrieved it, tucking it into the folds of his rags before resuming his patient pose.

Danziger led them across the street, along a narrow alley and into a shady courtyard. There he knocked on a door twice, and twice again. A few moments later the door was opened by a young Moor.

"This is Amin," Danziger said, and introduced Ned and Gabriel in fluent Arabic.

Amin showed them into a small room with a cool tiled floor and cushioned benches set around a low table of hammered brass.

"I'm courting his cousin," Danziger whispered when Amin had left. "Lovely creature, eyes like a doe and..." He mimed generous curves in the air. "I'll have to convert to Islam, of course, but that seems a small price to pay."

"You really mean to settle here?"

"Why not? I have better prospects here than back home."

"You keep talking about this venture," Ned said, pacing the small room. "What does it involve, exactly? Piracy?"

"In a manner of speaking. The Pasha's favourite slave has been kidnapped by the Spanish, and I intend to steal him back."

"And you think the Pasha will reward you for this?"

"I know he will. You see, the slave is also worth a great deal to the Spanish, and the Pasha would do anything to keep him from being shipped back to Spain."

"Why? Is he of noble blood? A cousin of King Philip?"

"No, he is one of the painted devils. What you would call a 'skrayling'."

Gabriel stared at him. "Where in God's name did the Pasha get his hands on a skrayling?"

"It seems that one of Murat Reis's galleys captured a skrayling vessel in the Adriatic and took its crew prisoner–"

"In the Adriatic? When?"

"Three years ago, I think. Many of the captives died or took their own lives, but their captain survived and was sold to the Pasha."

"Hennaq." Gabriel spat out the name.

"You know him?" Danziger stared at the two of them.

"Oh, yes, I know him," Gabriel said. "He promised to take some friends and I to France, but he turned on us as soon as we were out of sight of land. Very nearly shipped us off to the New World."

"Perhaps I should not take you on this voyage," Danziger said. "I hear vengeance in your voice."

"We have no desire to kill the skrayling," Ned put in quickly. "Do we, Gabe?"

"Certainly not." Gabriel folded his arms, his expression deadly serious. "But if we help you, we want a share of the ransom."

"That seems only fair. Shall we say one tenth?"

"A tenth? I was thinking more like a third. Between me and Ned, of course. A third for you, and a third for your other allies."

"A third?" Danziger spat on the floor. "Who do you think you are?"

"We are the only men here with intimate knowledge of the painted devils, as you call them. Do you want our help or not?"

Ned suppressed a grin. This was the Gabriel he remembered, fierce and fearless as his namesake.

The Dutchman considered for a moment. "A sixth. I have to reward Amin's family for their help, and Captain Youssef and any crew we hire."

"Very well, a sixth. In coin."

They shook on the deal, and soon afterwards the Englishmen were shown out into the street. Danziger stayed behind, perhaps to pursue his courtship further.

"This is madness," Ned muttered as they headed back to the quay. "You're going to get us killed, you know that?"

"Would you rather slowly rot to death here?"

"No."

"Well, then. If this all works, we'll have enough money to quit this life and go to Paris without Mal's help. There are theatres there–"

"All right, all right," Ned said. The light in Gabriel's eyes was irresistible. "But no more *hashish*, understand? We're going to need all our wits about us if we want to come out of this with our skins intact."

"Agreed." Gabriel linked his arm through Ned's. "From now on, we are sober and responsible brigands."

The hardest part was convincing Youssef to go along with the plan. Danziger contrived a meeting in the captain's cabin, ostensibly to discuss the state of the *Hayreddin*'s keel. Youssef seemed surprised that Gabriel was interested in carpentry, but made no objection to his presence.

"There's no point us both going," Gabriel had told Ned. "You don't speak French, and it will look strange if you just tag along. Youssef may turn a blind eye to our liaison, but we don't want to draw attention to it either."

"If you insist. But don't agree to anything that'll get us killed, all right?"

Gabriel smiled sadly to himself. Ned was always so protective. That was how he had lost his hand, defending Gabriel from the devourers. Foolish boy! Death would come when it willed.

Recalling himself, he turned his attention back to the discussion between Youssef and Danziger before either man could notice his fit of melancholy.

"This ship is old and in need of replacement," Danziger was saying. "I could build you a better one, captain. A faster one."

"And how much would that cost me?" Youssef replied, leaning back in his seat.

"I could put the money into your hands within the month."

"How?"

Danziger explained about Hennaq.

"Amin has discovered that the skrayling is being held in Mers-el-Kébir," he went on. "All you have to do is wait for us off the coast; the Englishmen and I will do the rest."

"And what if the Spanish catch us? As you point out, the *Hayreddin* is past her prime."

"That's the clever part. After we leave for Mers-el-Kébir, Amin will tip off the Pasha as to where his slave is being held, and the Spanish will be too busy fending off his fleet to notice us."

"If the Pasha is so eager to get the painted devil back, why hasn't he done it before?" Youssef asked.

"Because no one knew for certain where he was," said Danziger. "Mustapha Pasha can hardly take on the entire Spanish nation, can he? But the Ottomans have been itching to take back the town ever since the Spanish captured it nearly a century ago, and this might be the very excuse they've been looking for."

"So your plan hinges on tricking the Pasha into providing your diversion?"

"Not a trick. Amin is certain it is the truth. He swore a holy oath on it."

"And when am I to meet you, and take delivery of this slave?"

"In five days' time. It will take us about three days to sail to Mers-el-Kébir, and I have told Amin to give us two days' start."

"Only two days? It may take longer than that to convince the Pasha."

"It will be enough. It has to be enough." Danziger began to pace the small cabin, staring into empty space as if already seeing his route westwards. "The longer we leave it, the more likely it is the Spanish will sail away with this creature before we lay hands on him."

"And if the fleet does not come in time, or at all?"

"Then you will have to leave without us," Gabriel put in. "We cannot ask you to risk your life and livelihood on this venture, captain."

"So that is why you are here," Youssef said. "You are in league with my carpenter. Who else?"

"Only my countryman, Ned Faulkner."

"Though we will need more," Danziger said. "Amin's uncle is willing to lend us a small xebec, hardly more than a fishing boat, but it is too big for three men to handle alone. We'll need a dozen at least."

"You expect me to wager half my crew on this venture as well? Hire men in al-Jaza'ir to sail her."

"The Spanish will be suspicious of a Moorish crew," said Danziger. "I need fair-skinned men, like Gabriel here, and those can be hard to find."

Gabriel held his breath. Without Youssef's cooperation, this plan was suicide.

"Very well," the Moor said at last, "you can have three more men of your choice. But not the first mate. Or my cook."

"Seven men," Danziger replied. "And a quarter of the ransom for you, capitain. I cannot say fairer than that."

"You drive a hard bargain, Dutchman. But I accept. A quarter of the ransom."

"Thank you, capitain." Danziger held out his hand. "You won't regret this."

"I already do," he said with a smile. "But I would not be in this business if I were not willing to take a risk here and there. Now, be about your work, both of you, if you wish to remain in my good favour."

"Aye, captain." Gabriel took Danziger by the elbow and steered him towards the door before he could make any more demands.

"We sail at dawn tomorrow," the carpenter said as they emerged onto the deck. He pulled free of Gabriel's grasp and gestured towards the setting sun. "And we will light such a fire under the Spaniards' tails that our praises will be sung from al-Jaza'ir to Mecca itself."

Gabriel left the Dutchman to his plans and went in search of Ned. His lover might grumble and find reasons not to go, but Gabriel knew he was as bored and frustrated as himself, deep down. Hennaq's ransom would buy them a new life on land, away from the prying eyes of Youssef's crew. Now that was an incentive Ned would not be able to resist.

A few days later their borrowed xebec limped into the harbour of Mers-el-Kébir, or Mazalquivir as the Spanish named it. France now being at peace with Spain, their plan was to claim to be French smugglers who had narrowly escaped being taken by corsairs. That was one thing Ned did have experience of, though he didn't care to repeat it. He and Mal had crossed swords with the bastards on their voyage to Venice. Well, Mal had. Ned had thwacked one in the bollocks and then slithered back down the ladder into the relative safety of the hold.

"The Englishmen and I will go ashore," Danziger told his crew. "I need two others to accompany us."

One of the sailors stepped forward. A tall, black-bearded fellow with crooked teeth and gold rings in his ears, he looked more like a corsair than a smuggler.

"Raoul. Good." Danziger waved him over.

"Won't he be a bit... conspicuous?" Ned murmured to Gabriel.

Gabriel shrugged. "If the Spanish are looking at him, they won't be looking at us."

Danziger selected another man, a scrawny fellow named Pierre whom Ned recalled was an expert climber, as much at home in the rigging as a bird in a tree.

"Right," Danziger said. "The rest of you keelscrapings will man the ship and be ready to have us out of here at a moment's notice. Understand?"

The carpenter-turned-captain led his four companions ashore, and they stalked along the quay in a loose cluster, avoiding eye contact with the fishermen sitting mending their nets. Ned kept his false hand tucked in the pocket of his loose breeches; he had covered up the metal with a linen glove, but that in itself was conspicuous in this hot climate. But it was either that or wear a hook, an ugly thing that reminded him too much of the monsters that had taken his hand. At least with the metal arm he could pretend it was his own flesh, albeit dead and unfeeling.

The town of Mers-el-Kébir occupied the centre of a shallow crescent-shaped bay, embraced by two dark, tree-clad spurs of the distant mountains. Rows of Moorish-looking stone houses, thick-walled and flat-roofed, nestled in the narrow space between the steep mountain slopes and the sea. Near the centre a taller building thrust a spire towards the heavens, topped by a gilded cross that caught the harsh sunlight and flung it back into the eyes of the unwary. A mosque converted to a Christian church, by the look of it.

The church was not the only building repurposed by its new owners. Judging by the barrels outside and the scent of wine wafting across the quay on the hot breeze, several of the houses along the seafront had been converted to taverns. Ned's mouth watered at the prospect of a cup of good canary, or indeed any kind of wine at all. Before they could enter, however, their path was blocked by a squad of half-a-dozen Spanish soldiers. The Spaniards questioned Danziger at length and looked his companions over, suspicious that they had lost their cargo but not been taken prisoner by the corsairs. At last, however, the soldiers let them go, recommending a shipwright who could assist with repairs but warning them not to stay in Mazalquivir overlong. Danziger assured them very sincerely that he would not.

"So what now?" Ned whispered as they followed Danziger into the tavern. "How are we to find Hennaq?"

"I don't know," Gabriel replied. "How did Mal find the one he rescued in Corsica?"

"How do you think?" Ned rolled his eyes.

"I thought it was the Venetian courtesan who taught him magic."

"She taught him a few extra tricks, all right, and not just magic." Ned winked. "But I reckon he had a few of his own to begin with. If he and Sandy really do share a soul…"

"That doesn't help us, though, does it? We neither of us have a drop of skrayling blood between us."

"We'll just have to use our God-given wits."

Ned thought he heard Gabriel mutter "Then God help us" under his breath. He elbowed his lover in the ribs.

"Hush!" Gabriel whispered. "We're supposed to not be attracting attention, remember?"

The tavern was blissfully cool and shady after the sunlit quay. Ned sank down on a bench and wiped the sweat from his forehead with a grimy neckerchief. A few moments later Gabriel pushed a cup of wine across the tabletop. Ned took a gulp and sighed with contentment as the sweet burn of alcohol spread through his limbs.

"It's hardly worth savouring," Gabriel said, pulling a face as he sipped his own drink.

"Don't care. Christ's balls, I'd rather be back in the Marshalsea than in this Godforsaken place."

"*Taisez-vous!*" Danziger glared at them. Of course. They were supposed to be masquerading as Frenchmen.

Ned spent the rest of the afternoon in grim silence, curled around the cup of sour wine like a miser around his box of gold angels. The rest of the crew chattered away in French, even Gabriel occasionally making a comment in that same language. For all his complaining the actor seemed almost at home here, and Ned couldn't help wondering about his lover's adventures in the Mediterranean before they were reunited in Venice. At first he had been too happy to ask questions, and afterwards… With his good hand he rubbed the junction between the stump of his right arm and the base of the brass replacement.

"*Messieurs?*"

Ned looked up to see Danziger leaning over their end of the table.

"*Qu'est-ce que c'est?*" Gabriel replied.

Danziger muttered something, too quietly for Ned to make out even those few words he knew. Gabriel nodded and said something that sounded like agreement. When the captain returned to his seat, Gabriel leaned across the table.

"Hennaq is in the fortress, as we feared."

Ned cursed under his breath. "What do we do?"

"Danziger wants to stay the night here, try to find out more. If he can't come up with a plan, we abandon the attempt and sail back to al-Jaza'ir." Gabriel sighed and slumped down in his seat.

"He has a point. We can hardly storm the fortress with five men."

"Don't you want to go home to England?"

"Of course. But we have to survive this madcap venture first."

Gabriel smiled. "I thought you were the one with the Devil's own luck?"

"My luck ran out in Venice, remember."

"You're alive. I'd call that luck enough."

Ned shrugged. Gabriel reached out a hand across the table.

"Don't you dare get yourself killed, or you'll have me to face."

"I don't think they allow angels into Hell. Not since Lucifer."

Gabriel smiled sadly. "I don't think either of us gets a choice."

CHAPTER XIII

He was back at the theatre, hammering on the tiring-house door as the other actors pressed at his back. Smoke seared his throat. Someone was screaming–

Gabriel jerked awake. Another low rumble. Just a thunderstorm, he told himself. Go back to sleep.

A moment later the ground shook. A crack of breaking timbers, followed by the scrape and whisper of falling roof-tiles that smashed on the ground below. Not thunder; cannon fire. He rolled over on the thin mattress and shook Ned awake.

"Get up! The town is under fire!"

Ned blinked at him. "What?"

"The Pasha's fleet, I'm guessing, come to rescue Hennaq."

They snatched up their few belongings – the knives and purses they'd kept under their pillows – and joined the other men pushing and jostling their way down the inn stairs to the common room. Gabriel suppressed a yelp as the rough sole of someone's boot scraped the back of his bare calf, and prayed none of them would fall in the press and be crushed to death.

At last they emerged into the common room and the pressure eased as the men dispersed.

"Which way?" Ned panted.

"Front door," Gabriel replied. "I think I saw Danziger heading that way."

They ran out onto the quayside. Dawn was breaking, and against the rose-gold light they could make out a line of galleys, their sails reefed, spanning the bay. The cannons were silent, waiting, but perhaps they would not remain so for long.

"I thought they weren't supposed to get here until the day after tomorrow," Gabriel said to Danziger, who was likewise staring into the sunrise.

"Evidently Amin was more persuasive than we expected," the Dutchman said quietly.

Someone pushed past them, running northwards towards the fort that stood on an arrowhead-shaped promontory at the northern end of the bay.

"Come on, this is our chance!" Ned tugged at Gabriel's sleeve.

"What?" He could hardly drag his eyes away from the advancing ships.

"Everyone's fleeing to the fort. This is our chance to get inside, find Hennaq."

"You are right," Danziger said. "Raoul! Pierre! With me!"

Gabriel turned away and hurried after Ned, trying not to lose him in the throng which grew thicker the nearer they came to the red-walled fort.

"You think this will work?" he muttered in Ned's ear as they halted about fifty yards from the gate, squeezed between a heavily laden mule and a man carrying a child on his shoulders.

Ned craned his neck round. "You have a better idea? Besides, we can hardly sail away with that lot blockading the port. Our crew are all Christians; that was part of Danziger's cunning plan, after all."

Gabriel's retort was cut off by a blare of trumpets from the gate. One of the guards shouted something in Spanish. He went on at great length; Gabriel could only make out a word here and there, but it sounded like regulations on who would be allowed inside the fort. His heart sank.

A tap on his shoulder made him start. He turned to see Danziger behind him. Their young captain grinned and rubbed his thumb against his first two fingers. Gabriel grinned back. Money could always be relied on to get around the rules.

It took them the best part of an hour to get inside the fort, and by then the chill of morning was giving way to the oppressive heat of another Moroccan day. Gabriel's throat was as dry as the desert and the stink of humans and animals crammed together in the hot sun threatened to make him pass out, but he shuffled along patiently, taking comfort from Ned's closeness. He daren't reach out for his lover's hand in case he found someone else's, but just seeing him there was enough.

At last they stumbled into the shade of the gateway and Danziger spoke with the guard, pointing out his crew with one hand whilst slipping coins to the man with the other. The guard waved them through and they found themselves in the outer ward, a narrow low-walled enclosure against the western end of the fortress. The southern half, closest to the harbour, had been fenced off and all the townsfolk's livestock was being herded inside: sheep, goats, donkeys, mules and pigs mingling together, all competing to see who could make the most noise. Outside the corral, families sat huddled around their belongings, women and children weeping or simply blank-faced in terror. They knew they were the intruders here, but perhaps they had not expected the Moors to reclaim the port just yet.

The fort's southernmost cannons were firing now, keeping the Pasha's fleet from getting any closer. Between the constant barrage and the noise of the refugees, Gabriel felt like he was already in Hell. Still, he followed Ned and Danziger across the outer ward as far as they were allowed, which was still some distance from the gate into the main fortress. The captain paused and gathered them all round.

"Well, gentlemen," he said in French, "we have penetrated the enemy's initial defences. I suggest we wait for nightfall, then try to advance further."

"What if the Moors capture the town first?" Gabriel asked.

Danziger shrugged. "We will have to take that chance. God is on our side, is he not?"

The day dragged by in a haze of thirst and boredom. The Spanish soldiers came round with baskets of bread at noon, but with only a single jug of water between the five of them and no prospect of getting more, Ned could barely choke down his share of the half-stale loaf. At least as the afternoon wore on the sun began to sink below the western wall, throwing long shadows across the outer ward.

"I've been watching the guards," Gabriel said softly, leaning his shoulder against Ned's. "Most of them seem to be on the walls and the outer gatehouse; they can't spare many for the refugees or the inner gate, so those men are on longer shifts."

"So they'll be weary, and bored," Ned replied.

"Exactly."

"So we wait until dusk, when their sight is dimmest; that's a trick Mal taught me."

"And when their thoughts, and those of the refugees, are turning to supper."

"Still, how do we get through the gate?"

"I think we'll need a diversion." Gabriel beckoned Danziger over. "Can you ask Pierre and Raoul to start a fight on the other side of the ward? Perhaps when the soldiers next come round with food."

Danziger nodded and grinned. "I'm sure they would be happy to have something to do."

They didn't have long to wait. The scent of onions and herbs drifted across the ward as a pair of soldiers carried out a cauldron slung on a couple of pole-arms balanced across their shoulders. The refugees began to get to their feet and close in on the food. Danziger nodded to his men, who pushed their way through the crowd.

At this distance Ned couldn't see who threw the first punch, but soon there was shouting from the direction of the cauldron and the crowd shifted and swirled like a swarm of flies disturbed from a dungheap. He exchanged glances with Gabriel. It was now or never.

The guards on the inner gatehouse were already moving forwards to assist in subduing the riot. Ned, Gabriel and Danziger halted in the shadows until they were out of the guards' line of sight, then slipped through the gate.

"What if someone asks us who we are and where we're going?" Ned whispered.

"We kill them," Danziger growled. "Now quiet!"

The vast inner ward – twice as long as the entire plot of ground occupied by Tower of London but somewhat narrower – stretched before them, with, to either side of the gateway, a large fortress with crenelated walls. Smaller towers punctuated the curtain wall at intervals, and newer-looking outbuildings were ranged across the open space. A large pen held horses rather than livestock for eating, though Ned had heard enough of Mal's stories about sieges to know that they would serve double duty if need be. Christ forfend it should come to that, though.

"Look!" Gabriel pointed to an outbuilding from which men were emerging at intervals with baskets of bread and covered pots. Some went towards the main fortress to their left, overlooking the harbour, others into the low triangular tower to their right. "Looks like it's supper time for the garrison."

"I wish it were my supper time as well," Ned muttered under his breath. Thankfully the others didn't hear him.

"Which do we choose?" Gabriel asked. "Hennaq could be anywhere."

"If I were expecting an attack from the harbour," Danziger said, "I'd put my prize prisoner as far away as possible. I say we try the north tower."

Gabriel ducked into the empty guardroom and emerged a few moments later with a basket covered in a napkin, a kettle and a couple of wine bottles.

"With any luck no one will notice they're mostly empty," he said, handing them round. "Come on, before the guards get back."

Danziger led the way, striding confidently towards the north tower as if he belonged there. Ned hefted the empty basket onto his shoulder and followed. This was all going a little too easily for his liking.

It was hard to make anything out inside the fortress; no torches burned anywhere, and the light was fading fast. Daylight. Ned looked up. The fortress was open to the sky.

"You know," Gabriel hissed, pressing his back against the stonework, "I don't think there's a building in here at all. Not like in an English castle. It's just a series of angled walls for the defenders to man, and stairs up to the wall-walk."

"So where's Hennaq?" Ned whispered back.

"I don't know. In one of those outbuildings, perhaps?"

Ned sighed. "I knew this was going too well. Which outbuilding? There must be at least a dozen just on this side of the ward."

"I think we can ignore the kitchens. And the open one that looks like a smithy."

Danziger re-joined them. "We should leave the 'supper' here; it'll look strange if we carry it out again."

Ned set down his basket. His stomach ached with more than hunger, clenched around a tight knot of fear.

"So we just wander around the buildings until we get arrested?"

"It's nearly dark. I say we wait here a while longer, then make our move. Find the skrayling, break him out and be gone before dawn."

"How? We can hardly smuggle him out through that lot," Ned said, pointing back towards the gatehouse.

"We'll have to climb over the walls."

"In the dark? You are completely insane, you know that?"

"So I'm told." Danziger showed his teeth in what could charitably be called a smile. "I like to think I'm just a little bolder than most men. It gives me the element of surprise."

Ned shook his head. They would be caught and executed as spies, he was sure of it.

The guns had fallen silent, both sides hoarding their ammunition for a last assault at dawn, most likely. The three men walked quietly across the near-empty ward, past the kitchen and the smithy. A long, low building appeared to be barracks; they skirted it cautiously, slipping from one shadow to the next. Beyond was a small solidly built brick shed, perhaps a powder store or armoury. However its door was bolted and barred, which seemed an unlikely way to leave an armoury in the middle of an attack. He nudged Gabriel and pointed to it. The actor nodded.

Thankfully the armoury door was shielded from direct view by the back of the barracks. Gabriel and Danziger gently lifted the bar and slid back the bolts. Ned winced at every squeak and scrape of metal, but no one raised the alarm or came running. Danziger took hold of the door handle and Gabriel hefted his cudgel. Ned remembered Mal's account of the Corsican watchtower and the skrayling captives who had killed themselves rather than be sold into slavery. Dear God, please say Hennaq had not resorted to the same.

The door swung open and they peered inside. At first Ned could see nothing, then the lines of shadow resolved into the tattooed face of a skrayling. Gabriel beckoned to him.

"Captain Hennaq?"

The skrayling didn't move. Ned stepped inside the hut and held out his hand.

"You want to leave here?"

A rough palm scraped against his own, and strong fingers closed around his hand. Ned pulled the skrayling to his feet, and sniffed.

"Is there still gunpowder in here, or has the smell of it seeped into the walls?"

The explosion made a perfect diversion. The entire garrison, or so it seemed, rushed to the south wall, convinced the fort was under attack again. The three men and their skrayling companion slipped into the north tower unseen and paused, panting, in the shadows. Ned wiped the sweat from his brow with his good hand and willed his heart to cease its frantic pounding.

"Well, that worked a treat!" Danziger said. "Now we just have to get over the wall."

"How?" Gabriel looked around at his companions. "We left our best climber in the outer ward, and in any case we have no rope."

"That's where you're wrong," the Dutchman said. He unwound his sash and pulled up his tunic to reveal a layer of rope wound about his torso.

"You've been wearing that all this time? Why didn't you tell us?"

Danziger shrugged. "We had no need of it until now."

"What about Pierre and Raoul?" Ned asked. "We can't just leave them here."

"They're no fools. Probably out of the front gates already and on their way to meet the *Hayreddin*. Come on!"

He led them up a flight of steps to the wall-walk, which was thankfully deserted. The four of them crouched behind the crenelated wall and peered out through the embrasures.

"Hah, as I hoped." He pointed out to sea. "I knew our good captain would not fail us."

Barely visible with the glare of burning buildings behind them, the *Hayreddin* stood out to sea about a mile offshore. Danziger lashed the end of his rope to one of the merlons and paid it out gently.

"How am I going to get down that with only one hand?" Ned muttered. "Rigging's one thing, but this…"

"I'll show you," Danziger replied.

He looped the rope under his right leg and over his left shoulder.

"Your bottom hand–" he took hold of the rope behind his back "–controls your descent, your top one–" he clasped the end tied to the merlon "–only steadies you. You can do that, yes?"

Before Ned could answer, Danziger climbed over the wall and began to lower himself down. Ned leaned over to watch. The young Dutchman made it look so easy…

Muttered curses came from below.

"What is it?" Ned hissed.

"The rope's a few yards too short. I'll have to jump."

He did so, landing on the rocks below with an ankle-crunching impact. To Ned's relief Danziger stood up, seemingly unhurt, and waved for the rest of them to come down.

"You go next," Ned told Gabriel.

"You're not planning something stupid, are you?"

"No, I just don't trust Danziger with Hennaq." It was part of the truth. Enough of it. He took Gabriel's head in both hands and kissed him soundly, sun-chapped lips grazing on stubble. "Now go."

The moment Gabriel disappeared over the wall, Ned turned back to the eastern side of the fortress. The soldiers were still running back and forth, loading muskets and cannon. He had only moments alone with the skrayling; better be quick.

"Tell me something, captain," he said softly. "What happened to that Venetian whore we sent west with you?"

Hennaq looked puzzled. Ned racked his brains for how to put it in Tradetalk.

"She-fellah you take of us to Vinland. She die?"

"She go," the skrayling answered. "With sea lord of south, he who take I."

"The Moors rescued her? Dark-skin fellahs?" Ned pointed east, towards Al-Jaza'ir.

"Yes."

"God's teeth, that's all we need," Ned muttered to himself. "Where is she now?"

Hennaq shrugged. "I slave. Not see, not hear."

Well, that put a different complexion on things. If Olivia was on the loose, he had no choice but to warn Mal. In person, if need be.

He peered over the wall. Gabriel was almost down. Ned held his breath as Gabriel dropped gracefully to the rocks, then hauled up the slack rope with shaking hands.

"Now you," he said to Hennaq.

He had been worried the skrayling would be weak from his captivity, but Hennaq wrapped the rope about his body and climbed over the wall with calm determination. Ned wished he felt half as confident.

All too soon the rope went slack again.

"Well then, this is it," Ned muttered to himself.

He pushed up his sleeve and slid the lever forward. The metal fist opened, and he placed the rope across the studded palm then returned the lever to its original position. He wound the next few feet of the rope under his left leg and over his shoulder in a mirror image of Danziger's demonstration. Finally he swung a leg over the battlements, reached behind his back and grasped the rope. A heart-stopping moment as he swung the other leg over, his bare feet scrabbling for purchase. Rough stone scraped against his toes, but at last he had his feet planted flat against the wall.

"Hurry, Englishman!" Danziger hissed up at him.

Ned swore under his breath and walked his feet down a yard or so, gritting his teeth as the rope scoured his thigh and shoulder.

He made it about halfway down without mishap, but now he was soaked in sweat which turned the rope burns into lines of agony across his flesh. To his relief he found a temporary foothold, a hole in the wall big enough to wedge both feet into. He pressed his cheek against the cool stone for a moment, wishing he were at the bottom already, but voices floated up from below: Danziger's impatient, Gabriel's encouraging.

He tightened his grip on the rope and prepared to resume his descent, but flung himself back against the wall as the rope burn on his shoulder erupted in fresh agony. His linen shirt had worn right through, exposing bare flesh. He took the weight on his feet again and used his teeth to shift the fabric over, covering the burn, then moved the rope along an inch or two. Now it would rub against his neck as well, but better that than be scoured to the bone. Tears stung his eyes, as much from shame as from the raw flesh. Have to go on or fall and – no, don't think about it, Christ, just do it…

With a final prayer he kicked off again and shuffled the rest of the way down, cursing under his breath with every yard. When he could no longer feel any rope below his left hand, he twisted round and saw Gabriel standing right below him, almost close enough to reach Ned's feet.

"Jump! I'll catch you."

Ned transferred his left hand to the taut rope in front of him, shook the loose end free of his trembling limbs, and let go. A heartbeat later he landed in Gabriel's arms and they collapsed onto the rocks together.

"Careful!" Gabriel held him tight when he tried to roll over and get to his feet. "These rocks slope down to the cliff. One misstep and you'll tumble to your death."

Rough hands helped them both up. Hennaq. The skrayling grinned at them, showing his fangs. Ned supposed it was meant as a friendly gesture, but he still found it disconcerting.

They climbed with painful slowness over the rough terrain, feeling their way like blind men. Ned's surefootedness compensated a little for his utter weariness, but it was tough going all the same. He flinched every time his feet kicked loose a chip of rock that rattled its way down the slope, and expected musket fire to erupt from the fortress wall at any moment. But gradually Mers-el-Kébir shrank behind them, and he began to breathe more easily. The dangerous part of this mission was over; now came the tricky bit.

"What do you mean, we're not going to hand him over to the Pasha?" Danziger crossed the tiny cabin in a couple of strides and grabbed Ned by the front of his ragged shirt. "Look here, Englishman, I didn't risk my life to let that creature go free. He's a slave, and he's worth a fortune to the man who can deliver him–"

"–to his own people," Ned replied. "You think the Pasha is rich? The skraylings come from a land dripping in gold and silver and jewels. Besides, you think the Pasha will really pay you for him? Most likely he'll reward the captains of his fleet first, and you and me'll be lucky to get enough for a round of drinks."

Danziger relaxed his grip and Ned shook him off.

"Look, we ransom him back to his clan, we can all retire on the proceeds. Everyone's happy."

"Apart from the Pasha," Danziger pointed out.

"How's he going to find out, unless one of the crew betrays us?"

"I agree with Ned," Gabriel said. "The Spanish will claim Hennaq escaped, the Moors won't believe them. Or they'll think he was smuggled out on a Spanish ship before the Pasha's fleet arrived."

"So you're going to sail all the way to the New World? In this old tub?"

"No need," said Ned. "We can take him to Sark. Plenty of skraylings there, and it's close to home for us."

"You planned this all along, didn't you?" He stormed out of the cabin, swearing in the mix of French and Arabic common on board their vessel. Ned didn't need to understand either language to get the gist of it.

"You think it's safe to go back to England?" Gabriel said.

"I don't know, but it's worth a try. Maybe Mal's been able to get us a pardon by now. It's not like he can write to us and tell us."

"What about the guisers?"

"Fuck the guisers. I reckon if I'm going to die, I want to die among friends, with beer in my belly and you–" he pulled Gabriel closer "–in my bed. Fat chance of either at sea."

"I can wait a few weeks longer," Gabriel replied, brushing his lips against Ned's brow. "Good work, my love."

CHAPTER XIV

Though he had not given up his fight against the guisers, Mal was far more circumspect over the next few months. He put all his energies into re-establishing his reputation as a gentleman of leisure, content to spend the long, hot summer days playing bowls, and the evenings drinking and trying not to lose too much of his modest fortune at cards. He was aided in the latter by a few tricks taught to him by Ned. Not cheating as such – he had no wish to throw his life away in a duel – but enough to give him an edge over his less sharp-eyed companions.

The main purpose of all these pleasures, however, was to gain as much intelligence on the men surrounding princes Robert and Arthur as possible. If zealots like the Huntsmen were of no use as allies, perhaps he could find others who were more reasonable: men who despised politicking and falsehood and would gladly see conspirators rooted out for no other reason. Alas, such men were as rare at court as hen's teeth. Here every smile concealed a hidden purpose: manipulation, seduction, betrayal. Though perhaps his enemies thought the same of him.

As summer turned to autumn, Prince Robert's thoughts turned to hunting. Mal was overjoyed when he was invited to accompany the prince to Richmond. The park attached to the palace was well-supplied with fallow deer, fat by now from summer grazing and more interested in the rut than in avoiding humans. The prospect put Robert in such a jovial mood that Mal was able to contrive an invitation for Sandy, whom he knew would be anxious to see Kit again. Thus a fine September day found the twins riding side-by-side in the prince's retinue, so alike in their matched habits that all the court commented on it. How he could use such confusion to his advantage, Mal was not certain, but at the very least it might make it easier to slip away and meet his informant.

"There!" Mal pointed westwards down the road, to where the towers of Richmond Palace rose above the trees. The midday sun, barely halfway to its zenith at this time of year, flashed on the gilded domes topping the towers, and he had to shade his eyes to see it clearly. "Can't be more than a mile now."

His heart lifted at the thought of seeing his wife and son again, and it was all he could do not to steer Hector out of line and kick him into a gallop. That would be an unforgivable discourtesy, however, so he contented himself with imagining his family's delighted faces when he arrived.

After a few moments he realised that Sandy was no longer riding at his side. He glanced back down the line to see his brother some yards behind. Sandy had reined his mount to a halt and was staring at the palace, heedless of the other riders' curses as they manoeuvred around him. Mal turned Hector's head and trotted back along the line.

"What's the matter?"

When Sandy did not answer, Mal looked back at the palace, and realisation dawned. The room where they had both been held by Suffolk had looked eastwards towards a very similar prospect. To Sandy, the sight of those towers meant only one thing: pain.

"We can go back to London if you'd like," he said, reaching out a gloved hand.

"No. I have to see Kit."

"Come on, then. We're getting in everyone's way."

Without any outward prompting from its rider, Sandy's horse resumed its steady walk as if it had never stopped. Mal's hands tightened involuntarily on the reins and Hector tossed his head.

"Sorry, boy." He could hardly take his brother to task in public, but using magic here, surrounded by potential enemies? He would have to have words with Sandy when they were alone together.

"I think I should stay," Sandy said, "when you go back to London."

"I'm not sure that's wise." Not wise at all. "Won't it bring back too many painful memories, being within sight of Ferrymead House?"

"Painful, yes, but happy also. It is here I was reunited with my *amayi*."

"Well. Good. But how are we to explain it? It's one thing for us to visit as part of the prince's retinue, but this is the princess's household. Men who linger here once their business is done are likely to become the subject of scurrilous gossip."

Sandy frowned. "I am Kiiren's *amayi*, and Kit's uncle. They cannot keep me from him."

"Why are you so anxious all of a sudden? I thought you said Kit would be safe from the guisers now that he's old enough to wear a spirit-guard." As safe as any other member of our family, at any rate.

"He is. But..." Sandy looked away.

"You think it might affect him badly, like it did you." Being fettered in iron had soothed Sandy's fits at first, but had only made them worse in the end. Though the noxious atmosphere of Bedlam could hardly have helped. "That was different. You and I were... are... incomplete souls. Broken."

"Perhaps."

The front of the cavalcade had reached the palace gates and was slowing down as everyone shuffled back into line. Mal kept a close eye on his brother, not wanting to get into an argument with any of the more senior courtiers about precedence, but Sandy had withdrawn into himself and didn't speak again until they had passed through the gates.

"I wish people wouldn't stare at us."

To either side, the grounds had been laid out in elaborate knot gardens. At this time of day they were empty but for the gardeners, who had left off clipping the box hedges and deadheading the roses to kneel as the prince rode past.

"Everyone used to stare when we were boys. Don't you remember?"

"Some of it, now and then. Mostly in dreams. But Kiiren said I had enough bad memories to deal with, without digging for more."

"Some say it is better to flush them out, like lancing a boil."

"Would you cut out a scar and expect it to heal more cleanly the second time?"

Mal rolled his left shoulder self-consciously, feeling the pull of scarred flesh above his collarbone. Another trophy of their escape from Ferrymead House. "Perhaps not."

At the main entrance they all dismounted and an army of stable-boys ran out to take their horses. Prince Robert, near the head of the line, had already disappeared into the palace, leaving his entourage to mill around in confusion. Mal took Sandy by the elbow and led him towards the nearest door.

"Let's see if we can find Coby and Kit ourselves," he said. "I know they have apartments in the north wing, on one of the upper floors."

Coby was not in her apartments, and Kit was asleep, so Mal left Sandy with him and went off in search of his wife. This was only the second time he had been to Richmond Palace, and he hoped he remembered the way to the royal presence chamber. The previous time he had been quaking in his boots, summoned in haste after his return from Venice to report to the Prince of Wales. A nerve-racking ride through the countryside under close escort, only to have to cool his heels for hours in an antechamber until Robert returned from the hunt. And then to learn that not only did the prince not intend to punish the twins for their various misdemeanours, but wished to knight Mal for his services to the crown.

The guards straightened their backs as he approached the double doors at the top of the stairs though more, he suspected, to try and intimidate him than out of respect. He walked straight past them without so much as a glance either side, through the antechamber – empty but for a maid rebuilding the fire – and paused at the doorway, where he was announced by a startled herald.

"Sir Maliverny Catlyn, of Rushdale!"

Mal stepped into the presence chamber, quickly taking in the princess seated at her embroidery frame, surrounded by her ladies-in-waiting. His eyes caught Coby's for an instant, and his heart quickened. He thought he saw an answering blush rise from her collar, but courtesy drew his eyes back to the princess. There was no sign of Robert or the other male courtiers; no doubt they were washing off the dust of the road and slaking their thirsts. Mal bowed, catching sight of his own scuffed and begrimed boots, and wished he had thought to do the same.

"Your Highness."

"Master Catlyn. How good of you to come and see me so promptly on your arrival."

"The court is much duller for the absence of its brightest jewel," he replied. The formulaic praise was sour on his tongue, but the middle-aged princess smiled nonetheless.

"Sit with us a while, sir. We were just enjoying a recital by my newest treasure, a castrato all the way from Italy."

"It would be my pleasure, Your Highness."

A servant brought forward a stool, and he settled down. His position was frustratingly far from his wife, but since she sat on the other side of the throne, they could exchange a glance or two without his having to turn his back on the princess. It would have to suffice for now.

A Dutch harpsichord had been placed on a table, and two figures stood by it: a woman at the keyboard, and a man by her side. More than that, he could not make out for the bright sunlight streaming in through the enormous windows that occupied almost the entire far wall. The lady at the harpsichord began to play, and a few bars later her companion joined in, singing a countermelody with words in Italian. A chill ran down Mal's spine. That voice. An image rose in his mind, of a darkened garden lit by glass lamps hanging from the trees, and a beautiful woman in an ivory silk half-mask, playing a lute. Olivia dalle Boccole. It was all he could do not to leap to his feet and denounce her on the spot, but a glance at Coby revealed that she was completely unaware of the danger. Perhaps he was mistaken. The singer was a eunuch, so of course his voice was high like a woman's, and he was singing in Olivia's native tongue, so of course he sounded a little like her. Mal forced himself to breathe slowly. Sandy's anxiety at visiting the neighbourhood of their former torment was catching.

When the song ended all the ladies clapped. Mal joined in belatedly, his hands still so tense they scarcely felt like his own.

"Mistress Catlyn tells me you play the lute," Princess Juliana said, when the applause had died down.

"Alas, I have not played much these past few years, Your Highness. I would sound foolish indeed after such a fine performance."

"You are too modest, sir, just like your wife. But never fear, I shall not press you. Music should be a cause for joy, not dread." She beckoned to the singer. "Come, let me introduce you to my servant, Bartolomeo Pellegrino, all the way from the choir of Santa Maria Maggiore in Rome."

The young man approached the throne and bowed curtly. Mal rose from his seat but froze on the verge of returning the courtesy. He had been right all along. Dark olive skin, full lips, and eyes the colour of jade. Olivia, brazenly disguised as a young man. Remembering himself he completed the gesture before the ladies could notice. Olivia on the other hand had not missed his hesitation. Her eyes twinkled with amusement.

"A pleasure to meet you, Signor Catalin."

"And you. Sir."

Coby shot her husband a look of concern. The others surely hadn't noticed it, but after five years together there was no mistaking the tension in his voice. His expression was guarded and he did not look her way, but she saw his left hand moving where it rested on his sword hilt: two taps of his index finger, two taps of the middle finger, over and over. *Enemy sighted.* She got to her feet.

"Your Highness, may I beg your indulgence? My husband is no doubt weary from his ride, nor has he seen his son in many weeks, and I think Susanna will have roused Kit from his nap by now."

"Of course, my dear." Princess Juliana rose. "Perhaps later I will have the pleasure of a dance, sir, if you will not play?"

"I look forward to it, Your Highness."

He held out his arm, and Coby slipped her hand around his elbow as they walked out of the room.

"I was going to warn you," she whispered as they crossed the antechamber.

"Not here," he replied.

She fell silent, resisting the urge to look back over her shoulder. So, Mal had instantly guessed that Bartolomeo was a spy. But how?

The walk up to her apartments felt like it lasted an age, so anxious was she for answers. She kept glancing up at her husband, but his eyes were fixed straight ahead, his face pale. Coby's stomach roiled.

"Bad news?" she asked, the moment the outer door closed behind them.

"The worst. Our young Italian friend downstairs is none other than Olivia dalle Boccole."

"The courtesan?" She stared at him, aghast.

"Yes. Well, not a courtesan any more, of course. But still a guiser."

"How did she get away from Hennaq?"

"How should I know? All that matters is that she did, and she's here."

Sandy leapt up from the window seat. "Ilianwe, here?"

A vivid flash of memory: amber eyes gazing up at him, white petals stuck to their bare skin. Ilianwe was Olivia's soul-name, as Erishen was Sandy's – and his own. She had taught him dreamwalking... and much else.

"So it appears," Mal replied, hoping his wife hadn't noticed his discomposure. "And plotting revenge on the two of us, no doubt."

"What do we do?" Coby asked.

"You and Kit cannot stay here," Mal told her. "It is no longer safe."

"The Princess of Wales will think it very strange if I leave her service so soon. She may not even permit it."

"You are a married woman. If I say you must leave court, you must obey."

She frowned at him.

"In law, I mean," Mal said, putting an arm around her shoulder. She shrugged him off.

"I can be of more use to you here," she said. "If I leave, how do we spy on Olivia? You and Sandy can hardly stay here, especially with me gone."

"Then we will all stay here," Sandy said.

"No," Mal replied. "Someone has to keep an eye on Prince Henry. And we still have not discovered his *amayi*."

Sandy made a noise of reluctant agreement and went to sit cross-legged on the rug near his nephew, who was stacking wooden bricks with fierce concentration.

"I shall take Kit back to London," Mal said at last.

"What? No." Coby crossed the room and stood between her husband and their son.

"He will be safer there, with Sandy and me, than he could possibly be here. Olivia is vastly more powerful than any of the English guisers. In any case, soon he will be old enough for schooling. You must untie his leading strings sooner or later, my love."

"If you take him, Olivia will be suspicious. She will wonder why we are hiding him from her, and perhaps guess who he is."

"There is one way," Sandy said. "I have held back from it, but..."

"What?"

"I can make him forget who and what he is. He will just be another little boy, as I was."

"You can do that?" She looked down at Kit, who had stopped his play and was watching the adults with curiosity.

"Only with one so young. His soul is barely half-awake as it is."

"Isn't that dangerous?" Mal said. "How could you wish your fate on anyone?"

"This is different. He is whole, unbroken. And I will be there to help him when we no longer need him to hide."

For long moments no one spoke.

"Do it," Coby said softly.

Sandy knelt and whispered something in the skrayling tongue, then pressed his forehead to Kit's own. The boy's eyes closed, and after a while he gave a little gasp. Sandy released him, and Kit went back to playing with his toys as if nothing had happened.

Coby went to put a hand on Sandy's arm, but he turned away and went to stand staring out of the window.

"Well, that's that," Mal said. "Now, no more sadness. I have not ridden all this way for only a fleeting visit. Tonight we shall have a private supper together, and tomorrow you can show me the gardens."

"You just want to scout out secret ways into the palace," Coby said, trying to sound petulant and failing utterly.

"There, I knew that would put a smile on your face." He took her hands in his. "We can pretend it's the old days, just for a while."

She smiled up at him. "Yes, I'd like that. I'd like that a lot."

Mal threaded his way through the maze of courtyards and passages at the rear of Richmond Palace. He had still not had a chance to talk to the spy Lady Frances had spoken of, and he knew not how long the prince would want to stay at Richmond. If the hunting was poor, Robert might leave within the week. Mal had tried to arrange a rendezvous earlier, but Princess Juliana had held him to the promise of a dance and it was nearly midnight before he could get away. Coby had her own duties when the princess retired for the night, which left him with half an hour or so to fulfil his mission.

The service buildings had fallen silent, all the servants snatching a few precious hours' sleep before the whole great machine of court protocol started up again. The perfect time for a secret tryst. Mal slipped across another passage junction and out into a courtyard. Raindrops fell from the eaves into the hollows that millions of their predecessors had worn in the flagstones; the only other sound was the scuff and splash of Mal's boots as the flags gave way to equally ancient cobbles.

Lost in thought he turned a corner – and found himself face to face with the one person he did not wish to meet. Olivia. The former courtesan bowed and gave him an ironic smile.

"It has been too long, Signor Catalin," she said in that low husky voice that made the blood stir in his veins despite himself.

"Three years? I would hardly call that too long."

She tipped her head to one side. "I suppose it is but the blink of an eye to our kind."

Mal couldn't help glancing around. There was no one within sight, and all the windows in the surrounding walls were closed against the autumn chill.

"What are you doing here?" he asked, perhaps a little more abruptly than he had intended. Dammit, she knew just how to get under his skin.

"I grew lonely," she said, with a pout. "You abandoned me, if you recall. Betrayed me."

"I had no choice."

"There is always a choice," she hissed. She paused, as if reconsidering. "But it matters not. Thanks to you I have found a new home, with many companions to choose from."

Many? How many guisers were there in England? He reined in his impatience to question her. She was probably bluffing.

"I won't let you stay here," he said.

"Oh? And how will you get rid of me?" She folded her arms. "Expose my true sex, perhaps? That *would* be a scandal, a woman disguising herself as a young man for months at a time."

She fell silent, but the unspoken threat was as clear as day. Expose "Bartolomeo" as a woman, and Olivia would denounce Coby for the same and worse.

"The skraylings still want you back," he said. "I'm sure we can find you a safer route home this time."

Olivia laughed. "If the skraylings were so anxious to have me, I'm sure they would have done something by now. Alas for you, I think they value their trade with England more than one poor lost soul."

"They don't want to see a guiser on the throne any more than I do."

"But I'm not on the throne, am I? Besides, that was never my way, as well you know–"

Footsteps sounded behind him. Mal turned to see the source, and when he turned back, Olivia was gone. He cursed loudly, earning a startled look from the gardener's boy whose arrival had given Olivia the means to evade him.

"Master Catlyn?" the boy whispered. "I have the report you asked for."

Mal drew the boy aside, well away from any hiding places where they could be overheard, and listened to his recitation. The lad was illiterate, of course, but sometimes that was for the best. No written evidence to betray them.

"And you're certain the alchemist has not been seen at Syon House this past twelvemonth?" he asked when the boy was finished.

"Aye, sir. Jennet knows all the ways in and out and the secret places–" Even in the dark, Mal could tell the boy was blushing "–and she says he's not been there since before Michaelmas last."

Mal thanked him and gave him a handful of money for his pains; small coins that would not draw attention in the hand of an ill-paid servant. No use in pursuing an invitation to Syon House, then. Wherever Northumberland was keeping his pet alchemist, it wasn't at home.

CHAPTER XV

Though Mal's presence at Richmond did much to lighten her days, Coby had not forgotten her other duties. There was still the question of Lady Derby's visits to Syon House; if she was not going to meet Shawe or any of her lovers, what was she up to? Then there was Lady Frances's daughter to keep an eye on. Through patient coaxing Coby learnt that Elizabeth had grown up at her grandfather's house, Barn Elms, only a few miles east of Richmond Palace. It sounded a lonely childhood, with only nursemaids and tutors for company and occasional visits from her widowed mother. No wonder she was endlessly excited by even the dullest activities at court, though at the same time painfully shy and fearful of attention.

One afternoon they were sitting together in one of the window seats, making the most of the fading light. "Bartolomeo" had just finished entertaining them with a song and was refreshing his throat with a cup of honeyed wine.

"He sings so prettily," Elizabeth said, gazing at Bartolomeo with ill-disguised admiration. "I wish I could speak Italian. Mamma made sure I learnt French and Latin and even a little Greek, but Master Cottenham said Italian was not a fit tongue for ladies: too passionate and like to turn their thoughts astray."

"I think your tutor was right," Coby replied.

She was not about to encourage the girl by teaching her the few Italian phrases she remembered from her time in Venice. On the

contrary, the less Elizabeth had to do with Olivia the better, especially
if her betrothed was Jathekkil's *amayi*. Poor child, caught in the midst
of such scheming without the slightest idea of what was going on.

The room fell silent as a page in the livery of the Prince of Wales's
household entered.

"Your Highness," the youth said, staring straight ahead, "your royal
husband requests the pleasure of your company, and that of your
ladies and your servant Bartolomeo, at tomorrow morning's hunt."

Elizabeth immediately set her sewing down on her lap and leaned
forward, eyes bright with anticipation.

The princess's lips tightened briefly. "Please thank His Highness,
but as he well knows, I care little for the hunting."

A sigh of disappointment ran around the ladies-in-waiting.
Elizabeth's shoulders sagged, and Coby glimpsed bitter frustration in
Lady Derby's countenance before she managed to hide it. The countess
had set her sights higher than the Earl of Essex, it seemed. Perhaps it
would be wise to find out just where her ambitions lay.

"Such a pity," Coby said brightly. "I expect the Earl of Rutland will
want to ride out with his betrothed, but she cannot go alone."

The princess frowned at her. "Well, I suppose there can be no harm
if you accompany her, my dear. I would not keep the gentlemen from
their pleasures."

"Lady Catlyn cannot be relied upon to watch Mistress Sidney,"
Lady Derby said. "Her husband will surely be there, and he will
forever be distracting her."

The ladies giggled, and Coby flushed. She thought she and Mal had
been discreet here, far more discreet than back home in Derbyshire.

"Perhaps we should both go, Lady Derby," Coby said. "I am sure
you are far less easily distracted than I."

Juliana's eyes narrowed, and Coby cursed her misstep. Now it
looked as if the two of them were colluding to get Lady Derby and
the prince together.

"Oh no, I d-d-don't want to be any trouble," Elizabeth said, twisting
her hands in her lap. "I will gladly stay here, Your Highness–"

"Nonsense, my dear," Princess Juliana said stiffly. "Of course you must go, Lady Derby. You look so pinched and thin these days; a little fresh air will do you good."

Lady Derby bridled almost imperceptibly at the insult but forced a smile. "Thank you, Your Highness."

The atmosphere in the princess's presence chamber was frosty for the rest of the afternoon, and Coby was relieved beyond measure when she and the other ladies were finally excused. Lady Derby caught Coby's elbow as they left.

"Thank you for what you said earlier, Lady Catlyn. I swear I feel like a caged bird here."

Yes, well, nothing is keeping you here but your own wicked ambition.

"It is rather dull sometimes," Coby replied aloud. "I am glad to have a friend who feels the same way."

"We could be sisters," Lady Derby gave her a disarming smile. "Now, if you will excuse me, I had better tell my maidservant to unpack my riding habit."

Coby watched her leave with a sinking heart. A riding habit? That was not something she had thought of when she put together a wardrobe for her new station in life. She ran upstairs to look through her gowns in the hope of finding something suitable.

Early next morning Coby made her way down to the stable yard with Elizabeth Sidney. They had been invited to the formal breakfast before the hunt, but Elizabeth was so nervous and excited that she looked fit to vomit up the rich food. Instead they breakfasted in Coby's apartments on bread and small ale. Mal had already left to attend upon the prince, and Sandy was taking Kit for an early walk, so they had the place to themselves for a while. The peace and solitude seemed to soothe Elizabeth's nerves, and at last she felt able to take Coby's hand and go down to join the hunt.

The stable yard was such a mêlée of horses, hounds and men, Coby wondered that they had not already frightened away every deer within a dozen miles of Richmond Park.

"There he is!" Elizabeth cried, her hand tightening on Coby's. "Is he not handsome?"

For one moment Coby thought only of Mal, but there was no sign of her husband amongst the throng of courtiers, servants, foresters and kennel-masters required of such a grand enterprise.

"Who, dear?"

"Why, Rutland, of course. My betrothed."

Coby followed Elizabeth's gaze to a young gentleman with short red-brown hair beneath a high-crowned beaver hat. His moustache had been bleached a yellow colour and waxed so that it stuck out on either side in a sharp point, perhaps to divert attention from his equally pointed chin. Not an ill-favoured young man, but not what Coby would call handsome.

"There you are, my dears!" Lady Derby's smile did not quite reach her eyes, though the pleasure in her voice sounded genuine enough. "I wondered where you had got to; you missed the assembly and the displaying of the fewmets and everything."

The countess stepped around her mare, and Elizabeth's jaw dropped. Lady Derby wore an expertly tailored bodice of dark green wool, with a matching pair of knee-length breeches in the Venetian style. White silk stockings and embroidered leather shoes completed the ensemble, which showed off the countess's curvaceous figure to great advantage.

"Don't look so shocked, my dear," Lady Derby said with a laugh. "The Queen herself used to wear them for hunting when she was young. Far more practical than skirts, don't you think?"

Over Lady Derby's shoulder Coby could see Olivia watching them, green eyes twinkling with amusement. She was spared any further embarrassment, however, by the arrival of a groom with her own mount.

"We shall have to get you a proper hunter as well, Lady Catlyn," Lady Derby said, springing lithely into the saddle. "Now that you are at court, you must insist that your husband equips you properly."

Coby forced a smile. She had spent too many years making do with hand-me-downs to feel easy about spending an entire year's wages on one set of clothes – or on a horse she would seldom ride.

A change in the chaos around her heralded the arrival of Prince Robert. The heir to the throne was said to take after his late father a great deal, being tall and straight of build, with dark hair now turning silver at the temples. He wore a magnificent riding habit of black leather and red velvet, though with little other ornament: a hint of lace at collar and cuffs, a black plume in his cap affixed with a jewelled brooch, a heavy gold ring on his right hand. His solemn blue eyes seemed to take them all in, weigh their worth and stow the information away for later consideration.

Coby glanced across at Lady Derby but the countess had modestly lowered her gaze, though she was blushing furiously, no doubt from more than the chill morning air. Robert's gaze drifted down to take in the revealing garments. Cool appreciation, but no flicker of surprise, Coby noted. Had he been forewarned? Perhaps Lady Derby always dressed like this for riding, and it was only Coby who found it remarkable.

At last the hunting party was ready and they began to move out into the park. Mist lingered beneath the oak trees, turning the undergrowth into a maze of grey lacework. A place where one could be hidden from one's companions, though they were mere yards away.

"Found you at last."

Coby turned with a start to see her husband riding at her side.

"Where did you spring from?"

"So disappointed to see me?" He nudged his gelding closer, until Coby's skirts brushed against his calf.

"I was just thinking that a hunt is the perfect opportunity to slip away from prying eyes for a tryst."

He grinned. "My thoughts exactly."

"Not us," she hissed, waving her riding crop at him in mock chastisement. "Bartolomeo. Lady Derby. Rutland. We have three of them to keep an eye on, and only two of us. You should have brought Sandy."

"My brother does not care for hunting. I think you know why."

"Oh. Of course. Sorry." Mal had told her about how Erishen had been ridden down and murdered in the hills near Rushdale. She knew Mal still had nightmares about it from time to time, mostly when he was worried about Sandy.

"I'll follow Rutland," Mal said, breaking into her train of thought, "and you can take Lady Derby. If we see either of them with Olivia, we'll know who to suspect."

"Thank you," she whispered, as much to God as to her husband. She had prayed Mal would not suggest following Olivia himself. She ought to trust him – did trust him – but she did not trust the Venetian woman. Not an inch.

Ahead of them, the yipping of the hounds turned into a clamour of baying.

"The hunt is up!"

The formal procession along the trail dispersed as the leading horses broke into a canter. Mal's chestnut pulled ahead, disappearing into the throng. Coby cursed and clung to her little mare. As someone who had fled pursuit on too many occasions her heart was with the buck, not his hunters, and she rather hoped he would get away.

Coby had no idea how big the park was, but they seemed able to ride forever and not come to the end of it, as if the paths led into an enchanted world made up entirely of forest. She was soon totally disoriented and chilled to the bone, mist condensing on her hair and clothes in hundreds of minute beads like Venetian glass. She reined her mount to a halt and wiped her dripping nose on the back of a damp sleeve. The other riders were blurred shapes in the mist, melting into invisibility. She spurred her mare into a canter and caught up with the rest of the party again.

"Isn't this splendid?" Lady Derby turned and smiled at her. "I'm afraid the hounds have lost the scent again. Still, there's time yet."

The mist was starting to disperse now, though it was still cold and the sun little more than a white paper circle in a grey sky. The hunters had gathered in a clearing and servants were passing round cups of wine that had been warmed over a portable brazier. No wonder the deer were able to give them the slip, with all this noise and stink invading their woods. Coby accepted a cup of wine and looked around for Lady Derby, but there was no sign of her. Or of the prince. Spotting a side-path that led away from the main party, Coby dismounted and tied up her mare, then slipped away. If anyone remarked on her departure, she could always say she was looking for a quiet spot in which to relieve herself.

The prince and his companions paused for a stirrup-cup before riding on again in pursuit of the buck. Mal followed behind, keeping a close eye on Rutland. The young earl had lured his betrothed away from Lady Derby and they were riding side-by-side, laughing. Olivia was nowhere to be seen.

As the party cantered up a steep bank Elizabeth Sidney's mare sidestepped a tree root, causing her rider to tumble from the saddle into the path of the oncoming horses. Mal pulled Hector to an abrupt halt, leapt down and ran to her aid.

"Are you hurt, Mistress Sidney?"

She shook her head and clambered to her feet.

"No, thank you, sir."

She brushed the dead leaves from her clothes and hair, looking round anxiously for Rutland. The earl skidded down the muddy track, feet sideways on.

"Good God, what happened?"

"Is that any way to speak to a lady, my lord?" Mal said in the mildest tones he could manage.

"And who are you?" Rutland's yellow mustachios quivered with indignation. "Catlyn, isn't it?"

"Aye, my lord."

Having established this fact Rutland turned away, taking Elizabeth by the arm.

"Come, dearest one, I shall walk you back to the palace. Catlyn, bring our horses."

Mal bristled at being treated like a servant, but went to fetch the earl's bay gelding. The prince and the rest of the party had ridden on, leaving the three of them alone.

"I don't want to go back to the palace yet," Mal heard Elizabeth say as she and Rutland walked away. "It's so dull there."

"Very well," the earl replied. "What say we go looking for deer ourselves? There are plenty of does about, just waiting for the buck to find them."

The innuendo was lost on the girl, who happily let her beloved lead her down a bridlepath between two ancient oaks. Mal doubted that Grey would care much if his stepdaughter were deflowered by her betrothed before the wedding rather than after, and yet the thought made him uneasy. He looped Hector's reins over a nearby branch and told him to keep an eye on the other two horses. Hector ducked his head as if in acquiescence, and Mal set off after the two lovers. He hoped no one had been around to overhear that last exchange, or they would think his brother's madness was rubbing off on him.

Coby padded along the grassy path between walls of bracken nearly as high as her head. The noise of the hunt faded behind her, to be replaced by birdsong and the drip of water from the trees above. At last she heard voices up ahead: two of them. She gathered her skirts around her and crept forward.

As she drew nearer she realised the second voice was not quite as deep as a man's should be. Olivia? The bracken gave way to mixed scrub, and through the thinner cover Coby could make out two figures in a clearing to one side of the path, locked in a close embrace. The one facing her was indeed Olivia – and the other, in deep green doublet and Venetians, could be none other than Lady Derby. Coby halted, astonished. What were these two doing together, unless Lady Derby was the guiser after all? She held her breath and strained to make out their conversation, but they were speaking too low. At last Olivia broke off the embrace and walked towards Coby, her mouth set in a hard line. Lady Derby fell to her knees, weeping.

"I suggest you take care of your companion," Olivia said as she passed Coby on the path. "She aims too high, and the fall may have been too much for her."

Coby stared after the courtesan for a moment, then hurried to help Lady Derby to her feet.

"Oh, Lady Catlyn, thank the Lord!" Lady Derby dabbed at her nose with a lace handkerchief. "I–"

A horn blared in the near distance, and moments later an enormous buck charged through the undergrowth, his palmate antlers showering the two women with leaves. He froze, breath frothing from his flared nostrils, dark eyes swivelling back and forth between pursuers and those who blocked his path. Deciding at last, he lowered his massive head and charged. Lady Derby screamed and Coby pushed her aside out of the creature's path, expecting any moment to feel the antlers tear her flesh asunder. She slipped on the damp ground and fell. Above her the buck raised its head again... and snorted and trotted away as if he had forgotten the humans were even there. Coby rolled over onto hands and knees and looked up.

Olivia stood on the edge of the clearing, arms folded.

"What is it about you, Lady Catlyn, that draws the dangerous beasts?"

Coby had no chance to answer, since at that moment the hunters reached the clearing. She got to her feet.

"That way. The buck went that way."

Prince Robert saluted her and cantered off in pursuit, followed by the rest of his party. All but one. Lord Stafford dismounted and bowed.

"Lady Derby, Lady Catlyn. It appears to me you took an unpleasant fright from that beast. Allow me to escort you both back to the palace."

He took Lady Derby's arm and led her back towards the path.

"I should not leave Mistress Elizabeth here alone," Coby said. "Her mother would never forgive me if anything happened to her."

"As you wish, Lady Catlyn. Good luck with your own hunt!"

When they were out of earshot, Coby joined Olivia, who had been watching them all with curiosity.

"I suppose I should thank you," she told the guiser. "I fear that Lady Derby was not sufficiently in command of her wits to control the beast."

"You think her capable of such magics?"

"Is she not?"

Olivia laughed.

"She is as human as you, my dear Lady Catlyn. So, you owe me your life after all."

She turned and walked away, leaving Coby alone in the clearing, a triumphant smile spreading across her face. So, Lady Derby was not a guiser. That only left Rutland and Percy in the immediate running. She would have to find Mal straight away.

The path was broad and straight, but Mal could see no sign of the lovers, nor hear their voices. They must have turned aside into the thick brush for greater privacy. Quite what he was going to do when he eventually caught up with them, he had no idea. Challenge Rutland to a duel? If the earl really was Jathekkil's *amayi*, killing him would solve Mal's immediate problem, but at the price of arrest and possible execution. Nor could Mal attempt to use magic on a waking man; he would have to get too close, and in any case if he were right, Rutland would know himself betrayed.

Mal halted, alert for any sound that might give the lovers away. Nothing but the usual noises of the forest, and in the distance the winding of a hunting horn, receding rather than getting nearer. No help from that quarter then. He was about to move on when a man's voice, raised in anger, broke the stillness. Mal headed towards it, heedless of the twigs snapping under his boots.

A few moments later he emerged in a clearing. The girl was sitting on a tree stump, head in her hands. Alone. Mal halted a few yards away and sheathed his half-drawn rapier. Elizabeth started at the sound and looked up. Naught but a child, with her face as white as the mist and her eyes and nose red from weeping. Mal fought off the urge to chase after Rutland and give him the beating he deserved, but he could not leave the girl alone in the forest like this. He bowed but did not make any other move towards her, less she flee like a deer.

"Come, let me take you back to my wife," he said, gesturing towards the path.

Elizabeth hesitated, then got to her feet shakily. Mal held out his hand and she came to him, let him take her arm and guide her through the forest.

"Are you hurt?" he said after a while.

Elizabeth shook her head.

"It was all m-m-my fault," she said, so quietly Mal had to lean down to hear. "My lord Rutland was showing me a deer path, and we stopped to... to kiss and I–"

She broke off with a sob. Mal fished around in his pocket for a handkerchief, trying to remember the last time he had seen Coby weep, but memory failed him. Perhaps growing up pretending to be a boy had hardened her spirits. Unlike these delicate ladies of the court. Sooth, he wished she were here now dealing with this poor child instead of him.

After a while Elizabeth stopped crying.

"He'll n-n-never marry me now," she whispered.

"But you are betrothed to him, are you not? It will cause him a great deal of trouble to get out of the contract, even if you're not a virgin anymore."

Elizabeth wiped her nose and looked up at him. "Can you lose your virginity by kissing? Mamma told me the man had to lie on top of the woman and... well, you know." She blushed scarlet.

"Well, yes... So, he just kissed you?"

"Yes. And then... And then I puked all over his doublet." Elizabeth burst into tears again.

Mal stifled a laugh. Poor vain Rutland, doing his best to seduce a girl and eliciting only nausea.

"Well perhaps you'll be more careful in future, and not drink on an empty stomach."

Elizabeth nodded miserably.

Mal found Hector and the two other horses waiting patiently where he had left them. He helped Elizabeth into the saddle of her roan mare then took the reins of both geldings and led them back towards the palace.

So much for his plans. He might have rescued the girl, but he was no closer to determining whether Rutland was an enemy or merely an irritation. Perhaps he would have better luck back in London, where at least he would be on familiar territory.

CHAPTER XVI

Mal knocked on the door of his brother's bedchamber. They had come back to the capital with Robert and his retinue at the beginning of October, but instead of returning to his lodgings at Whitehall Palace, Mal had moved back into the house behind the Sign of the Parley. He needed quiet and sobriety to plan his next move, and finally the stratagem had paid off.

"Sandy! Are you awake?"

A faint groan was the only reply. Fearing some new trouble Mal threw open the door. To his relief naught appeared to be amiss, though the fug of *qoheetsakhan* smoke was thicker than usual. Sandy was sitting up in bed, calm if bleary-eyed, his hair curling in damp elf-locks around his pale brow.

"Rough night?" Mal said, leaning on the bedpost.

"Wearisome. For hours I could not sleep, try as I might–" Sandy gestured vaguely towards the small brazier where he burned the dream-herb "–and then when I did, I tried to patrol the city but was led astray by..."

He broke off, his grave expression turning Mal's breakfast to lead in his stomach.

"Devourers?"

"No. Something different. A presence, no more. Familiar, but hidden from me. I followed it for a long time, but could not find it."

"Perhaps it was Prince Henry," Mal said, sitting down on the end of the bed. "I hear he's come up from Hampton Court for his birthday celebrations."

"Perhaps." Sandy untangled himself from the sheets and went over to the basin to wash his face. He paused, hands cupped over the water. "What of your news?"

"Who says I have news?"

"I heard it in your voice, when you called out to me." He splashed his face and rubbed a flannel over his bare limbs.

"No news," Mal said after a moment, "but an idea. I was clearing out the pantry – you know the rats got in whilst we were away? – and it occurred to me. I don't need to see a rat to know where it's been."

"You're chasing rats now?"

"No, Shawe. We don't know where the man is, but we know damned well what he's up to."

"Alchemy."

"Exactly. And wherever he is, he can't very well stroll down to the village green and buy... I don't know, a dozen alembics and a pound of quicksilver, can he?"

"I suppose not," Sandy said, shooing Mal off the bed so he could strip the sweat-soaked sheets.

"So–" Mal scrambled to his feet "–we just need to find out who Shawe's supplier is here in London, and where the goods are being sent."

"We?"

"Well, me. Unless you really want to help." He tried to keep his tone neutral; two could cover the ground better than one, but his brother wasn't exactly trained in intelligence work, nor could he be relied upon to be subtle.

Sandy wasn't fooled.

"No, I have plenty to do here," he said, bundling up the sheets. "If we could keep a maid for more than a few weeks at a time..."

"You're the one that scares them away," Mal said, backing out of the room. "Don't work too hard, all right? I'll be back before supper."

He wandered into his own chamber, thoughts already preoccupied with how he was going to go about his search. Glass-blowers – that was the place to start. Shawe would be needing more glass rods like the one Mal had found in the workshop, and other vessels besides. The question was, what should be his own story? He sorted through his wardrobe and chanced upon the dark green silk doublet he had worn in Venice, the night he had met Olivia. Perfect.

His quest led him to the eastern end of Southwark where all the noxious industries were situated, well downwind of the rest of the suburb. As he made his way past a row of tanneries Mal pressed a perfume-drenched handkerchief to his nose, glad for once to be playing the foppish courtier. Barrels half-full of piss stood outside each building, an invitation to the suburb's male inhabitants to add their own contributions to the trade's raw materials.

Mal turned down a side street, broader than most if only to allow the passage of supply wagons. One blocked his way now, laden with heavy sacks that were being carried into a workshop. The sign over the door showed a bottle and goblet.

"You there!" Mal waved his handkerchief at one of the labourers. "Move this wagon immediately. I wish to visit your master."

The man hurried to obey, and after a few moments the wagon creaked forward a few yards to let Mal pass.

The front shop was almost as crowded as the street, piled with crates of beer bottles, perhaps waiting to be loaded onto the same wagon once it was emptied. Display shelves with wooden rails along the front showed off a selection of the workshop's wares: more bottles, mostly in green and amber glass; small flat sheets, some made up into lanterns or examples of window panels; goblets that mimicked the finer work of Venetian craftsmen for those who could not afford imported glass.

"Can I help you, sir?"

A man of middle years, coarse-featured from daily exposure to the heat and fumes of his trade, stood in the inner doorway. He wore a heavy leather apron covered in scorch-marks and thick gauntlets of the same. The flinty smell of hot glass drifted through the door, reminding Mal of the abandoned workshop at Shawe House.

"I'm here on behalf of my good friend Sir Walter Raleigh," Mal said. "He has developed an interest in alchemy, and wishes to purchase alembics and suchlike."

The man sucked in air over his uneven yellow teeth. "Costly work, sir, and I haven't done anything of its like in a while. But if Sir Walter could provide sketches, I'd be glad to oblige."

"Then you don't supply other alchemists?"

"Between you and me, sir–" the glassblower looked around conspiratorially "–most of these alchemist fellows never pay their bills. They may talk of turning lead into gold, but mostly they seem to turn it into debt."

Mal bristled. "Sir Walter Raleigh is a Member of Parliament and a wealthy man, sirrah, not some charlatan peddling false hope to the gullible."

"My apologies, sir, I didn't mean to offend you or Sir Walter. As I said, I'd be more than happy to oblige in whatever he needs."

Mal turned on his heel and walked out of the shop, leaving the glassblower to stammer further apologies in his wake.

There were a few other glass workshops in the district, but none proved any more fruitful than the first. It appeared that alchemical equipment was even harder to obtain than Mal had first thought. But if Shawe was not buying London-made wares, he must either be having them made elsewhere, or perhaps importing them. Mal took a wherry across the Thames and resumed his search amongst the merchant venturers of the City of London.

"Alchemical vessels?" The shopkeeper squinted at Mal over his horn-rimmed glasses. "Yes, we do import them on occasion, sir. Very expensive indeed, though, I must warn you."

Mal glanced around the showroom, where a king's ransom in fine glass twinkled in the light of carefully placed candles. Sets of decanters and matching goblets, each on a silver tray, covered a pair of marquetry-work display tables; empty candelabra dripping in glass beads stood among them or hung from the beams above. Behind the counter a row of wooden stands displayed ropes of manufactured pearls that would fool all but the keenest eye, pendant earrings of the same, and brooches studded with false gems of all colours.

"Venetian?" he asked. Some of the glass was a deep blue colour, like the *siiluhlankaar* crystals. If this trail went cold, perhaps he could find out who imported such rare minerals and trace Shawe that way.

"Naturally, sir. Shipped all the way from Murano, lovingly packed in lambswool and sawdust."

"So, you can obtain what Sir Walter requires?"

"Most assuredly, sir, though it may take a while. Our last shipment is already spoken for."

"I see. The wizard earl, I suppose?"

"My lord the Earl of Northumberland is a client, yes."

"Well of course." Mal fished a gold angel out of his purse and laid it on the counter. "But there must be many breakages on the way from Venice. Perhaps you cannot always fulfil my lord earl's orders. And if so, might we lay a deposit against that chance?"

The man ignored the coin, but a faint smile curved his lips and his hands twitched on the counter's edge as if longing to snatch up the bribe. So, money was assuredly the way to this fellow's shrivelled heart.

"We always order more than he requests, sir, for that very reason."

"Then it must chance that by good fortune you are sometimes left with a full shipment."

"It has happened, yes. An item or two to spare, certainly."

Mal slid another coin across the table. The shopkeeper's hands tensed and his eyes flicked rapidly towards the gold on the counter every few seconds as if expecting it to disappear. It was all Mal could do not to laugh in the man's face.

"Well, then. Perhaps if we are thus fortunate, you can divert any leftovers to Durham Place on your wagon's way to Syon House."

"Oh, we don't deliver to Syon House any more, sir. At least, not the alchemical wares."

"No?" Mal sniffed his handkerchief, affecting an air of indifference, though his sinews ached like a man readying himself to charge into battle. At last, a clue to Shawe's whereabouts.

"No. That was the peculiar thing."

He paused and licked his lips. Mal took out a third angel. Damn, but this was proving to be nigh as expensive as alchemy itself!

"About a year ago," the shopkeeper went on, "my lord earl gave instructions that further shipments were to be delivered to the Three Horseshoes in Aldgate Without. I assumed they were to be taken north, perhaps to Alnwick Castle itself."

"Most likely," Mal said, setting down the last angel next to its fellows. "Well, never mind. I'm sure Sir Walter can make it worth your while to send a delivery to the Strand as well."

"Of course, sir. It would be a pleasure." The shopkeeper opened his ledger and selected a pen from the inkstand. "Do you have a list of the items required?"

Mal made a show of searching his pockets.

"Damn, must have dropped the wretched thing in the street. I swear I had it when I set out."

"No matter, sir. Send a letter at your earliest convenience, and I will advise you when the consignment arrives."

"Much obliged," Mal said, and took his leave. The whisper of coins sliding across wood sounded behind him as the shopkeeper gave in to temptation at last.

Aldgate Without, eh? It was certainly on the northern edge of the city, but surely Bishopsgate would make more sense if one were heading for the Great North Road. Wherever Shawe was lurking, Mal would put good money on it not being Alnwick Castle.

The landlord of the Three Horseshoes proved far cheaper to get information out of. He described the two men who came with a wagon to collect Shawe's goods, but did not know where they came

from, only that they left by the Great Cambridge Road. That left the
whole of East Anglia as a hunting-ground, but on the other hand
if Northumberland had another shipment on its way, perhaps Mal
would not have to wait too long to follow it to its destination. He
left the landlord under the misapprehension that he worked for
Northumberland himself and was looking into an alleged misuse of
funds, and swore the man to secrecy in the matter.

With naught else to do until that ship came in, he made his way
to court. There was still the issue of Jathekkil's *amayi* to deal with:
Lady Derby might have been eliminated from the running, and young
Howard's continuing absence told against him, but that still left Rutland
and Percy. He could not afford to seek them out too directly, however, in
case they became suspicious. He therefore resigned himself to a tedious
afternoon of drifting around Whitehall Palace, from bowling green to
tennis court to hall and back, until he fell into suitable company.

As the day wore on, the skies darkened and Mal's humour with
them. So far there had been no sign of either Rutland or Percy, and all
he had to show for his afternoon's labour was a full bladder and a light
head from too much drinking. Only the thought of the coldness of his
empty bed kept him from going straight home to Southwark and leaving
his quest until the morrow. He paused in the shadow of a doorway to
take a piss and tried to decide where to go next. He could visit Prince
Arthur's lodgings, but if he got sucked into another game of cards with
Southampton he'd be lucky to still have an estate in the morning.

"And that was when I realised she was his sister!"

Raucous laughter echoed down a nearby passageway. Mal halted
mid-stream, hardly able to believe his luck. Judging by the accents,
the men heading this way were none other than Josceline Percy and
his northern cronies. He began fastening up his breeches.

"Not putting you off your stroke, are we?" one of them shouted at
Mal as they drew nearer.

Mal turned and made a clumsy bow, as if rather drunker than he
felt. In truth it made his head spin a little, so that his queasy grin was
not entirely feigned.

"No, sirs, I was quite done."

The men stepped out of the passage entrance into the light of a lantern. Their leader was indeed Jos Percy, little changed from the pale-faced youth Mal remembered, apart from a creditable attempt at a beard. His companions were other younger sons of noblemen, by the look of them poorer even than Mal but no doubt boasting an ancient lineage he could never match.

"Why, if it isn't Sir Maliverny Catlyn, toast of the court." The way Percy emphasised the word "toast", it was all Mal could do not to challenge him to a duel on the spot. The burning of Rushdale Hall had no doubt given Mal's enemies a good deal of amusing gossip behind his back.

"You are too kind, sir," he said through gritted teeth. Unable to resist, he added, "I see you have a new pomander."

Percy frowned down at the silver bauble pinned to his doublet. Mal had thrown its predecessor into the muck of a London gutter during their last encounter.

"Do you know, I'd forgotten all about that..."

For a moment Mal feared Percy would order his companions to take the price of the old one out of his hide, then the earl's brother laughed, a girlish giggle that grated on Mal's already jittery nerves.

"But that was long ago, when we were both young and foolish, eh, Catlyn?"

"You were young, sir," Mal slurred, "and mayhap I was foolish."

"There you go!" Percy slapped him on the arm. "Come, we're off to Bankside. What say you join us? It's on your way home, is it not?"

"Aye, it is."

"Where is it you're lodging these days, Catlyn?" one of Percy's companions asked. "In the George?"

"Not far away. Off Long Southwark, behind a printer's shop. The Sign of the Parley."

Was that a flicker of guilt in Percy's eyes? Hard to tell in this light.

"Splendid!" Percy said, throwing his arms around two of his companions' shoulders. "To Bankside!"

Mal followed in the younger men's wake with only half an ear to their chatter. If this lot were heading for Bankside at this time of night, it meant only one thing: he was faced with a choice between abandoning a perfect opportunity to get close to Jos Percy, or spending the evening at a brothel. Even if he somehow managed to avoid sampling the services on offer, his wife would never forgive him. He cursed Percy silently and hurried after the Northumbrians towards Westminster Pier.

"Where are we going?" Mal said as they disembarked at Falcon Stairs. "The Rose?"

"Somewhere far more select," Percy told him, taking Mal's arm in his.

They strolled along Bankside as far as the bull-baiting ring, then turned down a narrow side street. Where gardens and fishponds had once stood, new houses had sprung up, crowding out the diamond-studded sky. Every other building appeared to be a tavern or a brothel – or both. After a while Mal realised they were alone.

"Where are the others?" he asked, letting his free hand drift towards the hilt of his rapier.

Percy looked around. "What? Oh, you know Scrope; can't pass a pretty girl in the street but he has to stop and talk to her. And then Ewer has to outdo him in boasting…" He sighed theatrically. "They'll catch us up. Come, it's just down here."

He led Mal down a short alley towards the light of a lantern, and a moment later they emerged into an empty courtyard surrounded by closed doors and shuttered windows.

"Well, this can't be it," Percy said. "Perhaps it was left, not right…?"

He turned to leave, and yelped as four hooded men stepped out of the shadows around them.

"Going somewhere, gentlemen? Perhaps you'd like to leave those heavy purses. They'll only weigh you down."

Mal drew his rapier. "Get behind me, Percy."

The hooded men drew their own blades: rapiers like Mal's, flashing bright gold in the lantern light. Not footpads, then, for all their talk of robbery. Had Percy led him into a trap? Mal cursed his foolishness in thinking that the Northumbrians had happened upon him by chance.

He drew his dagger, using the movement as a distraction whilst he engaged the man to his right, slipping his blade beneath the other's guard. The man cried out and attempted to attack, but Mal leapt to the left, parrying the swordsman's incoming blade with his dagger. A rapid counterthrust with his rapier and one of the villains lay bleeding on the cobbles.

He heard the clash of blades behind him but had no time to pay further attention as his right-hand foe was joined by another. A left-hander. The two of them fought side by side, so close they were practically arm in arm, weaving a net of steel that threatened to overwhelm Mal in moments. The tip of a blade slipped past his guard and skewered his upper sleeve, slicing the skin just below his armpit. Damn, but they were good! No hired ruffians or idle courtiers, these… What the hell was Percy up to? Mal backed away, expecting to bump into Percy, but found himself alone in the centre of the courtyard.

"Put up your sword, sir."

The voice came from behind him.

"And if I do not?" Mal called over his shoulder.

"Then the lordling here will be joining his ancestors."

Mal turned to see Percy held tight by the third remaining man, a glint of steel beneath his too-high chin. The young nobleman was deathly pale, his eyes pleading. Mal laughed.

"You can kill him for all I care."

He turned back to his two assailants. If this was some scheme of Percy's, the villains would not kill their master, and there was still a chance he could fight his way out. If it were not, he was rid of one candidate for Jathekkil's *amayi* and could focus on the other. He crouched in a fighting stance, daring the hooded men to attack again.

This time they moved apart, trying to engage him from both sides so that he could not choose but to ignore one of them. He backed towards a doorway to limit their angle of attack. The man on the left lunged, overreaching himself. Mal sidestepped again and brought the pommel of his dagger down on the man's wrist, simultaneously thrusting his rapier through his opponent's unprotected ribs. The man clutched at his chest as the narrow blade withdrew, blood bubbling from his lips.

A strangled cry from the other side of the courtyard, and the remaining bravo turned tail and fled down the alley. Mal turned to see Percy, a blood-bright dagger in his hand, his former captor sinking to his knees and clutching his side. Percy wiped his blade on the man's doublet.

"Much use you were!" Percy slammed the blade home in its sheath and grimaced at Mal. "'Kill him for all I care.' I should have you arrested, you traitorous cur."

Mal paused in the act of wiping his own blade clean. The young nobleman looked shaken, though whether through frustration at a thwarted plan or genuine fear of death, it was hard to say. This had been a trap, all right, but not necessarily one of Percy's making. Perhaps Olivia's? Dark alleys and assassins were her stock in trade, after all. What better way to get rid of them both at a stroke than to use Percy as her bait and have her hirelings turn on him too when his job was done?

"Come, let's find your companions," he said to Percy. "Then I think I shall go home. I've had enough entertainment for one night."

CHAPTER XVII

"The skrayling is here, my lord."

"About time too." Grey took up his cane and rose from his seat, face set as if determined to conceal any pain. "We'll see her in the privy closet. Have a fire laid, and refreshments brought up."

"Of course, my lord."

The duke limped over to a bookcase and ran his fingers over the spines of a row at eye height. Mal suspected he was trying to ease his cramped limbs without seeming to do so.

"What do you suppose this is all about, Catlyn?"

"They must have found out about Olivia. Though why Adjaan would insist on meeting us here at the palace and not at the camp, I have no idea."

The privy closet was a small panelled chamber on the upper floor, perfect for discreet meetings. A single narrow window admitted some daylight, though on a dull October morning like this, that was little enough. Adjaan was standing by the fireplace, ignoring the hard wooden chairs that were so ill-suited to skrayling anatomy. She wore dark blue robes similar to the ones Ambassador Kiiren had worn to official ceremonies, though more sombre, and a single short braid threaded with turquoise beads hung over her left ear. Erishen's memories stirred in the back of Mal's mind; this was a Vinlandic custom, to mark the birth of a child. Those beads would be added to the child's spirit-guard when he or she was older.

"Suffolk-*tuur*, it is an honour to meet you at last," Adjaan said, bowing in the English manner.

"Likewise," Grey replied, taking a seat by the fire. "May I ask, to what do we owe such an unprecedented visit?"

Adjaan lowered herself carefully into the other chair, leaning forwards so as not to put pressure on her tail bone.

"I bring grave news from my kinfolk on Sark. And from your friends, Catlyn-*tuur*: Parrish and Faulkner."

"Something has happened to Ned?"

"Your friend is well, and his heart-mate also. But they have brought news of Captain Hennaq, and Ilianwe."

"Olivia escaped. Yes, we know."

"You knew and did not tell us?" Adjaan got to her feet. "Are we not allies, then?"

"I only found out a few weeks ago, and when I came to the camp I was told you had been called away. To Sark, presumably."

"I needed to bear my child amongst my own people, as far from yours as possible lest one of the *senzadheneth* try to take the place of the intended soul." She folded her arms across her full breasts. "I only returned to convey this news. It seems I should not have bothered."

"Forgive us, honoured one." Mal gestured for her to sit down again. "I should have told the elders in your absence, but since Olivia – Ilianwe – has not been near London yet, we thought the news could wait."

"You have seen her?"

"Yes. She is disguised as a young man, but I have no doubt it is her. She admitted as much to me herself."

"You must take me to her," Adjaan said.

"We must do nothing." Grey rapped his cane on the wooden floor, and Adjaan flinched. "This woman is dangerous, and I want her out of my kingdom. If it can be contrived, we will clap her in irons and hand her over to you for transportation to the New World."

Adjaan frowned. "I do not think that would be wise."

"What?"

"My people are mistrusted by yours as it is. How will it look if it is found out that we helped capture a human woman and took her over the sea?"

"We'll tell them she's a traitor." Even as Mal spoke the words, his conscience pricked him. *How many lies am I prepared to tell, to keep the truth from those who would never believe it?*

"The outspeaker is right," Grey said. "It's one thing to accuse a foreigner of treason, but why would we hand her over to the skraylings for punishment? The people will expect a public execution."

"We could fake her death and smuggle her out of the country," Mal said. "We've done it before, for our own people."

"I am well aware of your methods, Catlyn. I do not think they will help us in this case."

"With respect, my lord–"

"Enough!" The rap of the cane echoed like thunder in the little room. "Outspeaker, can I call upon your people to be vigilant? We need to be certain that this woman is not using her witchcraft on the Prince of Wales or his family."

"Of course, Suffolk-*tuur*."

"For my part, I will arrange for her to be brought to London, so you can do just that. Catlyn, I want a detailed report on her mundane activities. Who she speaks to, where she goes. If I am to arrest the Princess of Wales's pet, I need cast-iron evidence, do you understand?"

"Yes, sir. My wife already working on it."

"Good, then we are agreed. Outspeaker, it has been a pleasure."

After the skrayling had been escorted out, Mal sank to one knee before the duke's chair.

"My lord, if you have any mind to clemency... Faulkner and Parrish–"

"A pardon, is that what you're asking?" He barked a laugh. "I should have all three of you hanged. I have not forgotten that you disobeyed my orders."

"I know, my lord." Mal swallowed his hatred of this man who held all their lives in his vindictive grasp. "I am most truly sorry, my lord. Loyalty to my friends is my besetting sin."

"Get up." Grey prodded him in the shoulder with his cane. "I cannot abide false modesty."

"Yes, my lord."

Mal got to his feet and stood at attention, though he kept his gaze on the floor.

"Mayhap," said Grey, "these friends of yours know more about what happened than the skrayling woman can or will tell us. Whoever brought the charges against them never did put forward any evidence, so I don't suppose it will be difficult to persuade Robert it was all a mistake."

"Thank you, my lord. I and my friends will be eternally in your debt."

"I shall remember those words, Catlyn, you can be sure of that. Now get out of here. I have work to do."

Mal backed out of the room, bowing low, and strode off down the corridor, whistling a merry jig. Ned and Parrish back in London! It was the best news he had had in months.

Life at court did not come to a standstill, however, whilst Mal waited for his friends to return. The Prince of Wales had announced that his younger son would be breeched on his next birthday, and that a tournament would therefore be held in the little prince's honour, in addition to all the usual court ceremonial. The Princess of Wales had of course come back to London for the occasion, and Mal had at last been able to join his wife and son in their guest apartments at Whitehall Palace.

"What's beeching, Daddy?" Kit asked as they set off for the tiltyard.

Mal smiled. "Breeching. It's when a boy is put into grownup clothes."

Kit nodded. "Will I be beeched, um, breeched?"

"Soon. When you're old enough."

"How old?"

"Perhaps when you're five, like Prince Henry."

"I'm three an' a quarter." Kit looked up at him with wide brown eyes. "I'm a big boy."

"I know. Now watch where you're walking. We don't want you falling down the stairs, do we?"

At the Holbein Gate they had to wait with the other minor courtiers whilst an army of heralds and palace servants guided all the spectators to the correct seats.

"Sir Maliverny Catlyn," he said to the steward when they reached the gateway. "And family."

"This way, sir. Gentlemen's seats on the left."

They followed the steward's directions, past a great canopied stand where the Prince and Princess of Wales were enthroned. Prince Arthur sat at his brother's right hand, along with senior courtiers including the earls of Northumberland and Essex, and in front of them the birthday boy himself, Prince Henry, resplendent in... full armour? Mal stared for a moment, slack-jawed, then remembered himself and looked away.

They found Sandy already seated about halfway up the stand, glaring at anyone who tried to sit too close to him. He broke into a smile at the sight of Kit, but when the boy did not immediately run to him like he used to do, the expression on his face was heartbreaking. We did the right thing, Mal told himself, and forced a smile as he took his own place, next to his wife. She had tactfully placed Kit on the bench between herself and Sandy.

"Prince Arthur's idea, no doubt," Mal muttered to her, nodding towards the lists below. "He does like to remind people how much he takes after his grandfather."

"Did you see Prince Henry all in armour?" Coby whispered. "I thought this was an entertainment for his benefit. He is participating?"

"Looks like it. And his older brother too. See, there's Edward, by the tents."

He pointed to the competitors' pavilion, where eight year-old Prince Edward, likewise clad head to foot in plate armour, was talking animatedly to a man whom Mal did not recognise.

"That sounds somewhat rash," Coby said, "to risk both the Prince's heirs like that. What if one or both is hurt?"

What indeed? A simple accident, and Prince Henry would be heir to the throne after his father's death. Mal's hand strayed to the hilt of his rapier. He should stop this, before something terrible happened. But who would listen? He could hardly denounce Prince Henry before the crowd, not if he wanted to keep his own head.

Trumpets blared, and Mal's heart turned over in his chest. He had never cared much for jousting, but too much was at stake today.

"I want to see, I want to see!" Kit bounced up and down ineffectually.

Coby lifted the boy up onto the bench, steadying him with a hand around his waist. "There, see the horses now?"

To Mal's relief the first jousters were adults: the Earl of Southampton, and... He frowned at the banner. The Earl of Rutland? Were the guisers out in force today, or was Manners simply showing off in front of his betrothed? The two combatants trotted up to the royal stand and saluted the Prince of Wales, their blued-steel armour flashing in the rich autumn sunlight. Hours of painstaking craftsmanship, costing hundreds of pounds, only to dent and scratch it for an afternoon's entertainment. Mal supposed a lack of concern for such matters was what separated the nobility from a mere gentleman commoner like himself.

The two earls wheeled their mounts and cantered to opposite ends of the list. Trumpets sounded again, the herald lowered his flag and the riders kicked their horses into a gallop, thundering towards one another down the narrow field. The ground trembled under their passing hooves, and the crowd held its collective breath until the moment of impact. The lances clashed and shivered into splinters and the crowd roared.

Mal turned to his son. Kit was staring silently at the Earl of Southampton, who rode past with shattered lance held high.

"Why are the men fighting, Daddy?" he asked, his brow furrowed in concern.

"It's just a game, pet. They're showing what good riders they are, to stay on their horses even when they've been hit."

"Oh."

"Don't worry, no one will get hurt." God willing.

Southampton and Rutland made two more passes, equally without mishap, though Rutland won the bout for breaking all three of his lances to only two of Southampton's. They trotted back to the royal stand and saluted the princes again. Prince Henry sounded happy as he congratulated Rutland in his piping child's voice, but the formal words robbed the exchange of any personal meaning. Damn it, there had to be a better way to identify their enemies! If only they bore a mark, like witches were said to do, or had some vulnerability that was simple to test. As it was, a guiser bound in iron was indistinguishable from any other human. Bound in iron. Or steel. Such as armour...

A shiver of horror and hope ran over Mal's skin. If Prince Henry died jousting, Jathekkil might be destroyed. He looked across at Sandy, who frowned slightly. Mal leaned around behind Coby to whisper in his brother's ear, but his words were drowned out by another fanfare. A squire dressed in royal livery brought a pony up to the stand, and Prince Henry was escorted down to it by his uncle. Prince Arthur hoisted the boy into the saddle from the offside, being careful to avoid the large shield that had been affixed to the saddlebow. So, they were taking no chances after all.

Prince Henry shook the reins and kicked his armoured heels, and the pony trotted to the far end of the lists. At the other end his brother already waited, his face serene. Had he been bewitched, to ensure his youthful enthusiasm did not get the better of him – or to ensure that it would? The two boys' ponies broke into a canter. Ten yards... five... and they were past one another, without a point having been scored. Just a warm-up pass, then. He breathed out unsteadily.

The princes turned in unison and couched their lances for a second pass. With their visors down, neither boy's mood could be judged. Mal motioned wordlessly to Coby. Taking the hint she pulled Kit closer, ready to hide his face if things went amiss.

Again the ponies cantered down the long narrow space, their riders barely able to see over the barrier between them. This time as they clashed, their lances struck home, impacting their shields. Prince

Edward gave a muffled whoop as he rode past, but the buffet had been too much for Prince Henry and he slid from the saddle. The crowd's roar of approval turned to cries of anguish, but one voice rose above them all.

"*Amayiiii!*"

A slight figure vaulted down from the royal stand and ran to the prince, skidding to a kneeling halt over him. Stewards and squires ran up, surrounding them, but for a few brief moments Mal's view was clear, and he locked gazes with the young man who had cried out. It was Josceline Percy.

Mal exchanged glances with his brother. Kit was watching the scene wide-eyed and silent.

"We could hardly have planned it better ourselves," he whispered. "Now we know another of them."

"You think this was our enemies' doing?"

Mal shrugged. "I cannot see the purpose in it, but who else would be able to convince Prince Robert to put his sons' life in danger?"

The news was soon announced: Prince Henry had suffered a broken collarbone. This was not immediately life-threatening, but in Mal's experience a severe fracture could lead to infection and even death. On the other hand the royal physicians often had some training in skrayling medicine, so the likelihood of the prince recovering was good.

Nevertheless the rest of the tournament was cancelled, and the crowd slowly dispersed amid a rumble of gossip. All attention seemed to be on the two young princes, of course; no skraylings had been invited to the event, not even Outspeaker Adjaan, so no one outside Mal, Sandy, Coby and the guisers themselves was likely to have any idea of the significance of Josceline Percy's outburst.

"Take Kit to bed, but come and find me later when he's asleep," Mal told Coby. He turned to his brother, "Perhaps you'd better go with them, in case this accident sets off a fit."

Sandy nodded and lifted Kit onto his shoulders, the better to avoid being trampled by the throng.

Mal bade his son good night and watched until the three of them had disappeared through the gatehouse, Kit swaying on his uncle's shoulders as he pretended to aim a lance at the guards' partisans. Mal smiled ruefully. Children forgot so quickly; they did not brood over upsets like their elders were prone to do. He turned on his heel and headed for the Prince's lodgings. Little Henry had no doubt been conveyed to his apartments there, as soon as the court physician had ascertained he was in no immediate danger.

Most of Prince Robert's household were gathered in the great hall, standing around in knots with grave expressions on their faces. Mal passed through the crowd, but the one face he was seeking was absent. Most likely Percy was with his *amayi*, ready to see him through another rebirth should things go badly. Mal didn't envy him; no doubt the little prince was surrounded by his mother and her women, fussing and weeping and getting in everyone's way. He just hoped Coby could get away from her duties soon. He needed someone to talk this over with, someone clearer-headed than his brother.

He circulated among the courtiers for a little longer, but learned nothing new. No one dared blame Prince Robert for letting his sons indulge in such a dangerous activity, so everyone else connected with the tournament came under scrutiny: the armourers for failing to make the shields large enough, the master of arms for not training Prince Edward properly, even Prince Henry's pony for not bearing him safely. Mal soon left them to their pointless arguments and went up to his own room to await Coby's return.

The household being in chaos, he hailed the first servant he saw and ordered the man to bring up some supper and a flagon of wine. The hearth in his room was cold, so he laid a new fire himself and had it underway by the time the servant appeared with bread, a wedge of veal pie, and a half-burnt apple and cinnamon tart.

"Sorry, sir," the man said, setting them down on the table. "We had everything going for His Highness's birthday supper, and then this..."

"No matter." Mal gave him a penny and sent him on his way.

Rain had set in, rattling against the windowpanes and creeping through the gaps to pool on the stone sill. The fire crackled to itself in the silence of a palace holding its breath for fear of bad news on the heels of the good. Mal finished off the tart – gratifyingly tasty despite the burnt bits – and licked the crumbs from his fingers, leaning back in his chair by the fireplace. Better to rest now; unless the prince died, it would be some hours before he was needed again.

It seemed only moments later that he jerked awake. Someone was knocking softly at the door. He leapt to his feet, crossed the room in a few swift strides and opened the door, expecting to see his wife.

"Catlyn? May I come in?"

Mal hesitated. Well, he had wanted to speak to Josceline Percy in private. He just hadn't expected Percy to come to him.

"Very well." He stood back and opened the door to admit his visitor.

The younger man looked as though he hadn't slept in a week. Stubble darkened his jaw either side of a once-neat beard, and his skin was as grey and clammy as a day-old corpse. Mal closed the door behind him and leant back against it, arms folded.

"So, what brings you here at this time of night, sir? Is there some bad news about Prince Henry?" Feigning ignorance would not fool Percy for long, but Mal wasn't about to admit to anything he didn't have to.

Percy crossed to the table, poured himself a cup of wine and took several large gulps. A little colour returned to his face.

"This is all your fault," he said, glowering at Mal.

"Mine? Why, what have I done?"

"Don't play the innocent with me, Catlyn. I know what you are. And I think you know what I am."

"You are weary and distraught, sir. And who would not be, after such a day?"

"Such a day indeed. You brought this upon us–"

"I? You blame me for today's accident? It was not I who suggested letting the princes joust."

"No. It was that... creature." Percy took another swig of wine. "The one you unleashed upon us."

"I don't know what you mean."

"Oh I think you do. I've heard all about what happened in Venice. You made a powerful enemy, and now he's here for revenge."

"Ah. You mean Bartolomeo Pellegrino?"

"Yes, I mean Pellegrino." Percy approached until he was almost nose-to-nose with Mal, his wine-scented breath puffing up into Mal's face with every syllable. "It's your fault he's here, so what are you going to do about it?"

"Why should I do anything? It looks to me like he's doing my job for me."

"Your job?"

"Ridding the kingdom of you usurping villains."

Percy's eyes narrowed, and for a moment his lips drew back in a snarl like a dog's. Mal held his breath, expecting the guiser to fly at his throat, but at last Percy regained his composure.

"And what do you think he'll do when he's finished with us? Leave you and your brother in peace and go back to his little republic?"

"I was rather hoping the two sides would wipe one another out, and save me the trouble," Mal said, feigning more confidence than he felt. The possibility of having to take on the victor of this civil war was not appealing.

"Pellegrino betrayed us both, you know. You were supposed to die in that alley, and me with you."

"Then it's lucky for you I know how to handle myself in a fight. My lord."

They locked eyes, and Mal's fingers itched to draw his blade, but killing Percy now would only be doing Olivia a favour. After a long moment Percy breathed out heavily and took a step backward.

"Think about what I have said, Catlyn. I have money, and powerful friends."

"Is that a threat, sir?"

"Or an invitation. Depending on your answer."

"Then I will bid you goodnight, sir," Mal said, moving aside and putting a hand on the latch. "I'm sure your beloved prince will be wondering where you've got to."

Percy pushed past him.

"If he dies," Percy said in a low voice, "I will personally hunt you both down, you and your brother, and tear that abomination Erishen's soul from your screaming bodies."

Mal said nothing, only opened the door and ushered him out with a curt bow. He waited for several moments, listening to Percy's footfalls fade down the stairwell, then quietly slid the bolts into place and went to refill his own cup. His hands shook just a little as he poured the wine.

CHAPTER XVIII

The prince did not die, thank the Lord, but his household remained at Whitehall for the rest of the year, as did his mother's. No news had come from the glass importer about the shipment of alchemical equipment, so Mal was able to spend a few quiet weeks with his family once more. Ned and Gabriel arrived from Sark at last, and the house rang with laughter and the raucous singing of bawdy French ballads, though Mal caught Ned looking grave whenever Parrish left for a rehearsal.

"Don't fret," Mal told him, "the guisers have worse things to worry about these days than you and me. Olivia's arrival has thrown them into complete disarray."

"And what happens if – when – she brings them all under her thumb?"

"We came close to beating Ilianwe before," Sandy said, looking up from his book. "With the skraylings' help, we can defeat her for certain."

"The skraylings don't want to help us," Mal reminded him. "They'd rather sit back and watch us fight it out."

"Are you boys arguing again?" Coby stood in the kitchen doorway, dressed in her best gown and clutching a ruff in one hand. "Where's my goffering iron? And why aren't you all dressed yet? It's a good half an hour to the palace and the play starts at five."

Mal scrambled to his feet and headed upstairs, glad to get out of the conversation. The thought of their enemies uniting under Olivia was too horrible to contemplate, and yet he could not see any way to prevent it, short of allying himself with Percy against her. And that cure was even worse than the disease. At least a play would be a distraction for an hour or two.

The great hall had been set up like a theatre, with a stage at one end and rows of benches, crammed with courtiers dressed in Christmas finery, filling the rest. Mal and Coby found places near the back, wedged between an elderly man in a faded black doublet and hose that perhaps had been new when the Queen came to the throne, and a young couple who were far more interested in flirting with one another than in the entertainments.

Sandy had declined attending, saying he took no pleasure in playgoing without Kiiren to share it with, and Mal had left his brother behind with a heavy heart. At first he put on a merry face for his wife's benefit, but the laughter of the audience only seemed to sour his mood further, so he distracted himself by turning his attention to the royal party seated at the front of the hall. Little could be seen of the Queen or her two sons, whose high-backed chairs blocked the view of the unfortunate courtiers behind them, nor could he see her young grandsons over the heads of the crowd. He knew they were there, however, and he was most interested in seeing whose eyes turned that way more often than to the stage. His efforts were thwarted, however, by nine year-old Prince Edward, whose frequent loud observations on the play attracted the looks and amused comments of those about him.

His attention was drawn back to the stage by the entrance of Will Shakespeare, Gabriel Parrish and another actor he did not recognise, speaking of music. A few moments later Olivia stepped out of the wings, accompanied by the strains of music from a hidden lutenist.

"Come, Balthasar, we'll hear that song again," said the unknown actor.

"O, good my lord," Olivia replied, "tax not so bad a voice to slander music any more than once."

After several more such exchanges, which brought gales of laughter from the audience, the musician Balthasar was prevailed upon by his master to comply.

"A fine jest," Mal muttered to his wife.

"Or an unkind jibe at Princess Juliana," Coby whispered back.

"You think so?"

"To have her favourite singer mocked before all the court, even if only in pretence? Yes, I think it a calculated insult."

"But not of Shakespeare's doing, surely?"

"You would have to ask Parrish that. He might know."

The musician struck up again, and Olivia began to sing: "Sigh no more, ladies, sigh no more, men were deceivers ever..."

"That is true enough," Coby muttered, staring straight ahead.

Mal bit his tongue. He was not going to get into a quarrel with his wife here, and attract the ire of Her Majesty.

Thankfully the song was soon over, and Olivia departed. There followed some nonsense involving a plot to bring together a young man and woman who despised both love and one another. *A fool's errand, if you ask me. Trouble enough comes when a man and woman love one another from the outset.*

The rest of the play did not improve his mood, and he was relieved when the villain was unmasked, the lovers reconciled and at last all was over. He joined in the applause, however, after his wife glared at him. The actors gave their last bows, then Her Majesty rose and led the way out of the hall to the nearby banqueting chamber. The rest of the court followed in order of precedence, meaning that Mal and Coby had to wait until almost everyone else had left.

"Attend upon Her Highness," Mal whispered. "I think I shall speak to the actors, as you suggested."

Before she could protest he turned away and leapt up onto the stage. A few strides took him across the narrow space and through the curtains into the makeshift tiring-house beyond. A few of the actors turned to stare at him.

"I'm looking for Gabriel Parrish," he said, peering over the heads of the throng. There was no sign of Olivia, but he did not really expect it: Balthasar had appeared in only the one scene.

"Here, Catlyn!" Parrish waved a hand from the other side of the room.

Mal pushed his way through the actors.

"Can we talk?"

"Of course." Parrish handed him a silk doublet. "Hang that up over there, will you? There's a love."

Mal raised an eyebrow but did as he was instructed. Parrish pulled the shirt over his head and threw it onto the nearby bench.

"Well, what did you want to say?"

"In private, if we may…?"

Parrish shrugged. "If you must. Though there's few secrets that escape this lot for long."

"Only because you can't keep your mouth shut, Angel," one of the other actors shouted.

"Ignore him, he's only jealous," Parrish said to Mal in a stage whisper.

Mal lowered his own voice. "This is business, Parrish."

"Oh." The actor winked at him, then added more loudly, "Well, if you'd said that in the first place, love… I'm sure I can make an exception for a handsome fellow like you."

The tiring-house erupted in laughter. Mal stared at the wall, playing the part of the embarrassed admirer. Truth was, once upon a time he would have taken pleasure in the proximity of a half-naked man, especially one as handsome as Gabriel Parrish. Now, though, he was married and content, and Gabriel belonged to Ned, as much as any man could belong to another. Still, he stole a glance or three as Parrish stripped to his drawers and dressed in his own clothes. Just for the look of it, of course.

Parrish brushed the sleeves of his doublet, picked up his hat and took Mal's arm.

"Come along then, dear. I know just where we can get a bit of peace and quiet."

He steered Mal out of the tiring-house, through a servants' area where dishes waited before being taken through into the dining hall, down a flight of stairs, across a passageway and up two more flights of stairs to a low door.

"It's just an attic room," Parrish said in far more business-like tones as he showed Mal inside, "but well away from flapping ears. I checked it very thoroughly when I arrived; no one will hear a thing."

"Afraid someone's spying on you?"

"That too," the actor replied with a hint of his earlier insouciance, and threw himself down on the bed. "So, what can I do you for?"

Mal leant against the wall, for want of anywhere else to sit.

"Shakespeare's new play…"

"'Much Ado'? It's good, isn't it? Of course he has to go and set it in Italy, despite never having been there. I blame myself, of course, I've been telling him so much about my time in Venice and Spalato–"

"Parrish, I don't care if the play is set in Italy, Egypt or the court of the Great Khan himself. When did he write it?"

The actor frowned at him. "Why, is it important?"

"I wouldn't be asking if I didn't think it were."

"Oh. Yes. Well, he started it last year, before Ned and I went away. I'm pretty sure that was when I first heard him mention the idea. But that was just the seeds of it, because he was working on Henry the Fourth as well, and having a beast of a time with Falstaff's speech, and then Kemp went and left…"

"So he wrote it recently?"

"Not that recently. He's been saving it for a special occasion. I know he wanted to rewrite a few scenes but he hasn't had time, what with everything else happening–"

Mal sighed. Parrish was full of information, but getting it out of him could take a while.

"Did anyone else contribute to the play? I know you've mentioned collaborations before."

Parrish shook his head. "Not on this one, not to my knowledge."

"So no one changed any of it at any point?"

"Well, if you mean did we say every line exactly as written, then no. The clown always has licence to improvise, though Will is less patient than most with other men's embroiderings. And of course someone always forgets his lines and the rest of us have to make it up until we can get it back on track."

"But the scene about Balthasar being a poor singer; that was Shakespeare's work?"

Comprehension dawned on Parrish's face. "You think someone was taking a swipe at Olivia?"

"Could be."

"No. I saw the script in its first draft, from before 'Bartolomeo' arrived at court, and the part of Balthasar was as you heard it. Shakespeare seldom changes things once written."

"If it was not the script, perhaps the malice lay with whomever assigned the role."

"That was not Shakespeare, I can vouch that he was most vexed about it."

"Then who?"

"Burbage, most likely. He's our manager, and running a theatre company isn't cheap, even with the Prince's patronage. I dare say anyone with the chinks to spare could have persuaded him to do it."

Even as Coby ascended the stairs to the princess's apartments, she could hear raised voices. None were shriller than that of "Signor Bartolomeo", who was cursing and spitting like a kettle come to the boil. The fact that no one else understood the stream of Italian invectives did not lessen its impact. Coby winced as she slipped through the door, unseen behind a wall of brocade skirts and wired gauze headpieces that stood out like butterfly wings.

"I am sure no offence was meant, sir." Princess Juliana sounded on the verge of tears herself. "Everyone there was enchanted by your singing. The jest was on Don Pedro, for having such a poor ear for music."

Coby moved to stand by one of the bedposts, where she could see around the curtains but not easily be seen by the actors in this new drama.

"You truly think so, Your Highness?" Olivia looked decidedly calm, considering her recent outburst.

"I am sure of it," Juliana replied. "Don't you agree, ladies?"

The ladies-in-waiting chorused their agreement. They reminded Coby of nothing so much as an aviary of songbirds, pretty but useless.

"Begging your pardon, Your Highness, but I disagree," said Lady Derby. All heads turned to stare at her.

"Explain."

"Well…" Lady Derby cast a glance at Olivia. "Surely someone knew it would be taken as an insult. Signor Bartolomeo may not have seen the whole script, but others must have done. The playwright himself, of course, but also the Master of the Revels, and probably the actors' patron."

"Do you accuse my brother-in-law of plotting this jest at my expense?"

The ladies fell silent, and most of them suddenly found something more interesting to look at. Like the floor.

"Oh no, Your Highness," Lady Derby said quickly. "I accuse no one."

Princess Juliana stared at her former lady-in-waiting for a long moment. Perhaps thinking no one was looking at her, Olivia smiled, her pupils dilated like those of a cat that has spotted a mouse within pouncing distance. Coby shrank behind the bed-hanging, her fingers tightening on the rough woollen fabric. Whether it had been Olivia's scheme from the beginning or not, this was all going just the way the guiser wanted it. She slipped back out of the presence chamber and went in search of her husband.

"You're sure?" Mal whispered.

"Yes," Coby replied. "Whether Arthur did it or not, that's what Olivia wants everyone to think."

"But why? Is he another of them, like Percy, that she must overthrow if she is to rule the kingdom?"

"Surely not. If he were, why would Jathekkil have been so desperate to reincarnate as Prince Henry? Better to take another host, any host, so that Arthur could seize the throne and murder his nephews like wicked King Richard."

"You have a point. Most likely she is simply making mischief to throw her opponents off guard." He sighed. "Very well, I'll deal with the prince. You go to bed, and I'll join you when I can. This may take a while."

He bent and kissed her, then waited until he had seen her going back into the palace before descending to the courtyard and heading eastwards through the Holbein Gate into the tiltyard. On the south side stood the banqueting house, a massive timber and canvas pavilion that had been built twenty years ago for the wedding of Robert and Juliana. Tonight it was lit by hundreds of blown-glass lanterns, some containing candles but many filled with lightwater. Prince Arthur had spared no expense to ensure that tonight's entertainments would be remembered long after the last sweetmeats had been eaten.

Lit by the yellow and green skrayling lamps, the pavilion looked more like a sunlit glade than the dank tent it appeared by daylight, and felt deliciously warm compared to the chill night air. Most of the court and their servants were here, milling around tables set out with every delicacy the nearby kitchens could supply: spiced tartlets, roast songbirds, and marchpane painted and gilded and shaped into a hundred fantastical forms. The centrepiece was an enormous red dragon – Arthur's personal badge – with smoke curling up from its nostrils.

The prince himself was seated to one side of the central area, surrounded by hangers-on, including the senior members of his company of players. Some of the other courtiers were eyeing the actors with disdain, but Arthur seemed unperturbed. He laughed and joked with highborn and lowborn alike, and Mal began to see why he was so popular with the ordinary folk. More popular than his elder brother – but it took more than a dazzling smile and a name out of legend to rule a kingdom.

Mal made his way through the throng towards the prince. Perhaps this was not the best time to broach an awkward subject, but he might not get another chance to get this close to Arthur for a while. Sidestepping a rotund gentleman in scarlet velvet, he tried to slip inconspicuously into the group surrounding the prince. He needn't have bothered.

"Catlyn!" The prince waved him over and Mal obeyed, cursing his height that made him stand out in any crowd. "For God's sake smile, man! Anyone would think someone had died."

"My apologies, Your Highness."

"And sit down. I cannot talk to you up there."

Parrish scrambled to his feet and offered Mal his cushion.

"Please excuse me, Your Highness," the actor said. "I need to pluck a rose."

Arthur grinned and waved him away.

"Such a polite young man," he said as Mal sat down. "Now, Catlyn, tell me what makes you so grave. Have you fallen out of love with your wife at last?"

The prince beamed at his hangers-on, who laughed on cue.

"I am merely concerned about Your Highness," Mal said when the laughter had died down.

"That is very touching, but I would not have you melancholy on my account. Besides, what is there to be concerned about? I am well, and the play was a resounding success!" He reached out and tousled Shakespeare's thinning curls. "This man–" he leant towards Mal and lowered his voice to a stage whisper "–this man is a genius. Mark my words."

The prince's eyelids drooped as he gazed at Mal; he was already halfway to being dead drunk, by the looks of it.

"It was beyond compare," Mal said, careful not to give his frank opinion, "but it may have earned you a new enemy."

Arthur frowned at him.

"Signor Bartolomeo," Mal went on, "who played Balthasar. I cannot think he enjoyed being mocked before all the court."

"And what care I for the wounded feelings of a... of a foreign eunuch?" Arthur slurred. The hangers-on laughed again. "Really,

Catlyn, if that's all that's bothering you, I command you to forget it this instant. Have a cup of wine and be merry!"

"Very well, Your Highness. But my heart would rest easier if I knew you had trustworthy men around you." He doubted the prince was in any immediate danger, but one could never be too sure with Olivia. At the very least she might disturb his sleep with nightmares. Perhaps there was some way to convince Arthur to wear a spirit-guard?

The prince eyed his circle suspiciously.

"You know, you're right," he said in a low voice, sounding much more sober than he had a few moments ago. "Perhaps you should be my bodyguard for the night, eh?"

"It would be my honour, Your Highness."

"Yes, yes it would." Arthur leant back in his chair and raised his silver cup, the picture of an idle, dissolute prince once more. "Servants, more wine for my companions!"

The rest of the evening passed in a tedious meandering of conversation. Shakespeare was prevailed upon to recite one of his new sonnets, something about a lying mistress, or lying with his mistress: Mal was not clear on the details. By the time midnight rolled around most of them had drunk more than was good for them, and even the prince's inebriation was no longer much of an act. When he stood to leave, Mal had to leap to his feet to steady him.

"Good man," Arthur mumbled, patting his hand. "Now, shall we to bed?"

A few of the courtiers made obscene remarks and gestures at this, which Mal laughed off, though he hoped the prince had not meant it literally. It would not do to offend the brother of the heir to the throne.

As they weaved their way through the crowd, Mal expected some of the prince's circle to fall in behind them. Some of them, surely, must be his gentlemen of the chamber? But they emerged into the frosty night air alone. Perhaps they had taken their master's comment seriously, and were allowing him some privacy? Mal began rehearsing a polite but heartfelt refusal.

Arthur sobered up somewhat in the cold and walked steadily through the gatehouse, turning left into the gardens that fronted the Prince's lodgings. Mal followed him down the gravel path, one hand on his rapier hilt, scanning the shadows for any sign of movement, but they reached the entrance to the royal apartments unchallenged.

Mal had to help Arthur up the narrow winding stair and open the door one-handed whilst keeping his other hand under the prince's elbow. The last thing he needed was for his charge to take a tumble and break his head. That would play far too nicely into his enemies' hands.

The antechamber beyond was dark and empty. He paused, suspicious.

"Should there not be attendants, Your Highness? At least a page waiting, to summon them at your need?"

"Is no one here?" Arthur peered around the room. "Haslingfield? De la Pole?"

There was no reply, nor even a footfall or sleep-fuddled groan. Mal retrieved a candle from a niche by the door and found flint and tinder to light it. The small glow did little to light the room.

"Stay behind me, Your Highness." He drew his rapier, holding up the candlestick in his left hand out of his line of sight.

The door of the prince's bedchamber stood ajar, but no light showed. Mal nudged the door wide open with his foot. This room was as empty as the last, the scarlet-curtained bed a massive presence against the far wall.

"It seems your servants are a-merrymaking, Your Highness," Mal said loudly. He guided Arthur to a chair. "Sit down, if you will, my prince. I shall call for a page."

He did no such thing, but padded across the rugs to the bed, slid the point of his rapier between the curtains and eased the heavy fabric aside. In the dim light of the candle he could just make out a pale shape lying on the coverlet. A mistress, fallen asleep waiting for her lover to return? He drew back the curtain – and froze. It was no woman lying there, but a man, naked as a newborn babe, his head thrown back so that his face could not clearly be seen. Perhaps the courtiers' jibes were not so far off the mark.

Mal was about to call the prince over when he realised the man was not moving. Not even breathing. He pulled the curtains aside to get a better view. Sweet Jesu! It was Josceline Percy; and judging by the line of bruises around his throat, he had been strangled.

"What is it, Catlyn?" Arthur called out. "Where is that young scoundrel of a page?"

"I'm sorry, Your Highness, it seems that someone has decided to play a foul jest at your expense." *Yours. Or mine.* "Stay there, I will go and find a servant."

CHAPTER XIX

Having found a sleepy page and put the fear of God into him, Mal swiftly examined the body before anyone could come and disturb the evidence. The bruises round Percy's neck formed a series of small circular indentations, suggesting he had been strangled with a string of beads. A rosary perhaps, but if Mal's suspicions were correct, more likely a spirit-guard. In which case, Josceline Percy was unlikely to be reborn to trouble them in future.

The question was, who had committed the murder, and how had they persuaded Percy to come here? Carrying a body through the palace would have been far too conspicuous. No, he must have come here on his own two feet, probably willingly, and been killed right here. Afterwards the murderer had stripped the corpse and carried away the clothing. That suggested he – and it seemed most likely to have been a man, since Percy was neither old nor feeble – had been disguised as a servant. Another of Olivia's assassins? Or one of the English guisers, perhaps someone fearing that Percy had gone too far at the tournament and exposed them all. But then why leave it so long, and why leave his corpse in Prince Arthur's bed? No, Olivia was the most likely culprit. Not that he could prove anything. Though he had no idea where the former courtesan had been all evening, he did not doubt she had been careful. She had survived too many intrigues in Venice to make a foolish mistake now.

His deliberations were interrupted by the arrival of several young courtiers, the same men who had hung back earlier and allowed Mal to escort the prince alone. Had they been bribed or coerced into doing so? It seemed too much of a coincidence otherwise – and he had walked right into the trap. Or perhaps he had just been a convenient scapegoat, and one of them would have had to draw the short straw if he had not turned up.

"What's going on here? Your Highness?" The Earl of Rutland strode across the chamber and halted with a curse, his yellow mustachios bristling. "What is this wickedness?"

"We found him like this," Mal said. "I found him–"

Rutland's eyebrows twitched. "Catlyn again. Well, well."

Time to take charge of the situation, before Rutland ordered his arrest.

"If His Highness's servants and gentlemen of the chamber had not all abandoned him, this might not have happened," Mal said, look round the assembled courtiers. "Whose turn was it to wait upon the Prince tonight?"

"Well, I..." Rutland looked put out. "I was under the impression that His Highness wished to be alone–"

"As did we all," another young man put in.

"In any case the servants are always here to attend him," Rutland said. "It is they who should be called to account."

"I am sure they shall," Mal said. "But first someone needs to take care of the Prince. I'm sure there must be other bedchambers where His Highness can be made comfortable for the night."

"Of course," replied Rutland. "I would be only too glad to surrender my own bed. Your Highness?"

Arthur looked up at last, his bloodshot eyes livid against his pale skin. "Rutland?"

"Come this way, Your Highness. My own servants will see you to bed."

He escorted the befuddled prince out through the antechamber, leaving Mal with the younger gentlemen-in-waiting. They stared at him like rabbits confronted by a fox.

"You there," Mal pointed to one at random. "Find the Earl of Northumberland and tell him the bad news. You, find the steward and ask him to make arrangements for the collection and storage of the body. You, fetch servants to strip this bed. His Highness will not want to lie in the sweat of a dead man."

The three men scattered, leaving Mal with a boy of about seventeen with red-brown hair fashionably curled about his wide brow and falling to a lovelock over his left shoulder, and the beginnings of a moustache darkening his upper lip. In other circumstances Mal would have judged him handsome; right now he looked as though he was going to be sick, though whether from the sight of the corpse on the bed or merely too much sack on an empty stomach, Mal neither knew nor cared.

"Who are you?"

"D-D-Dudley North, sir. My father is Baron North. I'm down from Cambridge for Christmas."

"Cambridge man, eh? Which college?"

"Trinity, sir." The boy looked a little less glassy-eyed. Good. Talk of everyday matters would distract him from unwholesome curiosity about the night's events.

"I'm a Peterhouse man, myself," Mal said. He put an arm about North's shoulders. "Tell me about the other gentlemen in the prince's circle."

The boy unfortunately had little knowledge of his companions, but in his youthful enthusiasm he rattled on about the games of cards they had played to while away the cold winter evenings, and the young ladies who had passed among the players, bestowing their favours on the winners.

"Not that I won many games," he said mournfully, fidgeting with the lovelock.

"And what about male visitors? Did His Highness have many of those?"

"There were a few who came along with the girls, and..." North flushed. "And were used in like fashion."

"I see. Well, don't worry, I'm not interested in who favoured which kind of whores. I'm talking about men visiting the prince on more usual business. Or pleasure. Was anyone out of the ordinary admitted to Prince Arthur's presence since you arrived?"

"There was one," North said slowly. "A dark-skinned foreign fellow, like to a Moor."

Mal breathed out. Olivia. "A young man, a eunuch singer from Princess Juliana's household?"

"I'm not sure." North bit his lip, staring deep into memory. "I think so."

"Did he talk to the prince about anything in particular?"

"Poetry, mostly. And plays. I think that was it. A lot of the time they spoke in French and I'm rotten at languages."

"Good lad, you've been very helpful."

He sent North to wait in the antechamber. The servants and gentlemen-in-waiting would be back any moment, and he had not yet searched the room for other clues. Not that he expected to find anything. Olivia was too clever for that. As for the identity of her latest pawn, plenty of courtiers had visited the princess since Olivia's arrival. Including Robert and his entire retinue. Mal cursed softly. It could be any one of a dozen men. Not that it really mattered. One did not fight the sword but the man behind it. Or in this case, the woman.

With Percy's murder, the fragile tranquility of Juliana's household was shattered once more. Prince Henry, only recently recovered from his fall at the tournament, was inconsolable, demanding his mother's presence as if he were an infant once more. Kit picked up the other boy's mood and was uncharacteristically fretful and sleepless, until Coby wondered if she should risk fetching his uncle Sandy to tend him. Perhaps it would be better to take Kit back to Southwark, away from the poisonous atmosphere at court. After all, if guiser assassins could strike even here, she and Kit would be just as safe in their own home, especially with Mal at hand to protect them. That decided it. She resolved to ask permission as soon as she caught the princess in a fair humour.

Not this morning, however. Juliana had returned from her son's apartments in a grim mood, and had already made one lady-in-waiting burst into tears with her unkind words. Coby kept her head down and concentrated on her embroidery.

When the Earl of Northumberland was announced, Coby knew it could not be good news. A moment later the earl strode into the presence chamber, his visage as dark as his mourning garb. To Coby's surprise he was accompanied by two guardsmen in royal livery of scarlet and gold.

"Percy, such a pleasure to see you," Princess Juliana cried, holding out a hand in welcome. "Please accept my condolences."

Northumberland bowed. "Alas I am not here on pleasure, Your Highness, but on my godson's business. Your son's business."

"Henry?" She got to her feet. "What? Is he unwell?"

"Nay, madam, calm yourself. Your son is as well as ever and quite recovered from his fall."

Juliana sat back down with a sigh. "What other business can he have with his mother?"

"It is not with you, Your Highness, but with Mistress Catlyn. And her son."

Coby's stomach clenched in fear. "My lord?"

"Mistress Catlyn, I must ask you to surrender your son into my custody."

"May I ask why, my lord?" It was as much as she could do to keep her voice from breaking.

"My godson requests his presence as a companion." The ladies-in-waiting gasped, and the earl smiled thinly. "I need hardly add that this is an unprecedented honour."

Coby stared at him for a long moment. "Of course, my lord. When...?"

"His Highness is impatient to meet his new playmate. I am instructed to collect him this afternoon, immediately after dinner."

"So soon...?" That would give hardly any time to alert Mal, which was undoubtedly their intention.

"Would you keep His Highness waiting?"

"N-no, of course not, my lord."

"Good." He looked her up and down. "You may accompany him to Hampton Court, to see him settled in his new lodgings. Good day, Lady Catlyn."

Northumberland bowed again, turned on his heel and left. All was silent for a moment, but as soon as the door closed behind him, the presence chamber erupted into chatter. Coby ignored the questions and congratulations as she got to her feet.

"If you will excuse me, Your Highness, I have much to do."

She barely waited for the princess's acknowledgement before fleeing the room half-blinded by tears.

Mal stared at the brief note from his wife. His son, taken into the guardianship of his worst enemy? It was not to be borne, and yet he could see no way around it. Henry might only be five years old, but he was a prince of the realm, third in line to the throne. It could not be the boy's idea, though, surely? Guiser children were precocious, but not by so much that they could make strategies like an adult. This was more of Olivia's scheming, he was certain of it. With Percy out of the way she was free to take control of the young prince and bring the entire country under her thumb. Mal shivered. He had taken Venice from her, and now she had taken his son in return.

Footsteps sounded on the stairs outside. Sandy. Mal's heart sank. How was he going to explain to his brother? He got to his feet, shoving the note into his pocket.

"Sandy–"

"I heard," his brother said. "I spoke to Susanna as she left."

He sat down on the edge of the bed, shoulders slumped.

"I will go to court." Mal picked up his rapier and began fastening the hanger about his hips. "If I petition Robert–"

"No."

"No?" He stared at Sandy. "They've taken my son. Your *amayi*."

"As a hostage against our good behaviour. As long as we make no further move against them, they will not harm him."

"And we can be certain of that, can we?"

"If they harm him, he becomes useless to them."

"Sandy, this is Kit we're talking about. He's my son, not a pawn in some game."

"No, he is Kiiren. Our one true ally in the fight against them." Sandy got to his feet. "He rescued us from Jathekkil. Or had you forgotten?"

"He doesn't even remember who he is; you saw to that. And he's still a child."

"He is *tjirzadh*, more than a century old. Childhood is but a passing phase for us, sweet but brief."

Mal shook his head. *He is a child. My child. Not of my flesh, perhaps, but of my heart.*

"We can get him back," he said. "Take him far away from here, somewhere they'll leave us alone."

"Will they? And in any case, what will you tell Kiiren in ten years' time, when he is old enough to learn the truth? That we were too craven to fight the guisers, and left England to their mercy? I thought you wanted them gone?"

"I do. But how do we fight them with Kit as their hostage?"

Sandy spread his hands. "We don't."

"So you're just going to let Olivia take him from you? Let them win?"

"No. We wait, and watch. Kiiren wants the renegades defeated as much as anyone, and as the childhood friend of their leader he will be better placed than anyone to work against them from the inside. Let them think they have won; then, when their guard is down, we will use this over-reaching blow against them."

"It could be years–"

"Yes, yes, it will. But *tjirzadheneth* plan for the long term, and so must we."

"I used to think we were so alike," Mal said. "But you're not even human any more. You've become as cold and heartless as they are."

"I am one of them. And so are you."

Don't remind me. "Well I don't care what you think. I'm going to get my son back, one way or another."

"No."

Sandy closed the space between them and took Mal's head in both hands. Mal swallowed, feeling the pressure of Sandy's mind against his own. If his brother tried to coerce him using his magic, could he stop him? For long moments they stood there, eye to eye, the roiling storm of his brother's frustration and... yes, grief beating against his resolve, then with a sudden movement Sandy threw him across the bed. Mal rolled, fighting the instinct to draw his dagger.

"Stop it, Sandy! You're playing into their hands, letting them turn us against one another."

"I am not Alexander. I am Erishen." He was weeping now, tears rolling down his cheeks to disappear into his beard.

"I know. And you love Kiiren and want nothing more than to protect him. All right, I'll trust you. But if anything happens to him, even a hint of mistreatment, I will fight my way into the prince's household and take him by force. Do you understand?"

Sandy nodded. "The guisers cannot keep you from him; it would look too suspicious. And if they harm him, I will know at once."

"I will wait," Mal said, half to himself. "But not forever."

PART TWO

"I can add colours to the chameleon,
Change shapes with Proteus for advantages,
And set the murderous Machiavel to school.
Can I do this, and cannot get a crown?
Tut, were it farther off, I'll pluck it down."
William Shakespeare, HENRY VI, part III

CHAPTER XX

Kit stole a glance out of the schoolroom window. Such a beautiful spring morning, with fat clouds scudding across the sky like the white sails of ships. Perhaps they would be allowed a game of cricket before dinner, if it didn't rain again. Not that he was very good at cricket, but being outdoors was better than history lessons. He could pretend the bat was a belaying pin and the bails his beloved ship *Unicorn* that he had to protect from enemy fire. It was his duty as captain, after all.

His daydream was interrupted by the *thwack!* of Master Weston's cane on the lectern.

"*Eduarde Princeps.*" Weston's cane pointed at twelve year-old Prince Edward. "*Ubi Francogallos vicit Henricus Quintus?*"

The prince stared down at his ink-stained fingers as if the answer was written on them. Weston tapped his cane on his palm. In the distance a bell began to toll, over and over, as if counting out the minutes it would take the prince to answer.

Edward swallowed. "*Anno millesimo… quinqua… um… quadri–*"

Thwack!

The schoolmaster's eyes narrowed. "How long have I been teaching you, Your Highness?"

"F-five years, sir."

"And yet you still have as poor a grasp of history – and Latin – as young Catlyn there," Weston pointed his cane at Kit, "who is scarcely more than seven years old."

"I am sorry, sir."

Edward really did appear sorry, and his face fell further when Weston beckoned forward William Neville, the prince's companion and proxy. Kit swallowed against the taste of bile and tried not to wince as the cane whistled down. Neville stuffed his fist in his mouth to muffle a sob; Prince Edward had already made several mistakes this morning. Kit was glad Henry was a lot better at his lessons than his older brother, otherwise it would be him up there with a tender arse.

Something damp hit Kit's temple and plopped onto the desk in front of him. A tiny paper pellet soaked in ink. He lifted his hand to his brow and his fingers came away stained black. He knew it was de Vere, even without looking, and he knew which one of them would get the blame if they were caught horsing around. Kit slipped his hand into his pocket, drew out his handkerchief and did his best to wipe the ink off whilst pretending to blow his nose.

Master Weston straightened up with a grunt of satisfaction and gestured impatiently at Neville, who got to his feet and limped back to his desk. The schoolmaster cast his eye over his pupils. Kit shrank down on his bench, hoping to be overlooked.

"*Henrice Princeps?*" Weston gestured to Edward's young brother and repeated his earlier question.

"*Ad proelium Asincurtense, magister.*"

"Very good, Your Highness. Though I think it was no challenge for you. Perhaps something more difficult?"

Before the schoolmaster could frame his next question, however, the schoolroom door burst open to reveal a tall man whom Kit did not recognise. From his embroidered and lace-trimmed clothing and rich jewellery, Kit took him to be a courtier. He leant on a stick, though he was not a very old man like Master Weston.

"May I help you, my lord?" the schoolmaster quavered, bowing low as the man limped past him to kneel awkwardly before the princes.

"Your Highnesses, I bring grave news," the man said. "Your grandmother Queen Elizabeth is dead, and your father is now King."

Edward turned pale and put a hand to his mouth. "Then…"

"You're Prince of Wales," his brother said with a grin. "Like Father was until just now."

The new heir to the throne got to his feet. "Thank you, Suffolk."

"His Majesty sent me to bring you to him," the duke told the princes. "This way, Your Highnesses."

The moment the door closed, the remaining boys burst into excited chatter.

"Gentlemen, quiet!" Master Weston glared at them. "This is not a fairground. You will continue with your lessons until I receive instructions as to what to do with the rest of you. De Vere, read the next page of the text. Catlyn, Sidney, pay attention. I will be asking questions at the end."

"Sir?" Kit put up his hand.

"Yes, Catlyn?"

"Will we be allowed to play cricket before dinner, sir?"

"Cricket? Certainly not. No cricket, no bowling, no riding for pleasure. The court will be in mourning until the King's coronation."

"And when will that be, sir?" De Vere asked.

"Not for several months, I expect. The Queen's funeral must come first, then preparations have to be made…"

Kit slumped down on his bench, not listening to the rest. Months and months without riding or games? This was going to be the worst summer ever.

Mal stared down at the pile of sketches on the table under the parlour window. Each showed a different design for wooden wall panelling: linenfold, squares enclosing decorative roundels, Roman arches, rectangles with smaller rectangles inside…

"I care not which, so long as it is not too dear," he said at last. "Pick out three or four of the most economical and send the sketches to my wife in London."

"Of course, sir." The architect gathered up the drawings into his satchel with a sniff of disappointment at his employer's indifference. "And the bathing chamber…?"

"Glazed tiles, I think. I may indulge my brother's whims so far, but imported marble is an unnecessary expense."

"Tiles it is, sir. I shall have some samples–" he glanced at Mal "–sent to your wife along with the sketches."

"Good man."

The architect made his obeisance and left, thankfully closing the door behind him. With the carpenters now at work on the main staircase, one could hardly hear oneself think for the racket of hammer and saw all day long. Mal stared through the window at the falling rain. If the weather were fairer he would have gone for a ride around the estate, but after a long, wet spring the hillside paths were little more than torrents of mud and half-rotted leaves.

Five long years since it had burnt to the ground, and at last Rushdale Hall was almost as good as new. Better, in fact, though he had resisted his architect's suggestion of extending the foundations and rebuilding in the latest style, all glass and stucco. Honest red bricks had been good enough for his father and grandfather; they would be good enough for his descendants. If, please God, Kit ever came home.

The grate of hooves on the gravel drive brought him to his feet. Through the rain-blurred glass he made out a cloaked figure dismounting, his right arm held awkwardly out of the way. Mal grinned and headed out into the hall, blinking against the clouds of sawdust filling the air.

"Ned!"

His old friend shrugged out of his sodden cloak and stepped into Mal's welcoming embrace. Mal stifled a sob in his throat, unprepared for the rush of joy that swept through his heart and set it aglow like a cloud lit from behind by the sun. Dear God, he had missed the comfort of a familiar body pressed against his own.

"You can let me go now." Ned's voice came muffled against his shoulder.

"Right. Sorry."

He released Ned and showed him through into the parlour, hiding his discomfiture in pleasantries.

"Most of the house is still unfurnished," he said, suddenly aware of how cramped and dark his temporary quarters were. "I had the one surviving bedstead brought in here, since it had the first fireplace to be finished. Come, get out of those wet clothes and warm yourself. I have spare linen enough for the both of us."

Whilst Ned stripped by the fire, Mal fetched dry clothing and a blanket from the press and filled a pewter jug with wine to warm over the flames.

"If you're here to tell me about the Queen, I already know," he said at last, pulling up a stool.

Ned grimaced as he peeled off a soaking wet stocking and added it the pile on the floor. "Bad news travels fast."

"Not bad news for Robert. He must have thought he would never get to wear the crown."

"True enough."

"So why are you here? It…" He swallowed. "It's not Kit, is it?"

"No. At least, I've not heard anything, from Sandy or your wife."

Ned wrapped the blanket around his shoulders and sat down by the fire to warm his naked flesh. Mal noticed he sat hunched over to one side; no doubt his maimed limb was causing him pain in this weather. He poured wine for them both, and passed Ned a cup. The heat seeped through the metal, not quite hot enough to burn his fingers.

"What, then? It's a long way to come for a drink and a chat."

"I'm to fetch you back to London."

"Oh." Mal rolled the cup between his palms. "And what if I refuse?"

"You can't sulk up here forever, you know."

"I'm not sulking, I have work to do."

"I don't see you sawing timbers or climbing the scaffolding." Ned gestured around the room, from the ranks of burnt-down candles on the mantelpiece to the drifts of paper covering the table and sliding down onto the floor. "In fact it looks to me like you've hardly stirred from your den all winter."

"You wouldn't know a Derbyshire winter if it bowed and introduced itself. I reckon this is the first time you've ever been north of Islington."

"Don't change the subject. Are you coming down to London or not?"

"I don't suppose you'll give me a moment's peace until I say yes, will you?"

Ned grinned. "You know me too well."

"All right, all right. Give me a day to set my affairs in order, and after that I shall be entirely at your disposal."

It took the rest of that day and most of the one after to go through his papers and make sure that his steward and foreman were well-versed in what needed to be done over the summer, but at last Mal ran out of excuses. He packed his saddlebags the following morning in a haze of dread. What if Coby refused to see him? What if she didn't? He had no idea what he was going to say to her after all this time. And then there was Kit. Mal had visited him last autumn and found him well but distant. Was Henry winning the boy over at last?

He found Ned waiting in the stable yard, his own horse and Mal's old gelding Hector already saddled and ready to go. Ned's expression was guarded, as if he feared Mal would change his mind at the last minute. Mal forced a smile, surprised himself with a genuine feeling of lighthearted anticipation.

"To London!" he cried, springing into the saddle.

Hector tossed his head, glad to stretch his legs after winter idleness. Ned fell in at Mal's side and they rode down the valley together in companionable silence. Mal recalled with a pang the many times he and Coby had ridden thus on Walsingham's business in France. They should have stayed there and never come back to England. Then perhaps the two of them and Kit would still be together. He swallowed against the gathering melancholy, lest Ned think he had undergone a change of heart.

The weather turned colder as they went south, as if winter itself had returned to grieve for the Queen. They arrived in London one April morning to find the city quieter than Mal had ever seen it. Windows were shuttered tight against the numbing cold, rags stuffed into the cracks to keep the wind out. Rows of icicles, some more than a foot long, hung from the eaves and dripped onto the travellers beneath. The few Londoners they passed barely looked up as they hurried along on their own business, muffled in hats and hoods and the thickest cloaks they possessed.

Mal and Ned parted ways at Saint Paul's, Ned going south to get a wherry back to Bankside whilst Mal continued westward through Ludgate and along the Strand to Whitehall. The approach to the palace was only a little more lively than the rest of the city, with a line of black-clad citizens braving the weather to pay their respects to the dead Queen. Under the gateway, torches burned in sconces even at midday and the friendly red-gold glow of braziers spilled out of the guardroom. Mal dismounted and gave his business, and Hector was led away to the stables.

Queen Juliana's household was lodged in the same rooms as before, on the far side of the formal gardens. Mal was shown up to an antechamber, cold and echoing. He ignored the empty hearth and the benches along the tapestry-covered walls, and instead went to stand at one of the windows looking out over the Thames. Some distance to his right Westminster Stairs jutted out into the river, boats moored to poles set along either side, like the gondolas of Venice. It was there that the ambassador's barge had been stopped and Mal himself arrested for assaulting Blaise Grey. Had it really been ten years ago? It felt like yesterday and half a lifetime, all at once.

The sound of a door opening came from his left and he turned, expecting to see a visitor leaving the presence chamber, or perhaps a servant coming to invite him in.

"My lord." His wife curtsied deeply.

Mourning garb suited her ill, with her pale hair caught back too tight under the black lace cap.

He bowed in response. "My lady."

They stood there for a long moment, each waiting for the other to make the next move. When did our marriage become a duel? *When you took your brother's part instead of hers*, a traitorous voice in his head replied.

"I trust your journey was not too tiresome, my lord."

"I had not expected such a frosty reception from my old home, but I shall weather it."

More silence.

"Mina–"

She flushed a little at his use of her pet name. "I suppose you have come for a report on your son."

"Our son." As soon as the words left his mouth, he realised it was the wrong thing to say.

"Not mine. As you made very clear. And as for a report, I can tell you little more than he says in his letters. You might do better to visit him yourself."

"I intend to do that. But..." He looked down at the floor, unable to meet her gaze. "I wanted to see you first."

When she did not answer, he glanced up – and saw her eyes shining with tears. He crossed the room in swift strides and knelt at her feet.

"Jacomina, please, forgive me. I cannot unmake my choices, so what good does it do to fight over them?"

He felt her hand on his head, then her fingers slid down his cheek and under his chin, pressing gently so that he had to look up.

"If you want to reconcile with me," she said as their eyes met, "you will free Kit."

He glanced towards the door and got to his feet. He had been expecting such a condition, and in truth his own heart had been urging him to do the same for a long time. What good would it do to save England or rebuild his home, if he lost everyone he loved?

"It will take careful planning," he said in a low voice, leading her away from the door and any twitching ears on the other side. "We cannot risk our enemies so much as suspecting what we are up to, or they might threaten him."

"How long...?" she whispered.

"I don't know. Not until after the funeral. Perhaps not until after the coronation. If we cause trouble before Robert is crowned, the guisers might use that to their advantage."

She nodded. "I have waited four years. I can wait four months."

Footsteps sounded in the next room, and they stepped apart. Mal snapped a curt bow to his wife and strode to the outer door without a backward glance. Like Orpheus leaving the underworld, except that he would not risk everything for one last sight of his beloved wife's face. More lives than their own were at stake this time.

Coby made her excuses to the queen, saying she had a headache, and fled to her bedchamber. She had been dreading this meeting ever since she had sent Ned to Derbyshire, and now it was over she was at a loss as to what to do next. She was not about to forgive Mal for what he had done, but touching him, looking into his eyes, she had very nearly weakened and kissed him. Even now she ached to run after him, tell him she still loved him… She brushed away tears with the heel of her hand. Loved him, yes, but could she ever trust him again?

"My lady?" Susanna's voice came softly from the doorway.

Coby took a deep breath, then another, before she dared speak.

"Bring me some wine. And the tincture of valerian."

"Yes, my lady."

By the time the Venetian girl returned, Coby had regained a semblance of calm, but she dripped the medicine into her wine nonetheless. Taking a seat by the window she sipped the tart liquid whilst Susanna bustled about the bedchamber, folding clean linen and putting it away in the press.

Coby sighed. Only three weeks into the period of official mourning and the already tedious court routine had turned into a cage of empty ritual. Even their daily prayers felt more like a burden than a release, which only added to her guilt and frustration.

"I'm not bothering you, am I, my lady?"

"No, not at all." Coby lowered her wine cup into her lap. "Come and sit down."

"My lady?"

Coby waved her over, and the girl complied, perching on the edge of the window seat as if ready to flee at a moment's notice.

"I know I have not been the best of mistresses of late," she began, staring down into her cup, "and I am sorry for that. But I hope that one day soon all our worries will be over."

"Master Cristoforo…" Susanna whispered.

"Yes." She looked up and smiled. "We must be patient, as we have been these past four years, but yes, God willing my son will be returned to us."

"But how?"

"That I cannot tell you. But I wanted you to know…" Because you are my only true friend in all this, she wanted to add. But a lady did not speak so candidly to servants. "Leave me. I think I shall sleep a while."

When the girl had gone, Coby drained the cup and set it down on the table. *A lady I may be now, but I never wanted to be one, and it has brought me no happiness. If this venture fails and we yet live, perhaps I shall become Jacob again and make my own way in the world once more. A life of poverty and peril is better than another year in this cage.*

Mal did not go straight to see Kit after visiting his wife. First he returned to the Sign of the Parley, and a reunion with his brother. He was expecting the haggard appearance of a man who had been spending too much time dreamwalking, but Sandy looked surprisingly well, if a little… unorthodox. He was clean-shaven again and had let his hair grow long, even going as far as to braid a few sections as he had done when living on Sark with Kiiren.

"I take it you've been spending time with the skraylings," Mal said, sitting down at the kitchen table.

"Adjaan has sailed back to Vinland with young Hretjaar," Sandy replied. "Until her replacement arrives, the skraylings have no outspeaker, so I have been deputised."

"The elders trust you with such a role? I thought we were abominations in their eyes?"

Sandy shrugged. "Sekharhjarret persuaded the other elders that they needed a liaison with the English more than ever, now that the

Queen is dead. And none of them speak enough of your tongue to pass muster at court."

Mal tried not to boggle at the idea of his unsubtle brother manoeuvring the tricky currents of Prince – now King – Robert's court.

"Perhaps I can use your new-found diplomatic talents," he said. "I want to see Kit."

He had already decided not to bring up his agreement with Coby until after the visit. Sandy was bound to object, and Mal was not willing to wait to see his son, nor to risk arousing the guisers' suspicions by being openly at odds with his brother.

"Now?"

"No time like the present. But dress like an Englishman, will you? We don't want to forcibly remind Prince Henry that we're hand-in-glove with the skraylings."

He took his saddlebags up to his old room and washed his face, and a few minutes later Sandy appeared at the door. He had combed out his braids and was wearing a wine-red doublet and hose, knee-length riding boots and a black velvet cap.

"Much better," Mal said, and led the way downstairs.

At Whitehall Palace they were admitted to the princes' chambers with surprising readiness. Mal couldn't help wondering if this was some stratagem of Henry's designed to throw them off-balance, or simply boyish impatience. Either way Mal intended to spend as little time in the princes' company as possible, lest any suspicion of his intent become apparent. He hoped he might be able to talk privily with Kit, however, and glean as much about his situation as possible before deciding on a plan.

The princes' antechamber had been pressed into service as a schoolroom, though it looked more like a battlefield at the moment. A line of chairs had been arranged at one end, and Prince Henry stood on the middle one, waving a wooden sword. A handful of other boys crouched in front of the improvised battlements, arguing among themselves. Mal caught something about "the heads of our enemies" before the princes' tutor, a thin-faced man with a shock of white hair, clapped his hands and called the boys to attention.

Prince Henry glared at Mal and Sandy. For a moment Mal thought that Jathekkil would get the better of him, but Henry was evidently in more control of himself than he had been as an infant. Instead he merely thrust his wooden sword through his belt and watched them, arms folded.

It was his elder brother, Edward, who addressed them.

"Gentlemen, what brings you here?"

Mal swept a low bow. "With your permission, Your Highness, I would like to speak to my son. In private."

"Very well." The prince gestured for Kit to rise.

Kit got to his feet but said nothing, only stared at the floor. Mal's heart sank. Had Henry broken his spirit after all?

"Catlyn!" The schoolmaster brought his springy cane down on a pile of books with a sharp thwack. Mal had to suppress his own urge to snap to attention. "Bid your father and uncle good day."

"Yes, Master Weston."

"In Latin, boy!"

"*Etiam, magister.*" Kit bowed, though he still did not meet Mal's eye. "*Salvete, pater et… patrue.*"

Mal returned the bow. "*Salve, mi fili.*"

"You are excused from your lessons, Catlyn," Weston added. "For one half hour."

The other boys groaned in envy until a snap from Weston's cane brought them back to order. Sandy made to cross the space to Kit's side, but Mal shook his head. He held out a hand, and Kit walked slowly towards him.

"It's been a long time, son," Mal said, putting an arm around Kit's shoulder and leading him towards the door.

Sandy closed in on his other side and tentatively ruffled the boy's hair. Kit looked up sharply, and Sandy withdrew his hand, a hurt expression in his eyes.

"Give him time," Mal murmured to his brother. He looked down at Kit. "You've grown so much I hardly recognised you."

Kit said nothing.

"Shall we go along to the gallery?" Mal said as the doors closed behind them. "It's a little cold outside to walk in the park."

"The girls walk in the gallery."

"Oh, well, we wouldn't want to disturb them, would we? How about the library, then? I think I saw a globe in there."

Kit shrugged, which Mal took for as much agreement as he was likely to get.

They made their way downstairs in silence, through a parlour where a handful of elderly courtiers snored by the fire, to the prince's library. Mal closed the double doors carefully behind them.

"How are you enjoying your lessons?" he asked.

Kit shrugged again, then glanced shyly up at him. "I like the *Odyssey*. We've just started reading it in Greek."

"The *Odyssey*? I always preferred the *Iliad*." Mal sat down by the globe. "What about you, Sandy?"

"I liked the plays, especially *The Birds*, with all the singing and dancing. I think they must have reminded me of home. Of Vinland."

Mal shot him a glance. Was he planning to awaken Kiiren? That was the last thing he needed.

"And the princes?" Mal quickly changed the subject. "Are they good companions?"

"Edward will be king one day. I will gladly serve him."

The boy had been well schooled, he had to give them that. "And Henry?"

Kit's eyes widened and he glanced from his father to his uncle and back again. Mal gave an inward sigh of relief. They did not own him, then.

"I do not ask you to say anything disloyal," he told Kit. "But you do not like him as well as his brother, is that it?"

Kit nodded, his mouth twisting in misery. Mal leaned over and kissed his brow.

"The boys at school used to tease me a lot too. But we are stronger than that, eh?"

Kit nodded again.

"Well." Mal clapped his hands together. "Enough of such gloomy thoughts. How about a game of Hoodman Blind? I think Uncle Sandy should go first."

They improvised a hood by pulling Sandy's hat down over his eyes, and Kit dodged around him, giggling. Sandy eventually caught him and made a play of not knowing whether it was Mal or Kit, which earned him some scorn from his nephew.

"Well if you're so clever, you can take a turn," Sandy said, and plopped the hat onto Kit's head. It didn't need much pulling down to obscure his vision.

Kit soon caught Mal and pulled him down onto his knees so that he could touch his face. Now, here was a dilemma: would Kit remember that his uncle was clean-shaven, or should Mal give him a clue? Kit chewed his bottom lip for a moment.

"Father," he said at last and pulled the hat off, grinning.

"How did you know?"

"I heard your sword scrape on the floor when you knelt down."

Mal laughed. "You knew all along? So why all the face-patting?"

Kit said nothing, only threw himself into Mal's arms. Mal hugged him back, tears pricking his eyes.

"I missed you too, son."

CHAPTER XXI

King Robert spared no expense on his mother's funeral, perhaps not wanting to be thought ungracious for having to wait so long for his throne. The horses drawing the hearse were draped in black velvet decorated with embroidered plaques of the royal arms, as was the lead coffin in which the late queen's body lay. Lady Frances Grey, as wife of the preeminent peer of the realm, led the procession of mourners along the short route from Whitehall Palace to Westminster Abbey. The surrounding houses were packed with onlookers leaning out of doors and windows, some even perched on the rooftops clinging to the gutter, and all weeping and sighing as if their own mother were in the coffin passing below. The funeral service was plainer than the Queen herself might have preferred, but no one could accuse it of lacking dignity, and the coffin was at last laid to rest in the vault of her father King Henry, until such time as a fitting monument could be constructed.

In the weeks that followed, Mal plotted the rescue of his son. The coronation procession would no doubt start from the Tower of London as was traditional, which meant a brief period of them all being lodged there together: himself, Sandy, Coby and Kit. Tempting as it was to make use of that proximity, he knew that the Tower guard would be more watchful than usual with so many important guests under their protection. No, it was at the banquet after the ceremony that their best chance lay. Everyone's guard would be down, and they could slip away together unnoticed. All he had to do was arrange for a swift boat to be waiting to take them downriver to Deptford and they could be on a skrayling ship to Sark before they were even missed.

And from there, who knew? Perhaps even as far as the New World. That was the one place the guisers would never follow them.

By the day of the coronation the Queen's household was as restless as Coby had ever known it. Or perhaps it was her own impatience to be out of the Tower and putting Mal's plan into action. Quite what his plan was she did not know, and he had refused to tell her, saying it was better she did not know in case Olivia caught a glimpse of her dreams. The thought of that woman poking around in her mind made Coby shudder, and she readily agreed to Mal's terms. All she knew was that he and Sandy would make their move at the coronation feast, and that she was to stay as close to Kit as possible. Were they planning to spirit her away, as Sandy had done to Mal from these very apartments ten years ago? It seemed unlikely with so many guisers around, but perhaps Mal was relying on the skraylings to back him up for once.

"Lady Catlyn?"

"Hmm? Oh, sorry!"

Coby finished lacing up the back of Queen Juliana's gown and stepped out of the way of the other ladies-in-waiting. As the lowliest of the Queen's attendants she got all the least popular tasks, particularly once the other ladies found out how good she was at mending.

"Why so serious?" Lady Derby whispered, nudging her in the ribs.

"A little tired, that's all," Coby lied.

"Not long now," her companion replied, as if reading her thoughts. "I shall be so glad to get out of this dreary old place. The traitors and the ravens are welcome to it."

The Queen stepped into her shoes, then the two of them knelt to restore the folds of her skirts to their former neatness.

"It's traditional," Coby said as they resumed their places at a discreet distance. Every English king since King William's day had started his coronation procession from the Tower.

"I heard a most alarming rumour about these apartments," Lady Derby whispered, glancing about the bedchamber. "They say the skrayling ambassador slept in this very room. In that very bed."

Coby suppressed a smile. Not in that bed, or so her husband had told her. The ambassador was not accustomed to English fashions, and had preferred the servant's bed on the floor. "So I believe."

"Were you here for the ambassador's arrival?"

"Alas, no." Another lie. She was hardly about to confess to masquerading as a boy, apprenticed to a theatre company. "It was before... before Sir Maliverny and I met."

Just saying his name brought back the pain of their separation. Only a few more hours, and his promise would be put to the test.

"Hard to believe it was ten years ago," Lady Derby said. "I wasn't at court then, of course, being but a girl."

They watched in silence as other ladies draped heavy ropes of pearl about the Queen's neck and fastened an elaborate standing collar of gauze and lace and beadwork to the back of her gown. Diamonds and gold thread winked in the sunlight reflecting off the Thames. Coby found herself unconsciously smoothing her gown, and clasped her hands in front of her. After so many weeks in drab black it was a relief to be wearing pale colours again, even if she couldn't help fretting about soiling the fine silk. Old habits died hard.

At last the Queen was ready and there was nothing left but to wait until they were summoned down to the outer ward to mount their palfreys. Some of the ladies offered to play cards with the Queen in the dining chamber, a suggestion Juliana gladly agreed to. Coby was debating whether or not to join them when a knock came at the door leading to the Wakefield Tower, on the other side of the ward. She crossed the room and opened the door a crack.

"Kit, what are you doing here?"

"Mother, can I come in?"

Coby looked around, but the bedchamber was now empty.

"Of course, sweetheart. What is it?" As Kit came through into the light, she took in his flushed features and over-bright eyes. "Have you been fighting with the other boys again?"

"No, Mother. But look what Father gave me for my saint's day!"

He turned his slender body to display a swept-hilt sword, the very image of his father's rapier in miniature, hanging from his left hip. Coby forced a smile. Dear Lord, how quickly they grow up!

"I hope it's not sharp," she said.

Kit pulled a face. "Father said it had to be blunted in case I hurt one of the princes and got sent to the Tower for good."

"Well, he's right. It's not a toy. And you know your Ten Commandments."

"I know. 'Thou shalt not kill.' But Father has killed men, hasn't he?"

"Only to protect the people he loves."

"Then it's all right for me to kill people too. If someone was hurting you, or Father, or Uncle Sandy."

"No!"

"Then why did Father give me a sword?"

"Because it's the mark of a gentleman to wear one."

"Why?"

"Because lesser men are not permitted to."

"Why?"

Coby sighed in exasperation. "Because then they would always be killing one another in the streets and God would be angry. Now run along before you're missed."

"Yes, Mother." He flashed a grin at her and disappeared through the door.

So like his father. She smiled to herself, and went to sit with the other ladies. Tonight could not come soon enough.

The inner ward looked like a cross between an army muster and a fairground, hundreds of people and horses milling around in a chaotic swirl of colour and noise. Mal guided Hector into line at the top of the slope leading down to the outer ward, in the second rank of courtiers behind the King's party. Sandy took his place at Mal's left hand, looking less assured on his mount. They were dressed identically in dark red damask, with only Sandy's clean-shaven chin and longer hair to tell them apart. Mal would rather have worn black, all the better to pass unnoticed on their escape from the palace, but black was the one colour that had been banned from this joyous occasion.

Below him the highest peers of the realm escorted their monarch to his coronation: the tall figure of Blaise Grey stood out at the head of the file on the King's left, and the King's younger brother, Prince Arthur, on the right, his copper-coloured hair bright in the morning sunlight. Robert himself looked every inch the king, draped in an ermine-trimmed red velvet cloak that fell over the haunches of his mount almost to the ground. Mal wondered idly what they would do if and when the horse relieved itself during the procession. The King could hardly walk into the abbey stinking of horse shit.

As Mal watched, the King turned to share a jest with the Earl of Northumberland and a fold of his cloak fell back. Sunlight flashed on gold-chased armour for a moment, and Mal had to blink away the spots dancing before his eyes. Armour, for a coronation? Robert seemed determined to hammer home to his subjects that they were ruled by a man once more, not a cautious old woman. He certainly sounded pleased with himself, as well he might, having gained by birth what his father and grandfather had both attempted by force and failed: the throne of England.

Behind the King, other senior courtiers rode either side of the two young princes, who were followed by their own escort of companions, including Kit. Mal smiled fondly at the sight of his son sitting so straight and proud on his little grey pony, the new sword on his hip. He noticed however that the other boys scarcely spoke to him. Had they noticed anything strange about him, or were they merely contemptuous of the son of a mere gentleman riding amongst them? Royal favour could be a two-edged sword.

At last trumpets sounded and the procession began to move out through the gate under the Bloody Tower, the horses' hooves rattling and slipping on the ancient cobbles. Hector tossed his head, unhappy with the combination of crowds and treacherous footing, and Mal patted him reassuringly on the neck. The cavalcade turned right at the bottom of the slope, where the Queen's party was waiting to follow behind them. Mal glanced over his shoulder, hoping to see Coby, but she was probably somewhere at the back behind the Queen's litter. Still, he was glad to know she was not far away. Perhaps after the coronation ceremony she would be able to sit with him and Sandy and Kit at the feast. It had been far too long since they ate together as a family. Too long since they had been together at all.

The procession moved slowly through the outer ward, out of the main gates and up the long causeway to the gatehouse. The lions in the menagerie watched them pass with languid amber eyes, the huge male flicking his tail idly at the flies buzzing around the bloody remains of his breakfast. From beyond the outer curtain wall of the castle came the muted rumble of voices, rising to a crescendo of cheers as the first mounted figures emerged from the shadows of the gatehouse. A few moments later Mal and Sandy rode into that same echoing darkness, and out again into the blinding light of a July morning. Mal blinked and shaded his eyes–

A shot rang out, echoing around the nearby stone walls. A woman screamed. Mal urged Hector forward, towards Kit.

"The King! The King is down!"

The orderly procession dissolved into a rout, riders scattering into the screaming crowds or turning their horses back against the relentless tide of courtiers still crossing the causeway. Another shot, more muffled this time. Mal scooped a startled Kit off his pony and passed him to Sandy, then turned Hector back towards the gatehouse.

"Stop the procession!" he shouted at them. "Get the Queen and the princesses back into the Tower!"

A familiar slender figure vaulted down from her palfrey and ran to the Queen's litter, shouting instructions at the bearers. Mal smiled. Trust his wife to take charge in a crisis. He gazed past the Queen's party, and groaned. The causeway was blocked by dozens of liveried guards bearing partizans. They were trapped here, and who knew how many more assassins lurked in the streets outside the Tower, waiting to pick off any royal target they spotted.

"Stay here," he told Sandy. "Get Kit into the gatehouse if you can."

His brother dismounted and led his horse under the gatehouse arch, and Mal steered Hector through the press towards where he had last seen the princes. To his relief Northumberland had mustered a cordon of men around Edward and Henry, backing them against the blank curtain wall in the shadow of the gatehouse. Edward's mouth was set in a taut line, as if he was readying himself for battle; Henry looked wary but calm. When the younger prince noticed Mal looking his way he smiled slowly, and Mal's blood ran cold. *Dear God, have I misjudged so badly, expecting Jathekkil to wait for his throne?*

"Don't just stand there, Catlyn!" Grey loomed over him, eyes blazing. "Get down to the quayside and commandeer the largest skiff you can find. Quickly, or the King may die."

Kit watched his father leave, swallowing past the lump in his own throat. What was happening? Had someone shot the King? He couldn't see much from here, even high up on his uncle's horse. Lots of splendidly dressed men were riding back and forth, like a tapestry picture of a battle come to life, but in the stories no one ever talked about the screaming. Kit wanted to put his fingers in his ears, but that would mean letting go of the reins. He looked around for Uncle Sandy, but it was dark under the gatehouse and all the women were screaming...

Movement caught his eye, and he turned back to the scene outside the castle gates. It was too bright out there to see properly, but he thought he saw a group of men riding towards him, their faces grim. Kit drew his sword. It was all right to kill people to protect your loved ones. He gripped the hilt tighter.

"Out of the way, you addle-pated knave! Make way for the Prince of Wales!"

Kit tried to steer his horse out of the men's path, but the gelding whinnied and stamped its feet. Kit grabbed for the mane with both hands, forgetting he was holding the sword. The horse reared as the blade slapped into its neck and Kit slid backwards, screaming – into the arms of his mother.

"There, I've got you." She set Kit down on his feet and slapped Hector's rump, sending him charging towards the princes' party.

"What in God's name do you think you're doing, woman!"

"Protecting the Queen," Kit's mother shouted back. "Come along, Kit."

She guided him towards a door in the archway. Prince Henry's big sisters were already there, trying to walk and cling to one another at the same time. Kit heard a laugh behind him.

"Go on, Catlyn, go with the other girls."

It was de Vere, Kit was sure of it, though he could not see the older boy in the darkness. He looked away, not wanting them to see his flushed cheeks. If only Father hadn't taken him from his pony, he'd be with the princes now, not shut away with the girls. It wasn't fair.

"Where's Uncle Sandy?" Kit asked as his mother hurried him into the gatehouse. "I want to go back to Father."

"And your father wants you safe in here. Come along."

Mal jogged back up Tower Hill, pushing his way through the remaining crowds. Some of the citizenry had fled in panic, but most seemed more interested in finding out what would happen next. At last he reached a cordon of Tower guardsmen, holding back the throng with levelled partizans. One of them pointed his weapon at Mal.

"Let me through, you fool. Or would you rather the King died?"

He was saved from further argument by Lord Grey beckoning him over. The guardsman muttered an apology and let him through.

The space inside the cordon was empty but for a knot of men surrounding the King, who had been laid on his crumpled velvet cloak. All his fine armour had been removed apart from the pieces covering his right leg. The padding of deep red quilted silk covering the rest of his body looked unpleasantly like flayed flesh. Mal tore his gaze away and addressed Prince Arthur, who was kneeling by his brother.

"Your Highness?"

Arthur's head jerked up. His fine-boned visage was pale as paper. "What is it?"

"Your Highness, I have a boat waiting to take the King to the palace."

When the prince did not immediately respond, Blaise Grey answered for him.

"Thank you, Catlyn. Come, let us clear the way."

Mal followed him back to the cordon. Grey shouted orders to the guards, who parted in the centre and began pushing the crowd apart, wielding the butts of their partizans against the more reluctant.

"Make way for King Robert! Make way for the King!"

For a moment Mal feared the crowd would fight back. If that happened, God help His Majesty. But at last they began to move, shuffling back against the curtain wall and the houses opposite to stand with heads respectfully bowed as their king was carried past.

Mal led the sorry procession down to the quayside, and the King was carefully lifted into the waiting skiff. To Mal's surprise, Grey did not get into the boat.

"You and I have work to do," he said in a low voice. "How much did you see of the assassin?"

"Nothing, my lord. I was too far back, and the light was in my eyes. Why, what happened?"

Grey gave him a strange look. "Find your brother. Quickly. And when you do, bring him to Seething Lane."

"Yes, my lord."

Mal soon found Sandy, and they arrived in Seething Lane on the heels of a peculiar little procession consisting of several Tower guards carrying a long, heavy bundle, with Grey bringing up the rear.

"The assassin's body?"

Grey looked from Mal to Sandy, and nodded. They followed him into the dining parlour, Mal still wondering what on Earth was going on. An attack on the King was a serious business, but there was clearly more to it than Grey was saying.

"Light the candles," the duke said, going over to the window to close the curtains.

Mal gathered up the candlesticks from the table and the soldiers dumped the corpse onto its polished expanse. It was still wrapped in a couple of the guardsmen's cloaks, now stained dark at what Mal guessed was the head end. Grey waved for the guardsmen to leave, then peeled back the blood-soaked fabric.

Mal winced. Most of the man's head was missing, his face no more than a bloody pulp of flesh and shattered bone.

"Shot, I assume?"

"He took his own life. My men tried to get to him first, but he must have had it all planned. One pistol for the King, the other for himself."

"How did it happen? Surely there were guards?"

"He came out of nowhere," the duke said. "One moment the crowds were cheering, the next his horse leapt the front line and he shot the King."

"He was mounted?"

"Yes. Damnedest thing, too. Beast looked half-crazed at first, rolling its eyes and curvetting, then it froze like a statue just before the assassin raised his pistol."

Mal glanced at his brother. "I have seen skraylings control frightened horses like that."

"Curious that you should mention skraylings," Grey said, uncovering the rest of the corpse.

It was wearing a loose tunic and trousers of cream and brown wool, woven in a pattern of stripes and triangles. Mal stared at it, dumbfounded.

"A skrayling attacked the King?"

He exchanged glances with his brother. At least now he knew why Grey had been acting so oddly.

"The skraylings would not do this," Sandy said. "We are a peaceful people."

Grey appeared not to notice the slip, and Mal could hardly say anything to Sandy without making things worse. He began to wish he had not brought his brother along.

"Perhaps we should look more closely at the body," he said, placing one of the candlesticks back on the table. The flickering yellow light restored a semblance of life to the pale flesh, and for a moment Mal imagined the man rising, headless, from the table.

"Here," he went on, trying to distract himself from the troubling vision, "see his hands? His nails are as pink as yours and mine. Skraylings have thick grey nails, more like a dog's claws."

He rolled the corpse over, and tugged at the waistband of the trousers. Grey grabbed his arm.

"What in God's name are you doing, Catlyn?"

"Look." Mal shook him off and pointed to the base of the man's spine. "No tail. This is not a skrayling, my lord, it is a human dressed up as to resemble one."

"He looked enough like a skrayling to me," Grey replied, though there was doubt in his voice. "Lines on his face and everything."

"Oh, I don't doubt they made a good job of it. But that was why he blew his head off, you see? Otherwise we would have too easily discovered it was an ordinary man in paint."

"They? You mean our traitors?"

"Most likely. Or it could be one of our foreign enemies. Anyone who would benefit if we severed our alliance with the skraylings."

Grey flicked the cloak back over the bloody corpse and rang for his servants.

"Thank you, Catlyn, you've been most helpful. Now, if you will excuse me, I would like to wash before I make my report to the Privy Council."

"Of course, my lord. Come, brother."

Once out in the street and well out of earshot of Grey, Mal gave vent to his frustration in a volley of curses. All his plans to rescue his family lay in ruins, unless he could somehow exploit this chaos to get Coby and Kit out of the Tower unnoticed.

"This is Olivia's doing, I'd wager my soul on it," he said, turning left towards Tower Hill. "Turn the city against the skraylings and get rid of Robert so that she can put a child king on the throne."

"Henry, or his older brother?"

"It hardly matters, does it? If she has half your talent in bending others to her will, Edward will dance to her tune and not even know he's doing it."

CHAPTER XXII

Coby stared out of the gatehouse window in horror. Now that the attack was over, the full extent of the damage was all too apparent. Whilst the nobles outside the gate had been intent on protecting the King, the panic on the causeway within had been devastating. Bodies lay strewn where they had fallen in the crush; a few floated face down in the moat, having leapt over the parapet heedless of their heavy robes. Those still standing had either retreated back into the castle or had braved the gate to disperse to their homes.

"We can't just leave them down there," she said, turning back to the other ladies. "Some of them may still be alive."

The ladies-in-waiting stared back at her like sheep confronted by a wolf. Only Lady Frances Grey stirred from where she had been comforting the overwrought queen.

"Lady Catlyn is right," Lady Frances said. "It is our Christian duty to help those men."

The duchess chose four of the least frightened-looking ladies-in-waiting, in addition to Coby, and told the rest to take good care of the Queen and the two princesses. Coby crouched by Kit.

"You can help protect the ladies, can't you?"

Kit nodded and rested his hand on the hilt of the little sword, his brown eyes wide.

"Yes, Mamma."

"Good lad." *Pray God it does not come to that.*

She followed Lady Frances down to the guardroom.

"I shall need any clean linen you may have, and we will have to improvise litters for carrying the dead and wounded away. You–" Lady Frances pointed to one of the guards "–fetch a surgeon; there's one in Water Lane."

The men seemed only too glad to have orders to follow, even if they were coming from a woman.

"Now, ladies, this will not be a pleasant task," the duchess went on. "Find the injured first, and if possible have them moved to the safety of the gatehouse. If you are not certain if a man is alive or dead, leave him for the surgeon to assess. Those that are clearly dead must be taken into the castle for laying out."

Lady Frances led them out onto the causeway. The devastation looked less severe from down here, perhaps because they could not see all the bodies at once, but the moans of the wounded and the stink of blood and bodily wastes gave the scene a far more hellish aspect. Was this what a battlefield looked like? No wonder Mal never spoke of the years he spent soldiering.

The women picked their way among the fallen. Here nearest the gatehouse the bodies were few in number, dressed in the livery of the Queen's household guard. Coby left the other ladies to weep and fret over the fallen guardsmen and pressed further on, to where the city guilds' banners lay abandoned. The men here were no warriors but merchants and craftsmen, ill-prepared for a violent rout. A stout man with an alderman's gold chain tangled in his white beard lay on his back, staring sightless at the blue sky, apparently uninjured but dead beyond question. Not far away another man lay face down and motionless, his fine robes crumpled and dusty. Coby gently turned him over. Dead also, his nose broken and bloody where he had been trampled to death. A whimper escaped her throat.

"Help me, for pity's sake!"

She looked up and saw a man stirring, half-hidden by a red and blue banner emblazoned with leaping fish and the crossed keys of

Saint Peter worked in gold thread. Coby hurried over and freed the man from the heavy fabric. He was no more than thirty, with receding hair and a face pale as whey above a gingery beard.

"I think my leg is broken," the fishmonger wheezed, grimacing as he tried to sit up.

"Don't move."

Coby lifted the banner and smashed it down on the parapet of the walkway, breaking off a length of about two feet. Perfect. She repeated the process, then took out her knife and began tearing strips from a discarded silk cape. Returning to her patient, she gently bound the lengths of pole either side of his broken leg.

"That should steady it until the surgeon can treat you," she told him.

She gave the man a final reassuring pat on the shoulder and continued with her search.

At the Tower gatehouse the guards blocked Mal's way with crossed partizans.

"Sorry, sir, no one is allowed into the Tower without a warrant from the Privy Council. King's orders."

"Which king?" Mal asked, dreading the answer.

"King Robert, of course." The warder squinted at him against the light. "Unless you know different, sir."

"No. But you know how rumour spreads in times like these. One knows not whom to trust."

"Quite, sir."

Mal hesitated. "My wife and son are within–"

"Sorry, sir, no exceptions. If you have a letter for them, I'd be glad to convey it…" The man looked hopeful, no doubt expecting a little silver for his troubles.

"Alas, I have neither pen nor paper." He looked over his shoulder at the sun, now well past its zenith. Still a good few hours until curfew. "I shall be back in all haste, with letters for both of them. Have you seen a gelding hereabouts? Chestnut, sixteen hands, white stocking on his near hind fetlock? I rode him in the procession, but I was called away on the King's business."

"A fair few beasts was rounded up, sir. Can't remember all of them."

An idea came to him. "What about the horse the assassin was riding?"

The guard shrugged.

"Send a message to the stables. I want that horse found and brought to me, immediately."

"The chestnut, or the other one?"

"Both." When the guard did not make a move to obey, he added, "Now. Or must I report your negligence to my lord the Duke of Suffolk?"

"No, sir. Right away, sir." He ducked into the gatehouse for a moment before setting off down the causeway.

Mal turned back to Sandy. "Go home, and let Ned know what's happened. I'll be back before curfew, God willing."

"I should–"

"There's nothing you can do. Kit will be as safe in there as anywhere. Please, Sandy."

His brother said nothing; the taut line of his mouth and the distrustful look he gave Mal made words unnecessary. After a moment he turned and walked away. Mal let out a long breath. He had more important things to deal with than Sandy's sulks.

In the time it took for the guard to return with the horses, Mal had managed to persuade his fellows to provide paper and ink to write a letter to Coby. There was nothing to seal it with, of course, and he dared not send anything too obviously ciphered, so he wrote a simple but heartfelt message wishing her well and praying that he would see both her and Kit soon. He handed it over, along with a few coins to speed it on its way.

"There you go, sir," the first guard said, passing him Hector's reins. "And here's the other one you was asking about."

"This is it? You're certain?"

The second horse was a sturdy grey nag, dwarfed by Hector. Mal looked it over, noting its well-worn shoes and the sores in the corners of its mouth where the bit had rubbed.

"A hard-worked beast."

"Aye, sir. The stablemaster says he would never have let a mangy beast like that go out in the King's coronation procession."

"Good. Now we shall find our man," Mal said with a smile. "He may have killed himself, but he forgot one rather large witness."

"Oh?"

"Every horse knows its way home. I intend to let this one loose, and follow it."

He mounted Hector, leaned over the pommel of his saddle and gave the nag a slap on its rump. It made no move. He slapped it again. The horse turned and looked at Hector. Mal sighed. Of course. It would not want to take the lead with a larger, more dominant animal around. He dismounted and handed Hector's reins to the guard.

"Keep him here, will you? I'll be back as soon as I can."

With a prayer to Saint Michael that the creature wouldn't outrun him in the crowded streets, he led the nag a little way down the street and gave it another slap on the rump. It whinnied and broke into a trot. Mal jogged along behind it, ignoring the strange looks he got from passers-by.

"You're going to have to run faster than that, my lord!" a man shouted, to uproarious laughter from his companions.

The nag led Mal about half a mile westwards then turned right, heading up Gracechurch Street towards Bishopsgate. Mal laboured after it, breath grating his throat, cursing his idleness these past few years. Time was he would have thought nothing of such a chase; now he was sweating and panting like an old man.

Thankfully his tormentor slowed as it approached the gate, finding its way blocked by the guards.

"Let it through," Mal wheezed as he jogged up. "We're on the King's business."

The gate guards stepped aside, and the chase began again. The street beyond was near empty, and the nag's steady trot increased in pace. At least the road was flatter here. Mal broke into a run, hoping that this burst of speed meant the beast was nearing home.

Sure enough it slowed after another quarter of a mile and trotted up to the gates of a livery stable. Mal stumbled to a halt, his heart sinking. It was as he feared. This was a hired horse. Most likely the assassin had given a false name and the trail would go cold. Still, he had to try.

By the time he reached the stable, a groom had taken hold of the grey nag's bridle and was leading it into a stall.

"You looking for a mount, sir?"

Mal turned to look at the man who had addressed him: a short, red-faced ostler in a greasy jerkin, stinking of his trade.

"That one," he wheezed, pointing a shaking hand at the nag.

The ostler looked Mal up and down. "I think you'll need a bigger beast than our Rosie, sir, if you don't mind me saying."

"Rosie? Is that the creature's name?"

"Aye, sir. Good little thing, steady pace, tireless. Why, what are you wanting a horse for? Would have thought a gentleman like you would keep his own, if you don't mind me saying."

"It's not for me. I'm Sir Maliverny Catlyn, here on the King's business. That horse was used in an attack on the King this morning."

The ostler turned pale. "I heard the news. Anything I can do to help the King's justice, my lord, anything."

"I need to know who hired that horse last."

"I heard it was a skrayling what shot His Majesty," the ostler said. "Haven't had any of those coming here in years."

"The assassin may have stolen the horse, but we need to know from whom." Much as he wanted to set the story straight and exonerate the skraylings, now was not the time.

The ostler cupped a hand to his mouth. "Davy! Who had the hire of Rosie last?"

A groom poked his head round the stall. "Master Nathaniel, same as always."

"Nathaniel?"

"A notary, Nathaniel Palmer. He has an account with us, seeing as he travels a lot with his work."

"And where can I find this Nathaniel Palmer?"

The ostler gave him directions to a house just off Bishopsgate Within. Mal thanked the man, and gave him a half-crown for his trouble.

"Feed the mare well, and let her rest," he told them. "She has been cruelly used, and is in no way to blame for the ill she has helped cause."

"Of course, sir. God save the King!"

"I hope he does," Mal replied softly as he left. *Otherwise we will have a child on the throne; a child with a monstrous brother who is bent on taking it – and the kingdom – for himself.*

When the soldiers came to take Kit back to the other boys, he wasn't sure whether to be happy or afraid. De Vere would probably not stop taunting him and calling him a girl, and in the Tower there was nowhere to hide from him. On the other hand it had been very boring cooped up with the princesses, who just cried all the time or worse, fussed over him like he was a baby. He stomped down the stairs after the soldiers, wishing his father or Uncle Sandy would come and take him away. At that thought he looked around eagerly. Perhaps the soldiers had lied and he was being taken to his father after all... but then they turned left instead of right and went through the gateway to the inner ward.

As he feared they led him up the stairs into the Bloody Tower, to the portcullis room where he and Robert Sidney shared a bed, and left him there. When they had arrived here two days ago, he and Sidney had pretended they were soldiers in a besieged castle, sent to man the defences and drop boiling water and molten lead on their enemies' heads. A portcullis wasn't much use, though, if you were trying to get out rather than stop someone getting in. He leaned over the mechanism, wondering if it were possible to squeeze through the gaps.

Someone pushed him and he toppled forwards, flailing for the nearest beam to steady himself. He turned, panting, to see Sidney smirking at him.

"Sidney, don't be an ass!"

"Made you squeal."

"Did not."

"I heard you. Bet you wet yourself too."

"Did not."

"*Pueri!*"

Both boys snapped to attention.

"*Magister.*"

"Is this any proper way for gentlemen to behave?" Master Weston glared at them both. "Cavorting like jugglers when your lord King lies in agonies?"

"*Non est, magister.*"

"Do not imagine that this unfortunate turn of events will prevent you from having lessons. The discipline of learning will take your minds off melancholy thoughts."

Sidney groaned and trudged through into their chamber. Kit made to follow him, but Master Weston blocked his path with his cane.

"Not you, Catlyn. The prince wishes to speak with you."

Kit bowed and made his way up the spiral stair to Prince Henry's chambers. The upper floor of the tower was divided by a wood-and-plaster wall into an L-shaped parlour and a separate bedchamber. Prince Henry sat in a chair by the window, watching him intently. There was no sign of de Vere, and Kit hoped his old enemy had gone back to the adjoining Wakefield Tower, where Prince Edward had his lodgings.

"Your Highness."

"How did you like my sisters?"

Kit blinked at the prince. "Um, they were very kind to me."

"Of course they were. And my beloved mother?"

"I didn't see her much. She looked sad and worried."

Henry stood up. "You don't like me, do you, Catlyn?"

Kit stared at the ground. "I..." He had never been very good at lying.

"It's all right, you can tell the truth." He stepped closer to Kit. "But we could be friends, if you wanted. Good friends."

"I don't understand."

"My father may die of his wounds, and then Edward will be king and I will be heir. Unless something happens to him before he has a son."

"I hope not–" Kit realised this was the wrong thing to say. "I-I-I mean that I hope your father doesn't die."

"No. Of course not. But whether he dies now or later, my friends will be important men. Even more important than they are now. I need friends who are loyal to me and no one else. Could you do that, Catlyn?"

Kit swallowed. "I can try, Your Highness."

"Then you will obey me, before your father or anyone else?"

"Anyone? Even the King?"

"Well, no." Henry looked annoyed. "That would be treason. And if you breathed a word that I said otherwise, I'd have to have you executed."

"What?" Kit backed away further, until he was up against the door. The nail heads pressed into his back.

The prince laughed. "You should see your face, Catlyn. Of course I'm not going to have you executed. Not yet, at any rate."

Kit did not feel reassured.

"You're pretty good at Latin, aren't you?" Henry said. "And you draw well, and I dare say you're itching to practise with that new sword."

"Yes, Your Highness."

"Good, I think you'll make a fine companion. Kneel and swear your loyalty to me, and I'll forgive you."

Kit knelt and placed his hands palm together, like he had seen knights do before their liege lords in tapestries and paintings. Please, Father, forgive me. He's the prince, I cannot refuse.

Henry clasped Kit's hands in his own. His palms were warm against Kit's knuckles, and yet the touch made him shiver. Kit longed to tear his hands away and run, regardless of what Henry did to him for it, but the prince had him trapped against the door.

"Do you, Christopher Catlyn, swear allegiance to me, Henry Tudor, your lord and prince, for all your days?"

"I so swear." His voice came out barely above a whisper.

"Louder, if you will."

"I so swear."

"Good. You may rise."

Kit got to his feet. He felt sure there ought to have been more words than that, something about God and a lord's duty to protect his vassals, but Henry had always been impatient.

"Now, give me your sword."

Kit hesitated. "It was a gift from my father–"

"And I am your liege lord now. Give it to me."

Kit swallowed past the lump in his throat and unbuckled the belt. It almost slipped from his fingers, and he could not look up at the prince as he handed it over. Henry turned away and stared out of the window at the White Tower. Kit supposed he was dismissed, and backed towards the door.

"One more thing," Henry said over his shoulder. "Don't think to betray me. I can read your thoughts as you sleep, and learn your innermost secrets."

"That's witchcraft," Kit said, before he could stop himself.

Henry turned, his face like thunder. "It is the divine power of princes. Or do you doubt me already?"

"N-n-no, Your Highness."

"No, of course not." He smiled. "You may leave us."

Henry turned away again, and Kit scrabbled for the door latch behind him. He had never been more grateful to have lessons to go to in his life.

Palmer's lodgings were in a courtyard off Cornhill Street, a short walk from the Royal Exchange. A sour-faced woman of middling years answered the door, looking him up and down before offering a begrudging curtsey.

"I'm looking for Nathaniel Palmer," Mal said. He watched the woman's reaction, but she betrayed no sign that she thought him dead.

"He ain't here. Gone to visit one of his merchant friends, I'll warrant."

"But you don't know for sure?"

She shrugged. "He left the house this morning, like he often does. I said to him, aren't you staying for the coronation, but he said he had pressing business."

"Did he say where?"

"No." The woman frowned. "That was the odd thing. Usually he told me where he was going and how long he would be, but this time he just said not to expect him for a while."

"Perhaps I had better come in. This is not a matter to discuss in the street."

"Who are you? And why should I let you into my house?"

"Sir Maliverny Catlyn, on the King's business. And you are…?"

"Mistress Bell. His landlady." Her eyes went wide. "This ain't nothing to do with the shooting, is it?"

Mal nodded curtly. Mistress Bell glanced up and down the street, then opened the door wider. Her dark eyes glinted in the shadows of the passage, eager for gossip.

"So what's Palmer's done, then?" she asked as she showed Mal up a flight of stairs. "I heard it was a foreigner what shot the King, not an Englishman."

"I'm afraid I can't say," Mal replied. "He may not be involved at all, but it was his horse the killer was riding."

"You think this villain knocked him on the head and made off with the beast?" She took a key from her pocket and unlocked one of the doors. "This is his room. I sweep it out once a week and collect his laundry. He's very little trouble."

The room was plainly furnished in sombre dark woods and woollen drapery, and as neat as one might expect of a tenant with legal training. A desk stood near the window, flanked by shelves and pigeonholes for storing great quantities of documents, all bound up with string and sealing wax. If Palmer were the assassin and had allies in this conspiracy, they had not yet thought to destroy all possible evidence. Mal smiled. This lot would keep Ned occupied for quite a while.

"What did... does Master Palmer look like?"

Mistress Bell gave a description that matched the body on Grey's table well enough. It was not proof in itself, but better than finding out that the horse had indisputably been stolen. Mal lit a candle, took a scrap of paper from the desk and wrote a note to Grey, sealing it with a plain blob of wax. They would have to confiscate all of Palmer's papers, and hope they contained clues to the man's associates.

"Send this to Suffolk House, as fast as you may." He pulled a handful of coins out of his pocket. "For your trouble."

"That's a lot of trouble, sir," Mistress Bell said, her eyes narrowing in suspicion.

"I'm afraid Master Palmer is in a great deal of trouble. One way or another, I doubt you will be seeing him again."

CHAPTER XXIII

The Queen's household was moved back to Saint Thomas' Tower as soon as the causeway had been cleared. Juliana had protested to the guardsmen that she should be by her husband's side in this time of crisis, but to no avail. The Privy Council had decreed, in the name of the King, that Robert's wife and children must stay in the Tower for their own safety until all the conspirators behind the assassination attempt had been arrested. And so they had returned to what had been intended as temporary quarters, feeling more like prisoners than guests under protection.

Coby tried to busy herself about the Queen's apartments but there was little to do apart from sewing, listening to one of the ladies-in-waiting read, or watching the skrayling ships depart the city. She spent far too much of her time on the latter, wondering where she and Mal would take Kit if the skraylings never returned. Of course she had to get Kit out of here first, the sooner the better.

A wail came from the bedchamber. The Queen. Coby rushed up the short flight of steps.

"Your Majesty?"

Queen Juliana had sunk to the floor in a puddle of silks, and would have fallen entirely if two of her ladies had not knelt and held her up. Coby noticed the door to the Wakefield Tower stood open, and a white-faced page hovered near it, twisting his black velvet bonnet in his hands. She left the Queen to her companions and crossed to him.

"What news?" she asked in a low voice, taking him by the elbow.

"P-P-Prince Edward, madam. He's taken sick. Naught but a summer fever, the doctor says, but–"

But the prince's great-uncle, after whom he had been named, had likewise fallen ill and died on the cusp of adulthood. Coby glanced back at the Queen. Poor woman, to have two beloved lives hanging in the thread and no means to save either.

"Take me to my son," she told the page.

"But–"

"Now!" she muttered, steering him across the bedchamber. "You and I can do nothing here."

She followed him through the parlour and dining room and down the steps to the outer ward, through the gateway under the Bloody Tower and up to the green. In truth there were few easy routes from one tower to the next, as was no doubt intentional; back when the castle was an important fortress, its strength lay in making it as difficult as possible to pass from the outer curtain wall to the inner.

At the foot of the steps up to the Bloody Tower's entrance stood a grey-haired yeoman warder. The scarlet tassels on his partizan swung wildly as he moved it to block her entrance. Odd, the little details that stood out in these moments.

"Name and business?"

Coby drew herself up to her full height, which was a good inch taller than the guard. "I am Lady Jacomina Catlyn, and I am here to see my son Christopher."

"Sorry, madam, no one is admitted to the princes' presence at the moment, not with fever running riot."

"Tush, man, there is naught wrong with me, I will not infect anyone."

The warder shrugged. "Those is my orders, madam, from the Prince of Wales hisself."

"The prince is but a child, and sick with fever," she said. "Besides, if everyone is so worried about him, surely he should be removed from here for his own safety?"

"Not my place to decide, madam."

"No, of course not." She paused. "But no doubt his uncle has been informed?"

"Couldn't say, madam."

Coby gave up. She was getting nowhere with this man, and if no one was allowed in or out, Kit might be safe for a while.

Kit sat in the window seat, pretending to read the opening verses of the *Iliad* but really gazing across the inner ward at the Beauchamp Tower. Prince Henry's grandfather, Robert Dudley, had been imprisoned there after plotting treason, and died there too.

"What are you staring at?" asked Robin Sidney, who was sitting opposite.

"Nothing," Kit replied.

He glanced at Prince Henry, who was playing chess with Master Weston. De Vere, who had joined them in the Bloody Tower when Edward first fell sick, put out his tongue. Kit resisted the urge to do the same back, in case Master Weston looked up and saw him.

Sidney leant forward across his book.

"Do you think Edward will haunt his tower when he dies, like the other two princes do here?"

"He's not dead yet." Kit whispered back. "Anyway, I don't believe in ghosts."

"You don't?" Sidney's eyes widened.

"Well, not apart from the Holy Ghost, and he's special because he's really God in disguise."

"But… what about all the stories? Luke the guardsman swears he's seen the princes at the windows, and heard them weeping."

"Why are you two boys talking?" Master Weston snapped. "I told you to read in silence. Open your mouths again and you'll feel my cane."

"*Etiam, magister,*" they chorused.

Sidney shot Kit a sulky look, as if it had been his fault. Kit glowered back. Thankfully Master Weston was distracted from observing them by the arrival of Prince Henry's physician, Doctor Renardi.

"Come, Your Highness, it is time for your morning treatment."

"Do I have to?" the prince asked, looking up from the chess board.

"I am afraid so, Your Highness. You do not want to catch the summer fever like your poor brother, do you?"

Henry got up from his seat. "Of course not. Although you would make me better if I did, wouldn't you, Renardi?"

"I would endeavour to do so, Highness. As I do now for your brother." He gestured towards the bedchamber. When the door had closed behind them, Master Weston rose from his chair.

"I think I shall take the air for a short while," he said to no one in particular. He carefully put all the chess pieces back in their starting positions and then left, talking to himself under his breath.

"Gone to help himself to the prince's wine stores, more like," de Vere said, heaving himself up from his cushion by the hearth.

"Why don't we get treatments for the fever?" Sidney asked.

"Because we're not princes," de Vere replied. He lowered his voice. "Besides, what if Renardi made Edward sick, and is trying to do the same to Henry with this 'treatment'?"

"Why would he do that?" Kit asked.

"Because he's a foreigner. You can't trust them, you know."

"Catlyn's a foreigner," Sidney said.

"I am not," Kit replied, though not with any conviction.

"Yes you are, the prince himself told me. Your grandmother was French, your mother is Dutch and you were born in France. That makes you a foreigner."

"Perhaps you poisoned Edward," de Vere said, looming over him.

"I did not." Kit backed away from the older boy.

De Vere's fist came flying towards him. Kit dodged, and de Vere yelped as his knuckles smashed against the rough wall. Kit raised his own fists, screaming with frustrated rage, but something else welled up inside him, a sadness that sucked the air from his lungs and left him feeling hollow and cold. The last thing he saw were his companions staring at him in wide-eyed horror before he fell into darkness.

●●●●

If the Queen's household had been quiet before, it was sepulchral now. Juliana's ladies were not permitted to speak unless spoken to, though the Queen spent so many hours in the little chapel that she was seldom there to give permission. The summer days seemed far too long, the hours endless. Coby tried to occupy her time with sewing, but that only left her mind free to worry about Kit and Mal. She had seen neither of them since the day of the coronation procession, did not even know if either of them were still alive, although she hoped that someone would have brought word if they were not.

Her one small consolation was that Olivia appeared even more frustrated by their confinement and silence than herself. The "castrato" was not permitted to sing, of course, not even a hymn or psalm at their daily worship. Olivia spent most of the day staring out of the window or hunched up on a cushion, eyes closed. Coby wondered if she was wandering the dreamlands or merely feigning sleep to avoid what little conversation the others dared attempt.

One thing Coby knew for sure: since Mal's plan had failed, she had no choice but to get Kit out of here herself. She considered petitioning the Queen, but if she were refused it would only make life ten times more awkward. It also felt discourteous to ask for herself what the Queen no doubt longed for and was unlikely to get. Reluctantly she put that option aside, to save as a last resort. The best plan was to rely on no one but herself, which meant finding a way out of the castle. And that required a reconnoitre. Getting out of Saint Thomas's Tower was easy enough; all she had to do was wait until Juliana went to prayer, then take herself off to her bedchamber complaining of womanly pains. If any of the other ladies discovered her absence and betrayed her, she would take the consequences.

She tarried in the outer ward for a while, examining possible exits whilst pretending to be enjoying the rose garden, just in case anyone was observing her from the surrounding towers' windows. The Cradle Tower's gate opened directly onto the moat, which was no use at all, but she had discovered there was a landward exit somewhere hereabouts used by the warders to get to Tower Hamlets. It was somewhere beyond the far wall of the rose garden, and with the skeleton keys she had brought hidden in her sewing basket, it would not be too hard to get through the locked gate in the garden wall. No doubt the causeway itself was guarded, but it seemed their best chance of escape.

With the exit from the outer ward accounted for, that just left the issue of getting into the Bloody Tower. In addition to the covered walkway to the Wakefield Tower on the same level as the Queen's bedchamber, there looked to be an open walkway above. Perhaps it was part of the guards' nightly round, though. She made her way into the inner ward and rapidly assessed possible entrances from that side; there might also be a way in from the lower level of the round Wakefield Tower, since it closely abutted the rectangular mass of the Bloody Tower. Nor was that entrance guarded, which was promising. Unless it meant there was no route through to the prince's chambers and hence no need for a guard. If only she could explore properly! With a grimace of frustration she walked up the slope to the coldharbour gate that guarded the small ward between the White Tower and the Great Hall. There might be nothing she could do for the dead who had been taken to the makeshift mortuary in the hall, but at least she could report to the Queen on how many had been claimed by their families.

For a brief moment she entertained the idea of disguising Kit as a dead body and having Ned come and take him away, but that would be far too hard to arrange given the lack of communication so far. No. Simple and fast was the only way that was likely to work, and even the chance of that was not good. But what other choice did she have?

Kit opened his eyes. His head hurt, and his back and legs were as sore as if Master Weston had taken a month's worth of misdemeanours from his hide. And what was he doing lying on the floor? He groaned and tried to sit up.

"Ah, you are awake, little signore! *Deo gratia!*"

Kit squinted against the sunlight pouring through the window. Doctor Renardi was leaning over him, smiling and nodding his head. Kit shrank back.

"What happened to me? Did... did I...?" He couldn't remember how he came to be on the floor, only that horrible feeling of sadness, like everyone he knew had died.

"It is the falling sickness, nothing worse, young master."

"I'm not going to die, am I?"

"No, young master, you will not die, at least not of this thing."

"But you said I had a sickness."

"Yes, the falling sickness. Has it happened to you before?"

"No, never."

The doctor frowned. "I shall ask your mother. Sometimes the patient is not even aware of the seizures, when they are mild."

"Will it happen again?"

"Perhaps today, perhaps next month, perhaps never. Only God can say."

He helped Kit to his feet. To Kit's relief the parlour was empty.

"Where is everyone?"

"Maestro Weston took the prince and the other boys down to the portcullis room for their lesson. Now, sit quietly and take your ease, and I will make up a sleeping draught for you to take tonight."

The doctor went into the prince's bedchamber. A few moments later the other door opened, and Sidney poked his head round. He hesitated before slipping through the door, but came no nearer to Kit. Long moments of silence passed, punctuated by the clink of bottles and the sound of muttered Italian from the prince's bedchamber.

"De Vere says you're possessed," Sidney said at last.

"Am not." Kit pulled up his knees and wrapped his arms around them. "He affrighted me, that's all."

The other boy sidled closer.

"But you were foaming at the mouth and shaking and everything." Sidney pulled a face. "De Vere is demanding to be allowed to go home, and if he does, I shall tell them to let me go as well."

"Don't leave me alone with the prince. Please, Robin."

He'd never called Sidney by his first name before. Sidney's face crumpled.

"I'm sorry, Catlyn. If they say I can go, I'll go."

Kit turned away so that Sidney couldn't see the tears welling in his eyes. They were all leaving him. That's why he had been so sad. It was a vision of the future. Saints had visions during their seizures, didn't they? He hoped God hadn't chosen him to be a saint. Most of them seemed to die horribly.

The Bull's Head was busier than Mal had ever seen it, men crowded around every table or just standing against the walls in grave-faced knots. In part that could be blamed on the closure of the theatres lest such mass gatherings foster further sedition, which left Southwark's actors with naught to do but drink and gossip in their favourite watering-hole. Mostly it was the natural desire of Londoners to congregate and chew over the unprecedented events of the past few days, and speculate on the likelihood of their new king living to see Christmas.

"The King's health!" someone shouted, and raised his tankard.

Everyone within earshot followed suit; you never knew when you were being observed by one of the many informants and spies who worked for various nobles and court officials. Such as Mal and his two companions. They mingled with the crowd, stopping to talk to old friends and making new acquaintances.

"Eaton?" Mal stopped and stared at a half-familiar grizzled figure with a patch over one eye.

"The very same," the former actor replied. "Catlyn, isn't it? You're quite the gentleman now, I hear."

Mal laughed. "Who'd have thought it, eh? And you?"

"I get by," Eaton replied. "Been working the box office for Henslowe. The missing eye fools folk into thinking I don't see 'em trying to sneak in without paying. They're wrong, of course."

"And what has your good eye noticed of late?" Mal said, slipping a shilling from his pocket and rubbing it idly between finger and thumb.

"You asking me to betray my employer's trust?"

"Not at all. I care naught for the affairs of the theatre. But you must hear things, standing at the gate every afternoon."

Eaton grinned. "Folk do seem to think a missing eye makes a man deaf as well."

"So...?"

"My news is stale, I fear. What with the theatres being closed and that."

"Still, there must have been murmurs, even before last week's tragedy."

"Just the usual. Bread and beer prices going up, worries that they'll go up again if we have another bad harvest…"

"Anything about the skraylings?"

Eaton shook his head. "They keep to themselves, and that's the way most folks like it."

"But you don't."

A pause. "I'm no traitor, Catlyn. One of them tried to kill the King."

"Of course. But before that…"

Eaton leaned in, as if fearing to be overheard.

"The skraylings like the theatre. When they stay at home, we all earn less."

Mal slipped him the coin. "Buy yourself a beer or three, and drink to Naismith's memory for me."

Eaton nodded in appreciation and pocketed the silver.

Mal made his way back through the crowd and eventually found Ned and Gabriel talking to Will Shakespeare. He made a discreet signal and they excused themselves.

"So, gentlemen, have you heard enough yet?"

The two men murmured their affirmations, and Mal led the way back to the Sign of the Parley in silence. When they were safe behind closed doors he poured them all another beer from his own supplies and they gathered around the kitchen table.

"Well," he said at last. "Olivia and her allies seem to have achieved their aim. Everyone believes it was the skraylings who plotted against the King and sent an assassin to kill him."

"That's not the half of it," Gabriel said. "At least two men stopped me and asked when Burbage was changing the company's name to 'The King's Men'."

Ned grimaced. "And one of my old journeymen told me they've had so many customers this week asking for histories of Richard the Third, it's beyond a jest. There's even new ballads about him."

They exchanged worried glances. With his nephews locked up in the Tower and his brother the King on his deathbed, the parallels between Prince Arthur and the hated King Richard were too close for comfort.

"You really think Arthur is preparing to take the throne if Robert dies?" Mal asked them.

"I think people think he is," Ned replied. "And he's doing bugger-all to convince them otherwise."

"Some are saying he's fled back to his stronghold at Kenilworth, to gather an army," Gabriel added. "Arrant nonsense, of course; we would have heard if he had."

"Olivia." Mal stared into the distance, seeing those jade-green eyes twinkle with mischief. "This is all part of her plan."

"After that business with Percy, people believe him capable of any wickedness." Gabriel sighed. "I wish he'd stop playing Crookback and let the princes out of the Tower. It's not helping his cause one bit."

"And Kit too. Don't forget he's still a hostage."

"What about the rumours that Edward is sick?" Ned asked. "You reckon there's anything in them?"

"I pray to God there isn't. If Edward dies too..." The unspoken words hung in the air. *Then Henry could soon be king.*

"So what do we do?"

"We try to unravel Olivia's plans and undo what has been done. Gabriel, you and Will Shakespeare are close to Prince Arthur. Speak to him, urge him to intervene and move his nephews to Whitehall to be with their father. Or to Richmond, if it is true that Edward is unwell."

"I'll try," the actor said. "Though he might not listen to us."

"Make him listen." Mal turned to Ned. "How are you doing on those papers of Palmer's?"

"Not well. For all he was neat and tidy, the whoreson had appalling handwriting. I'm starting to get the hang of it, though. Give me another day, and I might have your answers."

"A day, then, but no more. The longer we take, the harder it will be to change the tide of men's opinion."

CHAPTER XXIV

Ned rubbed his eyes and stood to stretch his aching back. Two days he'd been working on these damned papers of Palmer's, with precious little help from anyone. To be fair, most of it made little sense unless you were well-versed in reading legal documents, so Gabriel had been reduced to bringing Ned meals and forcing him to rest once in a while.

"Let me," Gabriel said, setting down the dirty dinner plates he'd been gathering up. "Sit back down."

He came round behind Ned and began kneading his shoulder muscles. Ned groaned in pleasure. After a while he recalled that he wasn't the only one who had been hard at work today.

"Any luck at the palace?"

"None." Gabriel pressed his thumb into a knot at the base of Ned's neck, as if for emphasis. "We waited two hours to see Arthur and when we were finally allowed in, that venomous bitch Olivia was there, curled around his chair like the serpent in Eden. All we could do was offer our condolences and leave."

"Unh. Mal's not going to be happy about that."

"You think I'm happy about it?"

On the floor below the front door opened, letting a breeze in to stir the dust on the stairs and blow a draught under the door of the upstairs parlour. Gabriel released Ned, kissed the nape of his neck – sending a delicious shiver down his spine – and went to gather up the dishes. Damn the boy, he could be such a distraction at times!

Gabriel blew a kiss from the doorway and headed downstairs. A few moments later a familiar voice swore loudly, then footsteps sounded on the landing outside, too heavy to be Gabriel's.

"You heard Gabe's news, then?"

"Aye." Mal shook the raindrops off his hat. "Find anything yet?"

"Watch what you're doing!"

Ned gathered up the documents nearest Mal as fast as he could. The brass-and-steel fingers of his right hand clattered uselessly against the tabletop, and he cursed under his breath.

"Sorry," Mal said. "Well?"

"Yes, I've found something. And it's more bad news, I'm afraid."

"Why does this not surprise me? Go on."

Ned put down the rain-spattered papers and picked out a sheet he'd put aside. "You might recognise the names and signatures on that one."

Mal took it from him with a raised eyebrow and scanned the first few lines.

"Dear God in Heaven."

"I told you, you wouldn't like it."

"I don't even remember dealing with Palmer. Mind you, it was six years ago, and there were a great many papers to sign when I came back to England. Not just the deeds to the estate; there were all of Sandy's affairs to sort out as well." He sighed and sat down by the fire. "This doesn't look good. If it gets out, Northumberland will have me on Tower Hill before you can say 'habeas corpus'."

"We could burn it," Ned said. "No one would have to know."

"As a last resort, perhaps. No, hold on to it, and we'll see if we can make an alternative case to distract attention from that particular connection."

"That won't be hard."

"Oh?"

"Palmer was a scrivener-notary." When Mal looked blank, he added, "They've got exclusive rights to deal with contracts and suchlike within the City of London. Lots of mercantile clients, foreign traders especially. A man like Palmer would probably have spoken half-a-dozen languages: French, Spanish, Portuguese, Tradetalk…"

"Skraylings."

"Skraylings." Ned gestured to the documents scattered across the table. "Nearly a quarter of his dealings involved skrayling merchants, one way or another."

"But why would a man who chose to make it his business to deal with the skraylings go and dress up as one and shoot the King?"

"Familiarity breeds contempt, so they say. Perhaps he'd had enough of them."

"Or perhaps he was a Huntsman, or one of their sympathisers." Mal shook the document with his name on it. "I had to deal with Palmer because he was one of my brother Charles's chosen agents. What if Charles singled him out because they had common interests, so to speak?"

"That doesn't help your case, though, does it?"

"Quite the opposite," Mal replied glumly.

"So what do we tell Grey?"

"Damned if I know."

Ned sank his head in his hands. "Time was I could have forged something, neat as you like. Now…" He gestured with his false hand.

"Don't blame yourself. Whoever set Palmer on this course knew exactly what they were doing."

"The guisers?"

"Olivia. Whoever was responsible for the earlier attacks on you and me – whether Percy or one of his allies – they were unsubtle to say the least. This new conspiracy relied on finding the one person in London who makes a plausible link between me and a plot to kill the King, and then convincing him to blow his brains out." Mal sprang to his feet with a curse. "Damn it, the woman probably even wagered on the possibility that I would become involved in the matter. Which means that we have to be very careful what we do next, or we could find ourselves in worse trouble than we are already."

"Worse? What's worse than being executed for treason?"

Mal made no answer, only gathered up the papers with a distracted air.

"What about you?" Ned asked, hoping for better news than his own. "Any chance that the horse was stolen and the assassin wasn't Palmer?"

"Nothing," Mal said, slamming the stack of documents back down on the table. "I made enquiries in all of Palmer's old haunts, but no one's seen or heard of him since before the coronation. Perhaps I should ride out tomorrow and talk to some of his associates outside London."

"What about Sandy?"

"What about him?"

"Well, he could go and talk to the skraylings, couldn't he? If anyone can get the truth out of them, surely it's your brother."

"A capital idea! I'll speak to him after supper." Mal pulled up a stool at the table and selected a quill from the inkstand. "In the meantime, I'll compile a summary of your findings and we'll take it to Grey in the morning."

The sun was sinking behind him as Erishen walked the length of Southwark towards the guild-house. People passed on either side, their faces set like stone. It had been three days, and still there was no good news of the King's recovery. It was strange to him, to think of a person gone forever with no chance of rebirth; the Christian heaven seemed a poor recompense for being exiled from life.

As he neared the guild-house the mood of the passers-by changed. They hurried along the street with heads bowed and eyes on the ground, as if they could make themselves invisible by not seeing anyone. He turned the corner and halted, staring.

The windows of the guild-house were boarded up – hastily, by the looks of it – and the front door was dented as if someone had taken a small battering ram to it. Excrement was smeared on the boards and on the whitewashed walls, and the sign hanging above the door had been ripped down. Even as he watched, a man walking past made an obscene gesture towards the building then crossed himself.

Erishen glanced up at the first floor windows. These had not been boarded over on the outside, of course, and the glass in them was mostly smashed and missing, but the inner shutters had evidently kept out most missiles. Some of those had been on fire, judging by the scorch marks. Erishen waited, and after a few moments one of the shutters opened a crack. He caught a glimpse of a tattooed face before the shutters closed again.

He waited several more minutes, whilst humans passed him and stared. Eventually the grille in the front door of the guild-house slid open, and he hurried across the street.

"Erishen-*tuur*?" a voice hissed.

"*Hä.*"

"Come in, quickly!"

The door itself opened and he was hauled inside, tripping over the threshold. It slammed shut again behind him; just in time. Something slammed into it from the outside, followed by a hammering and muffled shouting.

As Erishen's eyes adjusted to the dark, he began to make out the faces of nearly a dozen skraylings, tattooed lines stark against their pale skin.

"Erishen-*tuur*, what are you doing here?" one of them asked in Vinlandic.

"I was going to the camp to speak with Chief Merchant Sekharhjarret."

"Have you not heard? Sekharhjarret is dead."

Erishen stared at his kinsmen, but they all bobbed their heads in confirmation.

"Dead? How?"

"The humans attacked the camp, the night after their clan leader Robert was hurt. Sekharhjarret went out to try and calm them, but one threw a stone that struck him on the head and he died the next day."

"I should go."

"Please, stay, Erishen-*tuur*. The humans saw you come in; they know you are our friend and will hurt you."

"I need to warn my brother–"

"Tonight. We can protect you in the dreamlands as we cannot on the streets." Seeing Erishen hesitate, he added, "And if you cannot reach him, you can leave here before dawn, while the humans sleep."

That was true enough. It would mean dodging the night watchmen, but they were old and feeble. Safer than risking the streets in daylight.

"Very well."

They led him through the atrium and the now-empty trading hall, up the stairs into one of the wings that faced away from the street. The windows here were intact, at least on the side facing the courtyard.

"How long have you been here?" Sandy asked.

"Since the day of the attack. Some of our merchants were outside the Tower to cheer on the new leader, but they fled in boats."

"Did they see the killer?"

"No, there were too many humans in the way. But we have heard the stories, that it was one of us who did it. This is a lie."

"I know." Sandy told them what he had seen at the house in Seething Lane. "Do any of you know a human named Palmer? He is a scribe and contract lawyer."

They shrugged. "We deal with many humans. We seldom note their names apart from the principal merchants."

"No matter–"

"What is going on here?"

Erishen looked round to see an aged skrayling in crumpled robes peering at him. "Greetings, honoured one."

"Who let this human into our stronghold? And how does he know our tongue?"

One of the younger skraylings took him by the elbow. "This is Erishen-*tuur*, honoured one, come to offer his respects."

"Does he bring an offer of peace as well?"

"Alas, no, honoured one." He looked at Erishen. "At least, there has been no talk of peace yet."

"Hah, you youngsters! Stories first, business later, eh?"

"Business cannot be conducted without a sound understanding of the situation," Erishen put in.

"We understand the situation well enough. Blame has been put upon us, like the goat in the Christian story, and now we must prepare to leave."

Erishen looked round at all of them. "You are giving up so easily?"

"We are not warriors, you know that. It is fortunate the humans have not yet managed to set fire to this house of wood, but I think that is only through fear it would destroy their own homes as well."

"And what about the renegades? Do you abandon your watch over them? Abandon your English friends to their rule?"

The old skrayling made a placatory gesture. "We do not wish to see the Unbound rule any human nation, but what can we do once they have turned the people against us?"

"You believe this is their work, not that of other humans who hate you, such as the Huntsmen?"

Several of the skraylings flinched at the hated name.

"Yes," the elder said. "We do. Though how it was contrived, we cannot say. The killer was not one of the Unbound, of that we are certain."

"How?"

"We did not all stand idly in the street waving our handkerchiefs. Our patrols roamed the dreamlands as always, in anticipation of some attack against Elizabeth's son. They saw nothing untoward."

"Nothing?"

"Nothing."

Erishen looked at the gathered skraylings. It was true that they were not warriors, at least, not as the English understood it. There were skirmishes from time to time, back in Vinland, but the few deaths that resulted were mostly accidents. Fighting to kill was not the skrayling way.

"I want to go back," he said. "When you leave this land, take us with you. We are your kin–"

"You are stranger-born, like the others," the elder said. "It is not permitted."

Erishen fell to his knees and tipped his head back, baring his throat in submission. "Please, honoured one... at least take my *amayi*. He does not deserve exile."

"And whose fault is it that he now suffers this fate? You and your brother interfered with his mission and got him killed. You yourself broke our laws when you came to this land, and chose the path of the renegade."

Erishen had no answer to that, since it was all true.

"And yet," the elder went on, "you have suffered a great deal at the hands of the renegades, I am told. They burned your home and tried to destroy you, is that so?"

"Yes, honoured one."

The elder sighed. "I cannot promise you will be welcomed home, but if you are able to come to our ship before we sail, I will see you conveyed out of the reach of your enemies. What happens after that may be out of my hands."

"Thank you. My brother and I will be eternally grateful."

"Now, leave us. There is much to do before we go."

"Honoured one." The leader of the young skraylings made an obeisance. "We invited Erishen-*tuur* to stay until the streets are empty, that he may leave unnoticed."

"Very well." The old merchant turned away. "He may stay until midnight. Let him meditate upon his foolish actions until then."

Mal was woken in the night by Sandy's return from the skrayling guild-house. He listened in growing despondency to the news and resolved to report to the Privy Council immediately, in the hope of stopping this persecution before it went any further. After a swift early breakfast he saddled Hector and set off for the palace.

The wheels of state turn slowly, however, and the sun was approaching its zenith before a liveried servant arrived to announce that the council were ready to see him at last. He was escorted from the antechamber, across an inner courtyard and into the atrium of the Council Chamber itself, the guards' pole-arm butts clicking on the stone flags in time with the thud of their booted feet, until they came to a sudden halt before a pair of dark oak doors carved with the royal arms. Two more guards stood at attention either side; they opened the doors, and Mal was ushered inside.

The room beyond was not vast, but the space from the doors to the table at the far end seemed to stretch endlessly away from him. One of the men seated behind the table coughed. Mal remembered himself and bowed, low enough to show his respect for Prince Arthur, whose red hair was the only patch of colour in the sombre company. At the prince's right hand sat the short hunched figure of Sir Robert Cecil, the Secretary of State; on his left was the Lord High Admiral, Lord Howard of Effingham; and on the admiral's left the Lord Chancellor, Sir Thomas Egerton. The fifth member of the council was very like to Effingham in age and looks, though his silver beard was even longer; Mal guessed him to be Baron Buckhurst, the Lord High Treasurer. If Gabriel's report was correct, Olivia now had the prince under her thumb, but there was still hope she had not bewitched all of them.

Mal stopped a respectful distance from the polished table, his hands clasped behind his back, head up but eyes respectfully lowered. Sweat trickled down his back, and not only from the sticky heat of a July afternoon. The silence stretched out before him as the five men passed documents between themselves, reminding him of the Venetian Grand Chancellor and his secretaries. At least here he was not in imminent danger of torture. Not yet.

Cecil coughed and tossed aside the sheet of paper he had been reading.

"A very thorough investigation, Master Catlyn."

"Thank you, sir."

"You must have worked through the night to assemble such a long list of names from Palmer's paperwork."

"I had assistance. My colleagues in Lord Grey's service—"

"Ah yes. Still, such a pity."

"Pity?" Mal's stomach lurched.

"Yes, to spend so many hours on such a fruitless exercise."

"I do not think it fruitless, begging your pardons, sirs. It opens up many avenues of enquiry–"

"Do you presume to tell us how to conduct the administration of the realm, Master Catlyn?"

"No, sir, of course not." Was the prince in charge here, or Cecil? As Secretary of State, he had taken over many of Sir Francis Walsingham's responsibilities, if not his spy network.

"As I was saying, a fruitless exercise." Cecil leaned across the table, fixing Mal with his dark eyes. "I put it to you that Nathaniel Palmer is an innocent party in this. A decoy. You say it is he who fired at the King and then took his own life?"

"Aye, sir."

"A dreadful slander against an upright citizen, is it not? What cause have you to connect Palmer with the assassin?"

"His horse, sir. I followed it–"

"I read the report. A livery horse, open to hire by any that wants it. Is that right?"

Mal bit back the urge to point out that this too was in his report. "Aye, sir. And Palmer was the last to hire it."

"And this is the whole of your evidence against him?"

Mal hesitated, but he could not say any more without incriminating himself.

"Well?"

"Aye, sir."

Cecil picked up another sheet of paper, folded like a letter and bearing the greasy stain of a wax seal on its upper edge.

"Would it surprise you to learn that Master Palmer is alive and well?"

Mal stared at him. "Aye, sir, it would."

He took the proffered letter from Cecil and scanned the few short lines. *Regret to have inconvenienced your lordships… Called away on urgent business… Horse stolen north of Islington….* It looked credible enough, but Mal would stake his life on it being a forgery. If Palmer were alive, why would they need a letter as evidence?

"So you see, Master Catlyn, it could not possibly have been Palmer who shot the King, could it?"

"I suppose not, sir."

"Indeed I put it to you that your identification of the body was wholly mistaken and prompted by your well-known partisanship towards the skraylings."

"Sir?"

"The assassin, Master Catlyn, was a skrayling, not a Christian man."

"No, my lords, I swear. I examined it myself, and my brother confirmed–"

"Your brother Alexander." This from Egerton, a former lawyer elevated to one of the highest posts in the land and the man who had eventually issued Ned and Gabriel's pardon. Mal breathed a little more easily.

"Yes."

"Who spend many years in Bethlem Hospital, and then sojourned among the skraylings. Who last night went to their guild-house on some secret mission?"

So, Cecil and his intelligencers had swayed Egerton to their cause.

"He was making enquiries about Palmer, on my behalf," Mal said.

"Was he now?"

"Yes, sir."

Egerton snorted and looked at his colleagues. "I do not think a madman can be considered a very credible witness, do you?"

Mal had no answer. He was not about to agree with the lawyer, but neither was there much point in gainsaying the truth.

"So," Cecil said, "we have your word that the assassin was Palmer, and Palmer's own word – countersigned by credible witnesses – that he was nowhere near London on that day. Whom do you think I'm inclined to believe, Master Catlyn?"

The guisers who are pulling your strings. Unless you are one of them yourself.

"What do you intend to do about it?" he asked instead. "Hand the body over to the skraylings for identification?"

"Really, Catlyn, do you think us so naive? The body has already been quartered and displayed above the gates of the city. Such a pity the head did not survive in any useful condition. No–" Cecil laced his blunt fingers together "–we shall stamp out this rebellion before it spreads."

Prince Arthur spoke for the first time.

"The skraylings will be expelled from the realm," he said, "and forbidden to return on pain of death."

A little late for that, since they are probably leaving the city as we speak. "Does that include Sark, Your Highness?"

Arthur turned to his left.

"Eventually," Egerton conceded. "The island was gifted by Her Majesty the Queen, of blessed memory, and can therefore only be taken away by her heirs. God willing King Robert will recover and enact this reversal; if not, his heirs will surely do so."

His heirs. Then they are already planning for Edward's accession. Is Arthur complicit in all this?

"I think our business with Master Catlyn is concluded, don't you, gentlemen?" Cecil said, glancing around the table.

The other Privy Councillors nodded, and Mal breathed a sigh of relief.

"You are dismissed. But take care, sir; your bias in this matter has been noted."

Mal bowed and backed out of the council chamber. Though he was relieved beyond measure to have escaped arrest, it was now clear that the conspirators behind the assassin had achieved their principal goal: to expel the skraylings from England. From now on, the guisers would be free to exercise their powers in the capital, with no one to gainsay them.

CHAPTER XXV

The tolling of the city's bells could mean only one thing: another royal death. Mal stopped a palace servant in the passageway.

"What's happened? Is the King dead?"

"Prince Edward, God rest his soul," the man replied, making the sign of the cross.

Mal echoed the gesture absentmindedly. Dear God, that meant Henry was now Prince of Wales... He ran out into the courtyard and shouted to a groom to fetch his horse.

The city streets were crowded with citizens debating the latest news, but the people scattered as Mal spurred his mount onward, through Ludgate and down to London Bridge. One thought blazed in his mind: that he had to get Coby and Kit out of the Tower before another day dawned on this benighted kingdom.

After a brief stop in Southwark to gather everything he needed, he rode back into the city and along Thames Street to the Tower. Approaching the castle gate he adopted what he hoped was an authoritative air.

"I wish to speak to my wife, Lady Catlyn," he told the older of the two guards, a stout fellow of about forty with streaks of grey in his spade-shaped beard. "I've brought clean clothes for her and my son."

The guard squinted at Mal from the archway and stepped forward into the sunlight.

"Sorry, sir, no one's allowed in or out except to collect their dead. Privy Council's orders."

"But you could bring her to the gate, could you not? As long as I do not enter the Tower and she does not leave, there can be no problem."

The guard scratched his beard. "I suppose not."

"Well, then." Mal folded his arms and gave the man an expectant look. After a few seconds he took the hint.

"Right you are, sir."

Mal watched him cross the causeway and disappear through the gate of the Byward Tower, then turned his attention back to the gatehouse.

"This is where the Queen and her ladies were lodged after the attack on the king?" he asked the other guard.

"How'd you know that?" The younger man's brow wrinkled in suspicion.

"Because I was here that day, helping to convey His Majesty to safety."

The guard's eyes widened, and he looked at Mal with more respect.

"That's right, sir. The chamber above isn't used for much in peace time."

Mal nodded thoughtfully. It had a good view of the space in front of the gates, and perhaps of the causeway; an ideal place from which to direct operations. He wondered if Olivia had somehow managed to slip ahead of the procession and make her way up there. Afterwards, no one would have questioned her presence in the Queen's sanctuary. The woman left nothing to chance, that was plain.

The minutes passed painfully slowly, but at last the first guard returned with Coby. Her expression remained guarded, hands clasped tight at her waist as she crossed the causeway. He couldn't blame her. He had promised to get Kit out of London, and he had failed. The fact that it was none of his own fault didn't matter.

When at last she reached the shadow of the gatehouse, he allowed himself to step forward a pace and hold out his arms in greeting. She hesitated before stepping into his embrace.

"If you love our son, feign gladness," he whispered in her ear. "I must speak to you privily."

To his relief she slipped her arms around his waist, though she trembled almost as much as she had that very first time he held her, in the shadows of an alley where her male guise would not attract attention. Tentatively, still fearing she might recoil, he kissed her brow, then released her and went over to the first guard.

"Look here," he said in a low voice, glancing back towards Coby. "I haven't had the pleasure of my wife's company in many nights, if you know what I mean."

The guard gave him a quizzical look. Mal took a silver crown from his purse and pressed it into the man's hand.

"One of these for you and your comrade here, and another for yourself when we're done. For the hire of the chamber above."

"That's very generous, sir."

"Not at all. You men work hard in the defence of the Crown, you deserve a little pleasure of your own."

Mal took his wife's arm and they were shown up to the chamber above the guard-room. A couple of cots stood against the wall, surrounded by empty barrels, bundles of kindling and other detritus of soldiering. Mal thanked the man, then closed the door and waited, listening for his retreating footsteps. When he was certain no one was eavesdropping, he led Coby over to one of the cots.

"Just for the look of it," he said, "in case we're interrupted."

For a moment he thought she would refuse. Well, she had every right to doubt him until he had proven himself. He sat down on the cot and gestured for her to sit beside him. "First we need to get you and Kit out of here."

She smiled at last, with a shadow of the mischief they used to delight in sharing. "I was already working on a plan, but your advice would be welcome."

He listened to her description of the reconnoitre, nodding and prompting for more information at intervals.

"The eastern exit? That must be the one they call the Iron Gate. You will leave tonight?"

"The moon is scarce past new," she said, her eyes sparkling with excitement now. "There can be no better time."

He took her hand, and she did not resist. "Then I shall be waiting for you outside the gate, from midnight until an hour before dawn."

She leant forward a little, and to his surprise he realised she was inviting a kiss. He obliged, intending it to be only the briefest of caresses, but the touch of her lips on his shook him to the core. Before he knew it he had taken her in his arms and was kissing her jaw, her throat, weeping his regrets into her unbound hair.

"Ssh, my love," he heard her murmur, but that only made it worse.

With an effort he gathered the shreds of his dignity and pulled one hand free to wipe his eyes. When he looked up, her eyes were shining too. He opened his mouth to apologise for his past heartlessness, but she reached up and put a finger to his lips.

"What need we of words?" she whispered, and kissed him again.

By the time the guard knocked politely on the door half an hour later their reconciliation was complete, and they went their separate ways with lightened hearts and many a secret smile.

Kit spent a very dull morning and an even duller afternoon alone in his bedchamber, Doctor Renardi having forbidden him to attend lessons in case he overtaxed his mind too soon after his seizure. At first Kit had been delighted, but then the doctor also forbade reading or physical exertion, so he had nothing to do except stare out of the window. For a while he amused himself by watching the sentries patrolling the battlements and trying to count the ravens that flew around the little towers of the great keep, but even that became boring after a while.

A search of the room produced a couple of worn pennies with which to play shove-groat on the top of one of the chests, though it wasn't really smooth enough, and then he lost one of the coins when it skidded off and rolled into a crack in the floorboards, so that was the end of that. After what felt like hours, Master Weston sent Sidney to call him to supper, and Kit was never so glad to see the other boys in his life, even de Vere.

When supper was over, Doctor Renardi made more of his sleeping draught and sent both the younger boys to bed. To Kit's surprise the doctor brought two cups to their chamber.

"You both need your sleep," he said, "and you, Master Sidney, will disturb Master Catlyn less if you sleep soundly."

Sidney folded his arms. "Take it away. You're trying to poison us, like you did Prince Edward."

Kit looked doubtfully at the cups, then at Doctor Renardi. "It was all right last night."

"It is not poison, Master Sidney. See?" The doctor took a sip from one of the cups. "Now drink up."

"What's in it?" Sidney wrinkled his nose as he took the one that Renardi had drunk from.

"Chamomile and a little valerian."

"It's really not horrid." Kit took a gulp of the warm, sweet liquid. "There's honey too."

The doctor waited until they had both emptied their cups, then left them to undress.

"I hope I'm allowed to do lessons tomorrow," Kit said, climbing into bed.

"I wish I could swap places with you. I hate Latin."

"*Perodi linguam Latinam,*" Kit translated.

Sidney giggled. "You see? You're much better at it than me."

The bed-ropes creaked as Sidney got in and the two boys lay in silence, their usual squabbles over cold feet and farts forgotten. Kit pulled the covers up to his chin and prayed for the sleeping draught to work quickly. Tomorrow couldn't be any worse than today.

"I want to help," Sandy said, barring Mal's way out of the kitchen.

It was a childish gesture, one that took Mal back to old arguments won – and lost. He laid a hand on his brother's shoulder and looked into his dark eyes, wondering if there was anything really left of Sandy in there, or if Erishen had taken over entirely.

"And you can. By going to Deptford. If there's a single skrayling vessel left that can carry us out of England, you are the best person to approach her captain."

Sandy nodded slowly, as if digesting this. *You made me wait for this*, Mal could not help but think. *Now it's your turn.*

"So," he said aloud, "can I get on with my own business?"

Without waiting for a reply he gently pushed his brother aside and headed up the stairs. A moment later footsteps followed him.

"But I could transport Kit out of the Tower in the blink of an eye," Sandy said as he caught Mal up in the parlour. "You wouldn't need to go to all this trouble."

"Could you? With our enemies right there?"

Sandy opened his mouth to speak, but Mal held up a hand to silence him.

"Don't be a fool, Sandy. If anything went wrong, I could lose you as well as Coby and Kit."

His brother sagged, defeated. Mal closed the space between them, embraced him.

"It won't be long now," he murmured. "Just a few more hours, and we'll all be free."

That night Coby went to bed as usual with the other ladies, but just before midnight she rose and silently dressed in her boy's attire that Mal had thoughtfully included in the bundle of clothing. Her lock-pick roll went into one pocket, a purse of coins and jewellery in the other, and she tucked a sheathed dagger into the back of her belt, just in case. Last of all she fastened a spirit-guard around her throat, since there was a chance she might have to face Prince Henry or even Olivia tonight.

With her shoes in her left hand she padded down the stairs to the dining room in her stockinged feet. Now came the hardest part. In order to get to the walkway she had seen, she would have to go through the Queen's bedchamber. She tiptoed through the small parlour and up the steps, and pressed her ear against the door. To her relief she heard snoring. Hardly daring to breathe, she eased the latch down and opened the door just wide enough to slip through.

The Queen's bedchamber was pitch dark, the air thick with the smell of a used chamberpot. Coby sidled along the wall furthest from the bed, groping for the door that she knew was there. At last her fingers met wood studded with nail heads.

The bed creaked.

"…and don't do that again…"

Coby froze, heart pounding fit to burst out of her chest.

The voice died away into a mumble. Coby offered up silent thanks; it was only one of the ladies-in-waiting talking in her sleep. She opened the second door as quietly as the first and closed it behind her, then groped her way up the stairwell to the floor above. The scuff of boots on the outer wall-walk betrayed the guards' patrols, but she had become accustomed to their patterns after more than a week in the Tower. Far fewer guards patrolled the inner ward. After all, no one expected an attack from within.

The door to the walkway leading into the Wakefield Tower was locked but not bolted, for which she was vastly grateful. It suggested that the door at the other end might be similarly secured; if it were bolted from within, she would have to rethink her route. She knelt and unrolled her tools, and soon had the door open.

Out in the cool night air, her courage almost failed her. There was so far to go yet, and she still did not know if she could even get them out of the fortress. She closed her eyes for a moment and took a deep breath, then scuttled across the short walkway, hunched down low enough not to be easily spotted by a sentry.

Mal looked around the room, checking he hadn't forgotten something. He wore his blades and carried a modest sum of money in his purse, but that was all; he did not want to be laden down for this venture. All his spare clothes and other belongings had been packed and sent to Deptford with Sandy and Gabriel.

"Are you sure you won't come with us?" he said to Ned.

His friend shook his head. "We belong in London, Gabe and me. Anyway, with you lot gone for good, I doubt the guisers will care about us."

"You know I'd stay, if it weren't for Kit and Coby. 'Tis not cowardice that drives me away."

"I know." Ned clapped him on the shoulder, and gave him a sympathetic look. "I'd do the same for Gabe, if it came to it."

They made their way down to the courtyard, and Mal cautiously opened the wicket gate. The curfew bell had long since rung and the night was as black as he could wish, not even a glimmer of moonlight visible in the narrow streets. Here and there a lantern burned outside a house, enough to light their way but casting plenty of shadows too.

Mal stepped out into the street, ears alert for any sound of a watchman or a lurking footpad. This side of midnight there were still a few late revellers about, too emboldened by drink to care about the watch and too blinded by it to notice a predator in an alley-mouth until it was too late. Armed and sober men made an unattractive target in comparison, but Mal wanted no trouble tonight.

Slipping from shadow to shadow they made their way down Long Southwark and across Saint Olave's Street to a riverside lane. Dozens of wherries bobbed against the jetty, waiting for their owners to return at dawn. On the far bank, the Tower was lit up like a pleasure garden, torches burning at intervals along the wall-walks and around the tops of the towers. Mal's heart sank. It was a goodly distance from Saint Thomas's Tower to the easternmost corner of the castle; could Coby get that far without being caught?

"Too late to back out now," Ned whispered, catching his mood. "Help me untie one of these, will you?"

A few minutes later they were sliding across the murky waters of the Thames, with Mal at the oars and Ned crouched in the bows, steering them towards the darkness at the downriver end of the Tower. Mal wondered how the ferrymen managed to cross the river so easily when they couldn't see where they were going.

"Slow down!" Ned hissed. "I can hear another boat."

Mal glanced back over his shoulder. The waters all along the Tower quayside glittered gold in the torchlight, but in one spot the slow rhythm of the current was disturbed by a dark shape not much bigger than their own boat. As Mal watched, it disappeared into the tunnel under the wharf that led to Traitor's Gate.

"We should follow them," Ned said. "If the water gate's open, we can get right inside the castle, can't we?"

"No. The last thing we need is to be caught in a confined space, and anyway we could miss Coby and Kit altogether." He bent to the oars again. "We stick to the plan."

Kit woke in the night, his mouth dry as paper and his bladder aching. Perhaps the sleeping draught hadn't been as strong this time, or perhaps he was getting used to it already. Sidney was still snoring at his side, his arm flung out across the blankets. Kit thought of poor Edward, dying in his bed only a few yards from here. Perhaps he wouldn't get up and use the chamberpot just yet. It was easy enough to scoff at ghosts in the daytime, but at night when footsteps echoed and shadows shifted in the moonlight ... It couldn't be long until dawn, surely?

The ache in his bladder got worse, and he was just about to chance getting out of bed when he heard the door of their chamber creak. Was that Master Weston coming to wake them for breakfast, or the prince's ghost? He waited, heart pounding so loud he wondered that it didn't wake Sidney. The whisper of shoeleather on stone came nearer and nearer the bed. He wriggled upright, hardly daring to breathe. Should he wake Sidney? No, his companion would only tease him about it if it turned out to be nothing more than a servant.

The footsteps halted close to the bed. Light moved beyond the curtains, but not on the same side as the footsteps. There were two of them? Kit backed against the headboard, and next to him Sidney stirred.

"You awake, Catlyn?" the other boy mumbled.

At that moment the curtains were wrenched aside. Kit had a momentary glimpse of an unfamiliar man's face, yellow and black in the candlelight, then something was pulled down over his head, like Uncle Sandy's hat in the game of Hoodman Blind. A drawstring tightened about his throat and rough hands seized him. Kit kicked and tried to shout for help, but drawing breath only sucked the sacking dust into his mouth and made him choke. In his panic his full bladder gave way.

"Gah! Little bastard pissed all over me!"

"Less wriggling, little master," a second voice growled, "unless you want to feel the back of my hand."

Kit lay still, just as he was told, whilst they bound his wrists and ankles and wrapped him in something that felt like a blanket. One of the men hoisted him up, threw him over his shoulder and carried him out of the portcullis chamber, past the garderobe to the spiral stairs. At first Kit thought – hoped – they were going to the upper chamber, and that this was nothing worse than some cruel new jest of Prince Henry's, but the man went down and down, through a small room and down again into a great echoing space like a cellar. Finally they were out into the cool night air and the man halted as if waiting for something.

Kit twisted in the man's arms, determined to get free, but that only earned him a sharp slap around the head. Tears pricked his eyes. If only Henry had not taken his sword from him; he could have kept it by his bed and killed the man the moment he attacked.

A creak and a splashing sound, then Kit was carried rapidly downwards. The world lurched, and Kit cried out as he was thrown through the air, landing with a painful thud in what felt like the arms of another man.

"Just the two of them?" That was the man now holding him.

"For now," said another man, one Kit had not heard before. "Quick, before anyone sees the water gate is open."

Kit was lowered onto a hard surface that moved under him. After a moment he realised he was in a boat. Two of them, the man had said. Then at least he was not alone.

CHAPTER XXVI

Coby inched around the roof of the Bloody Tower just inside the battlements, praying she could not be heard in the room below. There must be a way into the tower here somewhere, otherwise why build the walkway across to the inner ward in the first place? At last she reached the far side and the low turret that topped the stairwell. Her hands were shaking so much she could scarcely hold the lock-picks, never mind fit them into the lock. Putting down the tool-roll for a moment she laced her fingers together and knelt in silent prayer. When the pounding of her heart had dimmed a little, she tried the latch, just in case – and the door swung open. Part of her wanted to believe it was Providence, but at the same time she feared there must be something badly wrong if the prince's lodgings were so ill-defended.

With a sick feeling in her stomach she went down the stair, which was so narrow her shoulders brushed both sides. Where would Kit be sleeping? In the prince's chamber, or somewhere else? She hoped it was the latter, so she kept going down until she reached the lower floor. A lantern burned down here and she had to shield her night-adjusted eyes against its light. The stink of a garderobe somewhere nearby explained the light's presence. Coby tiptoed past and found herself standing on a walkway above the tower's portcullis mechanism. On the other side of the passage, two doorways led into a chamber, and a door at the end was no doubt the one that had been guarded last time she was here. Now it stood open to the night, and Coby's feeling of dread worsened. She opened the nearest door and went in.

It took no more than a glance to confirm that the bed was empty. A chill crept over her heart. Where could the boys possibly have gone at this time of night?

"Kit?" she whispered, praying this was some prank.

Further examination only increased her anxiety. The bed had been slept in, but the bedding lay in tangled disarray and the hollows where its inhabitants had been lying were still warm.

"I thought you were done here?"

Coby whirled and dropped into a crouch, drawing her dagger. A man in black scholar's robes stood in the doorway, squinting at her through horn-rimmed spectacles perched on a prominent Roman nose. Steel-grey eyebrows sprouted over the spectacle rims, matching his neat silver beard.

"Where is my son?" she hissed. "What have you done with him?"

"Who are you?" His accent was Italian, and he looked familiar from somewhere.

Coby advanced on him, the dagger a reassuring weight in her hand.

"Tell me where–" she broke off, not wanting to give herself away "–where the Catlyn boy is."

The Italian shrugged. "I am not privy to His Highness's business."

"But you knew someone was coming here tonight. You left the doors unlocked and unbolted."

"Yes."

"What else do you know?"

When he did not reply, she backed him towards the portcullis mechanism.

"What else?"

He eyed the blade and licked his lips. "He'll kill me if I say more."

"And I'll kill you if you don't." She hoped she sounded more convincing than she felt. Shooting a man was hard enough; she didn't know if she could stab one.

"Cambridge. They were taking them to Cambridge. That's all I know, I swear on the Madonna."

She made a feint towards the Italian and he flinched back, giving her space to turn and run for the outer door. Behind her she could her him raising the alarm, but she ignored it, pounding down the stairs and across the inner ward to the gateway under the Bloody Tower.

She halted, panting. In the faint light of the torches it looked as though Traitor's Gate was open. So that was how they got out. Cursing under her breath she ran along the outer ward to the rose garden. Mal was still waiting for her, and if she was quick enough they might yet catch the villains who had stolen away her son.

Mal and Ned loitered in an angle of the wall that marked the end of the south moat, just round the corner from the Iron Gate. Midnight had come and gone, and still there was no sign of his wife and son. What if they had been captured? As if in answer, a bell began clanging on the far side of the castle.

"We should get out of here!" Ned hissed.

"No, we wait a while longer," Mal replied, clutching the curved hand-guard of his rapier so hard he almost expected the metal to bend.

Rapid footsteps echoed from the high walls of the castle. After a while a soft splashing sound came from the moat.

"What was that?"

He leaned over the moat wall and saw a small boat coming towards them.

"Coby?" he whispered under his breath.

It seemed like forever before the little craft bumped against the base of the wall.

"Mal? Is that you?"

"Aye. And Ned. Where's Kit? Hand him up to me."

A pause. "He's gone. Taken."

Mal swore.

"Ned, hold onto my legs." He leaned over the wall as far as he could reach without toppling into the moat himself. "Take my hands, my love."

She leapt and grasped his wrists, and he hauled her up, all the time horribly aware of how conspicuous they must be. Sure enough, a shout went up from a nearby tower, followed closely by the bark of a musket. A nearby capstone exploded, showering Mal with grit. Coby got a foot onto the edge of the wall and scrambled awkwardly over the top. The three of them crouched behind the wall for a moment.

"They took Kit and another boy, I think," Coby panted. "Through Traitor's Gate by boat."

Mal jerked his head towards the river. "Perhaps we can still catch them."

They broke cover and ran, and were soon hidden from view of the Tower by the houses that clustered around the river stairs. Mal untied the boat and waited for the others to get in.

"Come on!" Ned beckoned with his steel hand. "No time for courtesies. Get rowing!"

"Which way?"

"Downstream. The Italian said they were taking him to Cambridge."

"Italian?"

"I think he was the same man we saw at Ferrymead House. Suffolk's physician."

"Renardi. I might have known he'd be one of Jathekkil's lackeys."

Mal bent to the oars, glad that Coby had taken a seat in the stern where he could at least see her outlined against the lights of the Tower, even if her face was in shadow. Only her eyes were visible, glinting in the reflections off the water, cold and hard as obsidian. He didn't envy the men who had taken Kit, if she ever caught up with them.

Mal rowed for as long as he had strength, but they did not catch up with any boat that looked to contain the two young captives. Coby craned her neck, scanning both banks, though it was still too dark to make out much beyond the rough boundary between land and water.

"Do you think we're close yet?"

Mal released the oars with a sigh and stretched his back.

"I fear they are well ahead of us by now. It was a faint hope, my love, at best."

"But we have to find him." Her voice was overloud in the still pre-dawn air and edged with panic.

"We shall. But not this way." He turned and nudged Ned, who was dozing in the bow. "Take an oar, will you? Sandy and Gabriel will be wondering where we've got to."

Kit woke with a start, wondering why he felt so cold, and why his nightshirt was damp. Then he remembered wetting himself, and the men with the sacks and ropes, and he panicked, thrashing around and banging his head on something that felt like wooden panelling.

"Calm yourself, boy, or you'll roll overboard!"

A man's voice, gruff and unfamiliar. Kit lay still, his mind racing. Last night. Men who stole into his room, tied him up and carried him away. But how had they got into the castle? There were high walls and lots of guards; that was why the assassin had waited until the King came out. No one should be able to get inside unless Prince Henry allowed it.

Another thought came to him. What if they had taken him away thinking he was Henry? They were about the same age, and everyone always said they looked like brothers. When these men found out he wasn't the heir to the throne, they'd be angry and might throw him overboard to drown. He stifled a sob. Where were Father and Uncle Sandy? They would give these villains the beating they deserved.

The thought cheered him up and he lay there for a while imagining his father leaping into the boat, sword drawn, to dispatch both men, and then Uncle Sandy scooping him up and untying him. The boat rocked, and for a glorious moment Kit thought his imaginings had come true. Then someone pulled the sack off his head and he discovered the bitter truth: the only grownups here were three strangers. One looked like he might be the man who first attacked him, though it was hard to be sure. At any rate they all looked villainous, with their ill-kempt hair and beards and their eyes as hard as stones. Two of them wore stained shirts and baggy canvas breeches, like sailors or workmen; the third was better dressed, in a dark doublet and hose, but not a fine gentleman like his father.

One of the workmen helped Kit into a sitting position, then did the same for another small figure lying in the bottom of the boat. Sidney.

Kit knew better than to speak, but he tried to catch his companion's eye. Sidney didn't seem to notice; his face was pale and streaked with tears.

The man turned back.

"I'm going to untie your hands now, boy, so you can eat breakfast and relieve yourselves without my help. But no foolishness, do you hear me?"

Kit nodded.

"Good." The man drew a knife. "Because his lordship only said he wanted you boys in one piece. He didn't say nothing about not hurting you."

Kit flinched as the man seized his arm, but it was only to hold him steady whilst he cut his bonds. Kit chafed his sore wrists, then took the hunk of bread the man offered him. It was a couple of days old and turning hard, but at least it wasn't mouldy. De Vere liked to tell tall tales of the prisoners kept in the Tower, and how they were lucky to get anything to eat that the rats hadn't pissed on first, but then de Vere talked a lot of pigswill. Just because his father was an earl he fancied himself cleverer than the rest of them. Kit had once heard him say that his family was far older than the Tudors and should be on the throne instead of them. Perhaps that was what this was all about. Treason.

A little heartened by having some food in his stomach, Kit looked around properly for the first time. The sun was above the horizon now, on their right hand side, which meant they were travelling north. Quite where they were, though, he had no idea. A sea of reeds stretched in all directions, and the water their boat moved on was wreathed in mist. Little birds twittered all around them, like grasshoppers in a meadow. Craning his neck, Kit could just make out low hills on the western horizon, and a dark smudge that might be London. His throat tightened and he tugged the rough blanket closer about his shoulders. He wasn't going to cry, he wasn't.

But as the city slipped further behind them, his vision blurred. *Please, Uncle Sandy, it's your turn to come and find me this time.* He wasn't sure what he meant by that, but it comforted him a little.

••••

Sandy and Gabriel were waiting for them on Deptford Strand. As the boat bumped against the jetty and Sandy realised that Kit was not with them, he let out a pitiful wail. Mal leapt ashore and took his brother in his arms.

"We'll find him, I swear," he murmured, pressing his forehead to Sandy's and opening his mind willingly to the storm of grief.

It felt like hours later when Coby gently prised them apart, though the sun still hovered on the horizon so it could not have been more than a few minutes. Sandy was calm at last, but Mal felt as if the marrow had been scoured from his bones, leaving him hollow.

"Come on," she said quietly, "we can't stand around here all morning. We know where they're taking Kit, so we just have to catch up with them."

"How? They have a head start."

"I don't know how, but we have to try." She glanced over her shoulder. "Could Sandy find him, once we're away from the other guisers?"

"Perhaps. But I don't want to overtax him. You said they were taking Kit and the other boy to Cambridge."

"Yes, but… Oh. Shawe."

"Indeed. I don't know what the bastard is up to, but I cannot think it bodes well for our son. And we may need every ounce of strength that Sandy and I have if we are to overcome our enemies' magic."

"Well you can't cross the river here," Ned said. "Not unless you know your way across the Isle of Dogs and through the marshes to the Great Cambridge Road. And you can't go anywhere near the Tower, that's for sure."

Mal let out a growl of incoherent frustration. "And the city gates will all be watched. Henry must know by now that we know Kit has been taken. How the hell are we to get to Cambridge?"

"Leave it to me," Ned said with a wink.

Southwark was stirring by the time they got back to the Sign of the Parley. Ned unlocked the gate and ushered everyone inside, glancing nervously up and down the street. Just when he thought he and Gabriel might be able to forget about the guisers, the bastards went and did something like this. Poor little mite, stolen away from everyone he knew!

He shut and bolted the gate behind them and joined his friends in the kitchen.

"So, what's this plan of yours?" Mal asked.

Ned gestured to Gabriel, who was grinning like a child with a secret.

"Burbage has been thinking of sending the Prince's Men on the road," Gabriel said, "since the theatres are all closed now. You can travel with us until we're safely out of London, then ride ahead to Cambridge and we'll catch you up when we can."

"And Burbage can furnish you with disguises as well," Ned added. "Wigs, false beards, the lot."

"That's perfect," Coby said, and turned to Mal. "Isn't it perfect?"

He nodded cautiously. "How soon could you get the players together? We need to leave as soon as possible."

"I'll have them rounded up before noon," Gabriel said.

"Noon? That's too long," Mal muttered.

"You'll be of no use to the lad if the prince claps you in irons." Ned went over to the hearth and got out his tinderbox. "Besides, you can't leave without some breakfast inside you. You look fit to faint, the pair of you."

Mal glanced at his brother, who sat hunched over at the far end of the table, head in his hands.

"Very well."

"I'll be off then," Gabriel said, rising from his seat.

Sandy looked up abruptly.

"Can we trust these actors?" he asked. "We still don't know who all the guisers are, or their lackeys. What if Burbage, or Shakespeare, or–"

"Of course we can trust them," Ned said. "Shakespeare helped get me and Gabriel out of the Marshalsea, remember? If he's a guiser, I'm a Moor. And Burbage is too much the drunken whoremonger to be of any use to anyone."

"I'll go with you," Coby said to Gabriel. "I can pick out some costumes for disguises and run errands."

"No." Mal caught hold of her sleeve. "We stay here, the three of us. I won't risk you being caught."

"And you think here is safe? It's the first place they'll look."

A long silence whilst they all pondered this likelihood.

"She's right," Mal said at last. "Forget breakfast, Ned. Let's gather our belongings together and get out of here. Gabriel, we'll meet you, Ned and the Prince's Men at the Globe at noon."

Ned put down his ladle. "Where will you be?"

"Best you don't know. I have a few boltholes around Southwark; we'll be in one of those." He clapped Ned on the shoulder. "Try not to get arrested in the meantime, eh?"

Kit's spirits sank as the day wore on. The marshes seemed to go on forever, empty of people or roads or any means of escape. And yet he knew from studying maps that this was only one small corner of England. How big the world truly was, compared to the little globe that fitted within the compass of his arms.

They stopped for the night on an island in the marshes. The workman untied their ankle bonds once he had carried them ashore; like he said, it wasn't as if they could go anywhere. The well-dressed man threw some clothes at them and told them to put them on. Kit was vastly relieved; though the night was warm, he felt uncomfortable wearing just a nightshirt in the presence of strangers. At least it had dried out, even if it did still smell of piss a bit.

Sidney pulled a face. "These are peasant's clothes. I'm a cousin of the King; I can't wear these. I won't."

"You'll put them on or feel my belt," the well-dressed man told him. "Cousin or nephew or the prince hisself, I care not."

Kit pulled on the rough woollen slops, hoping that last comment had not been aimed at him. However the men hadn't addressed him as "Your Highness" yet, so perhaps they hadn't been trying to abduct the prince. But in that case, what did they want with him? His father wasn't rich or powerful...

"There's no drawers," Sidney whined, though not loudly enough for the man to hear him.

"Tuck your nightshirt around your bum," Kit said, showing him how. "That way they won't itch as much."

There were no stockings or shoes either, just jerkins of the same woollen stuff, threadbare and a bit musty-smelling.

Kit spread out his blanket as far from the water as possible whilst staying well away from their captors, and the two boys sat on it huddled together, more for mutual comfort than warmth. The bird noises had quieted, to be replaced by the croaking of frogs and the whine of mosquitos. The setting sun traced rose and gold ripples across the dark water, but there was not a building to be seen on the horizon nor any firelight nor smoke from a chimney. They were alone in this flat, watery wilderness.

The well-dressed man built a fire in the middle of the island and started grilling fish threaded on sticks. Kit's mouth began to water, and he tried to take his mind off his grumbling stomach by trying to work out how far away the frogs were, but it was no use. The younger of the two workmen must have heard it even over the croaking, because he brought them some more of the bread, but no fish. Sidney looked as though he was about to complain, but the man leered at them and he thought better of it.

"I want to go home," Sidney mumbled when the man had gone back to the fire.

"So do I," replied Kit. "But my father and uncle will find us soon and rescue us, I promise."

Sidney eyed him suspiciously. "How do they even know where we are?"

"I..." He shrugged. How could he explain it, when he didn't understand it himself? He just knew, as sure as if someone had told him.

"I think we should try to escape. Steal a couple of horses and ride away as fast as we can. I bet those two ruffians have never been on a horse in their lives."

Kit sighed. "Where are we going to find a horse out here, clotpole?"

"We have to wait until we're back on dry land. There's bound to be a house or a farm or something."

"And of course you know all about stealing horses."

"I know how to ride one, better than you."

"Do not."

"Do so."

"Oi, quiet, the pair of you!"

Something whistled through the air, and Kit yelped in pain. A stick, thrown by one of the men round the fire. He gave Sidney one last jab in the ribs then turned his attention to the bread he'd been given, and for a long time his jaws were occupied with something other than talking.

Afterwards he lay back down on the damp mossy ground and tried to get comfortable. The roots of the tree stuck in his back worse than Sidney's elbows had, back in the bed they shared in the tower. After a while the men put out the fire and settled down to sleep themselves. Kit lay awake staring at the stars, wishing he could fly up there amongst them. The thought gave him a shivery feeling, like he could make it happen if he really wished hard enough. He closed his eyes and concentrated for the longest time but nothing happened. With a sigh he rolled over and buried his face in the blanket.

CHAPTER XXVII

The first challenge was to get to the bolthole unnoticed. On a warm summer's morning they would be more conspicuous hooded and cloaked than with their faces uncovered, but on the other hand the twins stood out in any crowd.

"We'll wear our plainest clothes and go openly," Mal told them. "If we look like we're going about our lawful business, we're less likely to be noticed."

He led them through the quiet streets towards Bankside, crossing Long Southwark well away from the Great Stone Gate that guarded the southern end of London Bridge.

"Try to look less furtive," he hissed to Sandy, taking him by the arm. "We're just a trio of hardened carousers looking for an early start to our pleasures."

By way of demonstration he forced a laugh, as at a ribald jest from his companions. A Southwark matron sweeping her doorstep rolled her eyes at them and brushed the dirt more aggressively in their direction.

"I could cloud the memories of anyone who recognised us," Sandy said.

"You'll do no such thing. We might as well send out heralds to cry our names and whereabouts through the streets."

"Jathekkil and Ilianwe would not even notice, if I did it skin-to-skin–"

"No."

At last they came to the house Mal sought, in an alley not far from the courtyard where he and Percy had been ambushed. New and hastily built, its timbers were already warping in the damp English climate, and it leaned out so far there was scarcely an arm's length between its upper storey and its neighbour across the alley.

He knocked on the door thrice, paused and knocked again. The door opened to reveal a girl of about sixteen, beggarly thin apart from a belly swollen with child. Mal ushered the others inside.

"Upstairs, back room," he told them, slipping the girl a coin.

"What is this place?" Coby whispered. "A whorehouse?"

"Not exactly."

He followed Sandy and Coby upstairs, into the dingy bedchamber. Its shutters stood open, though the sun was not yet high enough to clear the roofs. Lines of laundry hung from the sill, crossing the courtyard behind the house. Coby pulled back the bed-hangings and wrinkled her nose.

"This *is* a whorehouse."

"It's where the whores come for their confinements," Mal said. "I pay them a small stipend, and they keep this room for me when I need it. What they do with it the rest of the time is none of my business."

He did not add that some men found pregnant women arousing, and thus there was a little truth in his wife's assessment. No point in sowing doubt in her mind, not when the breach between them was so recently healed.

The chest was under the bed where he had left it. He pulled it out, disabled the poisoned-needle trap and unlocked it.

"Now I believe you," Coby murmured, squatting down next to him. "Isn't that the box from Paris?"

"The very same." He lifted out a tray full of documents and set it aside. Underneath was a pouch of money and another, slightly larger bag, which he handed to Coby. "Steel shot. I had some made up, when I first returned to England. Hoped you'd never have to use it."

She grimaced. "I hope I don't have to, either."

He locked and rearmed the box and put it back in its place. There was nothing to do now but wait. He sat down on the edge of the bed and Coby drew a three-legged stool over and sat at his feet, leaning against one of his legs. He stroked her pale hair, schooling his heart to patience, though he wanted nothing more than to run through the streets in pursuit of his son's abductors. He was no use to Kit dead, he reminded himself again and again.

The sun had crept above the rooftops and was just casting a tentative beam over the windowsill when Mal was jerked out of his reverie by the sound of knocking downstairs.

Coby jumped to her feet. "Surely no one knows where we are, do they?"

Mal opened the door and stepped out onto the landing. Muffled voices in the street, and another knock, urgent and demanding.

"Both of you, this way!" he hissed at his companions. "Bring the saddlebags. Hurry!"

They crept down the stairs as fast as they could, Mal leading the way. At the bottom he signalled silently to Coby, who nodded.

"Hold fast there!" she shrieked in her best Bankside accent, "I'm on the pisspot."

"I don't care if you're on your deathbed, woman," a muffled voice came from beyond the door as they fled down the passageway. "Open up, in the name of the King!"

Mal pushed through the end door, through a dark and smoky kitchen and out into the courtyard. Another alley led westwards. Mal edged down it and peered out into the street. No soldiers here yet. He waved his companions across the road into another alley that ran behind the Rose Theatre. Not far to the Globe now.

Coby slipped through the gates after Mal and allowed herself a sigh of relief as the familiar smells of the theatre yard enveloped her: sawdust, stale beer and the fear-sweat tang of nervous actors. Or perhaps that was just her imagination. Her heart was still pounding from their flight through the back alleys of Bankside.

"Why is the wagon not loaded yet?" Mal said to Gabriel, gesturing at the stack of chests and crates in the yard.

"We still have to get you lot past two sets of gate guards," Gabriel replied. "And in truth, I do not trust the other actors not to give you away. The fewer who know you are with us, the safer you will be."

He opened one of the chests, which proved to be empty but for a bit of sacking in the bottom. Coby dumped her saddlebags into it and stepped in after them. The last thing she saw as she folded herself down into the box was Mal arguing quietly with his twin. Sweet Jesu! Could Sandy never do anything without complaint?

Gabriel brought an armful of costumes and dumped them on top of her, then shut the chest. She could hear the straps being buckled tight, and wondered how she would get out if no one came to free her. Would she be able to lift the lid high enough to saw through the leather with her belt knife? She drew a slow breath to quell her rising panic. She was with friends and loved ones. She was doing this for Kit. Whatever happened, it was worth it.

Her hiding place was lifted into the air and carried some distance before being thrown down onto a hard surface with a jolt. She pressed the back of her hand against her mouth to stifle a cry of panic. Someone pushed the chest so that it slid across the wagon bed and bumped up against something, sending her crashing into that same end, shoulder and head knocking painfully against the inside wall. Scarcely had she recovered from the shock when her feet and knees felt the impact of another chest pushed up against hers. Mal, perhaps, or Sandy.

It seemed like an age before the loading was completed and the wagon set off. Bouncing around in the bottom of the crate, Coby wished Gabriel had put the pile of costumes beneath her instead of on top. She would gladly risk discovery in return for fewer bruises.

Some distance further on the wagon turned, then turned again, and slowed to a halt. Was this the Great Stone Gate? She held her breath, hearing voices from the driver's seat that lay only inches beyond her head. The faint, demanding tones that must be the gate

guard, followed by the more mellifluous voice of the actor Richard
Burbage. She thought she heard Prince Arthur's name mentioned,
and imagined coins changing hands. At last the wagon lurched into
motion once more, juddering over the cobbles of London Bridge and
into the city itself.

Mal twisted in his confinement, trying to get comfortable. His legs
were too long: even with his feet braced against the far wall of the
crate, his knees were practically by his ears and his joints burning
with the strain. It brought to mind the scavenger's daughter, a cruel
device used to crush men until their ribs cracked and blood spurted
from their nostrils – or so the ballads said. A prayer came unbidden
to his lips, from the times long ago when he had woken often from
nightmares of blood and death.

*"Sancte Michael Archangele, deduc me per tenebras. Ferro tuo viam
illumina..."*

By the time the wagon finally halted and he heard the scrape of the
other crates being unloaded he was ready to weep with relief, but he
only kissed the pommel of the dagger he had been clasping between
his sweat-grimed hands and offered up a final thank-you to Saint
Michael. Even the bone-shaking impact of the chest being dumped on
the ground felt sweet as a release, until another prospect occurred to
him and his heart lurched in fear. What if this was not the inn outside
the city walls, but Aldgate? He braced himself for discovery, prepared
to come out fighting.

Scrape and rattle of buckles being undone, then a flood of blinding
light as the chest was opened and the concealing costumes pulled
aside. Mal looked up but could not make out the figure standing over
him, only a glare as of light reflecting off a steel helm. As he prepared
to draw the dagger, the blur resolved itself into the shape of a man,
bare-headed and haloed in light.

"Here, let me give you a hand," Gabriel said.

Mal accepted the offer gratefully, levering himself up on his elbow
whilst Gabriel hauled on his free arm. Cramped muscles screamed at

him and he staggered and nearly fell, but the other man caught and steadied him. Mal took a deep breath and sneezed in the dry dusty air. They were in a barn, bright speckled shafts of sunlight picking out the gilding on the actors' wagon. Coby ran over and flung her arms around him.

"We're not out of the woods yet," he murmured, brushing her hair back from her cheek with the edge of his thumb.

"I know." She turned her head and kissed the palm of his hand, sending a delicious shiver all the way down to his balls. He gently pushed her away; now was not the time for distractions.

"Is this the Three Horseshoes?" he asked Gabriel.

"Aye, just as you asked."

"You're hoping for news of Shawe?" Coby said.

"It seemed worth a try." He clapped her on the shoulder. "Speak to the landlord. Find out – discreetly – if he has any deliveries for Shawe. I'd go, but he might recognise me from last time and inform our enemies." He turned to his brother. "Stay here with the wagon. I don't want the landlord seeing you either."

Satisfied that everything was under control, he headed out into the street. There must be a livery stables around here somewhere. Of course Henry or one of his allies might have had the wits to send out warrants to all the stables and inns with descriptions of Mal and his brother, but he had to chance it. They had already lost a morning just getting out of London; God only knew how far ahead of them Kit might be by now.

The actors settled down to a lavish dinner of chops, pies and boiled meats whilst Coby approached the landlord, a balding man with a belly that proclaimed his trade as blatantly as the sign above his door.

"What can I do for you, lad?"

She thought quickly. "Master Burbage would like a jug or two of beer for the road."

"You one of them actors, then?" He looked her up and down. "I must say, you boys look a lot more convincing as women from a distance."

"Yes, I'm sure we do," Coby replied, not sure whether to be insulted, or grateful that he hadn't seen through her disguise. "Now, if you please, sir, the beer. We've a long way to go and it looks set to get even hotter this afternoon."

"You'll want to stop in Waltham Abbey, then, if you're heading north. Should get there by sunset, this time of year."

She peered past the landlord into the shadows of the storeroom behind him. A row of crates were stacked just inside the door. Could they be for Shawe? "You know, if you have any letters or packages you need delivering to Bedford or Cambridge or... or Lincoln, we'd be glad to take them."

The man frowned in thought and stared up at the rafters as if the information were written there in the soot.

"Can't say as we do, but I'll ask around."

Coby thanked him again and went to bid farewell to Ned and Gabriel, who promised to be in Cambridge within the week.

"Won't Burbage want you to play every tavern between here and Norwich?" she asked.

"He's not Naismith," Gabriel said. "The Prince's Men don't play for just any rabble. I'm more worried he'll want to stop at some country house for the summer."

"You mean like Lord Burghley's new place?" Ned said. "I hear it's fit for the King himself, God speed him to good health."

"Burghley House?" Gabriel looked thoughtful. "Now there's somewhere to aim for. It's north of Cambridge, so perhaps we can persuade Burbage to press on to the town itself first."

She bade them farewell again and ran out into the yard, just in time to see Mal arriving with the hired horses. Under cover of strapping their belongings behind the saddles, she told him what she had seen.

"Crates?" he said. "You're sure?"

"No, I imagined them. Yes, I'm sure. What do we do?"

He sighed. "Even if they are for Shawe, I doubt our enemies would conveniently label them with his place of residence. We'll go to Cambridge, and track him from there. That was the plan."

"When have our plans ever gone the way we intended?"

He squeezed her hand where it rested on the saddle's cantle.

"Don't think like that. We have to get him back." He patted the horse's rump. "Wait there. I'll go and fetch Sandy."

Mal cursed under his breath. Sandy was not in the wagon where he was supposed to be. Surely he could not have gone far? He strode down between the stalls, peering into each one. He didn't really expect to find his brother hiding in one of them, but perhaps the hayloft...

He was about to look around for a ladder when he heard a soft humming from the far end of the building, where the shadows were thickest. A single narrow beam of sunlight shone on the silken rump of a dapple grey, which was all Mal could see of the stall. Shielding his eyes against the light he moved forward.

"Sandy?"

His brother was standing by the horse's head, fussing with its mane.

"Sandy. Thank the Lord, I thought you had run off, or done something equally foolish."

"You mean like looking for Kit?" He smiled slowly. "Did that already."

"You what? Sandy–" Mal looked around to make sure they weren't being overheard. "You promised you wouldn't try and dreamwalk until we were well away from London."

Sandy ignored him. Mal realised he was braiding the horse's mane, separating it into neat sections, and humming what sounded like skrayling music.

"Well?" he said at last. "What did you find?"

"He's alive, and Shawe doesn't have him yet."

"Well, that's good news, at least."

"There's more. Kiiren is beginning to awaken."

"That's not so good." Mal went to step into the stall, but the grey stamped a back hoof. "Come on, we'd better find him before the guisers work out who and what he is."

"I think perhaps they already know, and that's why they took him."

"So what do we do?"

"We get closer, then we use him as an anchor to take us straight to Shawe."

"You think we have a chance against the alchemist?"

"The English guisers are weak compared to Ilianwe. I think we can–" Sandy grinned, his eyes seeming to flash gold in the beam of sunlight "–kick his arse."

CHAPTER XXVIII

Kit stumbled along the dusty road, wincing every time a sharp-edged pebble bit into the sole of his foot. They had reached the edge of the marsh after another day's travel and followed a little river northwestwards until it was crossed by a stone bridge. There they disembarked and took the road, which wound through low rolling hills. The boys' legs were left unbound so that they could walk, but their captors hemmed them in on all sides, and one of the workmen threw his knife into a gatepost as demonstration of what would happen if they tried to run for it.

Kit's feet were soon blistered and aching from walking barefoot, and he had to knuckle away the tears before Sidney or one of the men saw him. As the sun began to sink, however, they came to a lane that led off through a wood. Long cool grass grew on the raised strip between the wheel ruts, and Kit was able to ease his sore feet for a while.

At the end of the lane stood a ramshackle farmhouse, its windows no more than dark holes staring blindly across a weed-grown clearing. An equally shabby barn stood to one side, but to Kit's delight the sound of a horse stamping its hooves came from within. Sidney had been right. But what if they escaped and Uncle Sandy missed them? No, his uncle would find him wherever he was, he was certain of that. And he would rather ride away from here than spend another day walking.

The well-dressed man paused on the edge of the clearing and whistled like a song thrush, two short notes repeated twice, followed by a long trill. After a few moments a figure appeared in the doorway.

"About time," the stranger shouted. "I was beginning to think you'd been caught and strung up."

The well-dressed man laughed. "The way was cleared for us. Our masters have all under their command."

The two boys were hustled into the farmhouse and taken down some rickety stairs, where they were locked in a cellar without so much as a stick of furniture to make it comfortable. A few thin bars of moonlight crept in through the shuttered windows, which were too high up to reach.

"I wish I had my sword," Kit muttered, jumping ineffectually to try and reach the wooden slats. "We could hack this open, wriggle out and steal a horse."

"I'm not going anywhere," Sidney said with a sniff. He sat down on the floor and tried to examine his feet in the faint light of the waxing moon.

"Don't be a baby."

"I'm not a baby." He glared up at Kit. "I'm seven years old, older than–"

"Ssh!" Kit went to the other end of the cellar, ignoring his own stinging feet. The floorboards overhead were warped and uneven, with gaps between some of them big enough to stick his finger through. He craned his neck and listened.

"...still, it's a lot of trouble to go to for a pair of skinny wretches–"

"Our orders were very specific. The King's godson and the hedge-knight's brat, alive and whole."

Kit's mouth tightened. His father was no hedge-knight! He had lands and a patron at court and everything.

"Well I don't like it. Stealing kids ain't my idea of a good day's work."

"No one's asking you to like it. And it's a little late to complain now, don't you think?"

The first speaker – one of the workmen – grumbled something that Kit couldn't make out.

"Good, then. Now, gentlemen, get some sleep. One more day and we'll be done, then you can collect your pay and depart if you wish."

Kit sank back down to the ground, trembling with a mixture of panic and delight. Only one day left, which meant they had to escape tonight, but on the other hand their captors were going to sleep. He waited as long as he dared, fearing he might fall asleep himself, before padding across to the door. The lock was old and rusty, and anyway he had no idea how one was supposed to pick them; it was always made to sound so easy in stories. It would have to be the window, then.

"Here, Sidney, wake up!"

His companion woke with a cry. "Yes, Your Highness, I'm coming!"

"Ssh! It's me, Catlyn. We've been taken prisoner, remember?"

Sidney gave a sniff and a gulp. "What...?"

"Come on, we're going to escape."

"How?"

"You're going to climb onto my shoulders and pull the slats off one of the windows."

"I can't. My feet hurt too much."

"Yes, you can. Or do you want to be sold into slavery?"

Sidney squeaked. "Slaves? They can't do that, I'm—"

"The prince's cousin, yes, I know. So act like one." Kit sighed, and went over to the wall below the shutter with the widest gaps in it. "Come on."

Sidney got to his feet and limped over. Kit laced his hands together and gave the boy a boost up. Sidney scrambled wildly for purchase, slipped, and they fell in a painful heap on the floor.

"Ow! Clumsy ox! What did you do that for?"

"It wasn't me, you didn't stand still—"

"You were sticking your foot in my ear—"

"I had to put it somewhere—"

"Ssshh!"

Kit clamped his hand over Sidney's mouth. They lay there, locked together, for long minutes, waiting for the well-dressed man to come and tell them off.

"I don't think they heard us," Kit said at last, letting his breath out in a great sigh.

"It was your fault–"

"Hush! Or do you want to get us both killed?"

Sidney didn't answer.

"Come on, then, let's try again."

This time Sidney managed to climb onto his shoulders without mishap. He pulled at one of the slats.

"They're not coming away, Catlyn."

"Pull harder." Kit braced himself against the wall.

A moment later there was a creaking, tearing sound, followed by a dull clatter as the first slat fell to the cellar floor.

"I did it!"

Another slat fell, and another. Then nothing.

"What are you doing up there?" Kit whispered.

"I don't think I can pull any more loose. They're all too strong."

"Can you get through the hole?"

"I don't think so."

"Get down, let me have a go."

Sidney half-climbed, half-fell to the floor.

"I don't know if I can hold you," he said, his face paper-white in the moonlight.

"You have to try. Come on, I'm taller and skinnier than you. Just get down on all fours and I'll stand on your back."

Sidney did as he was told, and Kit placed a foot on the boy's trembling back. Holding himself steady against the wall he pushed upwards until he was standing with his eyes just below the level of the window. It wouldn't be easy, but there were a few slats he could reach. He took hold of one and carefully worked it loose.

"Yes!" he whispered in triumph as it came free.

He tossed it to the floor and set to work on the next one. That would do. He could probably get through a gap that big. He jumped down to the floor.

"Right, this is it," he said. "Come on, Sidney, give me a proper boost this time. I'm going to climb through."

Sidney pouted. "Why do you have to go first? I'm oldest."

"I'm the tallest, and it's my plan."

"Very well." Sidney crouched and laced his hands together. "Ready?"

"Ready."

Kit placed his left foot in Sidney's hands and pushed up with his right, leaping for the window frame and catching hold of it with both hands. A splinter dug into his palm and he nearly let go, but desperation drove him on. He pulled himself up until his head and shoulders were through the gap and wriggled for all he was worth, ignoring the scraping of the broken slats on his back and legs. A few moments later he rolled free of the window and lay on his back in the grass, panting.

A dark shape loomed over him.

"Going somewhere, gentlemen?"

Mal urged his mount on to as swift a pace as his companions could manage, and by nightfall they had reached the village of Hoddesdon on the Great Cambridge Road. Being a comfortable day's travel north of London the village was well supplied with inns, though most of them were full at this time of year with farmers going to and from the various summer fairs. Mal ended up paying over the odds for three spaces in the common room of the Swan, a large timbered building on the high street.

"No dreamwalking tonight," he warned his brother over supper. "The last thing we need is you shining out like a beacon to our enemies."

Sandy merely nodded, but his eyes spoke eloquently of his frustration.

Mal's own frustrations were of a less noble sort. He longed to curl up with his wife and forget his troubles for a while in the pleasure of her kisses, but would be impossible here. The best he could manage was to slip an arm around her waist under the thin blankets, and then only because the inn was so full that everyone was crammed cheek by jowl anyway.

"We'll get proper accommodation in Cambridge," he told both of them, as they set off next morning on fresh horses. "The town should be quiet, since most of the students will have gone home for the summer."

"Do you know anyone there?" Coby asked, guiding her nag alongside his.

"It's been a long time, but I dare say a few of the masters who taught me are still alive. One of them must surely be able to introduce me to someone who has met Shawe."

"We should have spoken to that friend of his before we left London. Harry someone-or-other?"

"Thomas Harriot?" Mal shook his head. "He's Northumberland's pet. If he knows where Shawe is, I doubt he'd tell us, and he'd certainly tell Northumberland we'd been asking after him. And Northumberland will tell Prince Henry, you can be sure of that."

Sandy spoke for the first time. "Jathekkil already knows where we are going. You left Renardi alive."

"I could hardly murder him in cold blood," Coby replied. "Anyway, even if I killed the doctor, Prince Henry would have guessed I spoke to him."

"Henry may have warned Shawe, but we can't let that stop us," Mal said. "Cambridge itself should be safe at any rate. Shawe prefers remote manorhouses, the better to conceal his alchemical experiments."

"So where is he?"

"Somewhere far enough outside the town for secrecy, but most likely not so far that he is cut off from his allies. The Fens are a lonely place; we should not have too much trouble finding him."

"Like looking for a needle on a bare floor instead of among the rushes."

"Exactly."

They rode on for a while in silence, past newly harvested cornfields and orchards heavy with blushing apples. Despite the cold spring the year had been a good one, an unexpected blessing to counteract the horror of events in London.

"You and Sandy should put on your disguises now, before we arrive," Coby said. "Best you get used to them."

They drew aside into a copse of ash and maple, and Coby handed out the clothes. For Sandy, a serving woman's gown with a linen coif to cover his hair and a broad-brimmed hat to hide his face; for Mal, a scholar's black robe and cap. Sandy shaved his chin smooth with his obsidian razor, and Coby applied a little powder to cover the remaining dark stubble.

"Don't you have a disguise?" Mal asked her.

She shook her head. "They're looking for Lady Catlyn. I'm better off like this."

"Renardi could have described you to our enemies."

"We'll have to take that chance. I will be of no use in a fight encumbered by skirts, and I have not the time nor skill to change my face."

After Mal had drawn the robe on over his other clothes, Coby carefully painted extra white hairs into his beard and hair, to make him seem older.

"You look half a skrayling now," Sandy jested. "Perhaps I should braid beads into your hair."

Mal pulled a face. "Perhaps I should cut off your hair, make you look more like a skrayling woman."

"Enough!" Coby stepped between them, her eyes bright with tears. "Kit lies captive, and all you can do is make merry?"

"I am sorry, my love." Mal drew her aside. "We only lighten our hearts to stop us from weeping."

She nodded as if in understanding, and Mal bent to kiss her brow.

"Mount up," he said. "We have delayed long enough."

"This is all your fault," Sidney muttered as they bounced around in the back of the covered wagon.

The well-dressed man had tied them up after the failed escape attempt, and next morning there had been no breakfast. Now it was well past noon and still they had not stopped for a rest nor been given dinner. Kit's stomach gnawed at his ribs, and his arms and legs hurt all over from being battered against the wooden floor and side of the wagon.

"We had to try and get away, didn't we?"

Sidney gave him a sullen look and turned his back. Kit sighed. He was too exhausted to argue with Sidney anyway. He lifted his bound hands to his mouth and tried to chew at the rope some more, but the fibres poking out of it were like needles in his chapped lips and he soon gave up. Licking the metal-tasting blood from his lips he wedged himself into a corner of the wagon. If he sat bolt upright, his head rested against the canvas covering instead of wood and it was almost comfortable.

He drifted off into something that was not quite sleep but not quite wakefulness either, and the next thing he knew it was getting dark. The cart had drawn off the side of the road into a field and their captors were making a fire. The smell of food made Kit's mouth water.

A canvas flap lifted, and one of the workmen peered inside.

"You lads hungry?"

Kit nodded warily.

"Tough. Master Waggoner says you're to have nothing until the morrow, to teach you what happens to lads what disobey."

Sidney let out a whimper that turned to a cough.

"Still, we don't want you arriving half-dead," he said, leaning into the wagon, "so you can have this between you."

He pushed a tankard towards Kit, who grabbed at it with his tied hands. The man laughed and left them.

Kit lifted the tankard to his face. It smelt like the small ale they usually had at breakfast. He took a sip, hoping they weren't drugging him again, then gulped about a third of it back.

"Here, save some for me!" Sidney launched himself across the wagon.

"Watch it, you'll spill it!" Kit clutched the tankard to his chest. The lukewarm liquid splashed against his shirt, filling the air with its heady scent.

"Give it here, then."

Kit passed the tankard to Sidney with shaking hands. Weak as it was, the ale was already going to his head. He lay back against the boards and fell asleep within moments.

Kit looked round dazedly as the wagon drew to a halt. The workmen hauled them out and untied their bonds, and Kit slumped down onto his hands and knees in the grass, head ringing.

"Come on, boy," the well-dressed man said, hauling him to his feet by the back of his shirt. "Don't you want to see your new home?"

Kit looked up, and his heart rose. In front of them stood a well-built house of pale grey stone with five gabled windows along the roofline and a tall chimney stack at each end. Diamond-paned glass glinted in the setting sun.

"Where are we?" Kit rasped. A small part of him still hoped that this had all been a horrible misunderstanding, and that the house before him was the home he had grown up in, rebuilt by his father after the fire.

"I don't suppose there's any harm in you knowing, seeing as you're not leaving any time soon," the well-dressed man said. "This is Anglesey Priory, a school for bright boys such as yourself."

Kit swallowed past his disappointment. "A school? But what about Master Weston?"

"I will teach you things that small-minded pedant never dreamed of."

Kit whirled to see a black-clad man standing at the lefthand corner of the house, as if he had appeared out of thin air. The man smiled and ran his eyes over the two boys, like a farmer sizing up sheep at the market.

"Perfect," he said at last. "Come."

He shepherded them towards the door.

"You'll want to watch out for that one, sir," the well-dressed man called out. "He's tried to run off once already."

"Really? We can't have that, can we?" Cold hard fingers dug into Kit's shoulder. "We'd better find somewhere safe to put you for the night."

He turned aside from the door and took the two boys around the back of the house to an outbuilding. Most of it was overgrown with ivy and looked as ancient as the Bloody Tower, but the stonework around the door had been repaired and the door itself was of new oak studded with gleaming iron nails. Kit opened his mouth to protest that they were hungry, but one look at their new captor's face told him this would only earn them worse punishment than simply being locked up for the night.

The schoolmaster unlocked the door with one of the keys from the bunch hanging from his belt, and pushed them inside. Kit glimpsed sacks and barrels stacked around the walls before the door closed, plunging them into darkness.

"My father will hear of this," Sidney wailed as the key turned in the lock. "He's the King's cousin, you know."

"I think he already knows that, clotpole," Kit muttered.

He felt his way towards where he had seen some empty sacks. If they couldn't escape right now, best to get some sleep and hope a better chance came along tomorrow.

CHAPTER XXIX

The storehouse door creaked open and Kit blinked against the light.

"Come out of there, both on yer!"

Kit clambered to his feet, expecting to see the schoolmaster again, but this was a different man. Clean-shaven like the other but younger, with long mouse-brown hair tied back from his face. He wore a plain brown doublet and hose, very neat and tidy apart from a ragged scarlet cloth tucked into his belt. He regarded the two boys with solemn hazel eyes.

"I'm Master Fox," he said, as if guessing Kit's next question before he had even thought it. His accent reminded Kit of his father and uncle. "Master Shawe sent me to fetch you two to breakfast."

"Breakfast?" Sidney whimpered, stumbling out behind Kit.

"Aye. Now come along."

"Are we in Derbyshire, sir?" Kit asked him as they walked back round the house.

"Nay. You see any hills round here, lad?"

"We came through some, yesterday."

Fox snorted. "Pimples. Nowt like back home."

The front door led directly into a large whitewashed chamber that looked like a cross between a classroom and a chapel. Fox showed them through a door on the far side and down half-a-dozen steps into a long gloomy stone hall with a vaulted ceiling like a wine cellar. A table ran the length of the room, and boys of varying ages sat along either side, the oldest at the far end. The scent of food met Kit's nostrils and he breathed in deeply, feeling a bit faint.

"Breakfast's on sideboard," Fox said. "Help thysens and sit down."

The two boys stammered their thanks and raced over to the trestle table, where baskets of bread and a vast tureen of pease porridge were laid out. Kit filled an earthenware bowl and took it to the end of the table nearest the door. Half the end bench was occupied by a couple of boys a bit older than him. Both had cropped hair and were dressed in blue-grey doublet and hose, as were the rest of the boys at the table.

"Excuse me? May I..." Kit inclined his head towards the seat.

One of the boys looked up from his breakfast with faraway eyes. Kit noticed he wore an earring in his left earlobe: a hoop of dull grey metal onto which had been threaded a bead of bright blue glass. It looked incongruously dandyish against his plain attire.

"You're new," the boy said slowly.

"Yes." Kit put down his bowl and held out his hand. "Kit Catlyn, if it please you."

The boy stared at his hand as if it were some exotic creature in a menagerie, then grinned up at Kit.

"Heron," he said.

"I..."

"This is Shrike," the boy continued, indicating his companion, who just stared at Kit with an unpleasant glint in his eye. He too wore a blue glass earring; was it some kind of badge of the school?

"Those are your names?" Kit asked.

Heron nodded. "We all have our brotherhood names. You'll get one too, once you've been tested."

Kit didn't like the sound of that, but he took the introduction as permission to sit down. For several minutes he ignored his new friends and stuffed his face with bread and porridge as fast as he could without choking. No one commented on his manners or even seemed to notice him. He glanced up at Sidney, who had taken the seat opposite.

"What is this place?" he whispered across the table.

Sidney shrugged and popped another chunk of bread in his mouth, chewing it determinedly. Kit scraped the last spoonful of porridge from his bowl. Not a moment too soon; a bell rang and the other boys got up from their places and began filing towards the sideboard with their empty bowls. Kit followed them.

After they had deposited their bowls in a stack, the boys skirted the far end of the table, making towards a spiral staircase halfway down the room.

"Not you two," Master Fox said, barring Kit's way with a calloused hand. "Sit down."

Kit and Sidney did as they were told. Fox went to a chest at the far end of the room and sorted through piles of clothing. At last he returned with two of the blue-grey suits, two pairs of shoes and a couple of changes of linen apiece.

"Well? Get 'em on, quick now."

Kit stripped under the cold gaze of the... what was Fox, anyway? He didn't dress like a schoolmaster but the way he ordered them round, he was no servant either.

Once they were both changed, Fox led them through a side door and round the back of the rear wing. Crumbling walls projected from the back of the house, as if it had once been part of a much bigger building. Master Shawe had called it a priory, which meant that monks had once lived here, before old King Henry, the prince's great grandfather, had sent them all away.

They followed Fox through a kitchen garden, past more ruins to a low outbuilding that looked cobbled together from more of the priory's old masonry, though its roof was of new red tiles. Its narrow windows were stopped with sheets of horn rather than glass. Smoke drifted up from the chimney, along with a few greenish sparks. Fireworks? Perhaps that was why all the ground around the building had been cleared and covered with a thick layer of crushed stone.

They crunched across the yard and Fox knocked on the door. Whilst they waited he turned and glared down at the boys.

"Touch nowt, understand?"

Kit nodded.

They were kept waiting for ages, but eventually the door opened to reveal Master Shawe. The headmaster was dressed in a long leather apron and tucked under his arm was a strange sort of helm with a visor made of glass. Kit took a step backwards, but Fox caught him by the scruff of the neck and shoved him over the threshold.

Inside, the building was dim as a cellar and stank of smoke, metal and something else Kit could not identify, at once acrid and chalky but sweet like stored apples. Some kind of oven or forge stood at the far end, its coals casting a faint red light that reflected back from dozens of bottles and jars on shelves ranged along one side of the workshop. Shawe laid the helm on a trestle table near the fire and opened a small wooden box.

"You." Master Shawe pointed at Kit. "Come here."

Kit walked towards the fire, trying not to show how scared he felt. He halted just out of arm's reach of Master Shawe. The man beckoned impatiently, and Kit shuffled a little closer. Shawe seized Kit's jaw and tilted his head to the right.

"You should have shorn them first," he snapped, over Kit's head. Before Fox could answer, he went on. "Never mind, you can do it later. One disturbance is more than enough for a morning."

He released Kit and turned away for a moment, uncorking a bottle and upending it against a wad of cloth. Taking Kit's jaw again in one hand, he swabbed his earlobe and tossed the cloth aside. Kit tried to see what he was up to out of the corner of his eye.

"Do not move, or this will be more painful than necessary."

A moment later something pinched his earlobe and popped through the skin with a sickening crunch. Kit clenched his teeth, and somewhere over on the other side of the workshop Sidney whimpered. Shawe rummaged in the box, then pinched Kit's ear again, or at least that's what it felt like. He pulled Kit nearer to the fire and lifted a tiny pair of red hot pincers out of the coals. Kit tensed, ready to run despite Shawe's warning, but all that happened was a sudden warmth behind his ear and a stink of hot metal and singed hair. At last Shawe let him go and he stumbled, panting with relief.

"Now the other one."

Kit weaved down the length of the workshop to where his friend was waiting. Sidney's breeches were dark where he had wet himself with fear; Kit was rather glad he'd gone first.

"It's all right," he whispered. "It really doesn't hurt very much."

That was true enough, though it was beginning to itch and burn now, like nettle rash. He lifted a hand tentatively to his ear and felt a small weight swinging from his earlobe. He remembered the blue beads worn by the other boys, Heron and Shrike.

"Was that the test?" he asked Master Fox as they waited for Sidney to get his ear pierced. "Do I get a special name now?"

Fox snorted a laugh. "Yer reckon that were a test? Nay, thou'll have to wait a spell longer for that. What thou's got there is a finding charm. You try to run away, Master Shawe'll track thee down and bring thee back here in a trice."

Kit lifted his hand towards his ear.

"And don't try and take it out neither," Fox added. "It's welded shut, so thou'll have to cut off thine own ear first."

Kit swallowed and wiped his bloody fingertips on his doublet. For the first time since that night on the marsh island he felt like crying, but he wasn't going to give this fellow the pleasure. Instead he crossed his arms and waited. He must have been missed by now, surely? His father and uncle would come and find him, and no amount of charms would stand in their way.

The players' wagon trundled northwards on the Great Cambridge Road at a leisurely two miles an hour, and Ned trudged along behind it. On the first day he had strolled arm-in-arm with Gabriel, chatting merrily about everything and nothing, but now his feet were sore, his shirt itchy from the sweat trickling down his back and his face gritty with the dust thrown up by the wagon.

"Why so glum?" Gabriel asked, dropping back to walk alongside Ned once more.

"Just reminded of our travels through France," Ned replied. "Feel like I'm going into exile again."

Gabriel laughed. "We're not two days out of London. Anyone would think you'd never left Southwark in your life."

"It's all very well for you. You've been everywhere with your actor friends. This–" he gestured towards the empty heath on either side of the road "–this might as well be France, for all I know of it. It looks godforsaken enough."

"Cheer up!" Gabriel poked him in the ribs. "We'll soon be stopping for the night, and good English beer is the same everywhere. Well, perhaps not quite"…"

Gabriel turned his head, looking back down the road to London. Ned followed his gaze and swore. A knot of seven or eight horsemen were galloping down the shallow slope of the road straight towards them. Sunlight glinted on steel helms and the hilts of swords. Soldiers or bandits? Either way, it looked like trouble. Ned backed towards the wagon, pulling Gabriel with him.

"Watch it, lads!" Burbage called out. "Someone's in a tearing hurry. Out of their way!"

The horsemen slowed as they approached the wagon, but instead of trotting past in single file they split into two groups, one circling round to block the wagon's path and the other reining to a halt at the rear. Several of the men drew pistols or short, well-used swords. A heavy-set man in a steel gorget and helm, evidently their leader, jerked his pistol towards Burbage.

"Where are the traitors? Bring them forth."

"What traitors, sir?" the actor replied. "We are all loyal servants of Prince Arthur."

The man sneered. "Loyal, eh? Well, that's no business of mine. I'm looking for Catlyn and his brother."

"Why? What have they done?"

"Only broke into the Tower and kidnapped the King's godson. Now hand 'em over."

"They're not here."

"They were seen near the Globe Theatre in Bankside. Your theatre. Where are they?"

"They parted from us on the road," Burbage said. "We kept company for a while, that is all."

"Where are they going?"

"How should I know? They are acquaintances of ours, nothing more."

"Acquaintances, eh? I hear Catlyn and his brood have been lodging with a one-armed printer and one of your actors, a fellow named Parrish. Which is he?"

Gabriel stepped forward before Ned could stop him.

"I am."

The man pointed his pistol at Gabriel. "Where are the Catlyns going?"

"I don't know," Gabriel said softly. "And I wouldn't tell you if I did."

The leader narrowed his eyes at them, then turned to the man at his right hand and jerked his head towards the actors. The riders dismounted, all except their leader, and closed in on the wagon. Ned stepped in front of Gabriel, staring the nearest man in the eye.

"Suits me," the ruffian growled. "I'll just spit you both together."

"Search the wagon," the leader shouted. "Rip up the floorboards if you have to, but find those two traitors."

Burbage made a strangled noise of protest as the men began throwing costumes onto the dusty ground, followed by the emptied chests and crates.

"They're not here, captain," one of them reported at last.

"Prince Arthur will hear of this." Burbage shook off the man holding him and approached the captain. "By whose authority do you harass me and my men?"

"Who do you think sent us, you fat oaf? Prince Arthur heads the Privy Council now."

Ned swore under his breath. Olivia had them all by the balls.

"And the King?" Gabriel asked.

The captain leant over his saddlebow and scratched his chin. "What's the fancy lawyers' phrase? 'No longer in command of his faculties.' Arthur is regent, until such time as the King recovers. Or dies."

"Orders, sir?" one of the riders called out.

"Arrest these two–" he pointed to Ned and Gabriel "–and send the rest of 'em on their way. We've wasted enough time here already."

Ned's arms were tied behind his back and he was lifted onto a horse in front of one of the soldiers.

"Don't wriggle, you little whoreson," the man growled in his ear. "And watch what you're doing with that hand, or I'll cut it off to match the other one. Or perhaps me and the lads'll just make merry with your pretty friend, whilst you watch. Bet that'll get you talking, eh?"

Ned swallowed the urge to turn and butt the man senseless. Two against ten was poor enough odds to begin with, even if he wasn't tied up.

"Good. Behave yourself and answer the captain's questions, and we might even let you go."

The man laughed and kicked his horse into a canter. Ned clung on with his knees, trying to work out a plan of escape. *Let us go, my arse. We'll be lucky to get out of this in one piece.*

The soldiers turned off the high road a few miles on, trotting in single file down a bridle-path leading through the sparsely wooded hills, and halted at last in a circle of beech trees. Ned was hauled off his mount and collapsed, light-headed, onto the thick golden leaf litter. At least it was shady here.

Someone hauled him upright by the back of his doublet, and a sharp metal edge pressed against his throat.

"Now, tell me where your friends went."

"Drink..." Ned gasped.

"Bring him a drink, so we can hear him speak," the captain told one of his men.

Thin wine splashed over Ned's lips and he gulped at it greedily. His head was still spinning, but he had enough wits to know that they would both die painfully if they didn't give these men the information they wanted. He considered lying, sending them off on a wild goose chase. That would buy Mal some time, but wouldn't help Ned get away. He had to lead them into a trap, somehow. And what better to bait a trap with than the truth?

"Well?" The captain leaned over him. "Speak up."

"Cambridge." Ned licked his lips. "They went to Cambridge."

"Ned, no!"

He shot Gabriel a helpless look. The captain looked from one to the other.

"Cambridge. Where in Cambridge?"

"An inn. The Pike or the Mackerel or something. I can't remember."

"Perhaps we should torture them anyway, sir, just to be sure," one of the soldiers said.

The captain frowned in thought. "No, torture takes too long. We'll save it for when they turn out to have lied to us."

Some of the soldiers dispersed into the trees to relieve themselves whilst their companions passed round the wineskin.

"Why did you tell them?" Gabriel whispered, leaning as close as he could reach.

"Would you rather be murdered and left to rot out here? If we lead them to Mal, they might keep us to use as hostages. If not, they'll kill us out of hand and hunt Mal down anyway."

"And that's your plan, is it?"

"Do you have a better one?"

Gabriel shook his head.

"Enough of the sweet talk, lover boy!" Ned's riding partner put a boot to Ned's shoulder and kicked him over. "Get on your feet. I'm not going to carry your stinking carcass any further than I have to."

Ned struggled upright and limped over to the man's horse. Poor creature, it looked exhausted already.

The captain evidently had the same thought.

"We'll rotate the prisoners to spare the horses," he said. "Dawson, you take the cripple; Jenkins, your mount looks fresh, you can have the actor."

Dawson, an ill-favoured fellow with yellow hair sticking out from under his helmet like a scarecrow's straw filling, glowered at Ned.

"We should hire a couple of mules at the next town, spare our own mounts," he said.

"Are you giving the orders now, Dawson?"

"No, sir. Just a suggestion, sir." He led his horse over to Ned, and boosted him into the saddle.

"Good. We're barely twenty miles from Cambridge. If we ride hard, we can catch up with Catlyn before sunset."

CHAPTER XXX

Master Fox conducted them back to the dining room and found a replacement pair of breeches for Sidney.

"Thou'll have to wash those thysen," he said, indicated the soiled clothing.

"But I'm the prince's cousin–"

"Aye, we know that. Thou dostn't think we choose just anyone, dost thou?"

He threw the breeches to Sidney and left them to their own devices. Kit explored the room, examining every window and piece of furniture, but found nothing of interest. After an hour or so the sound of footsteps came down the stairwell, followed by the boys themselves. They trooped past Kit without so much as a word and headed up the steps to the front hall. Even Heron and Shrike barely glanced in the newcomers' direction. It was all very odd, and Kit didn't like it one bit.

Master Fox returned and showed Kit and Sidney upstairs. The upper room was as large as the lower one, and served as a dormitory. The two boys were assigned beds near one end, then Fox set them to carrying buckets of water from the well in the rear courtyard back up to the dormitory and filling the jugs on the washstands. When they had done that he gave Sidney a wash-ball to clean the soiled breeches with and sent them back down to the yard.

"Don't they have any servants here?" Sidney grumbled as he draped the sodden breeches on a bush to dry. The branches bowed under their weight and they fell to the ground, getting dirty again. Sidney burst into tears. Kit picked the breeches up and rinsed off the worst of the muck, then hung them up properly. Wiping his hands on his own clothes he led the way back into the house. One day soon he would test Master Shawe's finding charm, but not yet. He needed to fill his belly a few more times, and work out where to steal some food from to take with him.

As they neared Cambridge, Coby realised she had never actually been through the town before. The college authorities did not allow companies of players within the bounds lest they distract students from their lectures, so Suffolk's Men had had to perform outdoors at Stourbridge Fair or avoid Cambridge altogether. On one visit they had skirted the northern edge of the town, where a somewhat decayed and neglected castle stood on a south-facing escarpment. There she had seen the whole town laid out below her like a map: the spires of churches poking up through the trees; the pale towers of the colleges, their new stone and gilded banners gleaming in the sunlight, and the river winding round the western edge and under the bridge at the foot of the hill.

Coming at it from the south, Cambridge was less impressive, its stonework half-hidden behind streets of timbered buildings such as one could see in any market town in England. Unless she raised her eyes to the rooftops she could pretend she was back in London, apart perhaps from the greater number of black-robed scholars in the streets.

"I thought you said the university term was over," she said to Mal as they approached the town centre.

"It is. If you think there are a lot of students here now, you should see it in a few weeks' time."

Coby stared up at a gatehouse as fine as any palace she had ever seen, with a gilded coat-of-arms above the door, topped by a statue of a woman wrapped in a blue cloak and flanked by a crowned red rose and a golden portcullis.

"Christ's College," Mal said. "That's the foundress, Lady Margaret Beaufort, grandmother of old King Henry."

"She must have been a very great lady, to have founded a college," Coby said.

"Two colleges. And yes, I believe she was."

"But you didn't go here, did you?"

"No. I was at Peterhouse. We'll visit it later, but first I want to find us rooms for the night."

They rode down the main street, past at least three more colleges and a great many shops, until they reached a bridge over the river. Ahead was a church, and the hill Coby had climbed all those years ago. Little remained of the castle now except an enormous gatehouse and the ruined keep on top of its mound. She wondered what had happened to the rest of the walls. Taken apart to build more colleges, perhaps.

Mal dismounted and led them to an inn on the far side of the bridge.

"The Pickerel was always my favourite," he told them. "We'd come here by boat, to avoid the watch."

The landlord greeted them as they went in, and when Mal explained he was a former student come to visit old friends, the man offered them his best bedchamber at a very reasonable price.

"He's probably short of guests this time of year," Mal said in a low voice once they were alone. "If we'd come here when the fair is on, we'd have been lucky to get a pallet on the common room floor."

"So what now?" Coby said, dumping her saddlebags next to the bed.

"Supper, I think, then tonight Sandy and I will explore the town whilst it sleeps." He put an arm around both their shoulders. "We're close, I'm sure of it. But we must be cautious. We're no help to Kit if the enemy captures us first."

After supper, Mal left his brother at the inn under a strict promise not to dreamwalk alone, and took Coby on a reconnoitre of Cambridge. A walk would sooth his nerves; to sit in one place when they were so close to Kit was nigh unbearable.

"What if we're seen?" Coby asked, as they crossed the bridge back into town.

"I'm willing to chance it," Mal replied. "It's more than fifteen years since I lived here, and if any of the town has changed greatly, we need to know about it in case we have to make a swift retreat that way. Besides, who is to notice a master showing his prospective student about the town, eh?"

He led Coby back down Bridge Street, past St John's with its gilded gate even more magnificent than Christ's, and his heart was eased a little to be able to walk arm-in-arm with her, showing her all the places he had known as a youth, before his father's death and Charles's disappearance had torn his life apart. It was fitting that it would be the place where his family were reunited at last.

"I only wish Sandy had been able to come here and study with me," he said as they crossed the market square, dodging the pigs that grubbed amongst the trampled debris for anything edible. "But he fell ill, after…"

"Why do you think they took the other boy?" Coby said, tactfully changing the subject. "The King's godson."

"Who knows? He may not be noble himself, but his family is very well connected. His grandmother was the Prince Consort's sister, and on his grandfather's side he's related by marriage to Lady Frances as well. His uncle was Sir Philip Sidney, her first husband."

"Elizabeth Sidney's father?" Coby sighed. "I shall never get all these families straight in my head; they all seem to marry one another."

"They do indeed."

"Did your father never plan your marriage to some pretty heiress?"

"Why, are you jealous all of a sudden?" He smiled down at her. "I suppose he must have, but Charles was the heir so he always came first."

They paused to admire the delicate towers of King's College Chapel rising above the timbered houses along the high street, glowing gold as the sun sank towards the rooftops.

"That's a chapel?" Coby breathed. "It's as big as Saint Paul's Cathedral."

"Not quite," Mal said with a laugh. "But it is rather ostentatious, isn't it?"

She chuckled. "Just a little. Where is your old college?"

"Down that way. It's the oldest in Cambridge, you know. But we'll see it tomorrow. I think we should get back to the inn; I don't like leaving Sandy alone for too long."

The walk back to the Pickerel felt much shorter than the walk into town, perhaps because he was hurrying now. He released her arm as they approached the inn and strode ahead. Something was amiss, though he could not put his finger on it.

The taproom was even quieter than when they left, only a couple of men seated at a table with their backs to the wall. They wore heavy jerkins despite the hot weather, and belts well-worn and bearing the marks of sword-hangers. Soldiers. Mal halted in the doorway, motioning for Coby to stay behind him.

A man in his mid-forties with a broken nose stepped out from behind an upright timber.

"Master Catlyn."

"Captain Monkton." Mal grimaced. "I should have known you'd be first in line to do the usurper's bidding."

Out of the corner of his eye he saw Coby walk past the front window of the inn without a second glance inside. Monkton paid her no attention.

"Usurper? Is that any name for an old friend, Catlyn? But then you did rather fall out of favour with Prince Arthur after you murdered Josceline Percy."

"I wasn't referring to Prince Arthur. And I did not murder Percy. If that's what you're here about, you can leave now."

Monkton smiled. "Percy is old news."

"Where's my brother?"

"I send some of my men upstairs to subdue him – and that trull you call a wife. Oh, don't fret." Monkton held up a hand. "I'm under orders to take you back alive and unharmed. Which is more than I can say for your other friends."

He stepped aside and gestured towards the other end of the taproom. Ned and Gabriel were gagged and tied back-to-back, straddling a bench. Another soldier with untidy straw-blond hair and a stubbly beard stood behind them, arms folded. Ned shook his head slightly, his eyes pleading.

"What happened to the landlord?" Mal asked.

"He knows to stay out of the King's business. Now, are you going to come along quietly, or do I have to make an example of one of your friends first?"

Monkton jerked his head, and Strawhair drew a knife and laid it against Ned's throat.

"First I want to see my wife," Mal said. "Do what you will with these two, but if you've harmed a hair of her head–"

"You don't care about them?" Monkton strolled over to the captives. "Perhaps I'll take out this fellow's eye. They'll make such a handsome pair of cripples."

He seized Gabriel's hair and pulled his head back, holding out his other hand for the knife. Ned squirmed against his bonds and made a desperate whining sound. Overhead the floorboards creaked, and someone coughed twice. *All clear.*

"All right." Mal held up his hands. "I'll come with you."

He stood motionless whilst the soldiers disarmed him.

"Good. I knew you'd see sense." Monkton flipped the knife, caught it by its blade and handed it back to his comrade. "Kill them both."

Ned lurched sideways, tipping the bench over and pulling Gabriel with him to the floor. Monkton stumbled as the two of them slammed into his legs, and groped for his sword. Mal punched the nearest soldier on the jaw before he could draw his pistol, seized his rapier from the table as the man crumpled and slashed it around in a backhand stroke that narrowly stopped an incoming blow from the second man. Disengage and counterthrust. The soldier clutched his bloodied ribs, gasping for breath.

Footsteps clattered on the stairs, but instead of the reinforcements Monkton was no doubt expecting it was Coby who appeared in the doorway, a brace of pistols at the ready. Behind her came Sandy, still in his woman's garb but bare-headed and with a bruise blooming on one cheekbone.

"Drop your weapons," Coby said. "All of you."

After a few heartbeats blades clattered to the floor, and the man with the pistol slowly drew it and placed it on the table where Mal's rapier had been. The room was silent but for the wheezing breath of the wounded man. Monkton edged forward a few inches, trying to regain control of the situation.

"Where are my men?"

"They're sleeping," Coby said. "Well, sort of sleeping. I'm not sure what my brother-in-law here does, but it knocks them out sure enough."

"Useless bastards!" Monkton spat on the floor.

"Tie him up." Mal kept his blade pointed at Monkton. "The university proctors can deal with this."

"Oh, I'm sure they'll be happy to arrest the ruffians who attacked men going about their lawful duties."

"My brother will persuade them to do the right thing, won't you, Sandy? After all, there were no other witnesses to this fight. Good of you to arrange that, Monkton, I'm much obliged."

Monkton's face twisted into a snarl. "You may have won this sortie, Catlyn, but the battle's far from over."

"Get him out of my sight." He drew his brother aside. "Find out what he knows about Shawe."

Sandy nodded. "It will be my pleasure."

When Coby had finished tying up Monkton and his two uninjured men, Sandy and Gabriel marched them upstairs to join their comrades.

"I think we could all do with a drink after that," Coby said, taking down five tankards from the bar.

"First I have to fetch the proctors' men," Mal said. "And a surgeon for that one."

The wounded man stared back at them, dull-eyed.

"I'll go," said Ned, brushing himself down.

"Don't be a fool. I know this town better than the rest of you put together. Just stay here and try not to get into any more trouble."

He pulled Coby close and kissed her brow.

"Good work," he murmured. "We would all have been dead without you."

"Sandy's the one you should thank," she replied. "He bewitched all three of his guards whilst they were tying him up; I just had to untie him again."

"Even so. You were brave and resourceful. As ever."

"I had a good teacher."

Ned coughed loudly. "If you two lovebirds have finished, I could do with that beer. My mouth's as dry as a Moorish tavern."

Mal laughed and made the sign of the fig at him, then unbolted the door.

"Lock this behind me," he told Coby. "And don't let anyone in, except the landlord."

He waited until he heard the bolts scrape back into their staples, then headed into town at a jog. If Sandy could get some useful intelligence out of Monkton and his men before Mal returned with the proctors, it would save them a lot of time. Time he feared they did not have.

By suppertime Kit was hungry as a hunter and exhausted from all the chores Master Fox had set them. Thankfully Sidney was too weary for once to complain, and Heron and Shrike ignored the two newcomers completely. No one said grace, nor were there prayers afterwards as there had been in the prince's household. Kit wondered if this were some secret academy for Papists, like they had read about in history. But surely Papists prayed too, even if the words were wrong?

After supper Master Fox gathered the older boys around him.

"Roebuck, Ash, Flint: you're on patrol tonight. Stay out of sight, but don't let anything through, understand?"

"Yes, sir," they chorused.

"Leveret, Crow: I think I shall need your special talents."

The last two boys grinned. One was as black-haired as his namesake, tall and thin with a pointed nose overshadowing his faint moustache; the other was shorter, with sandy hair and freckles. They turned as one and looked down the table towards Kit with bright eager eyes, like cats that had caught sight of a mouse. Kit looked away, not wanting them to see how scared he felt right now. This was something to do with the test Master Fox had spoken of, he was sure of it. He wondered if it was going to hurt more than the ear-piercing.

Despite their instructions, all of the boys retired to the dormitory and Master Fox snuffed out the candles one by one. Kit lay staring at the moonlight tracing the beams above him as the schoolmaster's footsteps retreated down the spiral stair.

He took a long time to fall asleep that night, despite the unaccustomed labour and the generous supper. His ear still itched terribly, and some of the other boys talked in their sleep or even cried out. When sleep did come, it was deep and dreamless, and he woke what felt like only moments later. The sun was already up, and the other boys were getting dressed. The bed next to him, however, was empty, its sheets thrown back. Kit lined up to wash his face and hands, expecting to see Sidney in the queue, but the prince's cousin was not there. They all went down to breakfast, and still Sidney did not appear. Heron gave Kit a sympathetic smile; Shrike peered over his shoulder, smirking like someone with a secret they were dying to reveal.

"What is it?" Kit said. "Where's Sidney?"

Heron just sighed.

"You'll find out, soon enough," Shrike said.

Kit forced down his porridge, feeling sick. Had Sidney run away in the night and not even woken him? Had he been caught and punished, perhaps locked up in the storehouse again? He waited until all the other boys had left the dining hall before approaching Master Fox, who was putting something away in the chest. It looked like a set of clothes, of a size to fit Kit. Or his friend.

Fox looked up at the question. "Sidney? He's gone."

"Gone where, sir?"

"Away. He failed his test."

Kit stared at him. "But he only just got here."

"We have no room for those who do not fit in."

Fox closed the lid and straightened up.

"And... when do I take my test, sir?"

"Tonight, I believe. Master Shawe is looking forward to it."

CHAPTER XXXI

To Coby's relief, Mal returned safely with the university's own watchmen, and the soldiers were escorted away to the prison in the old castle gatehouse. That night all five of them slept in the bedchamber Mal had rented; in truth the bed was big enough for them all, though Sandy ceded his place and instead sat in a borrowed armchair all night, whilst he used his magics in search of Kit.

Next morning they held council over a breakfast of yesterday's bread and flagons of small ale. The landlord had returned in the night and, whilst grateful to be rid of the "foreign ruffians" who had expelled him, had rightly guessed that it was Mal who had drawn them there in the first place, however unwittingly.

"We should find another place to stay," Coby said, grimacing as she tore the heel of the loaf in two.

"I hope there won't be need," Mal replied. He turned to Sandy. "Did you find anything last night?"

Sandy yawned and sank his head into his hands.

"Not a thing. Monkton and his men have never even heard of Shawe, and though I searched the entire town I found no sign of a skrayling soul, not even a dormant one. My *amayi* is not here."

"Damn." Mal got to his feet and brushed crumbs from his lap. "I'd better visit my old college and try to find out if he's been seen here. Coby, you can come with me; Sandy, get some rest. You can try further afield tonight if need be."

"What about us?" Ned asked, putting his good arm around Gabriel's waist.

"You should stay here and rest as well," Coby said quickly. Someone ought to keep an eye on Sandy. "You look like you've been to Hell and back."

Ned bristled. "We didn't come all this way to sit on our arses. We're fond of the lad too, you know."

Coby turned to Mal in wordless appeal, but he was too busy fussing with his rapier hanger to notice.

"Very well," Mal said. "Take our horses to the livery stable in town and hire fresh ones. If I get news of Shawe or Kit, I want to be able to leave immediately."

"Just don't be long," she told Ned as Mal left the room. "Monkton might not be the only one on our trail, and I don't want to be the one scraping you off the cobbles."

They walked back into town, retracing their steps to King's College Chapel and thence past more college buildings of red brick or creamy-yellow stone, until they reached the gates of what Coby assumed must be Peterhouse. Mal led the way inside, pausing in the lodge to speak to a grizzle-jawed porter who looked almost as ancient as the building he tended.

"Doctor Lambert?" The porter's wrinkled face creased still further, though not in what Coby would call a smile. "Aye, he lives, sir. Ye'll find him in the Old Court, in the same chambers he's had these thirty years."

Mal thanked him and led the way around an L-shaped courtyard surrounded by buildings that looked easily as old as Saint Thomas's Tower. Their rooflines were edged with battlements like a castle's, though their walls were pierced with many large arched windows framed in delicate stonework.

"This is where you lived and studied?" Coby asked as she trotted along at his side.

"Of course. Though it was smaller in my day." He pointed out a window high on the righthand side. "Those were my chambers. Well, mine and three other lads. I remember one time..."

"What?"

He shook his head. "No, that's a story for another day. Come, let's find Lambert."

Coby paused for a moment, staring at the distant window and wondering what mischief her husband could have got up to in his youth. A pity they were here on such serious business, or she would have wheedled it out of him on the spot.

The master's rooms were on the ground floor, just off one of the stairwells. Mal knocked and waited. When no one answered, he knocked again, more loudly this time.

"The poor old fellow's probably deaf by now, or blind," Mal said in a low voice. "Or both."

After several minutes' waiting the door opened, and a man of about sixty peered out. His bald head was covered by a black linen coif, its strings tied awkwardly under his chin so that they tangled in his long silver beard.

"I told you not to disturb me when I–" He squinted up at Mal. "You're not one of my students. Do I know you?"

"Maliverny Catlyn, *magister*. I came here in the autumn of eighty-three…"

"Catlyn, Catlyn…? Ah, yes, I remember. That business with Ponsonby and the bucket of eels–"

"Yes, that Catlyn."

Coby shot her husband a quizzical look. *I'll tell you later*, he mouthed. *I swear*.

"Well, come in, lad, come in." Lambert peered at Coby. "Though you seem to have a lad of your own now. Come to put him forward for the college, eh?"

"Aye. That is, no."

Mal glared at Coby, who shrank back a little, confused by this sudden turn of events. Was the old man so dim of sight that he really thought her a boy young enough to be starting college? She supposed it made a change from being a servant.

"The truth is, *magister*," Mal went on, as Lambert ushered them inside. "My son here neglects his studies atrociously, and I thought that a glimpse of the opportunities he is missing out on might spur him to greater efforts."

"Opportunity" was not the first word that sprang to Coby's mind upon entering the academic's chamber. "Squalor" was one, though "labyrinth" came close on its heels. Apart from a small bedstead in the far corner, little furniture could be seen, though she supposed it must be there somewhere, under the piles of books, boxes, and elaborate brass instruments which appeared to be sextants that had mated with clocks. Maps, of the night sky as well as the Earth and seas, covered the wall panels, and there were even objects hanging from the ceiling: model ships, bunches of desiccated herbs and, near the window, the skeleton of some flying creature, its bones cunningly reunited as in life. The place looked like a cross between Gabriel's old lodgings and an alchemist's workshop. No wonder Mal thought Lambert might be able to lead them to Shawe.

"You should beat him more often," Lambert said, clearing a pile of debris from what turned out to be a stool. "A good lashing sharpens the mind like a whetstone to a sword."

"Aye, *magister*. It always had that effect on me."

Lambert barked a laugh. "So I recall. Why are you here, then, if not to present your son?"

Mal took the offered seat, and Lambert lowered himself into a chair opposite, crushing several rolled-up documents in the process.

"I'm up here on the King's business," Mal said. "You know. The usual game."

Lambert ran a tongue around his gums and leaned forward. "Taken over from Walsingham, have you?"

"Could say that. So, do you have any likely lads among your students?"

Coby realised Mal was talking about recruiting spies. Had Walsingham come here just like this, twenty years ago, and been given Mal's name?

"There could be one or two. Though boys these days are not what they were." Lambert frowned at her, and Coby dropped her gaze, remembering she was playing the dutiful child. "Most of them are mutton-heads and wool-gatherers, and the ones from the Priory are the worst."

"The Priory?"

"Anglesey Priory. It's a new school out at Stow. Headmaster reckons he only takes the brightest boys, but I've yet to see one who was so much as your equal, Catlyn. And don't take that as a compliment."

"Of course not, *magister*." Mal got to his feet. "Well, that's a pity. I seem to have come all this way for nothing. Perhaps I should try one of the other colleges–"

"I did not say I had no one for you. But you will be the best judge of his suitability, I dare say."

"Is he here now?"

Lambert shook his head. "Gone home for the Long Vacation. You've chosen a bad time for such a venture." His eyes narrowed. "Indeed, a man clever enough to take over from Walsingham would have chosen almost any other time to come here."

Coby exchanged glances with Mal. The old man's wits were sharper than his eyesight, that was plain.

"You said yourself, *magister*, that I am not a clever man."

Lambert's mouth quirked. "So I did."

Mal walked over to what was probably a desk, hidden under drifts of paper.

"Your astronomical studies look to be a good deal advanced since I was last here," he said. "Are you acquainted with Thomas Harriot?"

"And now we come to the truth of the matter, eh?" Lambert eased himself round in his chair to watch Mal sifting through the papers. "I've corresponded with Harriot a little since he came back from the New World laden down with new-fangled devices and wild ideas. You know he claims there are spots on the sun? Blasphemous nonsense."

"Don't worry, *magister*, I'm not here to enquire into your orthodoxy."

"No? That's how you fellows proceed, is it not?"

Mal sighed and put down the document he had been perusing. "I shall be blunt, Master Lambert. I'm looking for a man named

Matthew Shawe, an acquaintance of Thomas Harriot. And yes, I seek him on the King's business."

"Shawe... Shawe..."

"He is an alchemist, among other things."

Lambert started. "Matthew Shawe, you say? Could it be...?"

"What?"

"A Matthew Shawe is the headmaster of Anglesey Priory School, the one I was telling you about."

"He is?" Mal turned to Coby. "That could well be our man."

"Excuse me, Master Lambert," Coby said, "but you mentioned you had boys from the Priory school here at the college."

"Yes, one or two. Why?"

"I think we should talk to them," Mal said. "If they're still here."

"As it happens there is one, but he's no longer a student. Sad case."

"Why, what happened?"

"Lost his wits, poor fellow. We thought perhaps whoever was paying his college stipend would take him back in, but then the money dried up. It was as if he had been disowned." Lambert shook his head. "We found him a position among the college servants rather than see him turned out to starve."

"I'd still like to talk to him, if I may," Mal said.

"Of course. You'll have to wait until he's finished in the kitchens, but perhaps you'd care to dine with me in the meantime?"

"I'd be honoured, sir, but I fear our business is very urgent. I'd like to see the boy now."

"Very well, if you must," Lambert muttered. "But much good it may do you."

"I hope you don't mind waiting here, sir," the porter said, showed Mal and Coby into an office at one end of the kitchens, "only Master Lambert thought it might alarm young Martin to be summoned to his lodgings."

"Of course," Mal said.

He sat down at the desk, where the college account ledger lay open. Out of habit he perused the recent entries: a late payment of a buttery bill from the end of the Easter term; deliveries of flour from the first wheat of the harvest, twelve dozen eggs from one of the college's farms in the village of Cherry Hinton, a side of beef from a butcher in King's Ditch. Nothing suspicious there.

Footsteps sounded in the passageway and the servant reappeared with a young man of twenty or so, bone-thin and stinking of woodsmoke and grease from his labours in the kitchens. Martin stared at the floor, work-reddened hands clasped before him. Mal gestured to the servant to leave them.

"You're Martin, the kitchen lad, aren't you?" Mal said gently.

The boy made no answer. He reminded Mal a great deal of Sandy back in Bedlam, at once oblivious to his surroundings and yet alert and on edge, if expecting a beating any moment.

"I won't hurt you," Mal said. "I just want to ask you a few questions. About the time before you came here. When you were at the school, Anglesey Priory."

Martin began to shake. "Don't take me back there, sir. I don't want to go back."

"I'm not here to take you back. I just want to know—"

Martin shook his head and flailed his hands before his face, like a man trying to shake off a troublesome wasp, before lapsing once more into immobility. Mal looked to Coby in mute appeal. Perhaps someone nearer his own age could elicit some sense?

"Martin…" she began.

"Aye, Martin," he muttered. "That's what they called me. Like the little bird in the eaves. Black and white; day and night. Except there's no day or night there, no sun or moon."

Mal stared at the boy.

"You've seen the dreamlands?"

Martin looked up at last. He stared at Mal for several heartbeats, then his blue eyes rolled upwards in their sockets. Mal dashed forward and caught him before he fell. He lowered the boy to the floor. Martin was twitching and moaning, rather like Sandy in one of his fits.

Coby hunkered down at Mal's side.

"I think it's pretty clear what we're up against," she said. "Guiser magic."

"Yes, but what kind?" Mal replied. "He's just a normal boy. Unless Sandy was wrong."

He gently brushed the hair back from Martin's face, studying the gaunt features as if that might give him a clue as to the boy's identity. He had said "they" called him Martin, so perhaps it wasn't his real name.

"What's that?" Coby pointed to the side of Martin's head, where the lower part of one of the boy's ears had been cut away.

"A self-inflicted injury, or perhaps a kitchen accident?"

"Perhaps. A kitchen is no place for a madman to work, with so many sharp blades and hot irons around."

"Irons..." Mal nodded thoughtfully. "If there's guiser magic at work here, he might be calmest where there's plenty of iron."

"I think we've learnt as much from him as we're going to," Coby said. "We should call the servants and have him carried to his bed."

"Aye. Poor fellow." He got to his feet and took a handkerchief from his pocket to wipe his greasy hands. "We'd best get back to the Pickerel and plan our next move."

Back at the inn they gathered in the bedchamber around a map of the county that Mal had borrowed from Master Lambert.

"Stow is scarce five miles away," Mal said. "It lies to the east of the river, though, so we'll need to go back through town and across Midsummer Common to the Newmarket Road. We have to assume that Henry has sent a message ahead of us, whether by courier or by magical means, so we must take all possible care when approaching the school."

"Do we all have spirit-guards?" Coby asked.

"We still have ours," Ned replied, patting his throat. "Monkton searched us for weapons, but either he didn't care about magic–"

"Or he doesn't know what his allies are," Gabriel finished for him.

"That wouldn't surprise me," Mal said. "There's no reason to advertise their powers to men like Monkton."

"I have a spare spirit-guard," Sandy said. "I brought it for Kit, in case."

"Good. Then we are protected from their magics, at least."

"Unless they have new magics," Coby said. "You said Shawe was up to something with his alchemy, something to do with iron that isn't iron?"

"I don't know what he's up to," Mal said. "But it won't be good, whatever it is. We need to get there before nightfall and scout the place out. Ned, you got us fresh horses?"

Ned shrugged. "Yes, of sorts."

"Show me." Mal folded up the map. "Everyone else, get ready to ride out."

He followed Ned down to the inn's stables.

"This is the best you could do?"

Mal walked along the line of stalls, surveying the motley collection of beasts. Three of the five seemed sound enough, but the chestnut pony looked to be well past his prime and the grey had an awkward stance that suggested he'd be lame before they reached the other side of town.

"The ostler wouldn't let me choose," Ned folded his arms, defensive. "Said I had to take the five nearest the stable door, or none."

"Did he now? We'll see about that." Mal untied the pony's lead rope. "Get the other three saddled up ready to leave."

He led the chestnut and the grey into the town, to the livery stables in Trumpington Street.

"Back so soon?" the ostler said, patting the pony's nose. "Your man said you wanted these for a week."

"I wanted five good horses, not these scrapings from the knacker's yard." Mal strolled down the stable, looking the horses over. "I'll take the bay gelding and that piebald nag."

"Sorry, sir, master's orders. You take the ones nearest the door or none. Otherwise the best beasts get worked too hard."

Mal drew his rapier and placed the tip below the ostler's chin. The man's eyebrows hitched up into his hairline.

"I'll take the bay gelding," Mal said slowly, "and the piebald nag."

"The burgesses will hear of this," the ostler squeaked, his eyes crossing as they tried to focus on the blade at his throat.

"And the King will hear of how you obstructed one of his officers in the course of his duty. Now get me those horses."

"Y-y-yes, sir."

Mal led the way back through Cambridge, Sandy riding at his side and Hendricks – Ned couldn't help thinking of her by her old name, now she was back in disguise – behind them. He and Gabriel brought up the rear on the two quietest beasts. Ned had packed bread, beer and cold meat, enough for a couple of days, since they didn't want to announce their presence by stopping at inns. At least the weather was warm and dry, so they could sleep outdoors if it came to it.

Beyond the town ditch the road sloped gently upwards from the riverside pastures. Vast fields of wheat and cut stubble stretched on either side, untrammelled by hedges. The sun beat down on their heads like a hammer. It was a bare, exposed landscape which made Ned feel as insignificant as an ant crawling across a paved courtyard.

"Such a beautiful day, it seems unfair we should be heading towards our deaths," Gabriel said softly.

"What?" Ned reined his pony in. "Who said anything about dying?"

"You think it will be easy, to snatch the boy from under the guisers' noses?"

"No, but… It's just a school. What threat can a few children be?"

"A school run by guisers," Gabriel said. "We'll be lucky to escape with our wits – and our souls – intact."

Ned made the sign of the cross.

"You knew what you were getting into when we left London," Gabriel added.

"Yes, but… It's not like we really had a choice, is it?" He looked ahead, to where the twins were disappearing into the hazy distance. "Besides, any guisers come near me, we'll see how much they like a buffet round the head with a steel fist."

He dropped the reins and worked the mechanism in his false arm, opening the brass fingers to reveal the bumpy surface of the palm, studded with beads from a former spirit-guard. Gabriel rolled his eyes and nudged his horse closer until their knees bumped together.

"Just be careful," his lover said in a low voice. "I don't want to lose any more bits of you."

"Any bits in particular you'd like me to hold onto?" Ned murmured, reaching across to squeeze Gabriel's thigh.

Gabriel slapped his hand away. "Be serious."

"I'm always serious," he said. "Especially when I'm jesting."

Gabriel sighed and kicked his mount into a canter. Ned followed, clutching the reins with his good hand and praying he would make it as far as Stow without falling off.

CHAPTER XXXII

They had to ask directions twice more, and each time Coby grew more nervous. Shawe undoubtedly had been warned of their coming, could have posted sentries or be using magical means to spy on them...

"We'll bring Kit home safe, don't you fear," Mal said at her elbow.

She turned with a start.

"I didn't even see you ride up–"

"Too busy looking ahead, eh?"

He gestured down the road. All that could be seen from here was smoke rising from behind a wall of trees, but she guessed they had reached the priory. She told him about her concerns.

"Undoubtedly true, but what choice do we have?"

"None," she sighed.

She reached out, and he took her hand and bent to kiss it. The mismatched trots of their mounts slammed her knuckles against his mouth.

"Ouch!"

"Sorry."

He looked up and grinned at her. "There, that's better. It's good to see you smile, if only for a moment."

She nodded and looked away, tears welling in her eyes again. Even a kind word was more than she could bear right now. Better to be firm of purpose and think only of what was needed to defeat their enemies. Cold steel, in hand and heart.

"You've done this before," Mal said, seeming to catch her mood. "How do we go about it?"

"We should ride straight past the priory as if we were on our way elsewhere. Then tie up the horses and double back, look for a way onto the land without being seen. There must be gardens around the back, or outbuildings or something."

"Of course. You did something similar at Suffolk's house, when you rescued me."

Coby managed a brief smile. "Just like old times. Though I'm glad it's not just me and Ned this time."

They rode a good half-mile past the entrance gate until they found a narrow path cutting through the woodland. Mal dismounted and motioned to the others to do likewise, and they led their horses deep into the trees. After a few hundred yards they came to a clearing, where a large blackened patch of ground marked the site of a charcoal-burner's activity. The nearby hut was sound but clearly had not been occupied in weeks; a thick flush of summer weeds blocked the door.

"This is a good a place as any to leave the horses, I reckon," Mal said.

He forced his way into the hut, and he and Ned deposited their supplies. Meanwhile Sandy went round the horses, touching his forehead to each one's muzzle and murmuring something to it in a foreign tongue. When he was done, the beasts went back to grazing the long grass around the edge of the clearing.

"What did you do to them?" Gabriel asked.

"I simply calmed their thoughts, so that they will stay here without needing to be fettered. Much easier to flee quickly that way."

"We'll scout out the grounds first," Mal said as he emerged from the hut. "One of us should wait here with the horses, just in case."

Gabriel stared pointedly at Ned, who reluctantly put up his hand.

"I'll stay. I won't be much use in a fight anyway."

"Very well. Everyone else, weapons at the ready. Shawe has no doubt been alerted by his allies in London, so they'll be expecting us."

"Are we going to have to fight our way in, like Venice?" Coby asked, trying to keep her voice level for Mal's sake.

"Not if I can help it. We don't want to give them an excuse to threaten Kit."

"Then how...?"

"We'll work that out when we've scouted the grounds and gained a better estimate of how many of them there are and what their defences might be."

"What if there are children in there, as young as Kit?" Coby said. "It's one thing to take on a grown man like Shawe, but I won't harm the little ones."

"I know. Leave one pistol unloaded, if you must, and use it only to threaten. But charge one with steel shot and powder, just in case."

They walked in single file down the path, Mal and Sandy going first as they had done on the road. Coby winced at every crack of twig underfoot; sneaking around muddy alleys was much easier than this.

Distracted by worrying about where to put her feet, Coby almost collided with Mal, who turned and raised a finger to his lips. The wood thinned out ahead, revealing a jumble of ruined walls half-submerged in ivy and brambles. The remains of the former priory, dissolved around seventy years ago. Coby frowned. There was nothing here to hide from.

Then she saw him: a boy of sixteen or so, pale as death, walking glazed-eyed amongst the ruins as if in a dream. The boy skimmed his hands over the brambles, heedless of their scratching, until blood dripped from his palms. He wandered in what they assumed was the direction of the school, then turned and retraced his steps like a sleepwalking sentry. After a few moments he passed through a gap in a waist-high wall and disappeared into the ruins. She glanced at Mal, who shook his head and mouthed one word. *Wait.*

The boy repeated his patrol twice more. The next time he went into the ruins, Mal beckoned them all close.

"What was that?" Gabriel hissed.

"Another of Shawe's victims?" Coby said. "It looks like Martin's not the only madman they've created."

"Still, it gives me an idea," Mal replied. "Parrish, wait here. Sandy, the spare spirit-guard, if I may?"

••••

Mal crouched by the entrance to the ruins, his brother at his side. On the opposite side of the broken doorway Coby crouched likewise. Mal flicked his fingers at her, urging her further back. She nodded and obeyed, until she was hidden in the shadowed undergrowth. He turned his attention back to the path and took hold of the other end of the spirit-guard so that it hung between his hands like a garrotte.

Slow, erratic footsteps approached. Mal tensed, ready to spring up. As the youth stepped out through the doorway a bleating noise came from Coby's direction, like a lost lamb calling for its mother. The boy's head whipped round and he halted. Took a step towards her.

Mal leapt to his feet and threw the string of steel beads around the throat of the boy, who cried out briefly before Sandy could get his hand over his mouth. Mal cursed and snapped the clasp of the spirit-guard shut.

"Not another sound," he hissed, drawing his dagger and putting it to the boy's throat.

Coby emerged from the bushes looking dishevelled.

"Tie his wrists," Mal told her. "Now, lad, how many of you are there at the house?"

The boy's eyes darted from Mal to Sandy and back.

"What? Who are you? Where am I?" He made a whimpering sound in the back of his throat. "Sweet Jesu, what have you done to my hands?"

"The iron must have dispelled whatever enchantments were put on him," Coby said. She bent and began cleaning his scratched palms with her handkerchief.

"Or he feigns very well," Mal said. "Sandy, can you get anything out of him?"

His brother shook his head.

"Not with this on," he said, gesturing to the spirit-guard.

"Well we can't very well take it off him." Mal took hold of the boy's jaw and turned his head to one side. "What's this?"

He frowned at the blue crystal dangling from the boy's left earlobe. It looked remarkably like the one he had found in Shawe's workshop.

"Well, if we ever doubted this was the right place..."

"What's it for, do you reckon?" Coby asked.

"Some kind of spirit-guard that doesn't impede their own magic, perhaps?" Mal replied. "I dare say we'll find out soon enough."

He seized the boy's elbow and marched him back to where Gabriel was waiting.

"Take care of this one. Gag him and bind him further if need be, but whatever you do, don't remove his necklace." He ushered them back towards the clearing. "Come, we have to be quick, before he's missed. It can't be long until suppertime."

"What are we going to do?" Coby asked, trotting by his side.

He grinned at her. "What we do best."

"Catlyn?"

Kit blinked and looked up. He had been left alone in the dormitory whilst the other boys had their lessons, and after much pacing and fretting about Sidney he had finally settled down for a nap, thinking to save his strength for an escape before nightfall.

"Is it time for supper?"

"Not for you." One of the older boys – Flint, he thought his name was – was leaning over him. "We have more important business. Get up."

Kit did so, heart fluttering in his throat.

"Is this the test?" he whispered. "I thought that wasn't until tonight."

For an answer, Flint threw a bundle of something at him.

"Put that on."

It was a pale woollen robe with no fastenings, just a hole to put your head through and long sleeves that came down to Kit's knuckles, as if it had been made for a taller boy. It dragged on the floor a little too, and he had to lift it like a girl as he followed Flint across the dormitory to the stairwell and pattered down the cold steps on bare feet. Flint opened the door at the far end of the dining hall and ushered Kit through.

Even though it was not dark outside yet, the great chamber was lit with dozens of candles, illuminating a low bench draped in dark blue velvet that stood in the centre of the room. Master Fox stood at one end, holding a brass bowl from which rose thin wisps of smoke; Master Shawe stood at the other with a knife whose blade glinted like frozen night air. Kit halted. What was all this?

"Come, acolyte, and be reborn into our brotherhood," Master Shawe intoned. "Lie down, and waken as an immortal."

"I... I'm not sure I want to be immortal," Kit said, backing towards the door.

But Flint was there, blocking his way. Kit looked up into his grey eyes and swallowed. If a hulking fellow like Flint could do this, so could he. He turned back to the bench.

"What must I do?" he said, trying to sound brave.

"Lie down." Master Shawe indicated a cushion at the end of the bench nearest to him. "And close your eyes."

Kit obeyed, nearly tripping on the over-long robe as he climbed onto the bench. It was hard underneath the crunchy layer of velvet, harder even than the beds upstairs. He hoped this wouldn't take long.

Mal adjusted the hang of his rapier under the black scholar's gown so that it wouldn't be too visible from the front. His beard and hair were stiff again with the white greasepaint; not a perfect disguise, but it would have to do. Shawe had not seen him in years, and none of the pupils except Kit and his friend knew any of them, or so he hoped.

"Ned, Gabriel, I need you to stay here and keep watch over my brother. He's going to distract any dreamwalkers looking for us whilst Coby and I talk our way into the house and find Kit. Be ready with the horses for when we return."

"And if you don't?" Ned asked, hugging his metal hand to his chest.

"Then you leave without us. Flee the country, as you did before. No–" Mal held up his hand "–no arguments. There's no use us all dying."

He embraced his brother. "If I find Kit and can open a passage back to you, I shall."

"We may not need to. He may be strong enough now–"

"We can't count on that. Nor do we know what forces Shawe can muster. Devourers may be only the half of it."

He released Sandy and bade farewell to his other friends, then beckoned to his wife. Her woollen cap was pulled down low over her eyes to shadow her features, though not enough to conceal the fake bruise that Gabriel had painted around one eye and down across her cheekbone. She turned her back to him and he fastened her wrists together with loosely tied cord.

"Ready?" he murmured in her ear.

"As I'll ever be."

He led the way towards the schoolhouse, stomach churning. So close now, he could almost sense Kit inside the building ahead, but surely that was just his imagination. He hadn't taken off his spirit-guard yet, and in any case Kiiren's soul still slept, so how could he?

The house loomed ahead of them, outlined against the hazy blue sky of a summer evening. Lights burned in the main wing at ground level, a whole row of windows glowing against the shadowed stone. The near wing was unlit, giving no clue as to the whereabouts of its occupants.

No one accosted them as they approached the side door. Mal knocked quietly and waited, one hand beneath his gown ready to draw his dagger, the other on Coby's shoulder. After a few minutes the door opened and a boy of about twelve peered out at them. A pair of horn-rimmed spectacles were perched on his snub nose and he wore the same blue earring as their captive, but otherwise he looked much like any schoolboy or apprentice.

"May I help you, sir?" he asked.

"I wish to see your headmaster about this saucy knave–" Mal shook Coby "–he sent me for a pupil."

"Master Shawe is at work. Please come back in the morning."

"I shall do no such thing," Mal replied, elbowing the door aside. "I will see him this very minute."

The boy opened his mouth to shriek a warning but stopped when Coby produced a pistol and aimed it at his head. The unloaded one,

Mal assumed. Still, it had the desired effect. The boy turned pale and stepped backwards.

"Good lad. And don't think of alerting your master any other way. Now, may we come in?"

Something rattled overhead, and Kit opened his eyes again. Master Fox was swinging the brass bowl on a chain, like the things the Papists used in their church services. The smoke swirled down around Kit's head and made him cough.

"Close your eyes," Master Shawe said again.

This time Kit had no choice but to obey; the smoke was making him feel sleepy and it was so much easier to just close his eyes. After a moment he realised someone was speaking, close to his ear. It sounded a bit like Latin, or perhaps Greek, but he did not know the words. He really should have paid more attention in lessons...

He blinked, and there he was, back in the classroom at Greenwich Palace with the other boys. Neville gave him an icy look as he walked to the front of the class, and Kit wondered why the other boy had been called up instead of him. When he looked closer, though, he realised that the figure kneeling before Master Weston wasn't Neville at all. It was his own father, stripped to the waist, with bloody welts covering his back. Kit reached out a hand to touch him and he turned round, but it was Uncle Sandy, not his father.

"*Amayi*," his uncle whispered. "Go to sleep, it's too soon..."

The room went dark, and Kit found himself standing somewhere cold and silent.

The boy let them into a long hall that appeared to be the school's refectory. It was empty at this hour, though bowls and plates were stacked on a trestle table ready for supper.

"Where are your new pupils?" Mal asked. "Catlyn and Sidney?"

"I-I don't know about Sidney, b-b-but Catlyn is in there with Master Shawe." He indicated a door at the top of a short flight of steps.

Mal drew his rapier and went up to the door to press his ear against the timbers. After a few moments he turned back to Coby.

"I can smell *qoheetsakhan*," he said in a low voice. "What in God's name are they doing in there?"

The boy smiled slyly. "Making him one of us."

Mal unfastened his spirit-guard and crossed the refectory to spread his free hand along the boy's temple and jaw and stare into his eyes. Focusing all his thoughts he tried to slip into the boy's mind but it parted under his mental fingers like fog, sucking him into darkness–

He withdrew, gasping. "What are you?"

The boy just smiled again.

"We don't have time for this," Coby muttered. "Hold him at sword's point whilst I tie him up."

Mal obeyed, unable to tear his gaze away. Despite the spectacles the boy's eyes seemed unfocused, the pupils huge as a cat's at night. Coby swiftly bound the boy's wrists with the bit of rope that had been around her own, tightening the loops that had been so loose before.

"Come on, we have to get to Kit," she said, shaking Mal out of his stupor.

Rubbing his forehead, Mal stumbled after her. Whatever Shawe was doing here, he had a feeling it wasn't going to have the same effect on Kit as the other boys.

"Where am I?" Kit shouted. The word his uncle had used came to his lips: "*Amayi!*"

Things stirred in the darkness, black shapes he was afraid to look at. Something burned in his chest and spread upwards, along his arms and into his head, blinding him as it poured out of his eyes and mouth and fingernails, a white light brighter than anything he'd ever seen. The dark shapes ran.

"I am Kiiren," he yelled after them, "Outspeaker of the Shajiilrekhurrnasheth, and I am not afraid of you."

He didn't know where the words came from, but they felt right. He opened his eyes, shaking off the lethargy of the *qoheetsakhan*, and saw the two humans staring at him, wide-eyed and angry. The older one held a night-blade, its obsidian edge sharper than any steel.

"Who are you?" Kiiren said. He felt small, smaller than he remembered. "The *hrrith*..."

He clutched at his belly, expecting his guts to leak out between his fingers. No. Stupid. He had died that night; this was a new body, a... oh *amayi* no, a human body.

"What have I done?" he whispered.

"*Tjirzadhen*," the man with the *qoheetsakhan* spat. It was the name for Kiiren's own kind in Vinlandic, meaning one who had been reborn more than once. He made it sound like an insult. "We should kill him."

"No," the other replied. "No, he is more valuable to us alive. But we need him subdued–"

Kiiren didn't wait to hear any more. He dodged around the man with the knife, his new body lithe and swift, and ran for the nearest door.

Something thudded against the inside of the far door, and the latch rattled. Coby drew her other pistol. A voice, masculine and somewhat nasal. Though she could not make out the words, the tone sent shivers down her back. She lifted the latch with the barrel of her unloaded pistol and kicked the door open. A man stared back at her, his hands around Kit's throat. Shawe, presumably.

"Take your filthy paws off my son, demon!" She waved the unloaded pistol at Shawe for emphasis. "Steel bullets, if you're wondering, so don't try any enchantments either."

Shawe raised his hands, and the chain he had been holding slithered to the floor. Kit dashed past her, into the refectory. Coby backed away, still pointing the gun at the alchemist. Another man appeared behind Shawe, younger and with a more contemptuous expression on his face than on Shawe's, if that were possible.

"Run," he said. "I enjoy a game of hide and seek."

Coby raised her other pistol and squeezed the trigger, tipping the barrel upwards at the last moment so that the shot went over both their heads. Both men ducked reflexively.

"Get Kit out of here," Mal said, stepping between her and the guisers. "I'll deal with these two."

Coby shoved the unloaded pistol into her belt, grabbed Kit's hand and dragged him, protesting, out of the house.

"I want my *amayi!*" he wailed.

"That's where we're going, lambkin," she replied, "but we have to run very fast, back to the horses."

Kit halted in the middle of the path and stared up at her. "I'm not your lambkin, I'm Kiiren."

She looked into his dark eyes and the truth hit her like a blow to the stomach. This was not her son any more. They were too late.

CHAPTER XXXIII

Mal blocked the doorway, steel in each hand. Shawe to the left of him, a nasty-looking obsidian dagger in his hand, a younger man to his right with naught but a thurible. The bitter smell of dream-herb filled the air. Another ritual like Suffolk's, no doubt, attempting to manipulate souls. How predictable these villains were!

"I'd like to kill you slowly and painfully for what you've done to my son," he said to Shawe, "but I really don't have time."

He advanced a few steps into the room. Shawe retreated, stumbled against the velvet-draped bench and fell backwards with a curse. The knife slipped from his fingers and shattered on the tiled floor. Mal ignored him and turned to the other, who swung the thurible like a morning-star. Burning embers fell onto the drapery and a cloud of *qoheetsakhan* smoke enveloped them both. Mal halted, and for a moment all he could see was the dreamlands, twilit and empty. No, he would not fight them on their home ground. Concentrating all his will on his physical self he slashed the blade of his dagger across the back of his right wrist. The moment blood touched steel, his vision cleared.

Just in time. He ducked as the thurible whistled through the air, trailing smoke and sparks. Some landed in his hair and he shook them free before they could burn through to the skin. The guiser danced out of reach.

"You won't get me this time, *kiaqnehet*."

He swung his thurible again. Mal knocked it aside with his dagger and thrust the rapier blade into the guiser's belly almost up to the forte. The man cried out and dropped the thurible with a clang.

"No. You cannot kill me again," he gasped, sinking to his knees and clutching the blade. "Not again."

"What do you mean, again?"

The dying man coughed twice and looked up, grinning through the blood now running from his nostrils. "Of course, you don't recognise me in this body. It has been twenty years, Huntsman."

Mal withdrew his blade, bile rising in his throat.

"Tanijeel?"

The guiser looked puzzled. "You know my name?"

"You're Hennaq's heartmate. The skrayling who was butchered for mine and Sandy's initiation." He shook his head. "I'm so sorry…"

Tanijeel's eyes glazed over and he collapsed in a spreading pool of blood. Mal spared a brief glance towards Shawe, who cowered on the far side of the now-smouldering bench, and stepped back towards the door. Enough killing. Time to get out of here.

Coby caught up with Kit on the edge of the clearing and managed to grab him before he could throw himself at Sandy. Her brother-in-law lay with his head in Gabriel's lap, hands and eyelids twitching like a cat dreaming of mice.

"Sssh!" she whispered in Kit's ear, hand clamped over his mouth. "See? Uncle Sandy – I mean Erishen – is fighting our enemies. We mustn't wake him."

Kit nodded, and she let him go. He walked over to Sandy and knelt by his side, but did not touch him or speak. Ned crossed the clearing, dread written all over his features.

"Mal?"

"He stayed behind to fight Shawe. I… I don't know…"

Ned put his arms about her and she gasped for breath, fought back tears that she could not spare, not right now.

"We have to get the horses," she said, her voice raw in her throat, "get Kit out of here. If Mal... if he comes in time–"

"He already has," Ned replied, releasing her.

Mal jogged down the path to where he had left Sandy and the horses. To his relief Coby was there ahead of him, and Kit was with his uncle.

"Wake him," Mal told Gabriel. "We have to leave. Now."

"The guiser?" Coby asked as he embraced her and Ned together.

"I killed the younger one. Shawe lives."

Ned shot him a doubtful look. When Mal didn't reply Ned walked back towards the horses, scooping Kit up on his way.

"Come along, little man."

"I'm not your little man, I'm Ambassador Kiiren."

"And I'm Queen Cleopatra of Egypt. Now, where's your mother's horse?"

"I want to ride with my *amayi*."

"Aye, well, your uncle is barely awake enough to sit his own horse, without having to hold onto you as well. Do you want to break both your necks?"

Kit shook his head, and Ned lifted him onto the grey's saddle.

"Now wait there until your mother comes."

Coby looked up at Mal, eyes filling with tears. "He's telling the truth. Whatever magic Shawe worked on him, he's Kiiren now."

Mal kissed her forehead.

"We always knew this was going to happen one day, love."

"Yes, but so soon?"

He had no answer to that. Gently releasing her he went to see to his brother.

They rode back out to the road at a walk, not daring to go any faster in the dark. Mal brought up the rear, ready to fend off another guiser attack, but the priory grounds were eerily silent. At the road he urged them into a trot, riding alongside his wife and son. Kit – Kiiren as he supposed he must call him now – had dozed off, exhausted.

"That was too easy," Coby whispered after a while.

"I know."

"The younger one said something about 'hide and seek'. Do you think he's spying on us somehow?"

"Not any more."

He told her about Tanijeel.

"I helped create a guiser," he said at last, glancing back over his shoulder. Still no sign of pursuit. "I'm certain Tanijeel would never have joined the renegades if he had not suffered so cruelly at our hands."

"It wasn't you. You told me you were just a boy at the time, and never even touched him."

"So I was. But—"

"Then stop feeling so guilty about it."

"But I killed him the second time."

"Killed who?" Kiiren's voice was childishly high but held a commanding note.

"No one," Coby said.

She began telling him a story; a sure-fire way to distract both the skrayling within and the child he surely still was. Mal listened with half an ear, and realised it was a story of Robin Hood and his fight against the injustices of wicked King John. He wondered idly if generations to come would tell similar tales about themselves and their fight against wicked King Henry. Of course they had to win first, and preferably live to tell the tale.

The road dipped into a tree-lined hollow. Mal turned his attention back to his surroundings. This was the perfect place for an ambush. What if Shawe had used his magics to persuade the constable to free Monkton and his men? They could be lying in wait even now…

He reached the bottom of the hollow and the ground began to rise again. The moon was rising, casting a pale glow through the trees… No, that was not moonlight. Coby's mount whinnied and balked, and Mal reined his gelding to a halt beside her.

"What is it?" she whispered to him, as the light grew.

The tunnel mouth coalesced, cutting them off from Sandy, Ned and Gabriel, and now he could see a figure at the far end.

"Shawe?"

The figure came closer. He was thin and dark-haired, but it was not the alchemist. This lad was no more than eighteen.

"Give him to me." The apparition held out his arms to Kiiren.

Mal wheeled his mount, but another tunnel was already forming behind them.

"How did they find us so easily?" Coby muttered.

"Never mind that," Mal replied. "Prepare to ride like the wind."

He dismounted, drew his rapier and turned back to face the guiser blocking their path. The youth could not step out and confront him, not if his aim was to take Kiiren back.

"Give him to me, or be destroyed."

"And how exactly do you intend to do that?" Mal grinned at him and hefted his blade. The cold steel felt reassuringly solid and unmagical.

The youth raised his hands and a wind began to pour from the tunnel, whipping his hair forwards and filling the air with dead leaves and... black feathers? A harsh cawing mingled with the sound of the wind, a dark shape soared over the youth's head, straight towards Mal, who raised his blade in an instinctive parry. The crow exploded in a rain of feathers and gore, but Mal had no time to wipe the mess from his face. Another was coming at him, and another. The rapier sang as he wove a steel net between the monstrous birds and his family. Its blunt edge sliced through the crows as if they were mist, but they felt solid enough when they dodged the blade and raked his scalp with their claws.

There were too many now to fight; his only hope was to stop them at the source. Mal pressed forward, shielding his face with his left hand and whirling the rapier in his right. At last he reached the mouth of the tunnel. The boy sneered at him, but his smile turned to a grimace of horror as Mal thrust the rapier straight towards his heart. Before the blade could touch him, however, the tunnel flashed a sickly yellow-green and collapsed in on itself, sending a shock like a hammer blow back up the rapier. Mal dropped his blade, shaking his stinging hand.

"Mal!"

He stooped and grabbed the weapon with his left hand, and turned to see Coby hunched in the saddle, trying to protect Kiiren from the last of the crows. Mal leapt onto his own mount and set about them with his sword. By the time he had dispatched the last one, the tunnel behind them was open, another guiser standing at its mouth. Mal glanced over his shoulder. The lane in front of them was clear.

"Go!" He slapped the mare on her haunch and the beast sprang forward. He turned back to the guiser and brandished the rapier, still in his left hand. "You want some of this as well?"

The boy paled, but began to raise his hands. Mal kicked the gelding forward, and it lashed out with an ironshod hoof that landed square on the boy's chest. The horse screamed and reared as the tunnel exploded, and Mal slithered backwards, landing in a bone-crunching heap on the cold ground. He rolled quickly out of the way as the animal foundered. What in God's name had just happened? None of the guisers in England had been this powerful before. He limped off in search of his family, hoping his enemies had spent their best strength against him already.

A few hundred yards down the road, Coby finally caught up with Sandy, Ned and Gabriel.

"What did you think you were doing, letting us get separated like that? We nearly lost him."

Sandy had the good grace to turn pale. He slid down from his mount and ran over to them to take Kiiren's hand in his.

"It was my fault, *amayi*. Our horses bolted when the guisers attacked, and by the time I got them under control it was all over."

"Give me the spirit-guard," she said. "We all need to be protected from their enchantments."

He took it out and passed it up to her. Kiiren protested, but she fastened the necklace about his throat.

"There, that's better, lambkin."

She took the lack of further complaint as indication that Kiiren had withdrawn for a while, as Erishen did when Sandy put on a spirit-guard.

"We cannot leave it on him for long," Sandy said, echoing her thoughts.

"I know. But surely it's the wise thing to do, until we get further from the guisers."

Hoofbeats sounded on the road. Coby whirled, but it was only Mal. Only? She grinned in relief, and it was all she could do not to ride back to meet him.

As Mal drew nearer he slowed his mount to a trot and reined it in by Coby's side.

"You're hurt," she said, rummaging in her pocket for a handkerchief.

"Just scratches." He wiped his bloody forehead with the back of his cuff and dismounted. "Sandy, what was that?"

His brother shrugged. "We saw nothing. One moment we were riding along, the next our horses reared and bolted as if *hrrith* were after them."

"The beasts weren't far wrong. Shawe's lads were using tunnels from the dreamlands, but they seemed able to bring things through. Wind and leaves. And crows."

"They came for me," Kit said.

"It's all right, sweetheart," Coby told him. "Your father fought them off, and with your spirit-guard on, their magics cannot–"

"No, they'll come again, they'll find me. I know it."

"How? How did they find us last time?"

Kit raised his hand to his earlobe. "This. Master Shawe told us it's a finding charm."

"Then we must take it out."

Coby felt around the back of the earring for a catch, but there was nothing, just a rough spot in the metal. She shot Mal a worried look.

"I think it's welded shut. I'll need my tools to break it–"

"No time," Mal said, glancing back down the road and drawing his dagger.

Coby recalled the boy Martin with his mutilated ear.

"No, you can't!"

"I have to. Now hold him still."

"What's the matter, Mamma?"

"It's going to be all right, lambkin, but you're going to have to be brave."

"Is Daddy going to cut off my ear?"

"No!" She hugged him closer. "Just a little cut. Now be still, and it'll soon be all over."

She closed her own eyes as Mal steadied Kit's head against her shoulder with one hand. The blade flashed and Kit cried out.

"Hush," she murmured, blinking back her own tears as the boy sobbed into her chest.

"Let me take it," Ned said, holding out his hand. "A diversion–"

"Don't be a fool." Mal said. "They'd destroy you, and for what? A few miles' gain?"

He drew back his arm and threw the earring far out into the field.

"Come on," he said, kicking his horse into a trot, "let's get as far away from that damned thing as we can, before they try again."

Coby followed suit, clutching the trembling Kit tight, and praying they had freed him from the guisers' snares. A mile or so further on, Mal drew his mount to a halt at a milestone marked CAMBRIDGE III NEWMARKET XVII. The quarter moon was riding high, illuminating the open landscape and revealing a second road leading south from the milestone.

"Shawe may be expecting us to return to Cambridge," he said, "so we shall confound him by skirting the town."

"We have to stop soon," Coby said. "Kit needs to rest."

"We can be in Saffron Walden by dawn if we press on. We'll rest there a while, and make our plans."

CHAPTER XXXIV

The night passed without any further sign of the strange dreamwalkers, and by dawn the rescuers were within sight of the town of Saffron Walden, nestled in the gently rolling hills where Cambridgeshire met Essex. Mal looked around at his companions' grey faces, and wondered what he was going to say if anyone enquired as to their business. They looked as disreputable a bunch of vagabonds as ever were arrested by a zealous parish constable.

"There's an inn, just up ahead," Coby said, evidently having the same thought. "Perhaps we should stop there, rather than draw attention to ourselves by going into the town."

"Agreed."

Smoke was rising from the inn's chimney and a maidservant stood in the doorway, sweeping dried mud and gravel back into the high road. She gave a sullen curtsey when Mal hailed her, but at the sight of his silver she let them in and went off to fetch breakfast.

They gathered in the corner of the taproom by the fireplace, with Kit curled up on one end of the settle, his head in Coby's lap.

"We can't outrun the guisers forever, you know," she said, idly stroking Kit's hair. "We have to leave England now, unless you have some idea of how to fight them."

"I've been giving it some thought," Mal said. "I went into this believing there was only a handful of them, but now we know Shawe has been recruiting others, that makes the task far more difficult."

"How many others?" Ned asked.

"I asked Kit on the road," Coby said, "and he thought there were about two dozen boys, in addition to Shawe and his lieutenant."

"They're only boys, though."

"Yes, but you didn't see what they can do," Mal said. "This wasn't just dream magic and illusions, it was... I don't know what it was, but anyone who can conjure stuff out of thin air cannot be underestimated as an opponent. Imagine if they came to London and started loosing devourers onto the streets."

They fell silent. The serving girl returned with jacks of small ale and plates of bread and cold meat which she set down on the table, but no one made a move to help themselves. She sniffed and left them to it, muttering under her breath about ungrateful foreigners.

"Another thing bothers me more," Coby said quietly. "Why did they take the other boy as well as Kit? Was he a guiser all along, or did they simply make a mistake? How did they find and assemble all these boys in the first place?"

"They plan for the long term, we know that," Mal said. "They must have started this scheme a good twenty years ago, long before the skraylings began seriously suspecting what they were up to."

"I don't think Shawe's apprentices are guisers," Sandy said.

"Not guisers? But I saw–"

"You saw them call upon the power of the dreamlands, yes. But those boys do not have skrayling souls. They are human."

"But how?"

"You don't remember our traditions, do you? Of how the *tjirzadheneth* came to discover the dreamlands and be reborn."

Mal shook his head.

"Many, many generations ago, the skraylings were just like humans: trapped in their own heads, their own dreams. Then our ancestors discovered *qoheetsakhan* and found they could use it to enhance their own dreams and even penetrate the dreams of others. Through practice and discipline they learnt to master their souls and even overcome death. Shawe is trying to do the same to humans."

For a while no one spoke. The scale... the enormity of Shawe's scheme was beyond anything that Mal had imagined. To make an army of humans with the power of skrayling adepts, able to live forever if they so wished, but only by stealing the bodies of the unborn...

"How do we stop this blasphemy?" Coby said.

Mal drew a deep breath.

"I think we have no choice but to return to the Tower."

"What?"

"I was not certain until I heard Kit's – I mean Kiiren's – account, but now I'm sure of it." He swept his gaze around the table, taking in their worried looks. "Jathekkil is afraid of Shawe and his dreamwalkers. Why else do you think he's still holed up in the Tower, the greatest armoury in the realm?"

"My brother is right," Sandy said. "Rivalry and dissension were ever the guisers' weaknesess."

Ned stared at them both.

"So you're suggesting we walk into one enemy's stronghold in order to escape another?"

"Something like that, yes."

"And what then?"

Mal shrugged. "I haven't worked out the details yet."

"Oh good. I was afraid you had some kind of bold plan that would end in us all dying."

"Gentlemen, please!" Coby cocked a head towards Kiiren, who was huddling against Sandy, eyes wide. "Mal's right. We have to get back to London before Shawe finds us. We're safer hidden among a countless multitude of souls than out here in the countryside."

"What's to stop the prince arresting us the moment we set foot inside the city?" Gabriel said.

"Simple. We don't."

"So we get a boat to Southwark?"

"No, we take refuge at Charing Cross with Lord Grey. Much as it pains me to say it, he's the one person in London we can trust."

He looked around the table, expecting objections, but no one would meet his eye.

"That's settled, then." He reached across the table to claim one of the jacks of ale. "Eat up and take whatever ease you can; I want to be off within the hour. It's at least a two-day ride back to London."

The distant curfew bell was ringing by the time they reached Clerkenwell, but the watch didn't venture out this far, even though London's suburbs were spreading north almost as rapidly as Southwark was spreading south. Skirting north to avoid Lincoln's Inn, the only witnesses to their passage westward were the herds of solemn-eyed cattle watching from the shelter of oak trees and flicking their ears against the swarms of flies that rose from the damp grass. From St Giles-in-the-Field the riders turned south down St Martin's Lane and buildings gradually closed in around them, cutting off the last light of evening. A few faint stars could now be seen overhead, distant and uncaring. Mal shivered despite the warm night and prayed to Saint Michael that he was not leading his family into a trap.

He bade the others wait in the shadows of the lane whilst he and Sandy crossed the Strand to the gates of Suffolk House. Though he had said he trusted Grey, in truth he knew not what reception they would get after all that had happened. The duke might not be a guiser, but where did his loyalties now lie?

The minutes ticked by with agonising slowness as he waited for someone to answer the door. He glanced down the street, alert for any sign of the watch or, worse still, a lord's retainers with nothing better to do than harass loiterers. He was just thinking it better to give up and find a way across the river to Southwark when the wicket gate opened.

"Master Catlyn?" The porter looked surprised, even a little alarmed. "Two Master Catlyns?"

"This is my brother," Mal replied. "May we come in? I need to see Lord Grey urgently."

"Of course, sirs. This way."

The porter handed them off to another retainer who escorted the twins across the outer courtyard and through into the privy apartments. Mal stole a sidelong glance at the man: one of Grey's personal guards by the look of him, broad-shouldered but light of step, staring straight ahead but nonetheless aware of everything around him. Including Mal's attention. Mal looked away, focused on the house they were entering. Quiet. No sounds of music or merriment as one might expect in a rich man's mansion on a summer's evening, but it was hard to imagine Grey hosting a masquerade. He wondered how the duke passed his leisure hours. No doubt he was one of those men who lived for his work, the way others lived for pleasure.

So sure was he of this picture of his employer that he was surprised to be shown up to a spacious parlour where Grey, his wife and his mother were sitting around a table playing cards. Candles lit the players' faces and the game in front of them, but the rest of the chamber was lost in shadows.

"Sir Maliverny Catlyn. And brother." The guard snapped a bow and withdrew.

"A little late for a social call, is it not?" Grey folded his cards and put them face down on the polished surface, but did not get up. "I thought you'd fled the country."

"My brother and I were called away on… business, my lord."

"And has it been concluded in a satisfactory manner?"

"In as much as it could be, my lord. But there have been consequences that require your immediate attention."

"Can it not wait until morning?" Grey yawned. "I fear I may have drunk rather more sack than is wise."

Mal was not fooled. The duke looked perfectly sober.

"I'm afraid not, my lord."

Grey gave an exaggerated sigh. "Noblesse oblige, I suppose. If you will excuse us, mother?"

"Really, Blaise, you need to come up with a new excuse for wriggling out of a losing hand." The dowager duchess put down her cards and stood up, taking her daughter-in-law's offered arm. "Let us leave the boys to their little games, my dear."

Lady Frances gave them a wistful look as she passed. Mal responded with what he hoped was an encouraging expression, and she grinned back, nodding almost imperceptibly.

"Well, what is so urgent that you must interrupt my evening's pleasures?" Grey asked when the door had closed behind the ladies.

"My lord, I must beg your indulgence a moment."

He nodded to Sandy, who stepped behind the duke's chair and put his hands either side of the duke's head.

"What in God's name are you–?" Grey's eyes rolled up into his head and his cane clattered to the floor.

Mal hurried back to the door, ready to intercept Lady Frances if she returned quickly. He glanced over his shoulder.

"Well?"

"He is untainted," Sandy replied, releasing Grey.

"Thank Christ for that." Mal stepped outside, just in time to see Lady Frances enter the adjoining room. "My lady, I need your aid. My wife and son are waiting out in the street, along with Ned Faulkner and Gabriel Parrish. Please could you send someone to bring them to us, and stable our horses for the night?"

"Of course. You will all be staying?"

"That is my intent."

She gave him a curious look but said no more. He guessed she would question his wife instead, hoping that womanly camaraderie would avail her where simple politeness had not. Perhaps he should have Sandy look at her too, but many more such incidents and they would become hard to conceal.

When he returned to the parlour Grey was rousing from the stupor that Sandy's mind-probing had pushed him into.

"Are you unwell, my lord?" Mal asked. "Shall I pour you another cup of wine?"

"Yes, if you would." Grey rubbed a hand over his eyes. "Came over somewhat giddy for a moment. Must be the heat."

"It is very close in here. Sandy, open a window, would you?" Mal took a candlestick over to the sideboard and half-filled a clean glass with honey-pale sack. "You asked me to tell you about my business, my lord. I'm afraid it may take a while."

Coby sat in the window-seat, arms around her knees, staring out of the window at the moonlight shimmering on the Thames. She was still wearing her boy's garb, though Lady Frances had offered to lend her clean clothes. Tomorrow, perhaps. Tonight all she could think about was Kit. Kiiren. Whoever he was now. She hugged her knees tighter and swallowed past the lump in her throat. When the door opened she ignored it. She didn't want to speak to anyone right now, not even Mal.

"Mamma?"

Her head jerked round. He was standing there in nothing but a shirt, a gleam of dark metal at his throat. His legs were skinny, and all red and scabby round the knees like an ordinary boy.

"Kit?"

He climbed onto the window-seat and wormed his way into her lap. His dark curls still smelt of the dream-herb smoke. It reminded her of Sandy, and she wondered if her brother-in-law was behind this.

"Kiiren says he's sorry for upsetting you," Kit said in matter-of-fact tones, as if talking about an errant younger sibling. "He was scared after being asleep for so long."

"I know, lambkin."

She wiped the betraying tears from her eyes with the back of her hand, then to cover the action she licked her thumb and cleaned a smudge from Kit's cheek. He grimaced and buried his face against her doublet. After a while he looked up at her again.

"It doesn't hurt, being him," he said. "It's exciting really. He knows so much, though he won't tell me everything. He says I'm not old enough yet."

"He's probably right." The former ambassador must have seen many things that were not good for a child to know.

"Father and Uncle Sandy are going to fight Prince Henry, aren't they?"

Coby hesitated.

"Aren't they?"

"Yes."

"I want to go with them."

"You're not old enough. It's far too dangerous."

"But I hate the prince. He lied to me. He said he wanted to be my friend, but he–" Kit broke off, frowning. "And then Shawe killed my friend Sidney."

"I know. I'm so sorry." She cradled his head against her shoulder, expecting him to cry.

"So." He pushed himself upright, mouth set in a hard line. "I want to kill Henry."

"Kit, darling, you can't go around killing people. Especially princes."

"But you said it was all right, to protect your loved ones. And Henry will hurt you and Daddy and Uncle Sandy if he's not stopped."

She sighed. "We'll talk about it again tomorrow. Now go to bed. You're tired, and so am I."

He scrambled out of her lap, still glowering. She walked him to the door – he and Sandy had the adjoining bedchamber – and closed it behind him. Going over to the bed she began unbuttoning her doublet, then remembered herself and knelt to pray. For all their souls, but Kit's most of all. If he had one left.

"Witchcraft?" Grey leaned forward in his chair. "How long have you known about this, Catlyn?"

Mal looked around uncomfortably. The two men were alone now, Sandy having excused himself as soon as his own part in this was done.

"A long time," he said at last. "But I had no proof. Shawe had a powerful protector in the Earl of Northumberland, and there is no law against alchemy."

"We must take this news to the Regency Council–"

"We cannot. They…" He halted as Grey's words sank in. "Regency? Robert is dead?"

"Yesterday. You did not hear the news?"

"We've been avoiding inns and other travellers." He shook his head. "Dear God… Then we must act quickly, or Prince Arthur too will be dead within the week."

"Arthur? What has he to do with all this?"

"Nothing, except that he is the only other man in the kingdom with an indisputable claim to the throne. The conspirators who planned the assassination of King Robert and the murder of Prince Edward have one thorn in their side, one obstacle to total domination of the new king." He leapt up from his seat and rounded on the duke. "It will take a couple of days' preparation, but I believe I know how to stop them."

CHAPTER XXXV

"I don't know why I let you talk me into this," Mal said as Grey's men snapped the manacles around his wrists.

He shuffled out of the stables into the courtyard, blinking against the sunlight. Sandy was likewise chained at wrist and ankle; Coby remained free, and was now dressed in women's attire again. Mal wondered if she had managed to conceal any lockpicks or weaponry under the full brocade skirts. If not, or if she was searched, this could be a very short mission.

"Henry wants us prisoner more than anything else in the world," she said in a low voice. "He will be too eager to take charge of us to think about anything else."

"She is right," Sandy put in. "Jathekkil may be a twice-reborn guiser, but he is at present a boy, and a boy's emotions rule him. He will strut and gloat a while, and not stop to consider that we came to him willingly."

Grey limped across the courtyard towards them, his pain-racked features smoothed into an approximation of a smile. The duke was taking far more pleasure in this plan than was entirely necessary.

"What of your men, my lord?" Mal said quietly. "Can they be trusted to play their part?"

"Of course. They are not amateurs like Frogmore. They may be Huntsmen, but I hold their loyalty."

"I hope so."

Grey's men fell in around them. Most were in the duke's blue-and-white livery with his scarlet unicorn badge on the left breast, but two were rough-looking fellows in leather jerkins and threadbare trews. Their pupils were still slightly dilated from last night's dose of *qoheetsakhan*.

"Henry won't notice, will he?" Mal asked Sandy.

"I hope he will be too pleased to see us to question the means of acquiring us."

"And Grey was telling the truth, that they are real Huntsmen?"

Sandy shuddered. "Oh yes."

"I'm sorry you had to go through that, but we need them to be able to fool Henry."

His brother nodded. It was a necessary part of the plan. If Olivia questioned the men, she would use nothing as clumsy as torture. Mal needed the men to have some genuine memories of hunting skraylings, to distract her from the false memories Sandy had given them of capturing the twins.

Four liveried men with pole-arms led the way out of Suffolk House, followed by the three prisoners. Behind them came more retainers, this time with crossbows, just in case the captives changed their mind and tried to run for it. Last of all came the Huntsmen, sauntering along the street with heads held high. After all, they truly believed they had captured the King's worst enemies and would be rewarded for it.

Passers-by stopped and stared as they walked along the Strand towards Ludgate. At first the duke's livery was enough to stop any questions, especially here on the road to Westminster where nearly all the houses belonged to the great lords of the realm. As they passed under the gate, however, the jeers began.

"You're a pretty pair," a man called out. "What yer done, eh? Both fucked the wench, or one another?"

One of Grey's men lashed out with the butt of his pole-arm and he withdrew, cursing. Mal tried to close his ears to the catcalls and obscenities, wishing his wife could be spared this ordeal. By the time they reached Tower Street they had attracted a following of street urchins armed with mud and worse, and he was almost thankful for the Huntsmen, whose glowering presence kept the wretches from coming too close.

At the end of the street they turned left up the hill and approached the first gatehouse.

"What is this?" The guard's eyes narrowed in suspicion as he took in their little procession.

"A gift for His Majesty from my lord the Duke of Suffolk," the lead retainer said. "An escaped prisoner, and two of the King's chief enemies."

"Here, I know 'im." The other guard pointed at Mal. "Didn't I see Captain Monkton flog you, that one time? Years ago, it was…"

"I'm glad to see we'll be among old friends," Mal replied.

"Oh, we'll be friends all right," the man said with a leer. "Come on, better get them safe inside."

They followed one of the Tower guards across the causeway into the castle proper. A feeling of unease came over Mal as they passed into the inner ward. How many times had he been here? More often than he cared to recall, but never under such dangerous circumstances. If this did not work… But he could not allow himself to doubt, not now.

To his surprise they were not taken to the Bloody Tower, where Henry's household had been based earlier, but into the inner ward and through a massive gatehouse to the White Tower itself. Tall double doors opened onto a flight of worn stone steps that led up to the great entrance, and Mal had to be careful where he trod.

At the top the guard directed them through another set of doors into the great hall of the keep. The vast chamber had been swept clean and its walls hung with every faded tapestry the castle could provide. At the far end a canopy had been set up over a wooden dais. A small dark-haired figure perched on the throne beneath, and even in the gloom the light glinted on the golden crown he wore.

The retainers' pole-arms thudded on the flagstones in time to their booted footsteps as they marched down the hall with their prisoners. As they got closer, Mal spotted a red-faced page kneeling by the dais, and courtiers standing amongst the pillars on either side. King Henry got to his feet.

"Sir Maliverny Catlyn." He looked the three of them over. "Where is your son?"

"My lord Grey did not think it appropriate to send him, Your Majesty. After all, he's the innocent party in all this. Besides, it might not be safe–"

"Not safe? Where could be safer than the greatest castle in my kingdom?"

"There was a fever, Your Majesty."

"No. There was no fever in this castle. No one here has been stricken down, have you?"

The courtiers shook their heads and murmured agreement.

"You see?"

"But your brother–" Coby put in.

"My brother was murdered." Henry folded his arms, as if daring anyone to disagree. "On my uncle's orders."

"Your uncle, sire?"

"Arthur, the would-be usurper. Why do you think he fled to his castle in Warwickshire? To avoid arrest, and to rally his own troops. Even now he plots to raise an army and seize the throne. My throne."

Mal kept his features carefully blank. Had Olivia's machinations come to fruition already, or did the boy-king believe the rumours about his uncle? Just how much in control of events was he, when it came down to it?

Henry seemed to remember his other visitors at last.

"Who are they?" he said, pointing at the Huntsmen.

One of the men bowed, not ungracefully. "Just loyal citizens, sire, what captured these traitors."

"You two captured them? Not the duke?"

The Huntsman shrugged. "We knew his father of old, if you get my drift, sire."

Henry's eyes narrowed like a cat spotting a mouse. "Really? Well, gentlemen, it seems we have much to talk about." He flicked a hand towards the prisoners. "Take them away and put them somewhere safe. I'll deal with them later."

A yeoman warder directed them to an all-too-familiar tower at the far end of the outer curtain wall.

"Is this Monkton's idea of a jest?" Mal asked the warder.

"Who?"

"Captain Monkton, of the Tower militia?"

"Oh, that Monkton. No, he ain't here."

So, Monkton was still rotting in prison in Cambridge. The thought brought a smile to Mal's lips.

"Oi, what are you looking so cheerful about, traitor?" The warder struck Mal in the back of the knees and he stumbled and fell, twisting sideways as he did so to avoid cracking his skull on the cobbles. Coby hurried to his side and helped him up.

"Is the woman a prisoner as well?" the warder asked Grey's men, unlocking the door at the base of the tower.

"I want to stay with my husband," Coby said, before any of them could answer.

"Right you are, madam," the warder said. "If you want to be locked up here, that's your business. My business is to keep the guilty ones in, not the innocent out."

He led them up a narrow flight of stairs and unlocked the door at the top.

"Plenty of room for both of you in there," he said, ushering Mal and Coby inside.

"What about my brother?" Mal cried out as the door began to close. "He's not well, he needs an attendant–"

"Sorry, sir, can't have you all in one cell. Your brother will be comfortable enough on the floor above."

He closed and locked the door, and their footsteps receded upwards.

"It was worth a try," Mal said, shuffling around the room in his chains. "Do you know, this is the very cell I was held in, all those years ago?"

"When Monkton had you hauled in off the streets of Southwark, do you mean?"

"Aye. Ten years, can you believe that?" He cocked his head on one side, peering at the wall. "I remember these carvings like it was yesterday. Though I think there are a few more of them now."

"Some of the prisoners must have been here a long time," Coby replied, crouching to examine an elaborately carved roundel resembling a zodiac or horoscope.

The note of fear in her voice was unmistakable. Mal crossed the cell, rattling his manacles in frustration. She looked up and stood to embrace him.

"I hope you've brought your lockpicks," he murmured against her headdress.

She looked towards the door. "As soon as the guards have gone, I'll free you."

They stood there in silence for what seemed like hours, and at last the footsteps came back down and past them and the door at the bottom of the stairwell slammed shut.

"Do you have a knife?"

"Just a seal-cutter, in the lining of my left boot. I thought they'd find anything larger."

"Good. Easier than using my teeth."

He sat down on the bed and she pulled the boot off and extracted the tiny blade, a thumb's length of wafer-thin steel made for cutting the seals from letters. She took off her bodice, turned it inside-out and began carefully cutting the seams.

"What are you doing?"

"I could hardly walk in here with my tool-roll, could I? Especially in these clothes." She bit her lip in concentration as she picked away some thread. "So, whilst you and Sandy were busy with Grey, I borrowed needle and thread from Lady Frances and made a few... alterations."

She put down the blade and pulled a metal rod from the unpicked seam with a grin of triumph.

"You've sewn your entire set of skeleton keys into your clothing?" he said, trying not to laugh.

"Not all of them. I left out the small ones that are only any use for jewellery boxes and the like, and a few of the very largest."

Within half an hour she had an impressive collection of metal tools laid out on the blanket between them, and she unlocked Mal's fetters in short order. The lining of the bodice lay in ruins, but she put the garment back on as tidily as she could. Mal took great pleasure in tucking all the stray bits of fabric inside: all around her waist, at the back of her neck, along the front where the stiffening plumped up her breasts... He bent to kiss the soft warm skin, taking her in his arms as the hunger enveloped him. She giggled and made ineffectual attempts to push him off.

"We don't have time for this," she murmured into his hair.

He raised his head. "We have until sunset. After that, we may never get time again."

Ned folded his arms and held his ground. Lady Frances might be a duchess, but she was only a woman when all was said and done.

"I swore to my best friend that I would guard his son with my life. I can't do that if he's half the breadth of the Thames away."

"You exaggerate, Master Faulkner. Christopher will be only a few yards distant from the guest apartments. If there is any trouble, you can be with us in moments."

"And how will I know if there's trouble, if there's half a dozen stone walls between us?"

She sighed and drew him towards the window.

"My husband has men on the main gate–" she gestured towards the streetward entrance to Suffolk House "–and in the gardens also, lest anyone approach from the river. If we are attacked from either side, the alarm will go up."

"And if we are attacked from within?"

"You are accusing my servants of treachery?"

Ned chewed his moustache. How much to tell her? Hell, fuck Mal's tiptoeing around the truth; secrecy was for sneaky bastards like Henry.

"Not your servants," he said. "The enemy. They're sorcerers; they can appear out of thin air, bringing devils and who knows what with them."

Lady Frances made the sign of the cross, though to her credit she did not quail.

"What are we to do?"

Ned thought back to their escape from Anglesey Priory.

"For a start, arm your men with all the crossbows you have. A few steel-tipped bolts should slow our enemies down. But most of all, make sure Kit – Master Christopher – doesn't take off that necklace he's wearing."

Mal woke to darkness. For a moment he thought he was dreamwalking, but this was no gloomy moor under a sullen starless sky. All was black as night save a pair of small, narrow windows glowing with the last light of day. Outlined against them, a figure bent over, not looking at him. A metallic clink, then another. Mal shook off sleep and sat up.

"Awake at last?" his wife said, turning to look at him.

"What are you doing?"

"I sewed a handful of steel shot into the hem of my gown." Another clink. "Thought we might need them."

"You have your pistols?"

"Alas, no, but we're in the royal armoury, aren't we?" She straightened up and came back to the bed. "All done. Shall we go?"

She unlocked the cell door that led onto the stairwell and went up to free Sandy whilst Mal stood watch. This room had two doors, one of which – flanked by the westward-facing windows – opened onto the wall-walk. At the far end a lone guardsman stood with his partizan, gazing out over the Thames. Mal wondered briefly if his and Coby's lovemaking had provided sufficient entertainment for the fellow. He returned to the stairwell door, and a few moments later descending footsteps announced the success of his wife's mission.

"The guard will be starting his next round soon," Mal told his brother. "You know what to do?"

"Of course. Now go."

They embraced briefly, then Mal led the way out of the cell, feeling his way down the unlit stairs to the ground floor. Whilst Coby picked the lock on the outer door he groped around the newel-stones at the base of the spiral stair.

"Aha!" He withdrew the sword from its hiding place and slid the sheathed blade through his belt. The hilt was plain and leather-wrapped, by the feel of it; for once he did not miss the graceful but moonlight-snaring curves of his own rapier. "It's shocking what people leave lying around in a prison."

"Another of Grey's gifts?"

"Who's to suspect the duke's guards of collaborating with their captives? Do you have it open yet?"

The snick of the lock giving way echoed around the stairwell and the door opened a crack, letting in the hazy purple light of evening. After several moments Coby nodded, and they crept out into the inner ward, hugging the shadows at the base of the wall as they made their way towards the vast dark shape of the White Tower. When they were opposite the entrance, Mal paused and waited.

On the wall-walk above, the sentry's footsteps halted. Mal put a finger to his lips. A few moments later a soft curse came from overhead, followed by hurried footsteps, then after a short pause a sigh and the sound of running water.

"Come on!" Mal whispered, and led the way across the inner ward and through the gatehouse to the foot of the stairs.

They hurried up and let themselves inside. Mal offered up a quick prayer of gratitude to Saint Michael for Henry's arrogance in not posting guards at every possible entrance and exit. Evidently the young king considered manning the walls to be sufficient safeguard. Mal would take great pleasure in proving him wrong.

Kit waited until Lady Frances's maid had tucked him up under the thick counterpane and closed the bedchamber door behind her before scrambling out of bed and running to the window.

For a while he watched the boats plying back and forth across the Thames, their lanterns bobbing like fireflies. There were other lights too, outside the buildings on the far bank, and the dark shapes of people strolling along the riverside, even though it was nearly curfew. He couldn't see the Tower from here, but it was only a short ride away, he was sure of that. If only Father had let him go along! He was old enough now, surely, or why else would Father have given him a sword?

Henry had the sword now, of course. Kit muttered a few rude words that would have earned him a beating from Master Weston. Well, Master Weston wasn't here now, and nor was Father. If Henry wouldn't give the sword back, Kit was going to have to fetch it.

He found his clothes and struggled into them. Lady Frances had found him some hand-me-downs so that he didn't have to wear the clothes Master Fox had given him. The doublet was a bit big but it was a fine silk brocade in deep ruby red, which made him feel more like a soldier than a schoolboy. Now there was only one other thing he needed. He reached up behind his neck for the clasp of the necklace.

"Now, Kiiren," he said aloud as he unfastened it. "I need your help. How do I get to the Tower?"

Kiiren blinked and the spirit-guard slipped from his fingers, falling to the floor with a clatter that echoed softly from the panelled walls. Where was he? Ah yes, Lord Grey's house. And his beloved Erishen had left to confront Jathekkil without him. That would not do. No time to lose; as he had done once before, he reached out across the dreamlands to his *amayi* – but this time it was he who stepped through.

CHAPTER XXXVI

Erishen drew back from the guard into the waking world, ready to take the next step in their plan. Scarcely had he opened his eyes, however, than he saw a tunnel of light open, shimmering blue-green like the ocean. Ilianwe? He backed away, reaching out for the discarded manacles.

The small figure at the far end of the tunnel resolved itself into an equally unwelcome form, though for different reasons.

"*Amayi*, what are you doing here? Go back!"

Kiiren did not heed him, but stepped out into the tower cell.

"You left me behind." There was a boyish sulkiness in his tone.

"You are too young for this, beloved."

"I am as old as Jathekkil. As old as him in body – and older in soul. Why should I not stand beside you?"

Erishen sighed. "And you always said I was the stubborn one."

"I learnt it from you."

Human though he was, in the dim evening light Kiiren looked a great deal like the skrayling boy Erishen had collected from his mother after his first reincarnation. Same dark hair as yet unmarked by the silver streaks of adulthood, same determined expression.

"Very well. Come and sit by me." He explained their half of the plan. "Can you do that?"

Kiiren made a rude noise. "Easily."

Erishen took him by the shoulders.

"Do not underestimate him, *amayi*. Jathekkil may be young and weak, but Ilianwe is at least as old as I am and far more cunning. Now, we have delayed long enough. Lie down here, next to me, and we will begin."

Erishen lay back and closed his eyes, focusing all his will on the dreamlands.

"Stop fidgeting," he murmured. "Forget your mortal body and leave it behind."

He did likewise himself, blocking out all the sounds of the city and the smells of the dank tower room. The darkness behind his eyelids shimmered, and he stepped out onto the twilit moor. A moment later Kiiren materialised at his side. Erishen held out his hand. Here in the dreamlands they were equal in height, though Kiiren's soul burned with a fainter, whiter light that marked his relative youth.

"Ready?"

"Ready," Kiiren replied.

Only a short distance away, a cluster of dreaming minds marked the position of the great keep. No sign of Jathekkil, but perhaps he was still awake.

"Extend your senses," Erishen said. "Unless he wears a spirit-guard, there will be traces of his connection to the dreamlands."

Kiiren nodded. Together they spread their awareness outwards, taking in the scatter of human dreamers in the keep, the rustle of grass that perhaps marked the approach of a devourer... So fine-tuned was his attention that when another dreamwalker materialised behind him, the power bludgeoned his mind and he could not help but flinch.

"Erishen. It has been too long." A soft, seductive voice, with an accent he could not put his finger on.

He turned around, stepping between Kiiren and the new arrival. "Ilianwe."

"And this must be Kiiren." The figure inclined its head, peering around him. "You were reborn as a Venetian, I hear. How fortunate for you."

"Fortunate?" Kiiren replied. "I had much rather been reborn in my true kind. Our true kind."

Ilianwe laughed and changed shape, into a skrayling female, short of hair and solidly built.

"Like this?" she said. "A form you so aspired to in your last incarnation."

"It is traditional–"

"Tradition. It is tradition that bars us all from our former homeland. How can you have any loyalty to them?"

"Enough," Erishen said. "She is trying to stall us. Kiiren, go and help my brother. I will detain her."

Before he had even finished speaking Ilianwe changed again, into a winged, clawed thing that flew over Erishen's head straight towards the fleeing Kiiren. Erishen launched himself after her in a blaze of white-hot light that scorched her wings and sent her tumbling to the ground.

"Go, *amayi*, now!"

Erishen had no more time to give Kiiren his attention, for Ilianwe was on her feet again. This time her shape was more humanoid, armoured in scales against his fire. She thrust her hands forward and dozens of tiny barbs flew from her fingertips, piercing his dream-flesh. He bit down on the cry of agony that threatened to burst from his throat, lest he distract Kiiren from his vital mission. Illusion, only illusion, he told himself. He circled round so that he was between Ilianwe and the keep once more.

"You cannot defeat me," Ilianwe said. "Not in your broken state. I am older than you, and stronger."

"We defeated you once."

"And yet I am here."

She gestured to either side; the air rippled and turned to stone that spread out and round and up, forming a dome that enclosed him on all sides. Erishen beat on it with his fists, but it only trembled and sifted dust down to choke his lungs. *Illusion. I have no body here to need breath.*

Laughing, Ilianwe turned into the winged beast once more and flew after Kiiren. She did not attack, however, but flew straight over his head, light flaring out green and gold and violet as she began to open a portal. Erishen threw himself against the walls of his prison but they were solid as ever. He looked down at his knuckles, raw and bleeding, and realised he was awake and pounding his fists into the stone wall of the tower room. He whirled around, but Kiiren was gone.

The great keep had been designed as the finest and most secure bolthole for a king who had only recently taken his place on the throne of England. Not Jathekkil, of course, but William the Conqueror. Even so, the place served the usurper well. A massive gatehouse defended the main approach on the west side of the keep. The entrance doors were high up on the first floor and could only be reached by a long flight of steps protected by another stone gatehouse. Once inside, any attackers had to cross the great hall to the north side of the keep in order to reach the main staircase to the upper floors.

All this, Mal had determined from their first, brief visit to see the prince. He anticipated guards on each level, probably human; the other guisers must be spread thinly if the usurper was relying on them to control his kingdom whilst he lurked in here. Mal drew his borrowed sword and took the lead, putting each foot down with care to avoid the scuff of leather on stone.

Torches flickered in cressets, making the shadows of the tattered banners dance on the ceiling, but that was the only movement to be seen. The whole keep seemed oddly deserted, as if Henry had already taken his court back to Whitehall Palace, and yet surely that could not have been done within the few short hours since Mal had been imprisoned? He advanced through the great hall, a sick feeling in his stomach.

The hall was divided into two unequal halves by a massive retaining wall pierced by arches. Mal slipped into the shadow of the nearest and peered around the corner, to where he knew a door opened onto the great staircase. At last, a living soul! More torches illuminated the heavily built figure of one of the Huntsmen, standing guard at the entrance to the stairwell, feet apart, hands braced on the halberd before him. Even more ominously, he wore an executioner's hood, so like the masks worn by the Huntsmen on their rides. The man's eyes glinted through the slits in the black leather.

"Stay back!" Mal hissed over his shoulder at Coby.

He strolled forward, sword point drooping towards the floor.

"Ho there, good fellow! Will you step aside and let me and my companion visit the King?"

The Huntsman said nothing.

"Or does your loyalty to Lord Grey not extend beyond his threshold?"

"What would you know about loyalty, demon?" The Huntsman crossed himself and hefted his pole-arm.

"There's been some mistake," Mal said. "That was all a play, to fool the King–"

"No mistake."

The Huntsman strode forward, sweeping the eighteen-inch blade in a lethal arc at belly height. Mal leapt back; a sword was useless at this range.

"Shoot him!" Mal yelled, throwing himself sideways and rolling as he hit the floor.

"I don't have a gun, remember?"

Mal cursed and got to his feet. Something small flew past his head, too slow and silent to be a bullet. The Huntsman flinched, and the missile pattered to the floor and rolled away. Mal laughed. In lieu of weapon or powder, Coby was throwing her ammunition.

Another bullet sailed past the Huntsman's head, and it was his turn to laugh – until the next caught him in the teeth with an audible *crack*. The man swore and spat blood, but the distraction was enough. Mal leapt forward and lunged, skewering the Huntsman's right hand between the base of the fingers and through his wrist, the tip at last emerging below his forearm. Screaming, the man tried to wield his weapon one-handed but the balance was off. The halberd blade rang like an ill-tuned bell as it slammed into the stone floor. Mal lunged again, well below the padded jerkin, stabbing into the meat of the man's thigh. As he withdrew the blade blood gushed forth and the Huntsman staggered and dropped his weapon, enfolding Mal in an embrace that threatened to crush the breath from his lungs. The two of them fell to the floor, the Huntsman closing his uninjured hand around Mal's windpipe. Mal smashed the hilt of his sword against the brute's skull to no avail.

As the world started to go dark, the pressure on Mal's chest and throat suddenly eased. He blinked and saw a pale figure standing over him. Coby.

"What happened?" he asked.

"I... I don't really know. I think I stabbed him. A lot."

Her doublet and hose were covered in a fine spray of blood, as of many small wounds. She looked down at the sword in her hand. Mal's borrowed sword.

"Well, someone had to," he said, getting to his feet. Dear God, he was as soaked in gore as a Smithfield butcher, the other man's blood sticky and disturbingly warm.

Coby looked pale enough to swoon. Best to get her moving; she could think about this later. He took the sword from her, gently, and wiped it on the dead man's jerkin.

"Come on. We made enough of a racket to announce our arrival; let's not keep the King waiting."

The great stair was wide enough for three men to walk side-by-side – or for one man to wield a blade with ease. Mal led the way up to another floor identical in its plan to the one below, apart from a pillared gallery running round all four sides, like a cloister. This one was stacked to head height with breastplates, helmets and rusted coats of mail. A narrow passage led through the armoury to one of the corner towers, where a much smaller staircase spiralled upwards. Mal sheathed his sword and helped himself to a dagger from a pile on top of a barrel, taking one of the torches in his free hand. He nodded towards a rack of pistols.

"Grab a brace," he whispered to Coby. "And a powder flask."

She nodded numbly but complied. *Damn, but I hate having to do this. I should send her back to Sandy, where she'll be safe.* But it was too late for that now. Nothing for it but to press on.

The stairs opened into a small room furnished as a bedchamber. The scents of *qoheetsakhan* and burnt flesh mingled unpleasantly in the air.

The body of the other Huntsman lay in the middle of the floor, face down and stripped to the waist. Either dead or unconscious, by the look of it.

"I thought you preferred to have someone else do your interrogation for you," Mal said to the slight figure sitting in the window-seat.

Jathekkil got to his feet and walked forward into the light of the candles.

"Did you think I would not see through your ridiculous little plot? That I would be blinded by my desire to have you captive once more?"

"I thought it worth the hazard, yes."

"I'm afraid you've overreached yourself this time, Catlyn." He smiled, and a glow began to form behind him. "Goodbye."

"What?"

"Where do you think my court has gone? Did I spirit them away, as I did your son? Or did I perhaps send them all down to the lowest level of the keep, to sit around the barrels of gunpowder and wait for my orders?"

"You… bastard craven whoreson."

"Farewell, Catlyn." He turned to greet the figure forming at the other end of the tunnel. "No. Oh no. Not you again."

Mal leapt forward, grabbed the boy-king from behind and slid his dagger across his cheek. No need to kill, not yet, but the touch of blood on steel would break any magic he tried to use.

"No!" Jathekkil squirmed in Mal's grasp as Kiiren stepped through the portal.

"Sorry, Your Majesty," Mal said, "but it looks like you lose after all." He turned to his wife. "Go and free the courtiers. Kiiren and I can look after this one."

Coby hesitated for a moment, unwilling to leave her son in the same room as that creature. Mal glared at her, and at last she turned and ran.

He's not my son anyway, she kept telling herself over and over. He's Kiiren now. And yet when she thought back to the little time she had spent with Ambassador Kiiren, the two were much alike: inquisitive, soft-hearted and fond of stories, but with a stubborn streak when it came to protecting those they loved. She wiped the tears from her eyes and ran on. If Henry's boast had not been an idle threat, the lives of dozens of people still depended on her.

Down and down the great spiral stair she went, until her legs were aching and her head swimming. She passed the great hall and continued on down to the lowest level, which was above ground but with walls several yards thick and only tiny slot-like windows to provide a little light and ventilation. A flask of near-exhausted lightwater hung from an empty cresset, casting a faint bluish glow over the last few steps. She reached the bottom of the stairwell to find a solid wooden door twice her own height, barred with a great beam as well as locked and bolted.

"Oh wonderful," she muttered, bending to get her shoulder under the beam.

It took several minutes and enough swearing to shock a Billingsgate porter, but at last she had the thing open. She heaved back the door. The darkness within was impenetrable, but the mingled stinks of gunpowder and sweat revealed the cellar's contents well enough. She fetched the lightwater lantern, swirling it to bring it back to some semblance of usefulness, and held it up. The pallid faces of a hundred courtiers stared back at her.

"Come on," she called to them. "All of you, out of here, quickly!"

When they did not move, she added, "The King commands it!"

At that they began to stir, and she ushered them up the stairs in ones and twos. They were all dusty and bedraggled, with puffy features as if they had been asleep too long. When she was sure that the last of them was out of there, she closed the door and ran up the stairs, leaving the barrels of gunpowder in peace.

Mal knelt, dragging the boy-king down with him.

"Undo my spirit-guard," he told Kiiren, "and put it on our prisoner."

"What have you done with her?" Jathekkil growled as Kiiren came round to stand in front of him, the metal necklace between his hands. "What have you done with my *amayi*?"

"No worse than you would have done to mine," Kiiren replied. He looped the necklace round the struggling boy's head and fastened the clasp. "She's not dead, not yet."

Mal tied Henry's hands behind his back and secured him to one of the bedposts, then took his son aside.

"What did you do?"

"Nothing," Kiiren replied, his dark eyes sorrowful. "She brought it upon herself."

"What do you mean?"

"The people in the cellar were afraid. *Hrrith* came… so Ilianwe had to flee. I thought she would go back to her body, but she flew up into the sky and disappeared north. I think she's gone to find Shawe."

Mal's innards twisted in fear. "Come on, we have to find her body before it's too late."

Mal ran down through the keep, Kiiren in his arms, and found his wife waiting at the bottom of the entrance stairs. Outside, courtiers milled around in confusion. Over the hubbub came the low thud of a battering ram.

"What's going on?"

"They're trying to break into the Jewel House." Coby pointed to the long building at the foot of the stairs.

"No matter. We have more important things to worry about than a bit of gold."

"You really are a skrayling at heart, aren't you?" she said with a grin as she ran after him.

They pushed their way out through the throng.

"We need to find Ilianwe. Olivia."

"Her chamber is in the Queen's apartments," Coby said. "In the little tower room in the corner."

"I know the place." Mal put Kiiren down. "Look after him. I'll see you soon."

Ignoring his wife's protests he raced through the castle grounds, pushing past startled guardsmen. At last he found himself in the outer ward, at the foot of the stairs up to the old royal apartments in St Thomas's Tower.

"Hold! Who goes there?" a guard shouted down at him.

"Sir Maliverny Catlyn. Please, let me through. The Queen is in danger."

"And why should I believe you?" The guard advanced down the stair, pointing his partizan at Mal. "I heard you were a traitor."

Mal raised his hands as if surrendering. The guard relaxed, and Mal leapt up the next three steps and seized the partizan by its decorative side-blades. Twisting out of the way he hauled on the weapon, sending its bearer tumbling down the stairs to land in a heap on the cobbles below.

"Sorry," he muttered, bounding up the rest of the stairs and pulling open the door.

The dining parlour was just as he remembered it, though it lay empty at this time of night. He ran over to the door in the corner and tried the latch. Locked, dammit! On the other hand, anything in there would take a while to get out. He went through into the other half of the main apartments, to the bedchamber where he and Coby had spent the night all those years ago.

"Ladies?"

One of the bed's occupants sat up and screamed, waking her companions. Mal belatedly remembered he was soaked in blood from the waist down.

"Please, ladies, I'm not here to harm you, I swear. My name is Sir Maliverny Catlyn; my wife served the Queen–"

"We know who you are, sirrah," one of them said, gathering a robe around her shoulders. "A traitor and a renegade."

"Please, whatever you think of me, rouse the Queen mother and get yourselves out of here this instant. You are all in great danger."

"What kind of–"

Her answer was a loud thud from the room behind Mal.

"Go!" he said, taking the nearest woman's arm and pushing her towards the door. "Get out through the Wakefield Tower and flee this place entirely if you can."

The women scattered, and Mal stalked back into the dining chamber, ready to face whatever came through the tower door.

CHAPTER XXXVII

Coby stood at the top of the steps, wondering how she was to get all these people out of the Tower. Fortunately the problem was solved for her by the arrival of a squad of militiamen. Coby pulled Kit back into the shadow of the great doors. The last thing she wanted was to be herded out of the castle with the rest of the courtiers.

"Come on, let's go and check on our prisoner," she said. "We don't want some well-meaning warder letting him loose, not after all the trouble we've been to."

She was half out of breath by the time they reached the little tower room, and half-expected Jathekkil to have vanished into thin air. But there he was, tied to the bedpost with the dark metal of a spirit-guard glinting dully at his throat.

"Come back to finish me off, have you?" he rasped.

"I could never kill a child," Coby replied softly. She looked from one boy to the other. "But I suppose neither of you are children, are you?"

The usurper's eyes widened in fear.

"Don't worry," she said. "You're quite safe with us."

She went over to the door and unlocked it. After a moment's consideration she slipped the heavy iron key into her pocket and returned to the bed, where she tore a strip from one of the sheets and gagged the young king and bound his ankles before untying him from the bedpost. He bucked in her arms as she scooped him up and threw him on the bed.

"One boy sounds much like another," she said. "And my son looks a good deal like you. Everyone comments on it. If the yeomen warders come, I'm sure we can persuade them nothing is amiss."

She closed the bed-curtains and opened a large cupboard. As she suspected, it was full of fine clothing, made for a boy of eight or nine years.

"Kit, why don't you change out of those dirty things into something a bit nicer?"

As Mal watched, the door to Olivia's chamber melted like wax into a tarry puddle on the floor. A young man of eighteen or so stood on the other side, tall and thin with skin pale as a shoot forced in darkness. Another of Shawe's young sorcerers, no doubt. He seemed to look straight through Mal as if he wasn't there. Beyond him, Mal could see someone lying on the floor, an arm clad in green silk flung wide, graceful hand limp as a flower. Olivia.

Mal drew his sword, and the youth finally appeared to notice him.

"Don't like this, do you?" Mal said, pointing the steel blade towards him.

The youth raised his hands, and a chair thudded into the back of Mal's knees. Mal stumbled and dropped the sword, and the youth pounced, turning into a great cat in mid-air. Mal rolled and retrieved his weapon. Sweet Christ! He had expected an attack on his mind, not his body. Still, if that's what they wanted, he was more than happy to oblige.

He scrambled to his feet, sweeping the blade in an ever-changing series of arcs that wove a shield of steel between them. Let the creature get its magic through that! But he could not keep it up forever, and the sorcerer seemed to guess as much. He changed back into a human youth and withdrew, arms crossed, waiting. His enemy was no fencer, however; moments later he gave himself away by glancing over Mal's shoulder. Mal edged round to see another boy, slightly younger, framed in the doorway. How many of them were there? Two dozen at least, or so Kiiren had said. He needed reinforcements.

Without taking his eyes off the two youths, he reached out with his mind and called to his brother. Green light flared behind him, and a moment later Sandy stepped through.

"Good work," he murmured, stepping round Mal.

The light did not fade however, but shimmered between the pair of them, binding them together. Sandy moved sideways and the light stretched with him, becoming a wall that cut off the sorcerers' escape route. After a moment the two youths retreated into the corner tower and the stone walls closed in as if a door had never been there. Mal released a breath he didn't know he had been holding, and the green light died.

"How in God's name are they doing that?" he said, to no one in particular.

"You mean shaping the fabric of the world as if it were the dreamlands?" his brother replied. "It appears to be a human talent, one we never suspected."

Mal shook his head. "We can philosophise about this later. Since we're too late to stop them coming through, all we can do now is—"

The magically sealed wall began to crumble into sand, and as it fell away Mal could make out not two but half a dozen young sorcerers behind it. He reached behind him and wrenched open the outer door of the Queen's apartments, pulling Sandy after him.

Gabriel finally caught up with Ned at the edge of Tower Hill, after chasing his lover all the way from the Strand through the darkened streets of London's northern suburbs.

"What do you think you're doing?" he panted, grasping at Ned's sleeve.

"We can't let Kit go in there. Mal will kill me."

"How do you know he went to the Tower? Lady Frances just said he was missing."

"Where else would he go, eh? Besides, Mal needs us."

"No, he doesn't. He needs... I don't know, an army. Or the skraylings. An army of skraylings, perhaps."

"And where is he going to find one of those, eh? They're gone. Forever. The guisers made sure of that."

"So you're going in their place?"

Ned shrugged helplessly. "I can't just sit around and wait for my friends to die."

Gabriel slipped his arm around his lover's waist. "And I don't want to see you die. It was bad enough the last time. Don't put me through that again."

Ned said nothing, only buried his head in the crook of Gabriel's neck. They stood there for several minutes, Gabriel resting his cheek against Ned's hair. Faint sounds drifted westwards on the night air: a dull thudding, and voices raised in panic. Gabriel watched the fortress over Ned's shoulder, feeling the tension in his lover's muscles and knowing he too was listening to the noises issuing from within. As Gabriel watched, the gates of the Byward Tower opened and a bedraggled column of people began making their way across the causeway to the landward gatehouse.

"What's going on?" he said softly. "Are the guisers fleeing after all?"

Ned twisted in his arms.

"Something's afoot. Come on!"

Before Gabriel could stop him Ned raced off down the hill towards the Tower. With a groan of resignation Gabriel set off after him.

Mal vaulted down the stairs outside the Queen's apartments only to find his way blocked by the stream of courtiers being guided towards the Byward Tower by anxious-faced warders.

"Get them out of here, as fast as you can!" he yelled. "You! Fetch a squad of militiamen to guard Saint Thomas's Tower."

The warder he had addressed glared back at him.

"On whose authority?"

"The Duke of Suffolk's."

"Well I answer to the King, sirrah. The duke can mind his own business." He went back to shepherding the dazed-looking nobles towards the gates.

"Mal!"

He turned to see Ned pushing through the throng towards him.

"What in God's name are you two doing here? I told you to stay at Suffolk House."

"I know. I'm sorry. It's Kit–"

"Yes, he's here, I know." Mal sighed. "If you want to make yourself useful, go and fetch any militiamen you can round up. I need that building cordoned off, now."

Ned grinned his acknowledgement and ran off.

"Can I help?" Gabriel asked.

"Get up into the Bloody Tower and prepare to lower the portcullis as soon as Ned gets back. We need to lure Shawe's apprentices further into the castle and trap them there, so they can't attack the rest of the city."

Gabriel nodded in acknowledgement.

"They'll walk straight through the portcullis, you do realise that?" Sandy said as they hurried through the gateway.

"Don't be too sure," Mal replied. "It's bound and shod with iron; it might at least give them pause."

They jogged up the slope to the green and turned right towards the low bulk of the keep's gatehouse.

"Wait here for Ned to come through," he told Sandy. "I'm going to check on the next line of defences."

Without waiting for a reply he clapped his brother on the shoulder and set about exploring the coldharbour gate. A door at the foot of one of the two gatehouse towers opened onto a stair that led up to a guard room. No portcullis, but a double line of holes along the floor marked the passageway below, allowing defenders to drop stones or boiling water on attackers. Or, more promisingly in this instance, the steel-headed pikes and crossbow bolts stacked along one side of the guardroom. He picked up a couple of crossbows and quivers and raced back down to the innermost ward to bark orders at a group of militiamen who were half-heartedly restraining a couple of their colleagues.

"You can arrest these men for looting if they survive," Mal told them. "Right now I want all of you manning the murder-holes in the gatehouse."

He left them to it and returned to his brother just as Ned came panting up the slope. Mal thrust the crossbows and quivers at him, and Ned began cranking one of them with his good hand.

"Any sign of them yet?"

As if in answer, a scream came from the outer ward. Mal caught Sandy by the arm.

"Come on, we're going to have to lure them in here."

They ran down to the gate under the Bloody Tower. A dozen youths in the livery of Anglesey Priory stood along the wall-walk, staring down at them.

"Here we are," Mal yelled up at them. "We're the ones you seek."

As one the sorcerers jumped, floating down to the ground as gently as autumn leaves. Mal recalled moving like that in the dreamlands; Sandy was right, they were shaping reality around them as easily as a dream.

He backed into the gateway, not too fast lest they lose interest. They closed in, moving as one. Mal glanced at Sandy out of the corner of his eye. Like hounds picking up the scent at last the sorcerers charged forward. Mal turned and ran.

"Now, Gabriel!"

The rattle of the Bloody Tower's portcullis mechanism filled the night air. Not a moment too soon. Two of the young sorcerers were crushed under the iron spikes but the rest ran up the slope, howling. Mal turned and drew his sword. They had to keep them here, away from the fleeing courtiers but away from Kit and Coby as well.

The tallest of the sorcerers stretched out his arms and clapped his hands together before him. The torches on either side of the portcullis flared, setting fire to the ancient wooden timbers. Outlined against the flames, he began to advance up the slope towards Mal. A crossbow quarrel zipped past Mal's ear, only to burst into flame as it flew. The steel head fell to the cobbles a few feet short of its target. The stink of burnt feathers hung in the air for a moment before it was drowned out by the smoke now billowing from the portcullis.

"Fall back to the coldharbour gate!" Mal yelled over the roar of the flames.

He held his position until Ned and Gabriel were behind him, then backed towards the gates where the militiamen hopefully waited around the murder-holes. Burning the shafts wouldn't make a difference if the missiles came from above.

Kiiren let the human woman, Hendricks, finish buttoning the unfamiliar clothes, then he shrugged her off and went over to the bed.

"What are you doing, lambkin?" she asked, coming towards him.

"Watch the door." When she hesitated, he recalled the best way to appeal to her. "Please, Mamma?"

She nodded and went to stand guard. Kiiren pulled back the curtain.

Jathekkil glared up at him and wriggled backwards across the bed.

"I'm not going to hurt you," Kiiren said truthfully. "I just want to talk."

He climbed onto the bed and loosened the gag, pulling it down over Jathekkil's chin, then removed the prince's spirit-guard.

Jathekkil spat fibres from his mouth. "I don't have anything to say to you, traitor."

Kiiren shook his head in pity.

"You have been human too long, Jathekkil. It does not suit your temperament."

"You always were a sanctimonious little prick, Outspeaker."

"Insults? Is that all you have learned from your time here?"

"You have no idea what the humans are like, do you?"

"I have studied–"

"Study. Ha!" Jathekkil licked his lips, warming to his subject. "Just wait until you've lived a lifetime or two among them. You'll see. They'll never stop, you know, these Christians. They want our gold and gemstones, and all our clever devices that bring light in the darkness and cold in the heat of summer. They want our lands and those of our human allies in the New World. They will not rest until they have it all."

"You have misjudged them–"

"No, it is you who misjudge. You are too soft-hearted, Outspeaker. You see the good in everyone. Well I see the evil, and the evil is stronger."

Kiiren retied the gag, replaced the spirit-guard and climbed off the bed.

"What was all that about?" Hendricks asked.

It was a moment before Kiiren realised he and Jathekkil had been talking in Vinlandic.

"Nothing, Mamma. Just idle boasting."

He went over to the window and looked out, but from here all he could see were the barracks ranged along the north wall, and a scatter of new houses on the slopes above the Tower. He sank down on the window seat with a sigh.

What if Jathekkil were right, and all his efforts at diplomacy were for naught? No, he could not give in to despair, not now. His *amayi* still needed him. And one day they would both go home. That he had sworn, a lifetime ago when he first came to England. There was still the small problem of Erishen's shattered soul, but they would work that out. Perhaps if they could capture Shawe, his alchemy would show them how.

Imbued with new purpose, he jumped down from the window seat. "Mamma, we need to capture one of the boys from the school. Alive, if we can."

The coldharbour gates held for mere seconds before the fire-wielding sorcerer reduced them to ashes. One or two of his more reckless fellows dashed forward, only to be brought down by a hail of iron missiles from above. The youths gathered at the outer end of the passage, considering their options.

"Not so cocksure now, are you?" Ned yelled at them.

One of the boys raised his arms and a freezing wind poured down the passageway, ice crystals tearing at the defenders' skin as they tried to stand their ground. Mal squinted through the onslaught, his free hand before his face. The wind-raiser's companions had transformed into flat, serpentine creatures that slid along the upper walls of the passage, too high to be hit by missiles from above. One of them squirmed through a murder-hole, and moments later screams echoed around the passageway. Mal swore. Their last line of defence breached.

Ned and Gabriel raised their crossbows and shot at the creatures as they slithered out around the walls of the gatehouse, momentarily out of sight of their fire-wielding companion. One of them fell, transforming in mid-air into a boy of about thirteen, naked and with a crossbow bolt through his chest.

"God's teeth, I hate these guisers!" Ned growled, cranking his crossbow again. "Using children as their soldiers, the craven bastards."

The two oldest youths advanced through the gatehouse and emerged into the innermost ward.

"This isn't working," Sandy panted. "They're not even drawing on the dreamlands for their magic any more, and I don't know how to fight them."

"No, but I do." Mal raised the sword in *prima guardia*, ready to fend off the next attack.

"You told me yourself you are tiring. How long can you keep them back?"

"As long as I have to."

Sandy sighed. "There is another way."

Mal glanced back over his shoulder. "I'm not going to like it, am I?"

"We have to finish what Jathekkil started."

"What?"

"Reforge our souls into one."

"No."

"Brother, you know it must be. Sooner or later. Or we are both lost, and Kiiren will be alone."

"No."

"They'll destroy us anyway, and Kiiren. And kill your wife."

Mal hesitated. "She would not want this either. She would call it blasphemy."

"And if they eat her soul too? Where is her God then?"

The weapon drooped in his hand as he acknowledged the inevitable. "What must I do?"

"We will need a quiet place, and a little time."

"We can give you that," said Ned. "Go on. Do whatever it is you have to do to destroy this lot."

Mal seized Ned's arm with his free hand. "I can't let you do this. They'll kill you both."

"Most likely. But isn't that what happens in war?"

Mal hugged him one-handed, holding his sword out of the way.

"I'll never forget this, or you," he murmured in Ned's ear.

"Oh, go on with you." Ned kissed his cheek. "I mean it. Go."

Mal retreated into the keep, Sandy still behind him. The last thing he heard was Ned's battle-cry.

"Right, you bastard sons of whores, which one of you is first?"

CHAPTER XXXVIII

They found a high-ceilinged side-chamber that had once been a chapel, though its rood screen and altar had long since been removed and its coloured glass windows were grimy with neglect. Mal supposed it was as good a place to die as any.

"So, what do we do?"

"Put aside all your weapons, and remove anything made of iron or steel from your person."

Mal unfastened his sword belt and placed his blades on the stone steps before the missing altar, like a knight of old commencing his vigil. After a moment's consideration he kicked off his boots and removed his doublet, in case any of the buckles or lace-ends were tainted with iron.

When he was done, Sandy gestured for Mal to join him in a corner by the doorway, where they would not immediately be seen by anyone approaching.

"Now, sit down on the floor. This will go better if you don't fall over once we get started."

Mal sat down, hands clamped around his raised knees to stop them shaking, as he used to sit and hide as a boy when their father was in an ill temper. Sandy sat down by his side so that they were shoulder to shoulder, hip to hip, like a mirror image. He took out a small wooden box and opened it. Inside was the obsidian blade he used for shaving.

"Where did you get that from?" Mal asked.

Sandy just smiled. "Ready?"

"As I'll ever be."

Mal held out his wrist. The fat blue-green vein leading to his palm twitched in time with his heartbeat, counting out these last moments–

"No, not you. Me."

"What?" Mal looked up. "No. Jathekkil said I was the one that must die–"

"He was wrong. Your half of our soul is too weak. It might not prevail against mine, and then you are simply dead."

"Prevail? You mean I would have to fight you?"

"Our souls have been apart too long. They cannot simply be fitted back together like a broken cup." Sandy bared his wrist and laid the black, glassy blade against his skin. "I have to do this."

"No!"

But it was too late. Dark blood was already welling from a long shallow cut along the veins of Sandy's wrist. As Mal watched in horror, his brother sliced open his other wrist. Mal saw again the piles of skrayling corpses in the watchtower on Corsica, smelt the copper tang of fresh blood. Sandy put the blade down on the floor between his feet and took Mal's hand in his own. Lifeblood, warm and sticky, pulsed over both their hands and dripped to the floor.

"Try not to fight too hard," Sandy whispered, and closed his eyes.

"No…"

Mal pulled his brother close, cradling his head against his shoulder. He mumbled something, he knew not what, and heard the whisper of Sandy's dying reply.

"*Amayi'o anosennowe…* I will never give up…"

Ned and Gabriel stood side by side at the foot of the great stair. The sorcerers advanced slowly at first, as if unable to believe that two mortals would dare to try to stop them. The foremost stepped forward, rising up until he was seven, eight feet tall, broad in the beam and muscular, his face horribly familiar. Armitage? But this was not the man Ned had killed; the shapeshifter made Suffolk's retainer look like a runt.

The Armitage-giant launched himself at Ned, swinging his massive fists. Ned dodged; it wasn't hard to get under the blows. Bending over he headbutted the giant in the groin, and it roared and brought down its fist. Ned narrowly dodged it but the other fist came down, catching him a glancing blow on the left shoulder. Something made a horrible crunching noise and pain exploded inside Ned's skull. He looked up and to his horror the giant was falling on him, trying to crush him out of existence. Ned held up his right arm in a desperate attempt to fend him off, but as the creature smashed into the steel-studded palm it shrank once more into a slight youth of no more than seventeen, pale-faced and disoriented. Still, his weight was enough to push Ned backwards, and they sprawled on the steps together. The shapeshifter started getting to his feet, growing as he did so, but with an almighty effort Ned swiped him round the head. His opponent grunted and slumped to the ground, out cold. A trickle of blood ran from his temple. He wasn't getting up any time soon.

Ned staggered to his feet and looked around, just in time to see Gabriel locked in combat with something hardly less horrific than the devourers they had fought in Venice. Lean and pale as an ox carcass on a butcher's hook it was, with burning red eyes and clawed hands. It lunged for Gabriel's throat and bit down, blood gouting over its pink-and-white skin. Ned screamed and went for it, battering it around the head, but by ill chance the metal hand had snapped back into a fist and only the brass knuckles were connecting with the monster's flesh. He swore and worked the lever, but before he could hit the creature again it dropped Gabriel and went still, as did the others. They all stared up at the keep, then as one they began to move towards the entrance, shifting back into their human forms and scrambling over the fallen.

A slow drumbeat, getting slower. It was dark here, darker than the dreamlands had ever been before, as if leaden clouds had blotted out even the faint smear of light that illuminated the void. He was dying, and his only hope was that battered fragment of a soul tied to flesh as familiar as his own. He reached out an insubstantial hand, groping in the dark for what he knew must be there, but feared it would not. No. He had to believe, or it would truly disappear. *Never give up. I will always find you. I will always come for you.* Amayi. *Brother. Soul of my soul.*

There. Such a fragile thing, like a cobweb, and yet strong as steel. He groped his way along the bond, feeling it grow thick and corded beneath his fingers like an umbilicus, the shared flesh of their birth. Pouring his essence into its fibres he swam through the darkness, towards the source, hearing the heartbeat grow louder and louder once more. The bond twisted, trembling under his touch, but he pushed on. *We cannot fail now.*

All at once he was falling from a great height and he screamed, expecting to smash against the stony earth of the dreamlands any moment. A light flared, so bright he could not see it, could not open his eyes and yet it was there, searing through him, limning his veins and sinews and the tip of every hair on his skin–

Erishen.

He screamed his name, and opened his eyes to the darkness of an abandoned chapel.

"Hendricks?"

It was Mal's voice, or more likely Sandy's; it was hard to tell the difference through the heavy oak door. Coby turned the key and drew back the bolts. Mal stood there, swaying on his feet, his shirt gleaming dark and wet in the candlelight to match his hose.

"What happened?" she cried. "Oh, sweet Jesu, you're covered…"

She peered around him, but there was no one on the stair.

"I don't think they've broken in yet." He placed his bloody hands on her shoulders. "I need you to do something for me."

"Anything."

"We need to finish what Jathekkil started."

He glanced back at their captive, then down at the floor. She followed his gaze. The cellars, full of gunpowder.

"You will have to be careful, on the way down–"

"No. I can't leave you here," she said. "Mal, please–"

He put a finger to her lips.

"I am Erishen. I must finish this."

"No." She backed away from him and went to put her arm around Kit, but he ran over to his father and flung his arms about his knees.

"*Amayi.*"

Mal ruffled the boy's hair, just the way she had seen her brother-in-law do so many times.

"Where's Sandy?" When he did not reply, she went to the door. "Where is he?"

"Gone," Mal said. "I told you, I am Erishen now. And you must go. Take Kiiren. Quickly!"

She took Kit's hand and was about to lead him away when her nerve broke. She ran back to her husband – if he still was her husband – and kissed him on the cheek, then turned her back and walked out with Kit in tow. After a while, however, it was Kit who led the way, since she could see nothing for the tears in her eyes.

"Come on, Mamma, we have to be quick! They'll be here soon."

He leapt down the stairs like a young mountain goat and she could only stumble after him, her heart a dead weight in her chest. What evil magic had transferred Erishen into her beloved Mal?

She had no time to wonder further, however. As they reached the exit to the great hall, the archways of the dividing wall lit up as the outer doors beyond burst into flame. She pulled Kit down the next turn of the spiral stair and watched with a pounding heart as monstrous creatures loped or flew or slithered across the hall and up the stairs, intent on their prey. Mal. She started back after them as if in a dream.

"No, Mamma! We have to do what Erishen – what Father asked of us. Or we will all die for nothing."

"How can you…" She broke off, shaking her head. This was all too much to take in.

They continued on down the dark stairs, Coby trailing after the ancient creature in the shape of her son. All her family, taken from her by those… things. She would gladly destroy them all.

When they reached the level of the great hall she told Kit to stay there and hide in the shadows, and went on without him.

Gunpowder. Why did it have to be gunpowder? She had never trusted the foul stuff, not since that day at the theatre. Mal had forced her to learn to use a pistol, to try and overcome her fear, but the sharp stink of the stuff still made her feel queasy. Still, she did as she had been instructed, taking a small keg and laying trails from each of the main stacks of barrels to the entrance, and then pouring a single trail from the threshold to the foot of the stairs. Further than that she could not go, not without proper fuses and she did not know how to set those. It would have to be enough.

She took out flint and tinder, and coaxed it into flame. With a whispered prayer she dropped it onto the end of the gunpowder trail and fled up the stairs without a backward glance. Scooping up Kiiren she ran across the great hall, through the ashes that were all that remained of the doors, and down the outer stair to the innermost ward. To her surprise Ned was there, with an unconscious – or perhaps dead – Gabriel in his arms.

"Run!" She pelted past him towards the old banqueting hall, where the ambassador's reception had been held. Its door stood open, its temporary roof awaiting repairs for King Henry's coronation. Coby stumbled and almost dropped Kiiren, but regained her footing and made it into the scant shelter of the ancient walls as the first explosion rumbled through the ground beneath her feet. Smoke and sparks poured out of the arrow-slit windows, and the thunder rolled on as one stack after another went up.

"Kiiren. Can you reach your *amayi*? With a… a tunnel of light?"

"I think so." He squeezed his eyes shut, then opened them. "I'm scared, Mamma."

"I know, lambkin. Just try your best."

He closed his eyes again. Coby sat back on her heels, clasped her hands at her breast and prayed.

••••

There was only one way to fight Shawe's creatures: on their own terms. They had learnt to dreamwalk whilst waking, to bend the world to their will as easily as a young skrayling shapes his dreams. The idea had never occurred to Erishen before, but now he had seen it with his own eyes, it appeared absurdly simple. This feeling would not last for long, though, he also knew that. It was the last echo of the soul-joining, reverberating through his mind and putting his thoughts out of joint. For these few moments, he knew how they did it, and he could do it too. He just had to make the feeling last until the girl had destroyed them all.

He turned and stood to face the door, hearing the rattle of claws upon the stairs. With a thought he turned the door to close-dressed stonework, sealing the entrance just as he had seen the first sorcerer do in Ilianwe's chamber. The creatures howled in rage and the stones trembled, shivering into tiny fragments that spilled down the stairs around their feet. The foremost of them filled the doorway, human once more apart from black leathery wings that sprouted from his back.

Erishen folded his arms.

"Is that the best you can come up with? A Christian devil out of the bible our father used to read from? I am not one of your human victims."

The devil folded its wings, and the horns that had begun to sprout from its temples retracted back into its skull.

"You are not one of us."

"No? Then how can I do this?"

Erishen glanced towards the canopied bed. The sheets and blankets rose up and flew at the dreamshaper, threatening to smother him. At the last moment the youth raised his hands and they melted into a storm of white down, as though someone had burst a pillow. The dreamshaper spat out a feather.

"Enough of these games. Where is the puppet king?"

"You mean Jathekkil? Poor fellow, he went to all that trouble to gain the throne and now everyone wants to rule through him."

"He is weak, and lacking in vision. Our master knew humans far better."

"Master Shawe."

The dreamshaper laughed. "Not that dabbler in potions and elixirs. Master Fox, who brought us together. Until you killed him."

"Tanijeel."

"Yes. He told us what humans are capable of, and what we should do to them."

"And Olivia. Ilianwe. What about her? Is she your leader now?"

The boy shrugged. "We do not need her anymore."

She was dead, then; perhaps seeking reincarnation at this very moment. She was a survivor, after all.

A rumbling beneath their feet made the dreamshaper look around.

"I'm afraid you're too late," Erishen said, glancing towards the heavy wooden chest in which he had concealed the young prince. "In a few moments this entire castle will explode, and there's rather a lot of steel armour and weaponry on the floor below. Your chances of survival are minimal."

He reached out to Kiiren and opened a tunnel into the dreamlands.

"Farewell."

As he stepped through, he felt something catch at his heels. Damn it, they were following him! He rolled over on the dry grass, kicking at the claw-like hands grasping his ankles. Winged things shot overhead as the dreamshapers made their desperate escape. Erishen looked around to see Kiiren at the far end of the tunnel, arms out, beckoning. No!

With the last fragments of magic at his command he slammed the exit shut before his opponents could get to it. It was a gamble, but he suspected that without Tanijeel or Ilianwe to aid them they were trapped in here. Trapped in the endless night of the dreamlands, for he would not open a door for them no matter what they did to him. Of course, first they had to catch him. Falling onto all fours he transformed into a silver hound and coursed away across the grass, his enemies in hot pursuit.

EPILOGUE

Winter came early, up in the hills. By November they woke every morning to a world rimed in frost; by December it snowed as often as not, turning the roads to filthy freezing slush over a layer of compacted ice. The stream of visitors and letters, never frequent so far from London, trickled to a halt, and the estate closed in on itself to await the return of spring.

Children do not heed the turn of the seasons, however, and Coby found herself spending most of her daylight hours making new clothes for Kit, or altering the ones he already had when she ran out of sufficient fabric to make them anew. Not that he was growing especially fast, but they had brought little with them from London and he could hardly wear his courtly finery to ride his pony or play in the walled orchard.

"My lady?"

Their ancient steward hobbled into the parlour.

"You should not have come all the way upstairs, Lynwood. I told you to send one of the lads with messages."

"I know, my lady. But even my old sinews need stretching from time to time."

She put down her sewing. "What is it?"

"I was thinking, my lady..." He wrung his hands together. "Next Friday being the coronation as well as New Year's Day, I reckon it might raise the household's spirits to broach a cask of claret, to toast the new king's health."

"The new king?"

"Arthur, my lady."

"Oh. Of course."

Robert's brother had been declared King after Henry was killed in the explosion at the Tower. The work of traitors, according to Lord Grey; the same men who had assassinated King Robert and laid the blame at the skraylings' door. Grey had produced an extensive list of their names, compiled by his loyal servant Sir Maliverny Catlyn shortly before his tragic death at the hands of the same villains.

"We could make do with beer, my lady–"

"No, open the claret. It will not keep forever."

"Thank you, my lady."

"Only the one, mind. More than that will lead to rowdiness, in my experience."

"Yes, my lady." He turned to go. "I... I had thought you and the young master might have gone down to London."

"Perhaps in the spring, when the theatres reopen." Wild horses would not drag her to a coronation, not after last time. "Master Parrish has been nagging me to go, and I cannot put him off forever."

The steward bowed and took his leave. Coby sat down, picked up her sewing and abandoned it again. A visit to London would do them both good, in truth. She could stay with Lady Frances for a while; Kit needed the company of other children, and the duchess's little boy was of an age to play with him now.

The pale winter sunlight moved across the parlour floor and she watched it dully, wrapped around the ache in her chest that she had thought was beginning to heal. If they did not go to London she would have to send for a tutor for Kit, but after all he had gone through he needed time to be a normal boy for a while. Normal? No, he would never be that, even though he had become more Kit and less Kiiren in the months since Sandy's death and Mal's... She swallowed. Kiiren had said that Erishen, in Mal's body, had gone into the dreamlands, but Erishen himself had once told her that no one knew what happened to someone who got trapped there.

Rapid footsteps sounded in the gallery outside, and the door burst open.

"Mamma, mamma, look who's here!"

Kit burst into the room, eyes bright and cheeks flushed as if he'd been outside playing in the snow, but his clothes and hair were dry.

"What are you talking about, lambkin?"

"Look," he said, turning back to the doorway.

Coby followed his gaze, and her breath caught in her throat. A familiar figure stood there; gaunt and wearing naught but rags and dried blood, but unmistakable.

"Mal?"

Throwing her work aside she leapt to her feet and ran to catch him as he fell.

He opened his eyes, blinking against the light that burned like the midday sun. It was a candle, set in a pewter candlestick. He watched the wax drip down one side, but no matter how hard he stared it took its own path, heedless of his will. Then it was true. He was back in the waking world.

He tried to sit up but fell back, his head spinning. He raised his hand to the light, wondering why he no longer had manacle scars on his wrists from his time in Bedlam. Of course. He was Mal now, not Sandy. The spareness of his flesh had fooled him for a moment.

A movement at his side caught his eye, and he realised that Kiiren was asleep on the bed next to him, fully clothed and curled up like a puppy. He reached out and stroked one of the dark curls with a fingertip, reluctant to disturb him.

"You're awake."

She stood in the doorway, her face alight with joy. His wife. Jacomina. He tried to speak, but his throat was dry as dust. She hurried over to the bed and poured him a cup of some pale, sour liquid.

"It's just small ale," she said, when he wrinkled his nose. "The doctor said you weren't to drink anything stronger until you're up on your feet. I'll send for some broth when you're ready."

He let her fuss over him.

"You've been asleep for three days." She helped him into a sitting position and straightened the blankets around him. "Kit never left your side. How…?"

"How did he find me? The same way he always does, by not giving up."

"He said you turned away, you chose to stay there, in the dreamlands."

"I had no choice." He stared into the distance. "I couldn't let those creatures get away, they were too dangerous. So, I drew them off, and when they tired of chasing me I hunted them down."

"You killed them."

He shrugged. "What would you have me do, take them back to the skraylings in chains, like Ilianwe? We know how well that turned out."

"And now?"

"Now we are safe. They are gone, and England is free."

She toyed with the chatelaine in her lap. "When… when I last saw you, in the Tower… you told me you were Erishen, and that Mal is no more."

"I know. I'm sorry."

Her head jerked up. "You lied?"

"No. But I had to surrender to Erishen, for the healing of our souls to work. For those first few hours he had free rein, and I could only stand by and listen."

"You were possessed."

"I suppose that's one way to describe it."

"And now?"

"Now… Now I know what Sandy meant. He is part of me." He took her hand again. "He is part of me, not I part of him."

"Sandy, or Erishen?"

"Both. But mostly Erishen. Sandy is gone, all but a few memories."

"I'm sorry."

"Me too. But it was the only way to defeat the guisers."

"And now they're gone, you'll stay." It was not a question.

"Aye, I'll stay." He sighed. "For a long time I hoped the skraylings would take us back, Kiiren and me. But I fear they will not. Not me, at any rate. Kiiren was an innocent in all this, and he is still young, with many lifetimes ahead of him."

"You can put aside your dearest companion so easily?"

Mal scanned her face, trying to read her thoughts without invading her mind. Was she talking about Kiiren still, or herself?

"I may not give him the choice," he said. "But we'll cross that bridge when we come to it, eh?"

He held out his free arm, and she lay down on the bed at his side, head pillowed on his chest. After a moment she leaned up and kissed him, tentatively, like she was afraid he might disappear again. He hesitated, expecting Erishen's memories to overwhelm him as they had on the journey to Venice, but the taste of her lips brought back newer and more joyous memories of his own and he returned her kiss at last with a passion he scarcely had strength for.

"Ssh, you need to rest," she said at last, and pulled him down so that she could lay her head upon his shoulder.

He watched the western sky darken from turquoise to cobalt to deep lapis blue. Rest now, but afterwards? He and his family might enjoy a respite for months, even years, but the guisers would be back; he would wager his soul on it.

The truth was, he could hardly wait.

ACKNOWLEDGMENTS

The masque is over, the leftover sweetmeats sent down to the servants' hall, and it's time to say farewell to Mal and friends – but not without thanking everyone who made his final adventure possible.

Once again I sought professional help with my Latin. The sentences and phrases in the classroom scenes in Part Two were created with the patient assistance of Mark Davies, ARC Research Associate (Classics) in the School of Humanities at the University of Adelaide. Any errors introduced during the writing process are mine.

It's not just the academic stuff that needs researching for these books, though. As an armchair adventuress, I don't have hands-on experience of all the practical skills my characters possess, particularly the more dangerous ones! In particular, I would like to thank fellow author Courtney Schafer for all her help with the climbing scene in Chapter XIII. I can't climb for toffee, so I had no idea what was really practical with the technology of the period.

I mustn't forget the yeoman warders (aka Beefeaters) at the Tower of London, who answered my slightly odd questions about how to get into and out of the Bloody Tower, and more crucially didn't arrest me when I ignored the armoury displays in the White Tower in favour of sketching the castle layout. OK, so maybe I *was* planning an act of terrorism – just not in this century!

As with previous books, my beta-readers Laura Lam and Alex Beecroft were invaluable in giving a fresh perspective on the story,

427

which always difficult when you know the series inside-out yourself. On that same front, I'd like to thank my editor Marc Gascoigne for his professional insight in catching the areas where I tend to have blind-spots. And speaking of Marc, I'd like to thank everyone at Angry Robot – it's been a pleasure working with you guys for the past three years.

Last but not least, thank you again to all you readers who have stuck with Mal through his adventures and expressed your appreciation via Twitter, Facebook, Goodreads, etc. I can't promise there will be any more – I'm working on a completely new setting for my next project – but you never know...

Anne Lyle
Cambridge, August 2013

ABOUT THE AUTHOR

Anne Lyle was born in what is known to the tourist industry in the UK as "Robin Hood Country", and grew up fascinated by English history, folklore, and swashbuckling heroes. Unfortunately there was little demand in 1970s Nottingham for diminutive swordswomen, so she studied sensible subjects like science and languages instead.

It appears that although you can take the girl out of Sherwood Forest, you can't take Sherwood Forest out of the girl. She now spends every spare hour writing (or at least planning) fantasy fiction about spies, actors, outlaws and other folk on the fringes of society.

Anne lives in Cambridge, a city full of medieval and Tudor buildings where cattle graze on the common land much as they did in Shakespeare's London. She prides herself on being able to ride a horse (badly), sew a sampler and cut a quill pen but hasn't the least idea how to drive one of those new-fangled automobile thingies.

www.annelyle.com
twitter.com/AnneLyle